PRAISE FOR THE NOVELS OF SUSAN MEISSNER

A Fall of Marigolds

"Meissner has crafted a thoughtful story about lost loves and times past, illustrating how quickly disaster can take away what we hold most dear, and how ultimately we must move forward with hope in our hearts."

—Margaret Dilloway, bestselling author of *The Care and Handling of Roses with Thorns*

"Like the golden threads of a scarf sprinkled with marigolds, Susan Meissner weaves two unspeakable New York tragedies—the Triangle Shirtwaist Fire and 9/11—into a shimmering novel of love and acceptance. Meissner's heroines, Clara and Taryn, live a century apart, but their stories are connected not just by a bright scrap of fabric but by love lost. A compelling novel, *A Fall of Marigolds* turns fate into a triumph of spirit."

—Sandra Dallas, *New York Times* bestselling author of *True Sisters*

"A transportive, heartwarming, and fascinating novel that will resonate with readers in search of emotionally satisfying stories connecting past and present, and demonstrating the healing power of love."

—Erika Robuck, bestselling author of *Call Me Zelda*

"Weaves a compelling tapestry of past and present, of love and loss and learning to love again, of two women connected through time in a rich and unique way."

—Lisa Wingate, bestselling author of *The Prayer Box* and *Tending Roses*

"Susan Meissner knits the past and the present with the seamless skill of a master storyteller. A beautifully written, moving novel that had me gripped from the first page."

—Kate Kerrigan, *New York Times* bestselling author of *Ellis Island*

continued . . .

The Girl in the Glass

"Beautifully crafted and captivating, *The Girl in the Glass* is a story to savor and get lost in."

—*New York Times* bestselling author Sarah Jio

"Susan Meissner's prose graces each woman's story with an intricate and fragile beauty that reflects Meg's desperate love for Florence in the heart of the reader before she even boards the plane. In fact, this might be the most romantic book you read this year."

—Serena Chase, *USA Today*

"Charming and smoothly paced, *The Girl in the Glass* re-creates the feeling of walking the streets of Florence, Italy, and is populated with warm, generous-hearted characters." —*BookPage*

A Sound Among the Trees

"Meissner transports readers to another time and place to weave her lyrical tale of love, loss, forgiveness, and letting go. Her beautifully drawn characters are flawed yet likable, their courage and resilience echoing in the halls of Holly Oak for generations. A surprising conclusion and startling redemption make this book a page-turner, but the setting—the beautiful old Holly Oak and all of its ghosts—is what will seep into the reader's bones, making *A Sound Among the Trees* a book you don't want to put down."

—*New York Times* bestselling author Karen White

"My eyes welled up more than once! And I thought it especially fitting that, having already shown us the shape of mercy in a previous novel, Susan Meissner is now showing us the many shapes of love. *A Sound Among the Trees* is a hauntingly lyrical book that will make you believe a house can indeed have a memory . . . and maybe a heart. A beautiful story of love, loss, and sacrifice, and of the bonds that connect us through time."

—*New York Times* bestselling author Susanna Kearsley

"Meissner delivers a delightful page-turner that will surely enthrall readers from beginning to end. The antebellum details, lively characters, and overlapping dramas particularly will excite history buffs and romance fans." —*Publishers Weekly*

Lady in Waiting

The Shape of Mercy

A FALL
of
MARIGOLDS

SUSAN MEISSNER

 New American Library

New American Library
Published by the Penguin Group
Penguin Group (USA) LLC, 375 Hudson Street,
New York, New York 10014, USA

USA | Canada | UK | Ireland | Australia
New Zealand | India | South Africa | China

Penguin Books Ltd., Registered Offices: 80 Strand, London WC2R 0RL,
England
For more information about the Penguin Group visit penguin.com.

First published by New American Library,
a division of Penguin Group (USA) LLC

First Printing, February 2014

REGISTERED TRADEMARK—MARCA REGISTRADA

LIBRARY OF CONGRESS CATALOGING-IN-PUBLICATION DATA:
Meissner, Susan, 1961–
A fall of marigolds/Susan Meissner.
p. cm.
ISBN 978-0-451-41991-0 (pbk.)
1. Ellis Island Immigration Station (N.Y. and N.J.)—Fiction.
2. Immigrants—United States—Fiction. I. Title.
PS3613.E435F355 2014
813'.6—dc23 2013033477

Printed in the United States of America
20 19 18 17 16 15

Set in Sabon
Designed by Spring Hoteling

For Frank

"Love (they say) sometimes flies, sometimes walks,
runs with one, creeps with another,
warms a third, burns a fourth,
wounding some, and slaying others.
In one moment it begins, performs and concludes its career;
lays siege in the morning to a fortress which is surrendered
   before night,
there being no fortress that can withstand its power."

—Miguel de Cervantes Saavedra
*The History and Adventures of
the Renowned Don Quixote*

A FALL
of
MARIGOLDS

One

TARYN

THE length of floral-patterned challis rested on the cutting table like a bridal bouquet undone. Its once white background had mellowed to a sleepy ivory and the blooms of bright magenta and violet now whispered vermilion and lavender, faint reminders of their former greatness. I fingered the century-old fabric, soft to the touch. It had been left to age in the sun, on a chair back perhaps, or as a dresser scarf near a south-facing window. Or maybe it had just been ignored for a period of time when something happened that caused its owner to forget where she had placed it.

"I think it used to be quite pretty." The sixty-year-old woman on the other side of the cutting table frowned apologetically, embarrassed perhaps that a piece of cloth that had survived for so long had been handled irresponsibly.

"It still is," I assured her. "The pattern is intact and I can envision what the color palette was like when it was first printed."

"Can you?" Her voice was hopeful. "I was worried that it was too old and too faded for anyone to match. I don't even know where my great-grandmother got it."

"It's French wool challis, late nineteenth century." I turned the material over to study the reverse side. "Most likely printed with an aniline dye—coal-tar based, which is why the colors were originally so vibrant."

She laughed. "You can tell all that just by looking at it?"

I smiled back at her. "Four years of textile school."

"I didn't know there was a school for that. I guess there's a school for everything."

I turned the fabric over to its right side. "I think I can find a match or something close to it."

"Oh, that's wonderful. But it doesn't have to be wool challis. I hear that's pretty expensive. Rayon would be fine."

"I'll do my best. May I hold on to this or would you like me to remove a swatch?"

"You can keep it while you look. In the meantime, I'd like a few yards of these."

She pushed two bolts of Batavian batiks in autumn shades across the table.

I pulled the bolts toward me and handed her an info form to fill out on the challis. "I'll need your contact information so that I can e-mail you when I have some possible matches for you. And if you let me know your price range, that's helpful, too." I also handed her a pen.

The customer took the form. "Wonderful."

I unfolded the first bolt of toasty gold fabric. "This is a beautiful print. Brand-new this season. How many yards?"

But the woman was staring at the sheet of paper I'd given her. "'Everything beautiful has a story it wants to tell,'" she said, reading aloud the store's tagline at the top of the form. "I love that."

"It's our motto here at the Heirloom Yard," I said. "One of my professors in textile school taught me that."

The professor had actually said that every textile design is based on a cherished universal truth; I had prettied up his long-ago statement, on a long-ago day.

"And how many yards would you like?" I repeated my question.

"Oh! Two. No. Three yards, please. Of each."

I measured out the yardage and began to cut.

"It's so well said," the woman continued. "Especially if you're a quilter. And I just love the name of this fabric store. Did you come up with that, too?"

I nodded toward my employer and best friend, Celine, whose silvery pixie haircut was visible among a kaleidoscope of Jinny Beyer prints as she waited on another customer in the middle of the store. "Celine over there came up with the name. This is her shop. And all the beautiful quilts on the walls are hers."

Celine looked back at us and winked a hello.

I pushed the first bolt aside and reached for the other one, a chocolate brown cotton flecked with gold swirls.

"Actually, make that one two and a half." The woman sighed gently and visually took in the Heirloom Yard's shelves and tables. "I am so glad I found your store, I can't even tell you. When I knew we were moving to Manhattan, the first thing I did was mourn the loss of my favorite fabric store. I didn't think there'd be one here to replace it. I guess I thought Manhattan would be too urban and refined for quilts."

Her comment made me laugh. I had come to the city years ago—a new bride, a new college graduate—with a few misconceptions of my own.

"My daughter lives in Connecticut. She's the one who told me to check on the Upper West Side," the woman went on. "She had read in one of her magazines about how you specialize in reproduction fabric. It was a few years ago, but she keeps all her back issues. That's how I found you."

That article, three years old, was still bringing in new business.

I straightened the unfolded length of the second fabric and began to cut. "It's my favorite thing to do, actually. Finding a match for an old fabric."

"And she's brilliant at it," Celine said, now from just a few feet away as she prepared to cut yardage at a second cutting table.

"I think that's so very interesting," the woman said. "And you can always find a match?"

My scissors paused for only a second. "Almost always."

"But sometimes you can't?"

Again the scissors lingered over the fabric for a breath of a second. "The older a textile is, the harder it is. If we can't find it, then it might mean we'll go to a designer. That can be expensive, but we can recommend some good ones."

"Most of the time you can find something, though? I mean, it's not the end of the world if you can't find that challis, but I sure hope you can."

The scissors snipped through the last of the cut. "Yes. Most of the time."

"You know," the woman went on, oblivious to the tiny interlude, "I'm going to have to bring in my grandmother's wedding dress. She was a mail-order bride during the expansion to the West and . . ."

I listened with polite interest. In truth, I welcomed the swift transition into a conversation that didn't remind me of the one fabric I'd been unable—for ten years—to match. Granted, I had no swatch, no photograph, nothing but the memory of the material to work with, and even that was hazy. It had been in my hands for less than one day. And, as Celine liked to remind me, *that* had been a day like no other. I should ease up on my expectations.

How many antique swatch books had I thumbed through; how many Web sites and textile houses had I browsed looking for its match? The scarf had been an Indienne textile, French-made from an Indian design, and surely a hundred years old. The name Lily had been stitched in black near one edge, and the repeating pattern was a burst of marigolds.

In nearly a decade I had found nothing close by way of a match.

There had been a few scattered moments when a quick glance at a bolt or a photograph or a swatch seemed to grab hold and the very air around me shouted, "There it is!" and with a thumping heart I'd look again and be nearly relieved to realize I was mistaken. I wanted to find it and yet I didn't.

Everything beautiful has a story it wants to tell. But not every story is beautiful.

The woman had finished her comments about her

grandmother and I whisked away the lingering thoughts. I handed the pile of folded fabric to her and retrieved the form she had filled out. "Leslie up at the front counter will ring that up for you. Bring in your grandmother's wedding dress anytime." I glanced down at her form to see what her name was. "So nice to meet you, Mrs. Courtenay. I will be in touch with you about the challis."

"Oh, please call me Ruth."

"And I'm Taryn."

Ruth Courtenay began to make her way to the front of the store, bypassing other customers, nearly all women. Most of them had in their hands a quilt pattern book open to a dog-eared page, or bolts in their arms carried like babies as they looked for the perfect blend of contrast and complement.

And though the long and narrow store was full of customers, it was library-quiet inside. Even the Pandora music station we had playing in the background was hushed by the blanketing effect of bolt after bolt of fabric. I liked the way the bolts cuddled the customer's voices as if to wrap everyone in a soft embrace. The shrill sounds of traffic and commerce and sirens disappeared when you stepped inside the Heirloom Yard.

My nine-year-old daughter, Kendal, often said it was too quiet, like being stuck inside someone's sleepy dream. And since she and I lived in the cozy apartment upstairs, the quiet nature of the store was an ever-present reality that she wasn't above complaining about every now and then. Fortunately, she didn't seem to mind that there wasn't much separating my work life from our home life.

I loved where we lived—not in the way I loved my daughter, or textiles, or color. I loved the way the apartment made me feel when I retreated to it at the end of the day.

The Yard's upper rooms were an answer to an unvoiced prayer. Celine had offered them to me before I told anyone else I was pregnant, even before I fully realized I wouldn't be able to keep the Brooklyn apartment on one income.

She could have charged a lot more for the apartment if she let someone else sublease it, but Celine always insisted the situation was a win-win. Kendal and I had a comfortable if tiny roof over our heads and she had someone she trusted living over her store.

I left Ruth Courtenay's fabric at my workstation in the back room, where I kept my laptop and shelves of old swatch books. And then I suddenly realized the afternoon was easing away. Kendal would be getting out of school in less than twenty minutes. It was the first day back after the long summer break. I pulled the apron up over my head, draped it on my desk chair, and went back into the main part of the store.

Off to get Kendal, I mouthed to Celine, and she nodded.

I stepped out into the September afternoon. Behind me, Eighty-ninth Street stretched several blocks to Riverside Park, a favorite place of mine and Kendal's. Just ahead the intersection at Broadway sparkled with a steady stream of cars and our neighboring retailers' windows. A man walking his dog nodded a wordless hello, and a mom with a baby in a stroller bent to pop a pacifier back into her unhappy child's mouth. A delivery truck double-parked and the car behind it honked its disapproval. The air held only a hint that summer was waning.

September used to be my favorite month. I liked the way it sweetly bade the summer pastels away and showered the Yard's shelves with auburn, mocha, and every shade of red. September brought in the serious quilters, those who loved spending frosty nights piecing, stitching, and creating fabric masterpieces. It was a time for getting down to business.

Even now as I headed out, I could feel the subtle notes of imminent change. The constancy of September's unflagging return still amazed me, but for different reasons.

I walked a couple of long blocks, past Amsterdam, quickening my pace as ahead I saw children beginning to congregate outside Kendal's school, surely the most beautiful public school in Manhattan. The cathedral windows, the sweeping interior staircase, and the sunny, high-ceilinged classrooms appealed to my love of old-world charm. Kendal's school was another reason I was happy with our living arrangements.

As I crossed the intersection, I saw my daughter standing in a clutch of other fourth-grade girls eyeing a group of boys who were pushing one another and laughing. Her brownish-black hair shone in the late-afternoon sun, straight and gleaming. So like Kent's.

Same with the dimple in her left cheek.

And the eyes that narrowed into slits when she laughed.

Kendal had grown over the summer, more than her friends had. She stood a few inches taller than the circle of girls she was with.

My daughter was going to be tall like Kent, too.

I waved discreetly and Kendal stared at me for a moment before excusing herself from her friends.

"So how was your first day back from summer vacation?" I asked brightly.

"It was fine. And, Mom. Remember at breakfast I told you I can totally get home by myself? It's only three blocks. And I'm going on ten."

I eased us away from nannies and other mothers performing the same picking-up ritual and we headed toward home. "I remember. I know you can totally get home by yourself."

"So you agree with me?"

She was even starting to sound like Kent. So practical and pragmatic. "I said I'd think about it. Besides, I like walking home with you."

"Yes, but I am going to be ten."

"I know you are."

Kendal sighed. "I don't see what the big deal is. It's broad daylight."

Broad daylight. Where had she heard that phrase? Did anyone even say it anymore? Those two words together had ceased to mean much to me a long time ago. "Lots of bad things happen in broad daylight, Kendal."

"Not every day, Mom."

"I know," I said, after a moment's pause.

I did know that bad things didn't happen every day. I wasn't terrified a kidnapper lay in wait to steal Kendal the moment I let her walk home from school by herself. Worry about what *might* happen wasn't what made me hesitant. It was knowing the decision whether or not to allow her to walk home alone was mine to make.

We had reached Amsterdam. Traffic zoomed all around us as we waited for the signal. "I said I'd think about it. And I will."

Kendal frowned. "That's like saying no."

The light changed and we stepped into the intersection. "Thinking about something and deciding about something are two different things," I said. "I promise I won't just say no. Now tell me what you did today."

Kendal sketched the highlights of her first day back at school, and as we stepped into the Heirloom Yard, she was telling me about the new art teacher's Australian accent. We had taken only a few steps when I saw that Celine, Leslie, and the owner of the coffee shop next door stood huddled at the cutting table in the middle of the store, obviously looking intently at something.

As soon as the three of them heard my voice, they raised their heads and turned toward me in unison. Concern and surprise were evident in their faces. Whatever they were looking at had alarmed them in some way.

"What's up?" I reached the table before any of them answered my question. Celine held out her hand to gently stop me before I could see what they had been looking at.

"Molly just got the new issue of *People*." Celine nodded toward our coffee shop neighbor.

"So?" I didn't read newsmagazines anymore.

"Some photographer found a memory card inside an old camera bag she had in a storage unit. She thought she had lost it. She hadn't seen it in ten years."

I laughed nervously. Celine wasn't one for dramatics, but she was scaring me a little. "And?"

Celine hesitated and then moved aside. A magazine was opened to a two-page photo spread titled, "Tenth Anniversary Preview: Newly Discovered Photos from 9/11." The largest photo was of a man and woman standing at a curb, staring up at a horror that the camera lens did not show.

I recognized the scarf I was clutching, with its splash of marigolds, before I saw my own face staring back at me.

Time seemed to crunch to a stop.

I leaned toward the table's edge so that I could grasp something solid as the full memory of that captured moment swirled around me.

"That's you," I heard Kendal say, and I closed my eyes to reorient myself to the here and now at the Heirloom Yard, at the cutting table, surrounded by yards and yards of beautiful fabric. A long-ago voice crept out of the folds of my memory.

Give me your hand.

I couldn't breathe.

Give me your hand!

I couldn't breathe!

"Taryn!"

Celine's arms were around me, pulling me back.

"You were there? You saw it?" Kendal's words stung, but I welcomed the pain that assured me of where I was. Safe. Alive. With Kendal beside me.

"I'm all right," I whispered to Celine. I felt her arms around me relax a little.

"I'm sorry, Taryn," Molly said. "I just thought you needed to see it before, you know, people start asking you about it. It will be on all the newsstands tomorrow."

"Is my name there?" I whispered.

"No," Celine answered quickly. "You're not identified in the photo, just that man behind you."

I steeled myself for a second look, but my eyes were drawn again to the photo itself, not to the caption beneath it.

The scarf shone like a flame as I held it to my mouth. Behind me, a man in a florist's uniform held a cell phone to his ear. His gaze—like mine—was skyward, toward the burning spectacle across the street. The embroidered script under Athena Florist told the world his name was Mick.

The photo didn't show that a second later I would be on my knees and the man named Mick would be grabbing me, pulling me to my feet as the world fell to pieces around us.

My gaze traveled to the caption. *The streets were crowded with bystanders and evacuees seconds before the South Tower fell. Manhattan florist Mick Demetriou (pictured above) said escaping the crush of people and debris was harrowing. "I didn't think we would survive," he said of himself and the unidentified woman next to him, whom he helped to safety. Demetriou's cousin, a New York City firefighter, perished in the North Tower.*

"I didn't know you were there," Kendal said. "Why didn't you tell me you were there? What does 'harrowing' mean?"

"Not now, Kendal," Celine said, and bent to look at me. "You can call the magazine and tell them not to print your name in any subsequent uses of this photo, you know."

I couldn't make sense of what she had just said. "What?"

"A lot of our customers are going to recognize you. They might call the magazine to tell them they know who the unidentified woman is. Want me to tell them you do not want your name to be released?"

I couldn't answer Celine. I couldn't explain to Kendal why I hadn't told her I'd been near the towers that day. Or what "harrowing" meant.

I could only stare at that other me on the shiny page, clutching the scarf of blazing marigolds that had saved my life, and Kendal's too.

But not Kent's.

An old, familiar companion rose up from the flat folds of the scarf, the same invisible tagalong that had haunted me for years after Kent died.

A rush of sound filled my ears as I stood there among the hushing bolts of cloth.

All the fabric in the world could not muffle the roar of my regret.

Two

CLARA

Ellis Island
August 1911

IT was the most in-between of places, the trio of islands that was my world after the fire. For the immigrants who arrived ill from wherever they came from, the Earth stopped its careful spinning while they waited to be made well. They were not back home where their previous life had ended; nor were they embracing the wide horizon of a reinvented life. They were poised between two worlds.

Just like me.

The windowed walkway of the ferry house connected the hospital's bits of borrowed earth to the bigger island known as Ellis: a word that by contrast seemed to whisper hope. Beyond the hospital where I worked as a nurse was Battery Park in Manhattan, a short boat ride away.

In the opposite direction were the Narrows and the blue satin expanse that led back to everyone's old country. The hospital at Ellis was the stationary middle place where what you were and what you would be were decided. If you could be cured, you would be welcomed onshore. If you could not, you would be sent back where you came from.

Except for this, I didn't mind living where the docks of America lay just beyond reach. I looked to her skyline with a different kind of hunger.

Five months had passed since I'd set foot on the streets of New York. I could see her shining buildings from my dormitory window, and on gusty mornings I could nearly hear the busy streets coming to life. But I was not ready to return to them. The ferry brought me everything I needed, and the nurses' quarters were tidy, new, and sea-breeze fresh, though a bit cramped. I shared a room with another nurse, Dolly McLeod, who also worked and lived on island number three, the bottom rung of Ellis's E-shaped figure. Our dormitory stood a pebble's throw from the wards where the sick of a hundred nations waited. Their sole desire was to be deemed healthy enough to meet their loved ones on the kissing steps and get off the island. We cooled their fevered brows, tended their wounds, and nurtured their flagging hopes. Some were sick children, separated from their healthy parents. Others were adults who had diseases they had had no idea they were carrying when they set sail. Others were too feebleminded to make their own way in life, and despite their healthy lungs and hearts, they would be sent back to their home countries.

They spoke in languages that bore no resemblance to anything familiar: long, ribboned sentences looped together with alphabetic sounds that had no rhyme or meter. Some phrases we nurses had learned from hearing them so often. It seemed there were a thousand words for dreams realized and only one common whimper for hopes interrupted. Many would leave the hospital island healthier than when they arrived, but not all, of course. A few would leave this world for heaven's shores.

The work kept us busy from dawn to dusk. Sleep came quickly at night. And there were no remnants of the fire here.

Dolly and a couple of other nurses looked forward to going ashore on their off days and they would come back to the island on the midnight ferry smelling of cologne and tobacco and salty perspiration from having danced the evening away. In the beginning they invited me to join them but it did not take them long to figure out I never left the island. Dolly, who knew in part what kept me here, told me she had survived a house fire once. When she was eight. I wouldn't always feel this way, she said. After a while the dread of fire would fall away like a snakeskin.

I was not afraid of fire. I was in dreadful awe of how everything you were sure of could be swept away in a moment.

I hadn't told Dolly everything. She knew, as did the other nurses, about the fire. Everyone in New York knew about the Triangle Shirtwaist fire. She and the other nurses here knew that I, and everyone else from the seventh floor on down, had escaped to safety when fire broke out on the top floors of the Asch Building. They knew that one hundred and forty-seven employees of Triangle Shirtwaist had not.

They knew that the door to the stairs for the Washington Street exit was locked—to prevent stealing—and that the only alarm signaling the blaze came from the fire itself, as there was no siren to warn anyone. And they knew that garment workers by the dozens—mostly women—fell from windows to die quickly on the pavement rather than minute by agonizing minute in the flames. They knew the death toll was staggering, because it was in all the papers.

Dolly and the others didn't know what it was like to have watched as people stepped out of high, fiery windows, and they didn't ask, because who would ask a question like that?

They didn't know about Edward because I had said nothing about him.

I had only just started working as a nurse at the doctor's office on the sixth floor and had few acquaintances in New York. Not even Dolly knew that Edward Brim stole my heart within hours of meeting me in the elevator on my first day.

I had dropped my umbrella and he retrieved it for me.

"Are we expecting rain?" he said, smiling wide. He was first-generation American like me. I could tell from the lilt in his voice that his parents were European. Like mine. His nut-brown hair was combed and waxed into place with neat precision, but his suit was slightly wrinkled and there was a tiny bit of fried egg on his cuff—just the tiniest bit—convincing me without a glance at his left hand that he was a bachelor. He was tall like my father, but slender. His eyes were the color of the dawn after a night of wind and rain. But he had the look of New York about him. His parents surely had stayed in the city after they had come through Ellis, unlike my parents.

"Smells like rain," I'd responded.

His smile widened as the elevator lurched upward. "Does it?"

"Can't you smell it?" I said, and immediately wished I hadn't. Of course he couldn't. He was from the city.

The man next to him laughed. "She's a country girl, Edward. They always know what's coming."

"Well, then. I guess I'm glad I didn't bother to shine my shoes this morning!" Edward and the man laughed.

He bent toward me. "Be glad you know when rain is coming, miss. There aren't many things we're given warning of."

I smiled back at him, unable to wrest my gaze from his.

"New to New York?" he said.

I nodded.

"Welcome to the city, then, Miss . . . ?"

"Wood. Clara Wood."

He bowed slightly. "Pleased to meet you, Miss Wood. Edward Brim, at your service."

The elevator swayed to a stop on the sixth floor and the doors parted.

"My floor." I reluctantly nodded my farewell. Edward tipped his hat. And his eyes stayed on mine as the doors closed and the elevator resumed its lumbering ascent.

I saw him later that day as he ran for a trolley car in the rain. And I saw him nearly every day after that, either on the elevator or in the lobby of the Asch Building. I heard him talk about his work as a bookkeeper at the Triangle Shirtwaist Factory on the tenth floor, and I knew the coworker who often rode the elevator with him was a fabric buyer named Oliver. I knew Edward liked Earl Grey tea and macaroons and spearmint, because I could smell the fragrance of all three on his clothes. I knew he liked baseball and his mother's pastries and English ales.

He always said good morning to me, always tipped

his hat to me, always seemed to be on the verge of asking me something when the elevator arrived at my floor and I had to get off. The day of the fire, just as the elevator doors parted, he asked me whether I might want to see the work floor just before the shift ended. It was a Saturday. The seamstresses on the ninth floor would be finishing at five. I said yes.

The nurses on Ellis didn't know I watched Edward leap from the ninth floor to meet me on the street, a screaming girl in tow, her hair and skirt ablaze. The girl had been afraid to jump alone and Edward had grasped her hand as the fire drove them out the window.

Dolly and the others thought I was spectacularly fortunate to have escaped.

"You're very lucky, Clara," they said.

I didn't feel lucky.

When I was little, luck was finding something you thought was lost for good, or winning a porcelain doll at the county fair, or getting a new hat, or having every dance filled on your dance card. Good luck made you feel kissed by heaven and smiled upon by the Fates.

Good luck made you feel giddy and invincible.

Good luck didn't leave you desperately needing a place that was forever in between yesterday and tomorrow.

My parents wanted me to come home to Pennsylvania when word of the fire reached them. My father assured me that he still had a place for me at his medical practice, that he would always have a place for me. But I didn't want to go back to what I had been, back to the rural landscape where everything is the same shade of brown or green. I had just celebrated my twenty-first birthday. I was living in New York City, where every hue audaciously shone somewhere, day or night. I had been on the cusp, or so it seemed, of the rest of my life. Edward would have asked me to dine with him or see a show if the fire had never come. We were destined to fall in love; I was sure of it, even though I had known him for only two weeks.

But as ashes and burned fabric fell like snow on Edward's broken body and on so many others, none of whom I could help, I knew I would need a place to make sense of what I had lost and yet never had. Only an in-between place could grant me that.

Three

THE hospital's two islands were made from dirt and stone pummeled out from beneath New York's streets to make way for the underground railway. I was amazed that you could dump shiploads of earth into water and convince it to stay in one place. Sometimes I wondered: If there should be a tremor below, would these islands crumble away? God didn't put them here, so was He inclined or disinclined to protect them? Long ago, when the finger of God was on the bay, there were long stretches of tidal flats and acres of oyster beds, or so the story goes. What God made disappeared long ago.

My parents came to America from Europe the year before I was born, before Ellis's hospital existed. The second and third islands rose up from the seafloor, one after the other, years after Ellis opened, when it was apparent that something had to be done for immigrants who arrived in America ill and contagious.

It didn't occur to me to seek a post here when I first completed nursing school in Philadelphia. I wouldn't have chosen this set-apart place. It was the streets of Manhattan that beckoned me. The vibrant hues of New York had attracted me since I was seven, following a visit to see a show that I never forgot. I had wanted to be a part of its stunning energy for as long as I could remember.

My sister, Henrietta, would likely never leave Pennsylvania. She had married there and was having babies there and she would rock her grandchildren there. Nothing surprising ever happened to her and this suited her. To her, there was only one shade to every color. This was the difference between us. She was happy with the one shade.

I had always been drawn to color. Always. The more vibrant or intense or deep or unique, the better. I never swooned like my sister did when Papa had me assist in the surgery and our sponges and instruments turned crimson. The color of blood mesmerized me, even if the pain of the patient kept me from admiring it outright. Henrietta said blood was the color of death. I told her it was the color of life. Isn't it? Isn't it the color of life?

When the bodies landed on the pavement on the day of the fire, it was their lives that spilled out of them.

Sometimes at night, I dreamed of the fire, and my mind conjured the blood puddles on the sidewalk, like flattened red bouquets. I was not aware of making a sound. Surely I must have been doing so, for Dolly would rouse me and whisper, "You are safe, Clara." Other times the part of me that orchestrates my dreams would create a scenario in which Edward survived the fire. Why couldn't my dream weavers just skip the blaze altogether? I would like to dream that there was no fire.

My island made no demands of me. It wasn't here when time began and no doubt it would not be here when time ended. The people in the wards came and went. Other nurses came and went. It was a convenient place to linger.

I saw tiny glimpses of the life I knew, which surely waited for me still, in the faces of the hopeful.

ON days when multiple ships arrived in New York Harbor, the ferries began arriving at dawn. Immigrants by the hundreds passed through Ellis. Their landing cards would be checked, their names recorded, and their health assessed. Those who failed the health inspection would make their way to us, either by gurney or wheelchair or on foot, most with chalked initials on their outer clothing to inform us what illness or disability they were presenting signs of. I tended a dozen people every day in my rotations in the contagious wards. On multiple-ships days, the number of new arrivals could easily grow beyond what I was able to keep track of.

On one cloudy day in August, my fellow nurses and I rose before the sun and ate our eggs and toast by lamplight. The first ferry arrived just as the sun broke across the face of Ellis's palacelike front. By noon the hospital was bustling with new arrivals from the farthest corners of the world, much like the day before and the day before that. But there was only one new arrival who caught my gaze that day and kept it.

The copper-colored scarf around the man's neck as he waited in the hospital's receiving line was the one spot of color in the montage of brown and gray jackets. It seemed to call out to me, as if it knew it resembled the necklace of fire Edward had around his neck when he took to the sky. The scarf looked as soft as lamb's wool. I knew the moment I saw it that it was a woman's scarf and this also intrigued me.

An orderly had opened the door to the outside and a bullying breeze yanked on the immigrants' hats as they walked up the steps of the main building, where we waited to receive them. Ahead of the man in the scarf, a woman holding the hand of a fair-haired child let go to reach for her bonnet when it whirled away from her. I watched the man catch the hat as it danced toward the water behind them. He handed it back. The woman clutched it to her chest with a nod of gratitude, something I'd seen often in my five months on the island. The clash of languages did not rob the immigrants of their desire to communicate thanks when a snippet of good fortune found them. Somehow, they figured out a way.

The man, golden haired and slender, wore a black felt cap and carried a simple satchel. I guessed him to be in his late twenties, perhaps younger. His face was stippled with a shimmery new beard that covered slightly hollowed cheekbones. The voyage across the Atlantic had no doubt thinned him, as it had thinned all third-class passengers who landed at Ellis. But there was an aching weariness in his eyes and even in the set of his jaw. The hard voyage lingered there, and something else, too.

He approached the table where I and three other nurses waited in our starched white uniforms. The matron, Mrs. Crowley, sat next to us, looking at registration tags and chalked collars, checking off names, and directing the immigrants to one of several hospital buildings, depending on their condition. A child reached up to rub a swollen, watery eye and his mother swatted his hand with a whispered reprimand. The child stuffed his hand into his pocket. If the eye was infected with trachoma, that child would never see the shores of New York and neither would his mother. The attending doctor—not me, thank God—would tell the mother that they would have to go back to their homeland. No one with trachoma made it to shore.

I stood ready to assist with any French-speaking immigrants. I'm not fluent, but my French-born mother taught me enough to understand simple sentences, such as, "But I'm not sick," and, "I'm supposed to meet my cousin in New Jersey," and, "I don't have money for a doctor." When a French speaker hears me begin a sentence in his native language, he will invariably launch into an impassioned entreaty that I never understand. Mrs. Crowley insists it doesn't matter that I don't understand. I need only know how to say, "For now you must report to the hospital building you have been assigned to. There are no exceptions at this table. I'm sorry."

Several in the first group of people at the table spoke German and Swedish. Another spoke English with a thick Scottish brogue. Since no one needed my limited French, I found my attention drawn to the scarf-wearing man, whose eyes glistened with something other than sickness. Our gazes met and the momentary connection surprised me. I didn't hear the matron speak to me.

"Miss Wood!"

I jumped slightly and the clipboard I held poked me in the ribs. "Yes, Mrs. Crowley?"

"I asked if you know any Hungarian!"

"No. I'm sorry."

The matron whipped her head around to the other nurses. "Anyone know any Hungarian?"

A chorus of nos rose up around us and I chanced a look at the man. His gaze was drawn to the sky that shimmered outside the tall windows next to us, or perhaps to the land in the distance. Or maybe he was looking for the ship that had brought him and now lay at anchor in New York's harbor.

"You'll need to take that up with the doctor when you see him," Mrs. Crowley was saying to the dark-haired woman who stood at the front of the table.

The woman began to cry and the man in the scarf turned from his reverie and toward the sound of sobs laced with a lyrical dialect that seemed to fall around the room in tatters. No one knew what the woman was trying to convey.

"I can't help you here, love," Mrs. Crowley said, soothingly but with authority. "You will need to report to the ward where you've been assigned. Miss Wood, if you please?"

I took a step near the woman to gently take her arm, but she pulled away from me and arched across the table, imploring Mrs. Crowley with words no one under stood.

Mrs. Crowley turned to orderlies lounging at the back of the room. "I need a little help here," she shouted. Then she swiveled back to me. "Tell her the instructions in French, Miss Wood. Perhaps she will understand that."

"I'm sorry," I said in French. "There are no exceptions at this table. The doctor must see you."

The woman grabbed me by the shoulders and my clipboard clattered to the floor.

"Je ne suis pas malade! Je ne suis pas malade!"

I am not sick.

Her accent was like mine. French was not her native language. But she knew enough to tell me that much.

"Orderly!" the matron yelled over her shoulder.

The man in the scarf bent to pick up the fallen clipboard as an orderly strode toward the distraught woman.

For several seconds there was only the sound of feet on tile, the orderly's and the woman's, and her soft cries.

"Next in line, please," Mrs. Crowley said, her voice shaking a bit.

The man in the scarf took a step forward. He handed me my clipboard but his eyes trailed the woman in the gentle hold of the orderly as they walked away.

"Thank you." I extended my hand to take the clipboard.

"And your name?" Mrs. Crowley asked.

The man in the scarf slowly turned his head back around. He said nothing.

"Mrs. Crowley stretched out her hand toward the registration tag clipped to the man's jacket lapel. "Your tag? Yes, your tag."

The man handed it to her.

Mrs. Crowley studied his card and checked her list. "Ah. Yes. Andrew . . . Gwynn." Then she looked up and past him to the others waiting for their turn. "And your wife? Lily. Is she with you?"

The man named Andrew Gwynn stared at his hands, wordless.

"Do you understand what I am asking you? Where is Mrs. Gwynn?" Mrs. Crowley asked.

Mr. Gwynn opened his mouth to speak, and then closed it.

The matron looked at his tag and then turned to the

nurses behind her. "Good Lord. He's a Welshman who doesn't speak the King's English. Can anyone ask him where his wife is? She's on the list."

"She's not here," Mr. Gwynn said softly, his Welsh accent lifting his words like musical notes on a breeze.

"What was that?" Mrs. Crowley said.

Mr. Gwynn sighed, as if saying it had been all he could manage.

"He . . . he said she's not here," I offered.

"She's on the list. She's supposed to be here. They were supposed to stay together." Mrs. Crowley shook her head, annoyed. "Simple instructions. How much simpler can they be? They're supposed to stay together." She redirected her attention to Mr. Gwynn. "Why didn't the two of you stay together?"

Mr. Gwynn looked at her with unknowing eyes, as though he hadn't understood a word she had said. Or didn't know how to explain.

Mrs. Crowley threw up her hands. "They're supposed to stay together." She leaned toward Mr. Gwynn. "Where is Mrs. Gwynn? Your *frau*?"

"That's German, Mrs. Crowley," said the nurse next to me.

"She is not here," Andrew Gwynn murmured, looking down at his hands.

"Does his paperwork say she boarded the ship with him?" I leaned over and looked at the sheaf of papers in Mrs. Crowley's hands.

"They boarded at Liverpool. Both of them. Together."

I peered over Mrs. Crowley's shoulder. Andrew Gwynn and his wife, Lily, had crossed on the *Seville*. I had heard at breakfast that morning that scarlet fever had claimed thirteen people on that ship.

I looked up at Andrew Gwynn and I understood the ache of loss I saw in his eyes.

I bent toward Mrs. Crowley. "I think perhaps she died en route, Mrs. Crowley. Look. They were on the *Seville*."

Mrs. Crowley's mouth dropped open as her cheeks blossomed crimson. She shut it and furrowed her brow. "Is it too much to ask to get the right information? If they'd only filled out the paperwork right, I wouldn't have asked him."

With her pencil, Mrs. Crowley lined out the name under Andrew Gwynn's. "I'm very sorry for your loss, Mr. Gwynn. Very, very sorry. But as you know, you were . . . you were in close contact with a victim of the fever on your ship, so you are required to be in quarantine until we are sure you are not carrying the disease."

Mrs. Crowley looked up at the man in front of her. "He doesn't understand a word I am saying." She turned to me and handed me Mr. Gwynn's papers. "You can escort Mr. Gwynn to Ward K, Miss Wood. And then, for heaven's sake, run over to the main island and tell them to be more careful! And to send me some interpreters."

I hesitated before taking a step toward him.

"Will you come with me, please, Mr. Gwynn?"

He neither answered nor nodded his head. I took a couple steps toward the door and he followed me with his eyes only.

"Come with me?"

Mr. Gwynn turned and walked toward me. Behind us Mrs. Crowley called for the next in line. At the door I reached for my cape on a hook, as it was uncharacteristically cool that day. When I'd pulled it on over my shoulders, Andrew Gwynn was standing at the door, holding it open.

"Thank you."

He nodded.

We walked down the steps and into the late-summer breeze without talking. After several paces on the cement path that led to the isolation pavilions, the heaviness of the silence proved too much for me. I had to fill it with something.

"I am so very sorry about your wife."

He looked at me, silent.

"I don't speak Welsh. I only know some French. And only a tiny bit of that. My parents emigrated here before I was born. My father is Irish and my mother is French. They met on their ship."

He looked down at his feet and hiked his satchel higher onto his shoulder.

We were close now to the collection of isolation wards at the far end of island three. There was no reason for me to step into the halls where scarlet fever, typhus, and cholera slithered like demons. On days we didn't have a reason to go inside, we didn't. I wasn't due to rotate to the isolation wards for another three days.

When we arrived at the door to Ward K, I stopped and handed him his papers. "Go inside. Give these to the nurse at the desk. Understand?"

He didn't answer.

"Mr. Gwynn?"

"I understand, Miss Wood."

We stood and stared at each other. I knew then that he had understood everything I had said. And everything Mrs. Crowley had said, including my name. His shock and grief had silenced him. He reminded me of me, on the day of the fire, when there was no language for how

I felt inside. The urge to reach out and touch him nearly overcame me.

"Will you be all right, Mr. Gwynn?" I asked instead.

He looked up at the bricked front of Ward K. "I don't know."

I needed to get back but I felt compelled to stay a moment longer, in that little space that we shared. "Is there anything else I can do for you?"

He turned his head back to face me. "I would like my trunk, please."

The common moment gently evaporated and after a second's pause, I delivered the answer I had been trained to give when immigrants sent to the contagious wards asked about their luggage. "Your trunk will be kept for you in the baggage room on the main island. When you are ready to leave, you may retrieve it then."

"I would like my trunk now, please." His eyes were languid and his tone cordial, but underneath the polite tone was a tendril of desperation.

"I'm sorry. They won't let you have it, Mr. Gwynn. Not in the contagious wards."

Andrew closed his eyes against my words as though I had tossed sand in his face. "I must have my father's pattern book," he said. "I have nothing else. I want my father's pattern book."

"A pattern book?"

"He was a tailor. I am a tailor. The book is all I have left. Please. If the trunk is stolen I will have nothing." He opened his eyes and they shone with determination.

"The baggage room is quite safe, Mr. Gwynn." But I could see he did not believe me. And there was no reason he should. With detainees numbering in the hundreds every day, the baggage room was a busy, crowded place. I would not wish anything I valued to be stowed there for longer than a day.

His compounded loss proved too much for me. Andrew's homeland was far behind him, his wife was dead, and he was about to enter the scarlet fever ward for who knew how long. All that was left to him now were his grief and his trunk. He was in an in-between place like me, but his was much worse. I knew that if I asked for permission to get the pattern book out of Andrew Gwynn's trunk, I would not be granted it. A sick man didn't need sewing patterns. And a well man would have them back in his possession within the week. But I also knew that I would have to try.

"I can't bring the trunk to you, Mr. Gwynn. No one will allow it. But I will try to get the pattern book for you. I will need your trunk's claim ticket. And is there a key?"

A measure of his dread lifted and he reached into his coat pocket and drew out a folded card with the claim numbers for his and his wife's luggage. He also handed me a looped shoelace with two keys dangling from it. "It is wrapped in canvas. On top."

I took the key and card from him and slipped them into my apron.

"Thank you, Miss Wood," he murmured, and I saw the hint of a grateful smile.

"I can only try, Mr. Gwynn. I may return to you with nothing but your keys and card."

He nodded and the thick layer of dazed astonishment returned, as though he might at any minute wake from a dream, for surely none of this was real.

I wondered whether he had family already in America

who were waiting for him. "Do you need me to contact someone for you? Is anyone expecting you onshore?" I asked.

"My brother, Nigel, and his wife. In New York. Greenwich Village."

"Would you like me to send word to them that . . . where you are?"

"I sent a telegram this morning. From the ship." He looked off toward the harbor behind us.

"That's good." I didn't know what to say next. Andrew made no move to turn from me and enter the building. He seemed to be lost in a new thought.

"He won't believe me."

"Pardon?"

He turned back to face me, surprised, it seemed, that I had heard him. "I'd only been married a week. And I had only known Lily for twelve days before we married." He shook his head and looked off in the distance. "Nigel will think I'm a fool," he said to the teasing August wind.

A vision of Edward handing me my umbrella filled my mind, and the scent of macaroons and Earl Grey tea crowded in around me. I knew how fast the heart could learn to love someone. A jab of sorrow poked me and I flinched.

"I don't think you're a fool," I said.

The scarf billowed up between us, soft and eager to fly. I caught a whiff of fragrance in its threads, delicate and sweet. In the sunlight it looked less like fire and more like a burst of monarch butterflies. I could see a cascading fall of marigolds splashed across the fabric.

Andrew caught the twin tails and smoothed them down over his chest.

If Mrs. Crowley knew the scarf had belonged to Andrew Gwynn's dead wife, she would have likely insisted it be taken from him to be incinerated.

Andrew seemed to notice I was staring at the scarf and putting the obvious together in my head. He looked down at it, and then tucked it quickly into his coat.

"Thank you for your help, Miss Wood," he said.

Then he opened the door, stepped inside, and closed it behind him.

Four

MY father said I was good at nursing because I didn't panic. Mama and Henrietta could sweep the floors of my father's practice and roll bandages and take medicine to those who couldn't get to town, but neither of them could help my father in the surgery like I could. I think it surprised him when I didn't head to nursing school the moment I finished high school. I was in no hurry to learn officially what I already knew unofficially. I stayed at my father's practice, working by his side, pondering what I might do with my life as my closest childhood friends married or went away to teachers college. I wanted to be in the city. Marriage to a Pennsylvanian farmer wouldn't take me there, and teachers college held no attraction for me. There was comfort in knowing it would be easy to find work as a nurse in Manhattan, and there was no other employment that called to me, despite my affection for color. I didn't paint and I didn't arrange flowers, and needlepoint and sewing bored me. The world was an immense, vibrant place. I knew this was true, despite my sole experience with the quiet country life. I wanted to see it in all its colorful vitality. New York was the place to be.

When I thought about what was taken from me, this secondary loss came to mind. The fire robbed me of a future with Edward in it, I am sure of that, but it also stole from me my affinity for the wild and wonderful. The hospital was busy, but it was not wild, or wonderful. It was a steady place, with its hum of ten thousand words that were unknown to me. Despite the hammer of illness, it was a very tame place. I saw only what I had lost when I slept at night. I didn't see it on that calm slab of earth surrounded by water.

AS I walked away from Ward K with Andrew Gwynn's trunk keys and claim ticket in my apron pocket, I was glad I'd already been requested by Mrs. Crowley to see that we had more interpreters. It gave me a bona fide reason to go to the main island, though I doubted more interpreters would be spared. If Ellis was as busy as we'd been led to believe at breakfast, all the interpreters would be needed in the great hall.

More of the infirm and the suspect were heading across to the hospital as I walked through the ferry house to the main immigration building. Several of them made eye contact with me, silently questioning me, it seemed, to explain how the medical inspectors could so adamantly insist they weren't well enough to chase their dreams. I kept my head down and moved quickly past them. The farther into the ferry house corridor I went, the more people I passed who were either just arriving or heading out to American shores at last. Once past the ferry house, I was on the main island.

Ellis's primary immigration building stood palatial on its rectangle of land. I loved its red bricks and creamy limestone trim, and its little towers and their domes. It was designed in the French Renaissance Revival style, which made me wonder what the Europeans thought when they saw it. Did it make them feel at home, or a little unsettled that their first glimpse of America was not so different from the place they had left?

The main building still smelled and looked new. The first station had burned to the ground more than a decade ago, a fact that had not gone unnoticed by me. That original building was made entirely of wood. Ellis's new buildings were made of stone and brick. There were no traces of that fire here.

As I made my way inside, I encountered a hive of activity, and as I suspected, there was a desperate need for interpreters at the inspection stations. I managed to convince someone from the Hebrew Immigrant Aid Society to pay a visit to the hospital later. And one of the nurses assisting the doctors in the medical inspection, who spoke German, said she would come over in the late afternoon, but the others could make no promises. That first errand complete, I set off to see about completing the second one.

I knew the baggage room would be bursting with commotion. On days with many ships arriving, trunks and cases would be coming and going until nightfall. That would work either to my favor or against it. If the handlers were too busy to attend to me, I would have to return to island three empty-handed. If they were too busy to wonder about my request and simply let me look inside the luggage, I could get Andrew his book and be in and out without much scrutiny.

Once inside the baggage and dormitory building behind the main station, I excused myself to the front of the queue. Transfers of luggage moved at a consistent pace and the reception area was busy but not chaotic. I looked for a baggage clerk who seemed young and new at his job. I spotted a lad not much older than sixteen—as near as I could tell—and handed him Andrew Gwynn's claim ticket.

"We've a patient in the hospital who needs something from inside his trunk," I said. "It's important."

The young man looked unsure; he'd no doubt been told that luggage came into the room and luggage went out of it. I wasn't a porter checking luggage and I wasn't an immigrant retrieving it.

I straightened my nurse's cap to draw attention to my uniform. "It's important," I said again.

"I'm not sure that—"

I cut him off. "Mr. Gwynn, the gentleman I am speaking of, arrived just this morning. He'd come for this himself but he's in isolation at present. Shouldn't be hard to find. He just arrived. I have the keys."

The other clerks were busy and I could tell the young man feared interrupting them to ask what to do for me. I played on that fear, I confess.

"Do you or do you not know how to do your job, young man?"

His eyes widened and I could see I had won. "Right away, miss."

He disappeared among the long rows of trunks and boxes and cases. I watched from several yards away as he checked the card I had given him against two pieces of luggage at his feet. He was clearly trying to decide which of the Gwynns' trunks was the one I needed. Lily's, no doubt, was also in the group of detained luggage from the *Seville*.

"Just bring them both," I called out to him.

He looked up at me, bewildered, and I smiled. "Bring them both. You are busy here. I will find what Mr. Gwynn needs."

The lad nodded and placed the two trunks, one much smaller than the other, on a dolly and pushed them toward me. A new delivery of luggage was now headed into the room and the boy was called over to assist.

"Thank you. I will leave these right here when I am done and you can put them back in a moment. I can see you are needed." I held out my hand for the claim ticket.

"Yes, miss." The boy dislodged the two trunks, returned the ticket to me, and dashed off with the dolly. I quickly knelt beside the smaller of the trunks, figuring that it was Andrew's. I tried the first key but it would not turn the lock. The second key slid in and the lock fell open. I raised the lid, eager to retrieve the pattern book and be away, but the moment the lid was lifted I saw it was Lily's luggage I had opened. Inside was a jumble of women's clothing, gloves, a felt jewelry box, a yellow hat, and a pair of honey-brown shoes. For a moment I just sat and stared at the spectrum of color that was Lily's life. Such a small trunk. So few things. And it was almost as if she had packed in a hurry. I realized at this same moment that I had no business looking in Lily Gwynn's trunk. I was about to snap the lid shut when I saw a slim book with papers sticking out of it resting just under a pair of gloves. I pulled at it and saw that it was a book of poetry by John Keats, and appeared to be well loved. Its spine was loose and the cover worn.

This woman had no doubt cherished the little book.

I pulled it completely out from under the gloves, set it on my lap, and snapped the trunk lid shut. Andrew might be spending a long two to three weeks or more battling the same terrible disease that had killed his new wife. He might like to have her book of poems at his bedside. I knew I would want it if I were him. I would take it to him. I would even read to him from it if he wanted me to.

I turned to the other trunk and opened it. The book of patterns was just as Andrew had said it would be, wrapped in a short length of canvas. The book was heavy and cumbersome and I set it on the floor as I shut the lid on the second trunk. I grabbed both the little book and the big one and rose to my feet.

There was much activity now in the area where the baggage was being arranged row by row. I sought the young lad whom I had somewhat tricked into helping me.

"I'm finished," I called to him.

His cheeks were flushed and a shimmer of sweat had broken out across his brow as he and another clerk pushed and prodded a huge steamer trunk into place. The young man nodded back to me. As I turned to walk away, I heard his coworker ask, "What's she doing here?" and I doubled my speed out of the room.

I hoisted the two books tight into my embrace and melted into the sea of humanity in case anyone in authority from the baggage room was to question the young man. I headed for the ferry house and the outer corridor past island two's hospital buildings to island three. It was nearly noon and the ferry house had quieted down, as many of the day's arrivals had moved into the dining room for a midday meal. I was also due for a meal break, but I needed to safely stow the two books in my room until I could get them to Andrew after my shift was over.

On island three I made a quick left down the first concrete path to the nurses' quarters. The halls were quiet and empty. Those who worked nights were asleep; those who worked days were all in the wards. I made my way to the room I shared with Dolly and stepped inside, going directly to my bed to shove the books under it.

As I knelt, the cumbersome weight of the pattern book allowed it to shift, and it slid partially from the canvas wrapping. I reached to catch it and the book of poetry fell out of my hands and onto the floor, dislodging its collection of loose papers. I rewrapped the pattern book and shoved it under my bed, and then I reached for the poetry book and the papers Lily Gwynn had folded inside.

I truly had no intention of looking at those papers. My only design was to put them back where Lily Gwynn had placed them. But when I picked up the first piece of paper, I saw without wanting to what was printed across the front:

CERTIFICATE OF ANNULMENT

The two printed names were Lily Kerani Gwynn and Andrew Paul Gwynn.

At the bottom of the certificate Lily had already signed her name. The place where Andrew's signature was needed was empty.

The second piece of paper was a handwritten letter containing a first line that my eyes devoured even as I tried to fold it quickly from my sight.

Dear Andrew, I hope in time you can find it possible to forgive me. . . .

Five

I knew with every fiber of my being that I shouldn't read the letter. I knew decency would have me return the letter to its private place inside Lily's book. But a force overcame me, a dreadful, relentless curiosity.

My father once told me that when a child is to be born, there is no stopping it from coming. Something inside the mother's body—something she cannot control—simply decides the child is to come out. The mother might want to wait until the doctor comes or for the snowstorm to end or the sun to rise or the husband to return, but she cannot press a lever to stop the baby from coming. It just comes. I've helped my father a time or two with birthings and I can say it's true. There are some things you can't stop even if you want to.

I could not stop reading the letter, though my face flamed crimson in shame as I did.

Dear Andrew,

I hope in time you can find it possible to forgive me.

Please do not come looking for me. I am not worthy for you to come after and I do not wish you to. What I want you to do is forget you ever met me.

It was always my plan to disappear when we arrived with our luggage at your brother's home. From the day I met you, I planned to run back to the hired cab for a forgotten glove, and to find someone on the street to give you the message to look inside my trunk, where I knew you would find this book. This was my plan from before I even knew your name, dear Andrew. This is why you are reading this letter at this moment.

I am not the person you think I am.

I have signed a letter of annulment so that you may move on with your life, but in truth, I do not think you will need it. We are not truly married, as I am already married to someone else. His name is Angus Ravenhouse and he is a monster.

You must know that the beast I was forced to wed stole everything from me when my father died: my life, my father's estate, and my father's good name. I do not love Angus. I married him six months ago to protect my mother from ruin and despair, but she died of a broken heart within weeks nonetheless. With her safe in heaven, there is nothing to keep me in the prison that is my marriage. Escaping Angus is my only goal. I had to leave England in a way in which he could not trace me, and get to America, where his money and influence meant nothing. I needed to have a different surname so that Lily Ravenhouse wouldn't appear on a passenger manifest. There are only so many ways to get a new surname. . . .

I fled London for Liverpool two months ago with the terrible hope that I would meet someone who could help me, knowing full well that only through deception could I get that help. I didn't have time to wait for you to get to know me, though when I met you on the street the day you got the letter from your brother, I knew you were the kind of man who would help me if you were able. I had to be on the ship with you, as your wife, with your name as my name. And you were leaving in such a short amount of time. So I led you to believe I had fallen in love with you in a matter of days, and I hoped against hope that you could believe it was possible. I could not extend to you then the honesty that you deserve. But I am extending it to you now.

I never wanted to hurt you. I swear before God I never wanted to hurt you. You deserve someone who loves you the way a man should be loved. I am not that person.

I am bound for the West and I ask you not to inquire about me, not that you should.

There is nothing in this trunk I need. You can do whatever you wish with its contents. If it helps you to forget me, burn it.

But please do not hate me for very long. I have lived with hate for six long months. It is like poison, black as pitch, and too dangerous to harbor.

I am and will always be in your debt.

Lily Broadman
Ravenhouse

The book of poetry lay open on my lap, and the certificate of annulment rested on its pages when I finished reading the letter. A stunning chill had sneaked in around me and I shivered, the thin paper of the letter rattling a bit and reminding me that I held it.

The weight of what I now knew astounded me. I could see in my mind's eye how Lily must have envisioned her plan playing out. Making port with Andrew at New York Harbor and then Ellis with their trunks in tow. Processing through immigration. Boarding a ferry that would take them to Manhattan. Meeting Andrew's brother at the docks. Hailing a cab and stowing their trunks. Arriving at Andrew's brother's place. Unloading the trunks. Lily, who runs back out to the street to retrieve a forgotten glove, is counting on Andrew and his brother to be distracted with maneuvering the trunks inside. She pays a beggar woman or a young boy on the street to give the man with the black felt hat a message when he comes out. She steps into the cab to retrieve the glove and instead pays the driver to make haste to the train station.

When the trunks were at last inside the flat, Andrew would look for Lily. He would head back outside but there would be no sign of her or the cab. He would look up and down the street, calling her name, perhaps. Then the paid messenger would approach him, saying he had a message from the lady with the orange scarf. "Look inside her trunk."

Andrew wouldn't believe this person at first. He would ask where the lady went. The person would shrug and repeat the message. Andrew would bend down and hold the boy by the shoulders or look deep into the eyes of the beggar woman. "Where did she go?" "In the cab," the person would say. "What do you mean, 'in the cab'?" And the messenger would point to the busy street where the cab is no longer in sight. "She went in the cab." Andrew would then dash back inside his brother's flat. He would fumble with the luggage keys. He might suggest to his brother that they summon a policeman. He would kneel at Lily's trunk and his fingers would tremble as he inserted the key into the lock. He wouldn't know what he was looking for. How long would it take him to find the letter inside the book? Two minutes? Five? Longer? Eventually he would find it. And he would read it. And the many minutes would have tick-tocked the passing of time.

And she'd be gone.

I don't know how long I sat imagining what would have happened had Lily not contracted the fever.

At some point I realized I couldn't continue to sit there. I had no business taking the book. Andrew hadn't asked me for anything from Lily's trunk. It was my own selfish desire to touch his grief that made me remove the book from Lily's trunk to give to him. I'd even contemplated reading verses aloud to him, to prove what an amazing caregiver I was. My own hunger for meaning had led me to take the book, because I wanted to be the angel-nurse who helped Andrew find his way out of his in-between place.

I ought never to have taken the book.

I folded the letter and placed it back inside, along with the certificate of annulment. I had to put the book back where it belonged, where it would play the part destiny had already assigned it. I winced at the thought of Andrew reading the letter when he at last arrived at his brother's. The cruelty of it was beyond belief, especially to a grieving man. But clearly it was not for me to decide the fate of this letter. It was already ordained that he should find it.

I rose, knowing that if I stayed and pondered the matter longer I might rip the terrible letter to shreds. *It is not mine to do anything with*, I whispered aloud as I dropped the little book back into my apron pocket and felt for the luggage keys so that I could return it to its rightful place. Not mine.

The dormitory hall was still quiet as I made my way back outside, into the corridor that led to the ferry house. The noon meal was concluding and the building was again starting to bustle with both new arrivals and those who'd passed their inspections and were waiting for ferries to take them to shore. I quickened my step and arrived breathless at the baggage building. It was as busy as it had been earlier, perhaps more so. I made my way to the front, and was disappointed to see that Lily's trunk had apparently already been put away. Andrew's still sat there. I looked for the boy who had helped me earlier. I found him stacking crates on a far wall. I called out to him. He made his way quickly to me, as if to quiet me.

"You're not supposed to be opening anyone's luggage. We don't open luggage here. We store it."

He'd asked for clarification while I was gone. And had gotten it.

"After this I promise I won't ask again. I doubly promise," I said. "I just need to know where the little trunk went. Mr. Gwynn's big trunk is right where I left it. But the little one is gone. I need to know where it is."

"They took it."

"Who took it?"

"I don't know. Inspectors. They had that one on a list."

"What do you mean? What list?" But even as I said this, a tremor of dread wriggled inside me. I knew even before he said it what kind of list Lily's trunk had been on. In that instant I knew why inspectors had taken it.

"There was a killing sickness on the ship that trunk was on. No one's sure which passenger had it first. They took all the luggage of the people that had it."

The luggage of the people who had died of it.

Lily's trunk was headed for the incinerator.

There would be no putting that letter back in the trunk where it belonged.

I sped away with my hand over the book in my pocket, the edges of Lily's letter crinkling under my fingertips.

Six

SCARLET fever begins its terrible work before you even know it is inside you. A menacing bacterium, too tiny to see with your eyes, finds its way to you from an avenue of exposure you aren't even aware of. The minute it is inside, it attacks. That is its only purpose. First you develop a sore throat, the kind that would have you think you've swallowed shards of glass. A fever follows, making you feel as if you are being cooked from the inside out. A tremendous headache arrives and by this time you have crawled into your bed and want nothing more than to disappear into sleep and not awaken until the sickness has left, if it indeed leaves. Your body is full of contagion now, and anyone who comes near must cover his or her nose and mouth, in case you cough and spew the sickness into the air he or she breathes. If your caregivers don't cleanse their hands after having attended you, they will soon have what you have. While you lie there, miserable in your bed, your body produces an angry scarlet rash that starts on your chest and spreads to your arms and legs. The rash is rough to the touch, like a cat's tongue. About the sixth day, the rash begins to fade and then it will peel like a sunburn. Your tongue blanches white, too, before turning a deep strawberry hue after the white layer sloughs off. This is good news, because it means you will likely survive.

But if the bacteria invades within the belly of a rocking ship in the middle of the Atlantic Ocean, it runs unfettered like a wild colt, from soul to soul. There is no doctor or nurse to rub your fevered body with carbolized oil or to soak your crimson limbs in a soda bath.

And if the infection goes deep into your bloodstream—if it finds its way to the very heart of you—you will develop sepsis or meningitis, and if that happens, there is no hope. Only heaven can cure you now.

The bacteria are so small, so quiet, there is no way to see where they linger. Are they on the clothes of the dead? Are they lurking in the bedcovers? Are they lying in wait in someone's luggage?

When the menace claims thirteen lives in the hold of one ship, the answer to those questions is always the same. There is only one way to be sure the disease isn't preparing to pounce from within the deceased's belongings and onto the shores of the greeting nation.

Burn the belongings.

Burn them all.

I could have walked straight to the incinerator with Lily's book and letter.

I didn't think her trunk was truly full of contagion.

From Andrew's numb responses to Mrs. Crowley's questions, I was certain Lily had died very recently. Perhaps within the last few days. I was also fairly sure her trunk had been secured in the baggage hold with the other steamer trunks when they left Liverpool and before she became ill. And even if she had opened her trunk after having been exposed to the disease, the incubation period had surely passed. The inspectors at Ellis would take no chances, of course, but I was in no danger.

The book in my pocket was no receptacle of disease.

As I walked back through the ferry house, I imagined the flames of the incinerator consuming Lily's letter and turning to ash her appalling confession. If I hadn't taken the book out of her trunk in the first place, that was exactly what would have become of it.

Had I not trifled with what wasn't mine, Andrew Gwynn would have lost forever the opportunity to learn of his bride's duplicity. He would have lived the rest of his life—however long that was to be—thinking the woman he had married within days of meeting her had loved him, that she had given up all that was familiar to marry him and sail to America because she was in love.

But now there was an opportunity for him to learn the truth.

And it rested with me.

It seemed I had two choices: dispose of the book and its contents and let Andrew believe his dead wife loved him, or give Andrew the letter and let him grieve for having been cruelly wronged.

Which was worse? Mourning the loss of something without knowing you never actually had it, or mourning the loss of what you thought you had and never had at all?

I thought of Edward, who, before he died, kissed me in my dreams and drew my gaze when I was awake.

I couldn't answer which was worse.

There could be no deciding at that moment what to do with Lily's letter. The incinerator would be hungry for it another day. Fire is always hungry for things that don't belong to it.

I hurried back to the main hospital building on island three. The midday meal was nearly over. There wasn't time to return to my dormitory room and find a place to put Lily's book. It jostled in my apron pocket as I ran to get back to my post. Dolly was returning from the staff dining room and I nearly ran into her in the main corridor.

She took in my breathless consternation and crooked an eyebrow. "Where've you been? I didn't see you in the dining hall. Are you all right?"

I forced a smile. "I'm fine. Was on an errand for Mrs. Crowley."

"Still? She was asking about you when I went in to eat. She was fixing to send someone after you."

"I'm fine," I echoed.

She touched my arm as we walked. "I saw you go into the nurses' quarters earlier. I nearly followed you to see if you were ill."

My hand reached instinctively for my apron pocket to cover it with my hand. Dolly's eyes traveled to it, and then she looked back at me.

"I'm fine." It sounded even less believable the third time. Dolly, being the only one who knew what I dreamed about when I slept, arched an eyebrow. Her concern suddenly seemed like something I could trust. I needed to figure out what to do with the letter, and Dolly wouldn't turn me in for my questionable acts in the baggage room. I could ask her what I should do.

"It's not about me. It's about that man who lost his wife on the *Seville*. I found out something about her. Something he doesn't know."

Dolly's eyes widened in interest. "The man you took to Ward K a bit ago?"

I nodded. "He asked me to get something out of his steamer trunk and when I did—"

"You did it?"

"Yes, I did. The man just lost his wife. Anyway, that's when I saw . . . when I learned something about her I am sure he doesn't know."

"What is it? What doesn't he know?"

We were now just yards from the main reception area. I could see the tip of Mrs. Crowley's hat as she sat at her table among a huddle of dark-coated immigrants. "Not here," I murmured. "I'll tell you later. But I need to find a way to see him again."

She lowered her voice, too. "To tell him?"

"I don't know what I'm going to do."

"When are you due to rotate to the wards?"

"Not for three days."

Dolly shrugged. "Let him find out on his own."

"He never will if I don't tell him."

Dolly looked dubious. "Why not?"

We were now back at the reception area and I snapped my mouth shut. I gave Dolly a wordless shake of my head and we pushed our way to the front to a scowling Mrs. Crowley.

Mrs. Crowley turned to me. "I asked you to find me

some interpreters, not travel to Europe to learn the languages!"

"I'm terribly sorry, Mrs. Crowley."

She rose from her chair. "I haven't had my dinner yet and there's a group of poor souls here from the *Seville* that need to be escorted over to Ward K. One of you needs to take them over and one of you needs to take my place at the table until the others get back from the dining hall."

"I can take your place at the table, Mrs. Crowley," Dolly said, even before Mrs. Crowley had fully finished her sentence. Dolly slid into her chair and looked up at me.

Mrs. Crowley handed me a short stack of registration cards and I turned to the group of sad-eyed people who had been aboard Andrew Gwynn's ship. There were a dozen maybe, mostly men, and three young women huddled together with long blond braids down their backs. The girl in the middle looked a bit pale and glassy eyed. I could tell already she was sick.

"I hope you ate when you were out strolling Ellis," Mrs. Crowley said as she brushed past me.

"I can eat later."

"Please tell me the long time you were away means you found some interpreters," she said over her shoulder as she started to amble away.

"No one can be spared now, I'm afraid. We might see a couple later in the afternoon."

She waved without turning her back.

I mouthed, "Thank you," to Dolly and then I faced the little crowd. "If you will follow me, please?"

A few blank stares told me not all of them spoke English. But the ones who did hoisted their haversacks and turned to walk in my direction. The others followed. We made our way quietly to the isolation wards.

This time I took the little group into the wards themselves to help the attending nurses sort them out. I knew Dolly probably needed me back at the reception area, but I also knew she had afforded me these moments for a purpose. As soon as the new arrivals had been shown to their wards, I confirmed where Andrew Gwynn had been taken earlier that morning. I was soon making my way to the far side of Ward K, where other men with suspected scarlet fever had been billeted.

The room held twelve metal beds and most were now occupied. Some of the men sat on the edges of their cots reading, some played cards with one another, and others were lying down with their hands folded across their chests, staring at the ceiling. Half of them were still in street clothes. That would likely change, would certainly change if they came down with the disease. A few lay sick and unmoving. A food cart was being pushed out by a male attendant. The men had just eaten.

I saw Andrew on the left side of the rows of beds. He was standing by a window with his hands in his trouser pockets, looking through the panes to the outstretched arm of the Liberty statue and the expanse of the world beyond. His shoulder bag sat open on his bed and the black felt hat rested against it. Without the hat, I could see that Andrew's hair was cropped short but hinting of curls that would grow if left alone. He had taken his jacket off and laid it on the chair next to his bed. A bit of sunshine-orange fabric peeked from the folds.

He seemed unaware of my approach. When I was just a few feet behind him I cleared my throat and he turned around. When he saw that it was me he glanced at my hands, no doubt to see whether I had his father's pattern book. I could feel the hardness of the poetry book at my hip as he looked at my empty hands. It appeared that I was carrying nothing.

"I was able to retrieve your pattern book, Mr. Gwynn," I said quickly. "I will try to get it to you later. I just wanted you to know it is safe in my room."

"You have it?" He seemed to doubt that something good could happen this day. He sought my eyes for confirmation that he had heard me correctly.

"I'm sorry you will have to wait for it, but there isn't a way to get it to you at the moment. My supervisor will be back from her dinner soon and I'm expected to finish my shift in the reception room."

"Is it safe in your room?" His accent colored his words with tones unfamiliar to me.

"The nurses' quarters are separate from the wards. And our doors are locked."

He nodded. "I do not mean to sound ungrateful. I just do not want to lose the last thing I have."

"You don't sound ungrateful, Mr. Gwynn."

He half turned back to the window. "If I should become sick, will you . . . could you possibly do something for me?"

I hesitated only a moment. "If I am able, yes."

He fully faced me again. "See that my brother gets the pattern book. Keep it safe for me until he comes to get . . . comes for me?"

It didn't seem too hard a task, though Mrs. Crowley would think it most improper for a nurse to safeguard a patient's belongings in her dormitory room. But I was already doing that. And had been for the better part of an hour.

"Shall I just keep it tucked away in my room until we see what the future holds?" I asked. "If you escape the fever, you will be able to leave in a few days. I can bring it to you then."

He nodded, relief evident in his careworn face. "And if I should get the fever, and if . . . if it kills me—"

"You will have much better care here than your . . . than anyone had on the ship, Mr. Gwynn. Many people who contract the fever survive if they receive proper medical treatment."

I clamped my mouth shut. There was no solace in pointing out the obvious: His wife had died because she had been on a ship in the middle of the ocean. If she had been here on Ellis when she became ill, she would have perhaps survived.

"But if I do not survive," Andrew went on, as if I had not interrupted him, "you will see that my brother gets the book?"

In the same moment that he asked me this I realized I had a stretch of space for deciding what to do with Lily's letter. If Andrew Gwynn succumbed to the fever just as his wife had, I wouldn't have to do anything. He could die in peace thinking his lovely new wife loved him. He would surely go looking for her in paradise and perhaps learn the truth at last in heaven. But heaven seems a place where truth cannot hurt. Here, the truth can be devastating.

If he fell ill and survived I had many days to decide.

If he wasn't to become ill at all, I had less than a week.

I had time.

He still waited for my answer.

I didn't want to tell Andrew that I'd make sure his brother got the book provided he came to the island to get it himself. That would have taken too much explaining.

"Of course," I said. "I am due to rotate into the

isolation wards on Monday. We can see how you're doing then."

He bowed slightly. "Thank you. I am in your debt."

"Not at all," I said quickly, shaking off those last five words.

He sat down on his bed slowly, as though contemplating what might be in store for him had exhausted him.

"I'll leave you to settle in, then," I said.

"Thank you." He held out his hand, palm up, toward me. It was the strangest gesture. Like a poor man asking for alms. I just stared, unsure what he expected me to do.

"My luggage keys?" he said.

"Oh! Of course!" I reached into my pocket, my hand firmly palming the book of poetry and my fingers grazing Lily's confession. I grasped for the shoelace and claim tickets and quickly drew them out. I placed them in his hands. "I am afraid they've sent your wife's . . . the other trunk to the incinerator. It's not in the baggage room anymore."

But this news did not surprise him.

"I was told that would likely happen. They told me they planned to destroy any of the belongings of those who had died. To be sure. It was a very bad case."

He closed his hand around the ticket and keys.

I started to walk away.

"You've a kind heart, Miss Wood."

I turned to look at Andrew but he was looking out the window again.

Kindness is always motivated by something nobler than just a desire to be kind.

I had a wounded heart. Like his. That is what I had.

Seven

THE afternoon passed quickly as more arrivals flowed into Ellis, typical for a Friday. Dolly and I and the other nurses in the reception area had little time for small talk as we escorted immigrants to the rooms that would be their holding place for at least the weekend. I could see that Dolly was anxious for the day to fully be at its close so that she could find out what I had discovered about Lily Gwynn. Late in the afternoon a large contingent of the suspected ill crowded into our lobby and I heard Dolly mutter under her breath, "Will this ever-lovin' day never end?"

Just before the sun went down I was sent on another errand to the main island for a Polish interpreter and by the time I returned with one, the reception area had finally closed for the day. Dolly was waiting for me in the staff dining room many minutes later, but the chairs around her had filled with our colleagues while she looked for my return. There would be no discussing Lily Gwynn until later, and disappointment made her stab her potatoes in annoyance.

When at last we were in our room in our nightgowns, with the needs of the day finally silenced, I pulled out Andrew Gwynn's pattern book from under my bed.

"What in the world is that?" Dolly asked as I unwrapped it from its canvas covering.

"It's a book of tailor's patterns. It belonged to Mr. Gwynn's father. He was afraid it might get stolen in the baggage room."

"It smells." Dolly wrinkled her nose.

I held the book close to my nostrils and breathed in the scent of old paper and muslin. "I like this smell."

"What has that book got to do with his dead wife?"

"Nothing. It's just the reason I went to the baggage room." I rewrapped the book in its canvas covering and shoved it back under my bed. I sat on my folded knees and withdrew the poetry book from the pocket of the apron I'd brought to the bed.

"Another book?" Dolly was unimpressed.

"This one was hers. I didn't know which of the two trunks on Mr. Gwynn's claim ticket was his. I thought his would be the smaller of the two. But I was wrong. The smaller one was Lily Gwynn's. And when I opened it by mistake, I saw this poetry book and thought maybe he would like to have this, too. It was hers and it looked as if it had been special to her. So I took it to give to him."

"And?"

"And when I got to our room to put them under my bed until later, I accidentally dropped the poetry book. These papers fell out of it."

I handed the papers to Dolly and watched her expression as she read the contents of both.

"Good Lord!" she gasped.

"I know. Isn't it terrible?"

"They had known each other only two weeks?"

"So sad, isn't it?"

"And he *married* her?"

The depth of her astonishment silenced me for a moment. She seemed appalled more by Andrew's marrying Lily than by Lily's deceit. "What is so wrong about his marrying her?" I finally said.

She held up the letter and waved it. "Need I explain? He didn't *know* her!"

A little geyser of indignation was working its way through me. "He thought he did. She wanted him to think he did. This is her terrible crime. Not his."

"Well, foolishness should be a crime, then. Marrying someone you just met is a daft thing to do."

"Give me those back." I pulled the letter and certificate from her hands, and Dolly's eyes widened like saucers.

"Why are you mad at me?"

"I'm not mad at you." I folded the documents and placed them back inside the poetry book.

"Yes, you are. Are you saying he was smart to marry someone he barely knew?"

"I'm saying it's not for anyone else to say how long it takes to fall in love with someone. Or how short."

"But that's my point! She *didn't* love him!"

"But he loved her." I huffed. "Isn't that obvious? You saw him today, wearing her scarf around his neck, barely able to answer any questions. He speaks English, you know. He understood everything Mrs. Crowley said to him. Grief made him act the way he did."

Dolly shook her head. "He didn't know her. How can you know someone you've only just met?"

She said it with such finality that I felt a weight, like a little cannonball, slam into my chest. I winced and she saw it.

"You think you can love someone you've only just met?" Her tone was soft and knowing, as if she had just figured something out, something that had been hidden before. She bent her head to make eye contact with me. "Did that happen to you once?"

I met her gaze, expecting to see laughing eyes, but I saw only compassion there. Had her face been wrapped in curious mirth I might have been able to stay angry. But her sympathetic expression melted my indignation, and tears that I had been holding for months started to spill out of me.

Dolly was at my side in an instant, wrapping her arms around me. The little book pressed against my chest, poking me in the ribs as I shook with the force of emotion unhinged. The tears ran down my face in rivulets but I refused to give voice to my sobs. I felt something deep and raging in my throat, scrabbling for release, but I locked my lips shut. A groan rumbled there but I did not let it out.

And all the while, Dolly rubbed my back and whispered, "There, there. There, there."

After a few moments, the tears ebbed and I found myself able to gather my wits. I had not cried since the day of the fire. I hadn't wanted to cry on the island at all. I'd been too afraid my tears would christen it with my sorrows. I wanted nothing about the fire to exist in my sacred in-between place. I wiped my cheeks with the sleeve of my nightgown and Dolly reached for a handkerchief from her bedside table. I declined it. There would be no spreading of my woes onto other surfaces.

"Did you lose someone you cared for in the fire?" Dolly asked gently, but the words felt prickled by barbs nonetheless.

I nodded without looking at her, embarrassed that I had been unable to keep this hidden from her any longer.

"Had you only just met him, then? Is that what this is about?"

Again I nodded.

"His name was Edward, wasn't it?"

I wrenched up my head to look at her. "How do you know that?"

Dolly fingered a sticky strand of hair away from my eyes. "You call out his name sometimes when you have . . . when you dream."

My face reddened. I felt the heat. "Do I?"

"Yes."

There was apparently little I could hide from the island after all. It had already heard Edward's name and my anguished cries—multiple times, apparently—as I lay asleep, re-creating the day of the fire over and over again in my nightmares.

"Who was he?" Dolly asked, gently inviting me to tell her.

I wiped the last bit of wetness from my eyes. "Only the kindest man I've ever known. I met him in the elevator. He was an accountant for Triangle and he worked on the tenth floor. I worked on the sixth. I saw him every day in the elevator. He always tipped his hat, always greeted me, always followed me with his eyes when I got off the elevator before him. I think he waited to get onto the elevator each day until he saw me. Must've been nerve-racking tim-ing it just right." I laughed lightly and so did Dolly.

"He had invited me to come up to see the factory floor the day of the fire." I recalled Edward asking me, remembering the slight hesitancy in his voice lest I found him too forward. But I'd smiled and told him I would like very much to see the sewing machines at work. And he had smiled broadly back at me. I looked up at Dolly. "He was going to ask me to dinner afterward. I'm sure of it. I could see it in his eyes. And I would have said yes."

"And he . . . he died in the fire."

The memory widened to include the rest of the day. Edward, far above me, standing at the edge of his mortal life. "He stepped out a window. I saw him on the ledge. His clothes were on fire. Flames were wrapped around his neck like a scarf."

"Oh, Clara."

"There was a young seamstress on the ledge with him. Her clothes were on fire, too. It was obvious she was afraid to step out alone, so he gave her his hand so that she wouldn't have to. He held on to her all the way down."

"Oh, dear sweet Jesus," Dolly murmured.

"He was such a kind man," I whispered, and my cheeks were wet again.

"And he . . . There was no saving him?"

I shook my head. "Only one person survived the jump. And she died later."

"Oh! I remember that now. That must have been horrible."

"It was. It is," I said. "There I stood with all my nurs-ing skills and I could do nothing for any of them. Or for him."

We were quiet for a moment. I wiped my eyes, and I saw from the corner of my vision that Dolly wiped hers, too.

After a moment, Dolly took my hands. "And here all this time I thought it was fear of fire that keeps you stuck on Ellis. It's not the fire. It's what it took from you, isn't it? That's why you never want to come ashore with us. Because of what you lost, not what you escaped."

"I'm not stuck here," I murmured. "I want to be here."

She covered my hands with hers. "You haven't been off the island in five months, Clara."

"That doesn't mean I'm stuck."

"But you're here just the same and you never leave. Are you afraid you might meet someone else? That you might actually get over him? Is that it?"

"I'm not afraid of that." The answer fell off my lips as if I'd rehearsed it.

"Well, what then?"

There was no answer at the ready this time.

"Are you afraid you'll find out he was married or something? That maybe he was just being kind because you were new?"

I covered the poetry book with my hand. "That's absurd. I'm not afraid of that. And he wasn't married." I opened my mouth and shut it again. A buzzing seemed to fill my ears. I couldn't think.

"It might do you good to find out who Edward was, Clara. You barely knew him. Maybe if you did know him, you'd be able to come to terms with this. Get off this island. Get on with your life."

The buzzing intensified. I reached my hand up to my ear and rubbed it. "I don't see how that would make a difference. What I knew I loved."

"What you knew?"

"It was enough."

"If it was enough I'm thinking you wouldn't be stuck here."

"I'm not stuck!"

"Well, it seems as if you are to me. And if you care at all for Andrew Gwynn, you should give him that letter and let him move on, lest he be stuck, too. I don't think he deserves to mourn all his days a wife who did not love him. Do you?"

Both of my ears felt ready to burst. "I don't know what I think."

Dolly leaned over and kissed me on top of my head. "Come with the girls and me to the city tomorrow night. We're going dancing."

"Maybe," I said slowly, with zero conviction.

She got into her bed and pulled up the covers. "Sleep on it, Clara. You don't have to do anything with that letter tonight." Dolly turned over, away from the light that still burned on my bedside table.

I sat there for a long while, afraid to get into my bed, give in to sleep, and revisit the fire.

I should never have opened Lily's trunk. I should never have taken the book. If only I had left it there. It would be ashes now.

Eight

THE first time I fell in love I was thirteen. His name was Otto Hertz and he was three years older than me. I had known him since early school days but he hadn't really caught my attention until he took a nasty fall from a barn roof while pushing snow off with a broom.

His father, a German who spoke little English, brought him into my father's surgery. It was a bitter cold and colorless day in February. My mother had been helping my father that morning, but when Otto was ushered in with a shiny point of bone poking out of the red-rimmed flesh of his arm, she promptly left the surgery holding her stomach. I stood at my father's side and helped him as he coaxed the angry pieces of bone back under muscle and skin and sewed up the tear. When the arm was bandaged and bound, I sat with Otto as the ether and morphine wore off, holding a cold compress to the goose egg on his forehead, also gifted him by his fall. He thanked me for my concern and told me I had pretty hair.

My immediate attraction to the blue-eyed boy was fierce and exciting. But I was alone in it. Other than his comment about my hair, Otto never intimated that he was likewise sweet on me.

Throughout his recovery, whenever Otto came into my father's surgery for a checkup or to have the stitches removed or the bandages changed, I made it a point to be in the room. I found ways to participate in his care, much to my father's chagrin, but Otto apparently never caught on. When his arm was finally healed, there were no more visits to the surgery. I had to hope for chance meetings on the street, which happened only twice the year after that. Both times Otto returned my effusive greeting, as polite boys are trained to do. But he clearly felt no reciprocating attraction to me. The following year I saw a girl on his arm when he came to town at Christmastime. A year later, when he was eighteen, he married her.

It wasn't until Otto married someone else that I reluctantly forced the feelings I still had for him to surface so I could release them like a bird to fly away. Hanging on to those feelings had been hard but also wonderful. At least I had had something of Otto while I clung to my one-sided affection for him.

The second time I fell in love I was eighteen. Daniel Borden was a medical student interning with my father to complete his schooling. He lived with us for two months, and I fell for him within the first three weeks. This time, the man of my affections felt the same way about me. When it was evident to all that we had feelings for each other, my father thought it prudent for Daniel to rent a room from the headmaster of the local school for the remainder of Daniel's four-month stay at my father's practice.

For the next eight weeks my feet didn't touch the ground. Daniel brought me flowers, wrote me love poems, read books to me, kissed me under the stars, showered me with words of affection, and told me every day how sad it would be when he returned to Boston. I fully expected him to ask my father for my hand before he left. But he did not.

The last evening before he was to leave us, he and I sat on the porch under a violet twilight and I asked him outright what he thought the future held for us. He kissed my hand and told me he wanted to be finished with school and have a job and a roof over his head before he spoke to my father about marrying me. He told me to be patient, that love would make the days go by fast.

And love did.

But distance also affects the speed of days.

After the first few months of his absence, Daniel's letters began to arrive less frequently. So I increased the number of letters I sent to him. His words of affection for me became less ardent, so I intensified mine. His promises regarding our future ceased to be included in his words to me, so I doubled the inclusions of my promises to him.

One day his letters stopped coming. In my head I knew there was a reason for this, but my heart refused to acknowledge what that reason was. I kept writing to Daniel as if nothing had changed between us. My parents saw that there were no more letters from Daniel, and stopped asking about him. Henrietta, who was married by now and living with her husband on a nearby farm, noticed that I was unable to provide any news of

Daniel's progress in school—or anything else about him—and she told me gently that it was time to face the truth: Daniel had fallen out of love with me. Henrietta said as sweetly as she could, though I hated her for it, that Daniel likely had feelings for someone else but lacked the courage to tell me.

I told Henrietta she didn't know what she was talking about and I didn't speak to her for a month. But in the end, Henrietta was right.

Daniel did finally send me a letter telling me he was sorry for treating me so abysmally and that he expected no forgiveness from me. He hadn't known how to tell me that he had met a young woman at a concert. He hadn't expected to fall in love with her, because he already loved me. He kept waiting for this startling attraction for this other woman to dissipate, but it only grew stronger. He confessed that he had asked her to marry him and she had said yes.

He was very sorry.

He never meant to hurt me.

He wished me all the best.

My parents, bless them, could tell without asking what Daniel had said in his letter. Henrietta figured it out, too, but begged for the details so that she could properly commiserate. I let her read the letter. Henrietta told me I deserved better, and that I should go away for a while to somewhere fabulous so that I could occupy my mind with thoughts wholly unrelated to Daniel Borden. She knew, as everyone close to me did, that before I had longed for Daniel Borden, I had longed for the colors of the big city.

I waited a few months for the wound to scab over, and decided Henrietta was right.

But I didn't want to go away just for a while. I wanted to get away permanently. I wanted to go to New York. Leaving as an unmarried woman meant I had to have a job.

There was really only one reason I chose nursing school.

The truth is I am good at fixing things. I like fixing things. Sick people are broken people and I like to make them whole again.

Nursing school was easy. My father had already taught me nearly everything I needed to know, and what he hadn't, I was able to learn quickly. School gave me wings to leave rural Pennsylvania for Philadelphia, and my diploma gave me wings to Manhattan.

Where I fell in love for the third time.

I awoke the morning after showing Dolly the letter, amazed and relieved that I hadn't dreamed of the fire. When I had finally crawled into bed the night before, it seemed the very room smelled like burned things and sleep seemed a very unsafe place to retreat to. I lay awake a long time thinking about what Dolly had said about my being unwilling to leave the island because I was afraid of finding out Edward didn't love me in return.

She had just about accused me of loving a dream.

Reality was a ferryboat ride away on the streets of New York and I was on the island, in an in-between place where dreams lived instead.

Dreams were all that was good on Ellis. Dreams kept the immigrants hopeful when complications loomed like a dark shadow and held them here with a heavy hand.

Sleep finally found me, and my dream makers were merciful. I slept soundly. Dolly had to shake me awake at sunrise.

I lay there for a few moments in the gray light of dawn, orienting myself to the day at hand. We ended our shift early on Saturday. Most of the staff would be on the ferry to the mainland before sunset. The only ones who stayed were the ones who had shifts to work on Sunday. I wasn't scheduled to work tomorrow. Nothing prevented me from accepting Dolly's invitation except that I had no desire to go. Stepping foot on Manhattan would be the beginning of something and the end of something else. I didn't want anything to end and I didn't want anything to begin. I turned over in my bed. The poetry book and its folded contents lay on my bedside table. I rose from bed, pulled up the blankets, and tucked the book under my pillow.

After I dressed, we walked to the staff dining hall for breakfast and then made our way to the reception area for Saturday's arrivals to the hospital.

"Did you decide?" Dolly asked quietly as we went down the corridor with the other nurses.

I honestly wasn't sure what she meant. I assumed she meant was I going to go to New York with her tonight.

"I'm not ready yet, Dolly."

"I mean the letter. It was as plain as day you weren't going to say yes to dancing with me tonight."

I frowned at her. "I thought about it. I'm just not ready for dancing."

"Suit yourself. What about the letter?"

I shrugged my shoulders. "Haven't decided."

"Want me to give it to him?"

I wheeled on her. "Why on earth would I want you to do that? I don't want you breathing a word of this to him. Or to anyone!"

"Oh, shush. I am not going to say anything to him. I

offered so that I could be the one to bring him the terrible news, not you. You can still be his lovely Florence Nightingale and I will just be the hated messenger."

My face felt rosy warm. "What do you mean, 'his lovely Florence Nightingale'?"

"I mean you don't have to be the one he will remember as having snooped in his dead wife's things, found out something terrible about her, and then had to tell him about it."

"I didn't snoop. I found it by accident."

"If you change your mind, let me know."

I was poised to defend myself but Dolly was clearly ready to change the subject. She saw other nurses ahead of us—the young women she usually went ashore with—and stepped up to talk with them. As we neared the reception area and the other nurses peeled off to report to the wards, one of them, named Ivy, turned to me. "Hope you change your mind and come tonight, Clara!"

I smiled and said nothing.

At the reception area, a queue of immigrants who'd failed their health inspections was waiting for us. And so the day began.

I did not go ashore.

I spent Saturday evening writing long letters to my parents and Henrietta, reading a book, and contemplating what the week ahead would be like when I rotated to the isolation wards.

I went to bed, alone in my room, before midnight and did not awaken when Dolly returned. In the morning, I left Dolly asleep in our room. I read from the psalms while I ate my breakfast, took a long walk across Ellis, sat and watched the New York skyline shining in the

Sunday noon sun. I read stories to the sick little tots in the children's wards, and waited for Dolly to emerge from our quarters.

She and the four girls she'd gone ashore with found me in the staff lounge. In their hands they held small boxes of chocolates.

I imagined I could still smell the city on them, could nearly hear its heartbeat.

That night, after Dolly and I had gone to bed, I knew the lingering aroma of the city would embolden my dream makers.

I dreamed I was in the elevator with Edward and the elevator was on fire. He smiled at me and reached for my hand. I gave it to him.

I had flowers in my hair and I was not afraid.

Nine

AS Dolly and I reported to island three's nurses' station early Monday morning, I secretly hoped I would be assigned to Andrew Gwynn's room so that I could watch him without being noticed that I watched him. As it turned out, I was assigned the children's measles ward and Dolly was to take Ward K, where the male scarlet fever patients were. Dolly piped up immediately and asked the matron whether we could switch. The matron in the contagious wards, a birdlike woman named Mrs. Nesbitt, wanted to know why. Dolly said she liked being with the little ones and besides, she had the scarlet fever ward the last rotation. Mrs. Nesbitt frowned, her storklike features looking even more pointed as she pouted, but she made the change on her schedule.

"See you at noon," Dolly said cheerfully when she

and I and the other nurses began to disperse for our posts. With my eyes I thanked her.

I made my way to Ward K, donning a high-necked cloak over my uniform to keep any stray particles of infection off my clothes. Inside the ward, the beds were now filled, mostly with immigrants who'd been in steerage on the *Seville*. Some lay abed, clearly with fever; some sat and ate their breakfasts; some stared off into space as they sat or lay on their cots, unable to summon any joy for the new day. At the far end of the room, I could see Andrew Gwynn still in his bed. A breakfast tray next to his bed appeared untouched.

The nurse who had been on duty during the night met me at the entrance, rattling off the conditions of the men who were now in my care.

"These three here"—and she pointed to a trio of black-haired men who lay shivering in their beds—"they came down with the fever Saturday night. Doctor saw them yesterday afternoon. You'll want to wear your mask when you care for them. Those on that wall say they are still feeling fine, no fever, no swollen glands. Those four down there"—and she pointed to the back of the room, including Andrew Gwynn's bed—"all seem to have come down with it since yesterday. I suggest a mask. The others will be released tomorrow if there's no other sign of disease. Doctor is due to make his rounds around ten. That one on the end"—she pointed to Andrew's bed—"he's not eaten anything yet and I've not been able to get down there to help him."

I nodded as I made my notes. The other nurse left and I slowly walked the length of the room, wishing those sitting on the edges of their beds a good morning and stopping at the bedsides of those who lay with fever to see who was awake and in need of something. I purposely saved Andrew Gwynn for last.

I approached his bedside while placing a gauze covering over my nose and mouth. "Mr. Gwynn," I said softly. "It's me. Nurse Wood. Would you like some breakfast?"

Andrew slowly turned in his bed to look at me. His face was flushed with the beginnings of fever and he raised a hand to his throat, grimacing as he swallowed.

I knew without the doctor having been by yet that the fever had Andrew firmly in its grasp. If this was his second day with it, then I could expect to have two weeks, closer to three, to decide what I would do with Lily's letter. Andrew's languid stare alarmed me a little. Grief would play a part in his battle with the disease; grief always played a part in whatever followed it.

I leaned over him and placed my hand on his brow to gauge his temperature. His skin was warm. He reached up to grab my wrist.

"Don't," he whispered.

I lifted my hand, surprised that my touch had hurt him. "You have the headache already, Mr. Gwynn?" The headache didn't usually show up until the third or fourth day.

"Don't get close. Sick. I'm sick."

He was worried my touching him would send me to my bed. He'd probably held his hand to Lily's brow just like I had held mine to his. And now he lay riddled with contagion.

"We are very careful here, Mr. Gwynn. I wash my hands a dozen times a day when I'm on the ward. They are beet red by the end of the day." I laughed lightly, but he only winced as he attempted to swallow again.

"How about a little breakfast, Mr. Gwynn?" I continued. "You will need your strength. And the doctor will ask why I was unable to get you to eat. You don't want him to be cross with me, do you?"

He turned his head to the breakfast tray. "Can't. Swallow," he murmured. His Welsh intonations accentuated the clipped words.

I surveyed the contents of his tray. The scrambled eggs and toast would be impossible. I reached behind him and pulled on his pillow to raise his head. "Let's try a little of the vegetable broth, shall we? Can you sit up a bit?"

Andrew slowly adjusted his body to a sitting position. I pulled the tray closer to him and handed him his spoon.

"It's actually pretty good," I said brightly. "Not too salty, not too bland."

He grasped the spoon and raised his arm. But when his hand began to tremble he lowered it.

"Did you eat anything yesterday?" I asked.

"Wasn't hungry."

"When was the last time you ate, Mr. Gwynn?"

He closed his eyes. "Don't remember."

I thought back to what his last few days had been like. If Lily's final hours were also the last of the voyage, and if he'd stayed at her bedside, it was possible he hadn't eaten in four or five days. I moved the tray and pulled up a chair to the side of his bed. I reached for the bowl of vegetable broth and the spoon that Andrew held loosely in his hand.

"Let me help you."

"No," he whispered.

"Yes." I placed a cloth napkin under his chin and dipped the spoon. He hesitated before opening his mouth and allowing me to feed him.

He took his time swallowing, screwing his eyes shut. "Can't eat," he whispered when he'd finished.

"Yes, you can." I ladled another serving. He obeyed.

The warmth of the broth massaged the inflammation in his throat bit by bit. As he took more from the spoon he began to wince less. His eyes were still glassy but he kept them open and trained on me. I found myself looking back at him. I fumbled for something to talk about.

"I would ask you what it's like to be a tailor, except I'm sure it hurts to talk and you need to eat anyway," I said nervously. "I'm sure it's very intricate work, being a tailor. You must enjoy it very much."

Andrew blinked and shrugged. "It's what I do."

I held the spoon aloft over the bowl. I could hear in his voice the same stoic resignation that I had in my voice when a person asked me what it was like to be a nurse.

"I know just what you mean," I said. "I'm a nurse because it's what I do. It's what I've always done. My father's a doctor in Pennsylvania. I've helped him in his practice since I was ten."

"I started sewing buttons when I was eight."

I smiled at this, this new little thing we had in common. While I continued to spoon more broth I told him about my parents, my easy-to-please sister, and before I knew it, my childhood longing for the bright lights and colors of the city, and that nursing had gotten me there.

"New York," he whispered, and again I sensed that underneath his words was an emotion I could keenly identify with. He had wanted New York, too. Tailoring would get him there.

"Yes, New York," I murmured.

He lay back on the pillow and I made no move to

encourage him to stay upright. For a moment we were both lost in the wonder of what we'd wanted and were willing to do to have it.

"May I be finished?" he finally said.

I looked at the bowl. He had eaten more than half. I placed it back on the tray. "I'll have the kitchen send up a more sensible lunch for you, Mr. Gwynn. No more toast for a while."

"How long?"

"How long before you can have toast?"

Andrew shook his head slowly. "How long will . . . Lily was gone in four days."

"We're going to take good care of you, Mr. Gwynn." I stood and reached for the small basin of water at his bedside, where a cloth lay folded on the rim. I gently plunged the cloth into the water and wrung out the excess. I placed the cloth on Andrew's brow, drawing out the heat with the coolness of the damp fabric.

He closed his eyes. "If she'd become sick later in the voyage she'd be here getting well. Yes?" He opened his eyes and looked at me, clearly expecting me to answer his question.

"Scarlet fever affects people in different ways, Mr. Gwynn. Many people do survive."

"But not all."

"No. Not all."

"I don't even know if there is someone I should write to," he said. "I don't know if there are cousins or aunts or uncles. She told me her parents are dead and she has no brothers or sisters. But surely there is someone I need to tell."

"Uh, perhaps. Perhaps not."

"How can she have no one in the world? There must be someone I should tell."

His voice was becoming raspy. The warmth of the broth on his vocal cords was dissipating.

"Shhh, Mr. Gwynn. Time to rest now." I held the cloth with one hand and adjusted the pillow with the other so that he could recline. "Comfortable?"

Andrew nodded.

"I need to see to the other patients in the ward now. Is there anything else I can get you?"

"No, thank you, Nurse. And thank you for . . . everything else."

I colored a bit. I felt the rosy shade warm my cheeks. "You are welcome."

"You'll keep the pattern book safe for me?"

"Of course."

He closed his eyes with another whispered word of gratitude.

As I walked away it occurred to me that I hadn't seen the scarf near his bed. I hoped it was tucked away inside the cabinet of his bedside table.

AT midmorning Dr. Treaver arrived to make his rounds.

Dr. Treaver, who had arrived on the island the same month I had, reminded me of my father in many ways, not only because he was about the same age and was a doctor like my father was. He had a soft voice like my father's, smoked the same pipe tobacco—I could smell the distinctive fruity blend on his clothes—and had the same neat, precise script. I never had any trouble reading Dr. Treaver's orders. I couldn't say the same about some of the other doctors on the island.

He arrived a few minutes after ten with another doctor trailing behind him. I was helping a young man get back into his cot after using the toilet. I washed my hands quickly and met them at the nurses' desk.

"Ah, Nurse Wood, nice to have you back on the ward," Dr. Treaver said, in his cotton-soft voice. He motioned to the doctor behind him, who looked to be a little older than me, with reddish-brown hair, shiny gold spectacles, and a ruddy pencil mustache. "This is Dr. Randall. He's a new intern and is just learning his way around the island. Dr. Randall, Nurse Wood."

I shook the new doctor's hand. "Very pleased to meet you, Doctor."

"Dr. Randall just finished his training in Boston," Dr. Treaver continued, and an unbidden image of Daniel Borden rose to the forefront of my mind. Daniel had also studied medicine in Boston. I pushed the image away. "I am taking him around to meet the patients in the wards today. Tomorrow he's on his own."

Dr. Treaver smiled and Dr. Randall laughed lightly. "I hope I don't get lost in the wards," Dr. Randall said. "This place is bigger than it appears from the docks."

Dr. Treaver started to head to the first bed. "Ah, well, the nurses here will keep you from falling off into the water. Nurse Wood knows her way around."

I retrieved my cart of supplies and the washing basin from behind the desk while the doctors donned cloaks over their clothes and put on masks. As we made our way around to the men on the cots, waiting a time or two for an interpreter to arrive, I caught Dr. Randall looking at me, sizing me up, or so it seemed. I kept my eyes glued to the patients, not wanting to encourage his stares. When we arrived at Andrew's cot, I retrieved the chart from the foot of the bed and dutifully recorded what Dr. Treaver dictated as he palpated Andrew's swollen glands, checked for early signs of the telltale rash, took Andrew's temperature, and gazed down his throat. Dr. Randall turned to me while Dr. Treaver listened to Andrew's heart.

"So I hear you escaped the Triangle Shirtwaist fire."

Three words that did not belong to my in-between place fell onto me like hot embers. Triangle Shirtwaist fire. I startled at their sizzling presence and nearly dropped the chart in my hands. Andrew turned his head to look at me.

Only a few of the other nurses knew what had sent me to the island. The topic never came up outside our sleeping quarters, which was exactly how I wanted it. My reason for taking a nursing post on Ellis was no one's business but my own. I desired very much to ask the new doctor how in God's name did he know this, but that is not what I said.

"Um, yes, Doctor."

"That must have been quite a terrible scene. I read about it in the *Globe*. One hundred forty-something dead?"

"Yes," I mumbled, searching for a way out of the conversation.

"And you were on the sixth floor of the building? That's just two floors down from where the fire began, isn't it?"

The air around me was growing warm. I felt a line of sweat appear above my brow. How did he know? Who had said this to him? Certainly not Dolly. Not Dolly. She would never. Not Dolly.

I could see Andrew staring at me, one eyebrow crooked in consternation.

"How very fortunate you were to have made it safely out," Dr. Randall continued.

He sounded genuinely glad for me, but I could think of nothing else to say except to ask him where he came by this information.

"Who told you this?" I asked.

Dr. Treaver looked up from Andrew, surprised at what must have seemed like a disrespectful question from me. He probably expected me to say something like, "Yes, I am so very grateful I made it out safely."

Dr. Randall hesitated only a second. "One of the nurses in the children's ward this morning."

Not Dolly. Please not Dolly.

"Carter. Nurse Carter, I think was her name."

Ivy.

I nodded, wordless.

"I'm sorry, Nurse Wood. You appear to be shaken. The topic came up quite by accident. I mentioned the fire and your colleague said there was a nurse here who survived it. My apologies for bringing up the matter. I only wished to say I am glad that you survived."

"Quite . . . quite all right," I stammered. "It's going on six months."

"Still, it was a terrible day in New York," Dr. Treaver said. "Six months, six years, it will always be a terrible day. So many lives lost. I had no idea you survived that fire, Nurse Wood."

I felt for the footboard of Andrew's bed to steady myself as the room seemed to gently spin. Neither doctor appeared to notice. But Andrew did.

Dr. Treaver asked Dr. Randall to step over to the bed and examine Andrew's throat and feel the swollen glands in his neck. Andrew opened his mouth when Dr. Treaver asked him to, but his gaze was on me.

The doctors conferred with each other and then Dr. Treaver told Andrew he was in very good hands and to mind the nurses, to take his medicine when we offered it to him, and that he and Dr. Randall would be back to see him the following day.

Then they washed their hands in the little basin on my cart, and proceeded to examine the man in the cot next to Andrew. I stayed at Andrew's bed for a moment longer, gathering my composure and letting the room— and what I could only describe as anger—settle, so that the island could slide back into its role as an in-between place where the fire did not exist.

I knew Andrew was watching me the whole time.

But what could I do about it?

He had already seen the dark place I had somehow emerged from. Just a tiny corner of it.

He knew I had survived something terrible that others had not.

THE day after the fire had been a Sunday. Churches all over lower Manhattan tolled bells of mourning for the senseless loss of life, but I could not bring myself to step inside one. Newspaper headlines lamented the city's sorrow in a typeface meant for unimaginable woe, but I didn't read the account. I didn't need to read what I had seen with my eyes and heard with my ears.

I looked out my apartment window over Washington Square Park, where the side of the stalwart Asch Building met my gaze. The outside showed hardly any evidence of the catastrophe that had taken place inside it the day before. Word on the street was that it was a fire-proof building. And indeed the building itself had survived marvelously. It was the people on the floors where the fire had raged—and the tinder-dry goods they worked with—that had not been fireproof.

The fire had already begun when I got on the elevator to meet Edward. As soon as the elevator doors opened on the ninth floor a rush of heat, smoke, and girls pressed in. "There's a fire!" one of the girls yelled, and the car instantly filled with as many people as it could hold. I could smell ash on their clothes and hair. I asked one of the girls where the fire was and she said it was everywhere, gobbling up shirtwaists in the workroom as they hung on their hangers. As soon as we were safely delivered to the lobby, the elevator operator bade us to quickly exit so that he could go back. I wanted to wait in the lobby for Edward to arrive, but after only a few minutes I was shooed outside as the building was being evacuated. I rushed out onto the other side of Greene Street, where a small crowd was gathering on the sidewalk. A fire engine was just arriving and police were cordoning off the area around the building. A ninth-floor seamstress who arrived after me said the elevator could make no more trips, as the fire was now in the elevator shaft. Several girls had fallen into the shaft and been killed, pushed into the abyss by panicked coworkers behind them.

I asked whether anyone had been using the stairs. She said no one could get to the stairs. The door was locked. There were others from the building standing where I stood but Edward was not among us.

The first faces appeared at the fire-laced windows as I prayed Edward had made it out safely. And then a man close to me gasped. "She's going to jump!" I looked to where he pointed, and as the crowd cried out in horror, the first girl stepped out of the smoke and into air that refused to hold her. She crashed onto a plate-glass protection over part of the sidewalk and it shattered with terrifying force. Even from many yards away we could see that her fall had reduced her to ribbons. Then there were more women at the windows, high above us, making their way out onto the sills.

"Don't jump! Don't jump," the bystanders all around me started yelling. I started yelling it, too. But girl after girl began to jump anyway.

A trio of firemen scrambled to spread open a net, but the distance was too high. The first girl to land in the net soared out of it and landed in an unmoving crumple many feet away.

I staggered forward into the street, my instinct to nurse the broken striking me like a lightning bolt. A man next to me, a greengrocer with the smell of cabbage on his hands, stopped me.

"Stay back, miss!"

"But I'm a nurse!" I exclaimed.

"They'll fall on you and kill you!"

The audacity of this notion immobilized me for a moment. That someone falling on me could kill me. Absurd.

I looked up then at these falling people, challenging reason to prove to me it could be true. And that was when I saw him: Edward, standing on a ledge a hundred feet above me. Fire wreathing his neck. A girl next to him. Flames ballooning her work dress. Her long hair on fire. Edward, moving toward the edge. The girl screaming. Reaching for Edward. Him taking her hand.

And as I shouted, "No!" they took to the sky.

The grocer reached for me as I dashed for the street, but I slipped from his grasp. I arrived at the cordon and a policeman held up his hand, ordering me to stop.

"I'm a nurse, I'm a nurse!" I yelled. Beyond him lay rag-doll people, broken and twisted, sprawled over red blooms that marked the spots where they had landed. I saw Edward's contorted body several yards away, saw his broken neck even from behind the rope, saw the girl he'd escorted to heaven with him, their hands no longer touching.

"You can't be here!" the policeman barked. "It's not safe. And there's not a one of these poor souls you can help. Now get back to the other side of the street!"

Above us came the sound of a terrible wail and a whoosh of air. The body of a black-haired girl landed a few feet away.

"Go!" the policeman yelled.

It was several seconds before I found the strength to obey him.

I don't remember getting back across Greene Street to where the greengrocer was. I didn't remember until later his wife folding me into her arms as I wept. And I don't remember at what point they brought me into the back room of their store and made me sip brandy. It was into the evening when they insisted their delivery boy walk me home. The crowd on Greene Street had not diminished. But the bodies had blessedly been removed.

The fire had long since been put out by then; it had lasted only half an hour.

Thirty minutes.

The owners of Triangle Shirtwaist, I learned later, were on the tenth floor when the fire broke out. But they had quickly evacuated onto the roof and then to the adjoining building, a way of escape that had not been available to the eighth- and ninth-floor workers.

Edward might have been with the owners at the top of the building when the fire started had he not made plans to be on the sewing floor at that moment. He was a bookkeeper, not a seamstress. There was only one reason he was on the ninth floor at twenty minutes to five.

He was waiting for me.

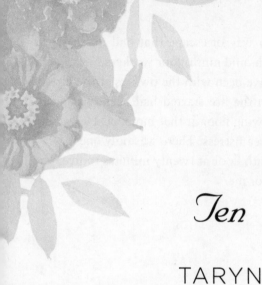

Ten

TARYN

Manhattan
September 2011

THE first reporter found me in two days.

I hadn't taken Celine up on her offer to call the magazine and tell them I didn't wish to be contacted. That would merely identify me.

"The magazine is going to find out it's you," Celine had countered. "It's a phenomenally emotional picture. Other publications are going to want to print it; I can guarantee it. You're going to get a call, probably several. A quarter of our customer base knows you lost your husband that day."

"Well, then I'll cross that bridge when I get to it."

Celine had been right. With the tenth anniversary only a week away, the dailies had the most interest in hearing how bystanders on the streets had escaped the collapse of the South Tower, the first one to fall. The photo had reacquainted the public with its horror of having witnessed the slaughter of so many innocents. The two faces in the photograph—one male and one female—resonated with every person on the planet who remembered that day, so the editorials said.

I politely turned down the first interview request, then the second, and then the subsequent morning TV talk shows. No one in the media pressured me to reconsider; that was one of the kindnesses extended to those of us who lost someone we loved on 9/11. We were not made to feel guilty for declining to speak of our heartaches.

But Kendal had questions that I did feel compelled to address, though I didn't know where to begin. For ten years I'd been able to crouch in between reality and regret and pretend neither had any influence on me, never moving forward, never looking backward. Residing above the Heirloom Yard was like living above the stuff of other people's dreams, not my own. It took the photograph for me to realize that.

The photographer who had happened upon the memory card said it had been a fluke, a chance rendezvous with a camera bag she didn't think she still owned.

But this wasn't the first time that what some would call a coincidence had shattered my notion that life is composed of mere random events, both lovely and terrible. It had happened to me an hour before the photographer snapped that shot.

As I lay in bed on the fourth night after the photo was published, I knew my flimsy truce with chance and destiny was gone. That in-between place had never really existed.

People who say everything happens for a reason usually say that only when they agree with the reason.

Those people are not the ones who wish they could fold back time and make different choices. They don't lie awake at night and whisper, *If only* . . .

THE sky that Tuesday morning was the sweetest shade of robin's-egg blue, cloudless and smooth.

Rays of a promising saffron sun were creeping over the bedspread as Kent walked across the bedroom to kiss me good-bye, a red travel mug in his hand.

His dress shirt was celery green, and his tie a silky charcoal.

I remember that day by its colors.

My yellow polka-dot pajamas as I lay in bed waiting for him to leave the apartment.

The white-and-sea-foam package I had hidden under my side of the bed.

The gray of waiting for several tense minutes.

The pink plus sign.

After so many years, a pink plus sign.

And then later, the marigold scarf—the last beautiful thing I saw that day.

I used to spend the nights when I couldn't sleep recreating that Tuesday in different colors. The sky not so blue, the sun coy behind puffy clouds, Kent in a yellow shirt and no travel mug. Me in my purple pajamas, telling him my period was late and did he want to stick around for a few minutes to see the test results even though it probably meant nothing?

Or the sky steel gray with rain. Kent in a blue-striped shirt and taupe raincoat, leaving the apartment while I still slept. Me in my teal nightgown with the little white daisies all over it, calling him as he was arriving at his office on the thirty-fourth floor, shouting into the phone those two words I'd been dying to say for four years: "I'm pregnant." And as we discussed plans for a celebratory dinner, I stepped out onto the balcony where red geraniums were nodding hello and there was no orange scarf that day. The unthinkable would still happen, but Kent would come home to me a few hours later, shaken and ash-covered, but he would come home. We would cry about what had occurred that day, both the good and the bad.

I've imagined that day in different colors so many times.

When I think back to the first waking moments, before the terrible sequence of events was set in motion, I am awed by how two simple phone calls changed everything. Two ordinary, seemingly unremarkable phone calls.

The first was mine to Kent a few minutes after seven. I knew he would be on a transatlantic conference call and unable to answer his BlackBerry. I held the little pregnancy test wand in my hand, barely able to contain myself as I left him the voice mail that would send him to the one hundred and sixth floor. *Hey, hon. Can you meet me for breakfast at Windows on the World at eight forty-five? There's something I want to show you, okay? It's pretty cool. Call me back if you can't make it. Love you.*

The second was to me from Rosalynn Stauer, one of Celine's best customers. Mrs. Stauer had a very old piece of fabric she desperately needed me to pick up before she left for Scotland that day so that I could begin the task of finding its match while she was away. Could I come on my way to work?

If I hadn't called Kent, he would have been on the

thirty-fourth floor when the first jet slammed into the North Tower.

If Rosalynn Stauer hadn't called me, I wouldn't have been late to meet Kent, and Kendal and I would be dead.

This was why I hadn't told Kendal I'd been there on the street when the towers fell and her father flew to heaven. It would mean telling her about those two phone calls, one that gave, and one that took.

I didn't want her to think that the day began to unravel when she became a part of it, just like I hadn't wanted to give Kent false hope when it had been so easy to protect him from it. I'd bought the pregnancy test in secret. If it had been negative, he would never have had to know.

Seeing that plus sign for the first time in my life was surreal. For several seconds I could only stare at the bit of plastic that quietly announced our baby was growing inside me. And then the joy that filled me was almost painful. It was too magnificent a feeling to experience alone. I wanted to be with Kent when I told him that finally, finally we were pregnant. That was the ache mixed with my joy: He wasn't with me.

I paced our Brooklyn apartment, over-the-moon happy as I contemplated how I should tell him. I didn't want to wait until he got home. I wasn't sure I could. I actually didn't think I could wait another hour. I wanted wings to fly over the river to tell him. I remembered Kent and I had enjoyed breakfast not too long before at Windows on the World for our sixth anniversary. The restaurant near the top of the North Tower was the perfect place to tell him, since, at one hundred and six floors off the ground, it was practically on cloud nine already.

I made the call to Kent, glad that I had to leave a voice mail. Then I showered and got ready, choosing a pale pink sundress patterned with tulips, as it was supposed to be eighty degrees for a high. The phone call from Rosalynn Stauer came as I was putting on earrings. At first I was annoyed by her intrusion and ridiculous request. She wanted me to essentially rearrange my morning so that I could pick up from her a piece of fabric she wanted me to match. Mrs. Stauer lived on Long Island, more than an hour's train ride away.

"We're leaving for Scotland today. I have to be at Newark at eleven," she said.

If she hadn't been Celine's best customer I would have told her she should've taken care of this before the day she had to leave.

"Can you stick it in the mail to me before you go?" I said instead, grabbing a pair of ballerina flats from my closet.

"Oh, I couldn't do that. It's a family heirloom, Taryn."

"I'm afraid I can't come to Long Island. I'm meeting someone downtown this morning, Mrs. Stauer. It's important."

"Oh! Didn't I mention it?" she said excitedly. "I'm already downtown! Roger had business to take care of before we head out, so we stayed overnight in the city. This is perfect."

I slipped on my shoes and looked at my watch. Celine was in Paris on a buying trip and I was in charge. I wanted her to be glad she had left me at the helm, as she had only recently made me assistant manager. If I left Brooklyn at that moment, I might have time to make a very quick stop before meeting Kent, depending on the location of her hotel. "Where are you?"

"At the Millenium."

The Millenium was just a five-minute walk from the

North Tower. Practically across the street from it. For just a moment, the strangest feeling came over me. It was as if it were no quirky twist that Mrs. Stauer had stayed downtown last night, that there was a reason I had this errand to run before meeting Kent.

But I shook that unfounded notion away. I didn't want to think about Mrs. Stauer or her fabric. I just wanted to get in, get out, and reach Kent.

"Okay. I'm leaving now, Mrs. Stauer. I should be there in twenty-five minutes. Can you meet me in the lobby?"

"Oh, splendid, Taryn. Just splendid. See you soon!"

She clicked off. I scooted into the kitchen to turn off the coffee and close the window above the sink—despite its squeaky protest—and then I dashed out the door.

The morning commute was in full swing and the High Street station was bustling with people heading into Manhattan. I sandwiched my way onto an A train and we took off. Ten minutes later I emerged onto Wall Street and I could feel how lovely the new day was going to be. The air was warm and fresh. And I was carrying a tiny speck of human life inside me.

After a quick five-minute walk, I was standing inside the Millenium's lobby and it was twenty-four minutes past eight. I still had plenty of time. But there was no Mrs. Stauer.

I waited five minutes and then went to the front desk to have the desk clerk phone her room.

"She wants you to come up," the clerk said as she replaced the phone. "Sixteenth floor, room sixteen twenty-four."

I sighed audibly but there was nothing the desk clerk could do for me. I headed for the elevators.

Seventy-plus Mrs. Stauer, sporting auburn curls of a

shade seen only on Irish setters, greeted me in her bathrobe.

"Oh, thanks for coming, Taryn. I am so glad we can take care of this before I go. Here, come in, come in." She opened the door wide.

"I really should be on my way. I've an appointment and—"

"But I'm not even dressed. And this won't take but a minute. I have it right here. Come in."

She waddled back inside her room and I followed. The door eased itself shut behind me. Mr. Stauer was apparently out getting a paper or coffee or fresh air. Several large suitcases filled one corner, and a service table in the middle of the room boasted two plates of nearly eaten blueberry pancakes.

Mrs. Stauer picked up a large handbag from off the floor and set it on the unmade king-size bed. She stuffed her hand inside and drew out a drawstring hosiery bag.

"We planned this trip to see my cousin in Glasgow ages ago and then I suddenly remembered yesterday that I'd promised her I would try to find a scarf like the one our auntie had. I wasn't sure where I had put this old thing." She looked up at me. "My side of the family is Scottish, you know. This particular aunt, my mother's youngest sister, came over in 1912, a month after the *Titanic*. Went through Ellis and everything. She had been a maid for a professor at the University of Edinburgh."

"Mrs. Stauer, I really must be going."

"Of course. Well, I found it buried in the cedar chest in the guest room." Mrs. Stauer opened the bag and pulled out a length of shining orange-red. Right away I could see the sweeping pattern of marigolds woven into the fabric's Indian design. The color palette was a soft mix of autumn hues, warm and inviting. Mrs. Stauer unfolded it and draped it across her ample front to show me the scarf in its entirety. It was beautiful.

Instinctively I reached for it.

Pleased with my interest, Mrs. Stauer laid it across my open hand. "Pretty, isn't it? It has to be near a hundred years old."

I fingered the silken threads. The scarf had no doubt been spun in France based on an Indian motif. Marigolds were used heavily in India in the worship of deities, the celebration of weddings, and in mourning the dead. A bit of black on the trailing edge caught my eye. Someone had stitched a name. Lily.

"Lily was your aunt?" I asked.

"Not sure who that was. My aunt's name was Eleanor. But she was given this scarf by someone who also worked for the professor, an American. That's why my aunt gave it to me instead of my cousin. There's only the one scarf, though, and two of us nieces. Corrine would love to have a replica of this scarf if that's possible. Our auntie wore it all the time. I'd like to get to Glasgow tonight and tell her you'll be able to find something for her."

"I'll do my best," I said, still intrigued with the scarf's beauty and the way it seemed to beckon me. But then I remembered I was to meet Kent at a quarter to nine and tell him the most amazing news. I looked at my watch. It was eight forty-two.

"I've got to go. I'm late. I promise I will get right on it, Mrs. Stauer." I rushed to the door. "Have a great time in Scotland."

I pulled the door open and flew out of it, folding the scarf into a rectangle as I sailed down the hallway toward the elevators. Behind me I heard Mrs. Stauer shout that I'd forgotten the bag. I hurriedly retraced my steps and took it from her. I hurried off again, rounded the corner to the elevators, and waited impatiently.

It seemed to take forever to reach the first-floor lobby. There was a faint tremor in the elevator car between the eighth and ninth floors, but I thought nothing of it. As soon as the elevator doors parted on the lobby level, I reached into my purse for my cell phone to let Kent know I was on my way. My fingers groped the inside but I could feel no phone. Had I left it at home? Had someone stolen it out of my purse during the standing-room-only commute? Distracted, I was only half-aware that people were coming to the lobby with strange looks on their faces. I heard someone ask a bellman what had happened outside, but I didn't listen for his answer. I looked at my watch again. Now it was eight forty-eight. It would take me five minutes to walk across the World Trade Center's central plaza and another five minutes to ascend to the one hundred and sixth floor. I was angry at Mrs. Stauer for stealing those minutes from me. Kent would wonder why I hadn't called or texted him.

As I neared the revolving front doors I heard someone say "plane crash" and someone else invoke the name of God. I stepped outside to the smell of smoke and fuel, and a strange sprinkling of paper and fluff.

I looked across the plaza. A fire-tinged scar marred the uppermost floors of the North Tower, high above me. Smoke poured out like a monster being released from the darkest cave imaginable.

"It was a jet!" someone shouted a few feet away from me. "I saw it. It flew right into it."

"I heard it," someone else said. "Shook the windows in my room."

Sirens began to punch the air from far away, and right in front of me as a trio of police cars went by me.

Kent.

I pushed past the people gathering outside the hotel and dashed across Church Street to enter the plaza. But police were already starting to fan out and prevent anyone from getting any closer to the North Tower.

Kent!

I plunged my hand again into my purse, desperate to find my phone. I had to call him. But there was no phone. Evacuees were soon filling the plaza and the sidewalks as bits of plastic and paper and metal continued to waft down. Police and security personnel were blocking all entrances to the complex so that I had to continually reposition myself to see the faces of the people fleeing the building. I had to find Kent among them to let him know I was okay, that I hadn't been in the elevator on my way to him. And I had to assure myself that he had been able to get to one of the fire exits.

Surely he could get to one of the fire exits.

I walked back to Church Street to try to see the top of the building, where Kent had surely been waiting for me. The smoking scar was below him. If he could just get to one of the fire exits . . . *God, let him get out!*

My tear-filled gaze was tilted toward the sky when a roaring whine shrieked above me, and to the left of my field of vision a whoosh of white soared into the South Tower. An explosion rocked the air above us and a fist of fire ballooned out from the upper half of the building. Screams and curses erupted all around me as those on the ground cried out in utter horror.

One plane flying into a building could be an accident. But not two. Something terrible and malevolent was happening. Fear coursed through me as more fragments fell from the sky.

I simply had to use a phone to call Kent and let him know where I was so that he could find me. I was afraid and I wanted him with me. I crossed the street in between wailing emergency vehicles and ran back inside the Millenium, now in a state of mini chaos as the hotel was being evacuated.

The television screens in the lounge were tuned to CNN. As I swept past I heard the news anchor declare that two planes had slammed into the twin towers: the first into the North Tower at eight forty-six a.m. and the other into the South Tower at just three minutes after nine.

"Please can I just use your phone," I yelled to frantic desk clerks who were attempting to help ten people at once. No one heard me.

I begged two people brushing past me for the use of their phone but they shook their heads.

Mrs. Stauer! I could go back to her room and use her phone. I skipped the elevators brimming with people getting off and headed for the stairs. I was breathless by the time I'd reached the sixteenth floor and pounded on the Stauers' door, but there was no answer.

It was now twenty minutes after nine.

Still breathing hard, I made my way back down to the lobby and was ushered out by hotel staff who clearly wished to be away as well. Outside, the smell of fuel and sense of destruction were intensifying. I was pushed with the crowd of fleeing people down Maiden Lane toward Broadway, where I stopped to catch my breath and to plant my feet. I would move no farther. I would stand there until every last evacuee ran past me. And I had to find someone who would loan me their phone just for a minute. As I gathered my wits I heard people around me talking and crying and cursing.

"God, what were those?" someone said.

And another one said, "Those are people. They're jumping."

I forced myself to swing my head up toward the North Tower as it belched black smoke. I saw a black speck, like a tiny pinprick on a swatch of ugly gray. The speck fell and disappeared from view.

"The ones on the top can't get out. They've been jumping," the first person said. "I saw probably fifty already."

I wheeled to the people around me. "My husband is in the North Tower!" I shouted. "For the love of God, can I please borrow someone's phone!"

"Here." A man in a florist's apron bearing the name Mick thrust his phone toward me. "But I don't know if you will get through."

I grabbed it and mumbled my thanks but my hands were shaking so badly I couldn't punch in the numbers. Tears blurred my vision. I could not stop them and I could not stop shaking.

The florist covered my hand with his. "Let me do it," he said gently. "What's the number?"

I was weeping now, unable to whisk away the vision of the falling speck and knowing it wasn't just a speck. It was a someone. A person. I handed the florist his phone and sputtered Kent's number. Then I reached into my purse for a tissue, knowing I didn't have any. My hand closed around the bag containing Mrs. Stauer's scarf, and it seemed that it reached for me, caressed my fingertips, urging me to draw it out. I pulled it free and brought the ancient fabric to my face to catch my tears. I caught a thousand different scents in its threads, some, it seemed, as old as love itself. At that moment I wanted to fall into those marigolds and never emerge. Had I been more aware of the other people around me I might have noticed the click of a camera shutter at that moment, but I heard nothing except the sound of my own anguish.

"I'm afraid it's not going through, ma'am," the florist said. "You can try texting him, maybe."

My hands were still shaking too badly. I started to reach for the phone but it was obvious I could not tap out a message.

"What do you want me to say?"

Was this to be my last communication with Kent? Was he still alive to even see it? I had to believe he was. "Tell him I am safe. Tell him I love him. Tell him . . . tell him he's going to be a father."

The florist was typing the message as I spoke, tears filling his eyes even as my own grief spilled down my cheeks.

"Thank you," I whispered.

He nodded and looked away from me while he flicked away the wetness at his eyes.

I turned my gaze back toward the smoke-filled sky.

"Maybe he's already out. What floor did he work on?" the florist said, a few minutes later.

"The thirty-fourth," I whispered numbly.

"Oh, well, then he probably got out."

"But that's not where he was."

For the next span of minutes, I don't even know how long it was, I saw the florist checking and rechecking his phone and I wanted to believe he was checking for me. I turned toward him a time or two, and he shook his head.

At some point, I heard someone tell another that it had been confirmed that terrorists had hijacked the two planes and deliberately flown them into the World Trade Center towers. Someone else said the Pentagon had also been hit. I put my hands over my ears to shut out their voices.

I continued to watch the faces of the people rushing past me, hoping against reason that I would see Kent among them.

Then there was an unearthly growl, a wrenching screech that split the tattered sky above us and the littered ground beneath our feet.

"The South Tower is falling!" someone shouted.

"That's not possible," another said.

"Run!" screamed a third.

I was knocked to my knees as a sudden press of people pushed me down, and then a wall of dust and rubble, like a tidal wave from the shores of hell, screamed toward us.

I was still struggling to rise when the wall of debris reached me. For a second there was only the movement of the wall. There was no light, no other sound, no cries for mercy.

No air.

I could see just a tiny tendril of the scarf clutched in front of my face, a last bit of something lovely as the abyss yanked me down.

I couldn't breathe.

Give me your hand.

The wall slammed against my chest.

Give me your hand.

I felt fingers reaching for me and there was a moment when I considered letting the wall have its way instead. If Kent was gone, then what was left for me?

The fingers grabbed hold of the scarf in my hand and pulled. I felt myself being raised. I only needed to let go of the scarf to be where Kent was. As a searing pain filled my lungs I wondered how much it would hurt to die this way.

But then I remembered the little pink plus sign. The wall could not touch the life tucked there.

Kent would want me to live.

I didn't let go.

With the scarf as my lifeline, the florist pulled me to my feet and we lurched away from the darkness.

Eleven

CLARA

I had discovered early at Ellis that a hospital nurse performs the same tasks day after day after day, and that an odd solace can be found in the monotony of those duties. Were it not for the steady thrum of the routine, the spectacle of unending human suffering would be a hospital nurse's undoing. There's only so much physical affliction the soul can witness. Concentrating on the task at hand and only the task kept me and my colleagues from being swallowed whole by what we saw every day.

As Dr. Randall prepared to leave the ward after the conversation about the fire, I sought to reclaim my equilibrium by reminding myself of this: Concentrate solely on the simple duties that lay before me. Dr. Randall's gaze on me was achingly apologetic as he and Dr. Treaver finished up their notes. I pretended not to notice.

Not long after the doctors had moved on to another ward, aides arrived to help me with sponge baths and bedpans. The men who were able walked to the toilet room just outside the ward as we steadied them. Andrew watched as one of the aides helped the man across from him, with only the smallest of privacy curtains, use the bedpan. Then he sat up slowly and swung his legs over the side of his bed. He started to stand and I rushed over to him from where I was changing sheets two beds away.

"Careful there, Mr. Gwynn." I reached for him, putting my arm around his back. I could feel the heat of his fever through his bedclothes. "What do you need?"

"I need to see if I can do this." The lilt of his words made me think of a faraway place with half-timbered cottages and thatched roofs.

"Do what?"

"Walk to the toilet."

"Let me help you."

"I don't want to trouble you."

I tightened my grip around his waist. "Let's just stand for a minute and see how that feels."

"I don't want you to help me . . . use the toilet."

His modesty was strangely alluring.

"How about we get there and see how you feel?" I said.

Andrew nodded and we made our way down the corridor in between the beds. He eased himself away from me a bit to test his steadiness.

"How are you doing? Feeling all right?"

"Yes. Yes, thank you." He paused, swallowed gingerly. "I'm very sorry about that fire."

The careful equilibrium that I had salvaged from the earlier conversation with Dr. Randall wavered a bit. But I did not feel the same blast of hot embers that I had felt before. It didn't seem to matter as much that Andrew spoke of the fire. I nodded.

"So many people died," he added.

"Yes."

"Were they not able to get out?"

"No. They couldn't."

"Were some of them your friends?"

I hesitated a moment. "One of them was."

He reached up to rub his throat. "I'm very sorry."

"I am sorry, too. Rest your voice now, Mr. Gwynn."

We reached the doorway and crossed the main hallway to the toilet room. I asked him whether he felt strong enough to go in alone.

"Yes. Thank you." He stepped into the room but then he turned toward me, held my gaze for a moment. "I'll be fine."

He shut the door gently.

AT my lunch break I found Dolly, Ivy, and a few of the other nurses at our usual table. I put down my tray and took the empty chair beside Dolly.

"Having a good day?" Dolly wanted some kind of cryptic message that would let her know whether I had made any headway with my secret quest.

"Busy," I answered. "I've ten men in the throes of scarlet fever."

Dolly frowned, but knew enough not to tell me that was not what she meant.

There would be no veiled conversations at the table about Lily Gwynn and her letter. Not with all the girls there.

Especially not with Ivy.

As if on cue, Ivy put down her fork to address our table. "Did everyone meet the new intern this morning? Isn't he dashing?"

"Oh, I don't know about that," Dolly said. "He's too skinny."

Ivy laughed and turned to me. "Don't you think he's handsome, Clara?"

I swallowed the bit of potato I had in my mouth. "I don't know. Maybe."

Margaret, a frequent member of Dolly's Saturday-night dancing entourage, piped up. "I'll fight you for him, Ivy. He's from Boston and he's a doctor. I wouldn't care if he had three eyes and a harelip."

"I heard he took a shine to Clara," another one, Nellie, said.

I snapped my head up. "What? He did not!"

"He came to the women's measles ward after yours. My ward. I heard him ask Dr. Treaver what your first name was."

"That doesn't mean anything," I protested.

"He's just interested in the fire, that's all!" Ivy chimed in, obviously wanting to claim the Boston doctor for herself and deflect any attention that might have erroneously fallen on me.

And, of course, she had to mention the fire.

"You told him about the fire?" Dolly was aghast, bless her.

"For heaven's sake, everyone knows about the fire. And he mentioned it first, not me. I told him there was a nurse here who was there that day."

"What did you do that for?" Dolly demanded.

"Do what? The fire was months ago." Ivy turned to me. "Right, Clara? Before I even got here."

"Right." I shoveled a piece of meat in my mouth and found I could not chew it. An awkward silence fell around us.

I stood and gathered my tray. "My meat's tough. I am going back for the soup."

I sensed the girls watching me. And I heard Dolly scold Ivy in a whisper as I walked away. "Just because it happened before you got here doesn't mean you can go tellin' people about it. That poor girl watched people jump from a burning building to their deaths! Dozens of them. She saw it all!"

I deposited my tray and kept walking.

Twelve

MY instructors at nursing school taught me there were three elements of responsibility I needed to be mindful of when nursing patients with scarlet fever. First, I had to understand the relationship between patient contact and aseptic care so that I would not also become infected. Second, I had to be vigilant regarding complications: secondary maladies brought on by the fever, such as nephritis. And last, I had to carefully safeguard anyone else in close proximity to the patient.

My father had told me the same general advice, only in far fewer words. *Respect the disease. It is powerful.*

He also told me the disease has no intent. It doesn't want anything. It has no malevolent desire to kill. If it could talk, it would not say, "I want to make you ill! I want to bring you to the brink of death! I want to kill!"

It would say only, "I make people ill. I bring them to the brink of death. I can kill."

The disease is like the machine that does what it does but has no cognizance of self. When a machine stops working, it does not care. And it doesn't celebrate when it starts working again.

I have seen enough cases of scarlet fever to know that to those who have it and to their loved ones, the disease seems heinous, deliberate, and personal. And of course I know why they feel this way. When you are in a fight for your life, then surely there is an adversary. There is something opposed to you. Something that desires to defeat you.

You want to believe your enemy is the disease.

You don't want to believe even for a minute that the enemy is your own body, this weak tent of flesh that cannot stand up against a speck of contagion, this fragile weave of muscle, bone, and soul that also cannot resist the power of flame nor the pull of the ground below it.

ANDREW and several others who had been on his ship developed the crimson rash on the second day. It showed up first on their chests and necks and rapidly spread. This rash is not like measles, where the skin appears as if someone has dotted it with a red pencil. The scarlet rash looks more like smears of rosy-red paint applied by the haphazard strokes of a mad artist.

The rash's angry blisters will not show up for another three days, and after they've had their way, their crusted remains will erupt into a sloughing, scaly waste that will have the men thinking they've been turned into lepers. The bits peel off like the scales of a fish, and the process is celebrated for only one reason: With each passing hour it signifies you will likely survive. But it is a nasty business that can last for days and it is often the reason clothes and belongings are burned. The confetti-like debris is akin to powdered poison.

Today my main concern as I entered the ward would be monitoring the men's fevers and the swelling in their throats. The fever and the swelling were always heightened on the second day. I went from bed to bed, checking on each patient, assisting with sips of water and a bedpan or two. I intentionally saved Andrew for last.

When I approached his bedside, Andrew barely acknowledged my presence. I placed my hand on his forehead and the heat of his skin warmed my hand like an iron. Andrew leaned into the coolness of my palm, moaning softly. The night nurse had written in his record that Andrew's temperature had been hovering at one hundred five degrees since before dawn. There was only one thing I could do for him as I waited for Dr. Treaver to arrive on his morning rounds: Draw the heat out with a cool cloth.

I had given hundreds of baths to men of every age, but I felt an unfamiliar bond with Andrew as I pressed a wet compress to his neck, chest, and back. I might have been running alongside him as he fought a dragon, handing him what he needed to fight. The dragon's hot breath seared into the cloth, wanting to take me on, too, it seemed. But I kept dousing the flame as I plunged and wrung out my cloth, again and again. Andrew shuddered at my touch, and each time I imagined him running toward the dragon with his sword raised high, poking the reptilian hide and looking for the place of weakness in the serpent's body.

Then he opened his eyes and gazed at me.

"Lily?" he whispered.

A drip of water slid down his temple and I caught it with the edge of the cloth. "It's Nurse Wood, Mr. Gwynn."

"Lily?"

"It's Nurse Wood. Remember me?"

"Lily, those aren't your clothes."

This wasn't the first time I had seen fever bring on delirium, but it was the first time I'd been mistaken for someone's dead wife. "You are at Ellis Island Hospital, Mr. Gwynn."

He said something in Welsh. At least, I think it was Welsh. He sounded very sad, and it pained my heart to hear the tone of his voice. He said it again louder and he seemed on the verge of having a fit. He raised his head a few inches off his pillow. I said something back to Andrew in French, because my mother would speak French to me when I lay sick in bed, hot with fever. It always calmed me. I hoped it might shatter the fever's spell.

"Ne t'inquiète pas, mon cœur."

Do not trouble yourself, sweetheart.

His shining eyes grew wide and he lay still.

"Fais des beaux rêves de lendemain."

Dream of sweet tomorrows.

Andrew lay back on his pillow but his eyes never left mine.

"Lily?"

"Shhh."

"Lily?"

I gave in. "What is it, Andrew?"

"I don't have money for a ring."

"It's all right."

"I wish I had my mother's ring."

"Shhh, now."

"You would have liked her, Lily. I wish you could have known her."

"Yes. Hush now. Time for rest."

He closed his eyes like an obedient child. I left my hand and the compress underneath it on his warm forehead until his breaths became slow and measured.

I sensed movement behind me.

I looked up expecting to see that Dr. Treaver had entered the room, but Dr. Randall was standing a few yards behind me, fastening the protective cloak tight around his neck. I remembered what Nellie had said at lunch the day before, about Dr. Randall asking my first name, and I rose with a start from Andrew's bedside.

"Good morning, Nurse Wood," he said as I made my way toward him. When I reached him I looked past the doorway to see whether Dr. Treaver was not far behind.

"It's just me today." Dr. Randall smiled.

"Oh. Of course. Good morning, Dr. Randall."

"And how are things this morning?" He walked over to the nurses' desk to look at our main chart for all the men in the ward. With a glance he could see the general state of all the patients in the room.

"Five confirmed new cases, then?" he said.

"Yes. The rash showed up this morning."

"And no temperatures higher than one hundred six? No convulsions? No edema?"

"No." I looked toward Andrew. "Mr. Gwynn was a bit delirious. I brought down his fever some with a cool bath. He's resting comfortably now."

"Delirious? How so?"

I swallowed. "He thought I was his wife. She . . .

she's one of those who died of the fever aboard the *Seville*."

Dr. Randall looked up from the chart. "Oh. How terrible. I hadn't heard that about him. Very sad."

There was nothing to say to this. I turned to prepare my cart so that I could assist him on his rounds. When I was finished readying it and tying on my mask, I turned to him and saw that he was watching me.

"You know, you have a gentle way about you, Nurse Wood. I saw you with Mr. Gwynn."

My cheeks grew instantly warm and I was glad he could not see it.

"I couldn't hear everything the two of you were saying but I could see that he was agitated and you calmed him with just your touch and a few words. I'm sure that wasn't taught at nursing school. Or was it?" His smile broadened.

I laughed nervously. "Did they not also teach you bedside manners at medical school, Dr. Randall?"

"They didn't teach us French."

I bumped a bottle of alcohol on my cart and it started to topple. He reached out and steadied it.

"That was French you were speaking, wasn't it?"

I pulled the bottle from his hand and righted it myself. "It was."

"But Mr. Gwynn is Welsh."

I shrugged. "My mother is French. She'd speak to me that way when I was sick. French sounds pretty. It soothes. I hoped it would soothe him."

"Indeed it did. How wise you were to think of that."

For a moment I thought perhaps he was mocking me, his smile and manner were so effusive. But he was being sincere.

"We do what we can here to ease the patients' discomfort," I said lamely, wincing a little at how rote it sounded.

"You do not give yourself enough credit, Nurse Wood. Or may I call you Clara?"

I pulled the cart close to me, and away from him. "You may call me Miss Wood."

His smile did not waver. "As you wish, Miss Wood. Shall we?"

We made the circuit from bed to bed. Many minutes later, when we arrived at Andrew's bed, the moments of delirium had clearly passed. Andrew stirred awake as Dr. Randall listened to his lungs and heart, palpated the glands of his throat, and observed the spread of the rash. He obeyed when Dr. Randall asked Andrew to open his mouth so that he could see inside. And he was able to hold the thermometer in his mouth. I was relieved to see the number had dropped to one hundred three, even though the decrease would likely not last. The third day would probably be worse.

"You're in very excellent hands here, Mr. Gwynn," Dr. Randall announced. "Nurse Wood is taking good care of you."

Andrew's gaze shifted to me and I smiled politely. I had no idea whether he remembered he had called me Lily. I suspected he did not.

We moved on to the next patient, who did not awaken when Dr. Randall performed his examination. And because Dr. Randall couldn't interact with the man in the bed, he addressed me. "Do you like to read, Miss Wood?"

"It depends on what it is, Doctor."

"Ah, yes. Of course it would. Do you like philosophy?"

I wasn't sure that I wanted to enlighten the doctor on what I liked to read. I thought of Lily's book of poetry up in my room. I hadn't read any poetry in years. I didn't think Dr. Randall had either.

"I like poetry," I blurted.

He looked up at me, happy, it seemed. "Truly?"

I nodded, a bit alarmed. I replaced the chart of the man he'd been examining and pushed my cart to the next bed. The patient who lay in it was in his second week with the disease, and was awake and sipping from a glass of water. His hands and neck were pasty white with scaling skin and spent blisters.

"Have a favorite?" Dr. Randall asked.

"A favorite what?"

"A favorite poet."

I bent toward the man in the bed. "Mind if I set your glass of water here on the table, Mr. Gianelli?" I asked, gently removing the cup from his hand.

"Surely you've a favorite poet."

"I like them all."

Dr. Randall laughed. "No one likes them all."

I placed the glass on the table next to the bed, eager as I had never been in my life to talk instead about swollen eustachian tubes, kidney pain, and desquamation. Dr. Randall set about examining Mr. Gianelli and giving new orders for increasing the number of scrubbing baths to twice a day to remove the rash residue.

The last two patients were also awake and conversant. When we finished, I headed for the sink at the end of the ward to scrub my hands. Dr. Randall followed me, unfastening the mask and cloak and dropping them into the bin to be sterilized for their next use.

He stood beside me and began to scrub his hands

also. "I don't mean to pry, Miss Wood, but there is little to entertain us after hours during the week. I thought it would be nice to discuss a book together in the staff commons after dinner. I was bored out of my mind last night."

"You were bored your first night?"

"It was my third night, and yes, I was bored."

I scrubbed and said nothing. Part of me longed for something to do in the evening besides read the social pages of the newspaper with Dolly and the other girls and listen to them gossip about people. But to sit in the commons with Dr. Randall and discuss a book? People would think I wanted him for a beau. That was an impossible scenario in my in-between place.

I dried my hands quickly and took a step away from the sink.

"Tell me who your favorite is," he said. "And I'll tell you if I've read him. Or her."

I could think of only the one name at that moment. Just the one.

"Keats."

He smiled. "Keats. I've read him. Shall we say later tonight? After supper?"

I shook my head. "I can't tonight."

"Tomorrow, then?" He dried his hands and turned to face me.

"I'm not . . . ready."

"Not what?"

"I'm . . ." But the next words dwindled away unrepeated. To my relief, at that very moment one of the patients called out for a drink of water. "I'm needed," I said, smiling with effort. "Good day, Doctor." I rushed to fill a pitcher of water and then made my way to the bedside of the man who had asked for it. Out of the corner of my eye, I saw Dr. Randall leave the ward.

When I had finished helping the man with his drink, I heard another voice ask me for water. Andrew.

I went to his bedside and poured his water. He sipped slowly and with effort as I held the glass.

"I like Keats, too," he said when I took the glass away. I was surprised he had heard the conversation at the sink. My eyes must have grown wide. "Wasn't trying to listen. The doctor's voice echoes in this tiled room," he continued.

I smiled a bit uneasily. "Then I shall have to be careful what secrets I tell in here."

He lay back on his pillow. "Your voice doesn't carry like his."

And it was as if he were really saying, *Your secrets will be safe with me.*

As I replaced his glass on his bedside table I wondered whether he knew Lily had also liked Keats. Did he know she had a volume of his poems in her baggage?

I didn't see how he could know that, considering what had been slipped inside it.

Thirteen

MY parents came to New York three days after the fire, arriving on the noon train with no luggage. Their plan was to help me pack my few things and then the three of us would be on the four o'clock to Philadelphia, where my father had no doubt left his motorcar for the hour drive home.

I should have met them at the station, but I couldn't summon the strength to do it. I hadn't been outside since the grocer's delivery boy escorted me home three days earlier. A cab brought my parents to the brownstone where I was renting a room on the top floor. It was a nice room in a well-kept building owned by a spinster named Miss Hatfield, who felt it was her mission in life to protect young single women from the perils of city living.

They arrived a few minutes after noon and Miss Hatfield insisted on making us lunch while we used her sitting room for our visit. It was clear she didn't want to lose me as a boarder, and she could tell, as I could, that my parents intended to take me home that day. She surely hoped her hospitality would nudge my parents into securing my room until my return, since I surely wouldn't be able to keep paying for it myself if I left with them.

My mother folded me into her arms as soon as Miss Hatfield left us to prepare our meal. I had not cried since the fire, and as I stood wrapped in motherly care, I felt a great wave of emotion rise to the surface of my being, as powerful as a storm surge. I pulled away from her so that we both wouldn't drown in it.

"I'm all right, I'm all right," I said, as I pushed back against the tide. "Let's sit."

We took seats on upholstered chairs adorned with lace doilies on their padded armrests. A canary in a bell-shaped cage twittered as we arranged ourselves.

"Oh, my darling. I can't believe this happened so soon after your arrival!" My mother leaned toward me and patted my arm, and I noticed for the first time that she was wearing a cornflower blue dress and matching hat that I'd never seen before. This suddenly struck me as odd. I had never seen her in a dress that I didn't know already. I'd been home for only a week in between graduation and moving to New York, and before that I had been away at nursing school. It occurred to me that if I went back with them, I would see that everything was slightly different—the size of the apple trees in the garden, the height of the little boy who lived across the lane from my parents, and even the dresses hanging in my mother's wardrobe. Everything would be slightly different except for me. I would go back to the exact spot where I'd been before I had met Edward. For me, that little tiny sliver of time and place would still be there, but only for me. For everyone and every-thing else, the world would have changed.

I couldn't go with them.

And I knew I couldn't stay.

Repairs to the top floors were under way at the Asch Building and I'd received a message from the clinic man-ager that businesses on the undamaged floors, which in-cluded the doctor's office where I worked, could expect to resume operating by the end of the week.

But I could never step inside the Asch Building again. Not ever.

"It must have been dreadful for those people who couldn't get out," my mother went on. "I feel so bad for their families, especially when we are so lucky that you—"

"It was dreadful. It was the most dreadful thing I've ever seen."

I'd been taught never to interrupt when someone else was speaking, and my intrusion surprised my mother. Surprised me, too.

"Seen? Did you . . . So you were on the street?" my father asked, unsure how to ask me what I had witnessed.

"From the time I got out of the building until the fire was out."

"The whole time?" My mother's eyes were wide.

"The fire burned for only half an hour."

"All . . . all those people and the fire lasted only half an hour?"

An ugly boldness seemed to sweep over me, as if I wanted to blame someone for how I felt that day. "Yes. All those people died in half an hour. None of us on the street could do anything about it. I'm a nurse and I could do nothing."

I hadn't meant to sound so blunt, and my mother

was certainly not expecting it. She sat back in her chair as if I had struck her.

I looked down at my feet and summoned the apology I owed her. "I'm sorry. None of this is your fault. I don't know what came over me."

"It's quite all right," my mother whispered, grace lacing her words together.

"Look, Clara," my father said gently. "Everything is all set for you to come back home with us. You don't have to give any of this another thought."

I smiled in spite of myself. He could not know that thoughts are not things you can give or not give. Thoughts are thrust upon you. You can only hope that thoughts that you don't want will tire of you at some point and flutter away. I think it was at this very moment that I realized I needed to be in an in-between place. Not home in Pennsylvania where my parents were. Nor in Manhattan where Edward had been. But someplace in between where I could wait for the heaviness to lift.

"I'm not going back with you," I said.

"Beg your pardon?" My father cocked his head as if he hadn't quite heard me.

"You . . . you want to stay here?" my mother asked.

"No. I don't want to stay here."

"I don't understand," my father said.

The truth was, I didn't understand either. I just knew that sitting with my parents in that room in Manhattan, I found I could barely breathe; it was as if I were suffocating on the fire's ashes. They were falling on top of me like January snow and if I didn't move, I would disappear underneath them.

I remembered then that in nursing school there was a fellow student, an aloof girl who kept to herself, who wanted to be stationed at Ellis Island Hospital when she graduated. When I asked her why, she told me it was because it was new, and big, the latest equipment was in use there, and nurses didn't have to enlist in the medical corps to work there like the doctors did. And she told me it was in the city without being in the city, and she liked that because she didn't like feeling pressed in. I had said something about its surely being a busy place nonetheless, and she said, "Yes, but it's a different busy. No one stays there for long. It's a place for the next thing to happen. It's Ellis. People don't live there. It's nobody's address." She dropped out before she graduated, but I remembered how she looked when she described it to me. It was the most animated I had ever seen her.

And her words were echoing in my head. *It's nobody's address. Nobody's address.* An in-between place.

"I want to get a post at the hospital on Ellis Island," I said. "I have heard there is a need for nurses."

My mother gasped, albeit quietly.

"Ellis? You want to work on Ellis? In public health?" My father blinked several times.

"It's such a . . . such a . . ." My mother couldn't finish.

"Such a what?"

"You don't want to work there," my father said soothingly, as if I were ten. "Cholera, typhus, measles, influenza— that's what they deal with there. It's no place to be, Clara."

And again my mother gasped. Even I started a bit at the mention of cholera and typhus. But I held my ground. "Unless you're a nurse. Then it's a perfectly reasonable place to be."

"Clara, what's happened to you?" My mother said it so softly I almost couldn't hear her. Before I could decide whether I truly had, my father spoke.

"I understand you've been through something . . . traumatic . . . and if you don't want to come home with us, that's fine. But don't punish yourself for surviving the fire by taking a post among the world's worst diseases. It's not your fault you couldn't save anyone."

For a moment I was rendered speechless. Punishing myself for surviving the fire? Was that what I was looking to do? The answer came swiftly.

I didn't need an island to do that.

"Clara?"

"If I wanted to punish myself, Papa, I could do that by staying here and stepping back inside that building. Or going home with you."

"You can't mean that?" My mother was now on the verge of tears.

"I don't mean home is a terrible place, Mama. I mean I am in a terrible place. And if I come home with you, nothing will change."

"Of course it will!"

"No, it won't."

My father cleared his throat. "You think that now because you witnessed a terrible fire, but when we get you home, what you saw will start to fade, Clara. You must trust me on this."

I turned to my father and saw strength and determination in his eyes. He was a fixer like me. He thought he could fix this just as he'd fixed every broken person whom he'd stitched back together. I had seen him do it a thousand times. But this was not a broken thing to be fixed. Or a disease to be cured. It was an abyss to climb out of.

"It's not what I saw, Papa. It's what I lost."

"What did you lose?" my mother asked, still clutching my hand.

I wanted to say, "Someone I was meant to love," and have the six words fall from my lips as sure and quick as the words "Merry Christmas" on the twenty-fifth of December. But I didn't think I could explain what I meant, and surely those words would need an explanation.

"I'm glad you came," I said instead. "And I know you think coming home would somehow make it seem as if I never left, that none of this happened. But in here"— and I pointed to my heart—"I know that it did."

"But do you have to go *there*?" my mother said, her eyes glassy with fear for me. "Those diseases . . . they are insidious; they are foreign!"

"I will be careful."

"But there are hospitals right here in Manhattan," she continued. "Why can't you work at one of those?"

"I promise I will be careful."

She turned to my father. "Tom! Talk to her!"

My father had grown silent in the last few moments, no doubt contemplating the last thing I had said to him. *It's what I lost.*

I could see him turning the sentence around in his head. Examining it as he would a wound or an illness. And I saw in his eyes the moment he realized that fixers like him and me can easily mend broken things. But we can't easily find lost things.

Finding something you lost takes a different kind of skill.

"Clara needs to handle this her way, Helene." He held my gaze and then faced my mother. "She will be careful."

"Tom."

But my father turned back to me. "How long do you want to work there?"

I shook my head. I didn't know.

But in my mind I answered him.

As long as it takes for what I lost to become what I release.

Lunch at Miss Hatfield's table was a stilted affair. And poor Miss Hatfield could sense it. By the time she served us slices of chocolate cake, she knew she was losing a boarder and my father's good money.

My father asked whether I wanted his assistance in getting a post on Ellis. He had an acquaintance in public health he would contact if I wanted him to. I would have turned him down were it not for the pressure of the invisible ashes inside my chest, bearing down on my soul. I agreed. And while he left to make his inquiries, my mother helped me box up the few trinkets in my room that I would not need in a dormitory room at Ellis Island Hospital.

When they left for the four o'clock train, I promised I would write them, that I would be careful, that I would tender my resignation the moment I didn't want to be at Ellis anymore.

As they drove away in a hired cab, I waved from the steps of Miss Hatfield's brownstone, breathing in the outside air tentatively.

There wasn't a hint of smoke or ash or death.

The pounding in my chest was the only evidence within and around me that I did not belong there anymore.

Fourteen

THE next few days of the fever were the worst for Andrew and the rest who'd come down with the disease after they arrived at Ellis. Another nurse, an older woman named Mrs. Meade, was assigned midweek to help me with the men in my care. We split the room in two, with those who were sickest at the back half of the room and those who were in various stages of recovery in the front half. I volunteered to take the back half, and Nurse Meade put up no protest.

I wanted to give every man there my kindest attention, but I found myself continually gravitating toward Andrew. Caring for his physical needs was the one thing I could do for him, and he was sick enough by Thursday not to care whether he needed help with a bedpan. Dr. Treaver made rounds Thursday, so I did not have to worry whether Dr. Randall would ask me again about joining him in the commons after hours to talk about a poet I'd lied about liking.

When I arrived at the ward on Friday morning, there seemed to be a slight improvement among the men at the back of the room. When I came to Andrew's bedside and placed my hand on his forehead, he opened his eyes and looked at me, something he had not done in the previous two days. The angry rash on his body was prickling into a poxlike explosion that would annoy him but hopefully would do no worse.

"Might you be feeling better today, Mr. Gwynn?" I asked.

He nodded.

I reached into the basin at his bedside, where fresh water had been brought only minutes earlier. I added some carbolized oil, plunged the rag into the cool water, and wrung it out. He closed his eyes as I laid the cool cloth on his forehead, and a soft sound escaped his throat.

"Does that feel all right?"

Again he nodded. "What day is it?" he whispered.

"It's Friday."

"It seems . . . seems longer."

I pressed the cloth now to his cheek and throat. "I think your fever is on its way out, Mr. Gwynn. The doctor will be here soon and he can tell you more."

He blinked slowly as I moved the compress over the top of his chest. "Lily died on this day. The fifth day."

"Yes. I am so sorry about that."

"She didn't even recognize me on this day."

It seemed he was inviting me into a conversation about his dead wife, the very thing I wanted to have so that I could reach a conclusion about her letter. And yet

I felt like an intruder. "I'm sure you gave her the best care you could, Mr. Gwynn. Surely you did."

We were silent for a moment as I soaked the rag in fresh water and then began to press the cool cloth against his forehead again.

"Would you like to tell me how you met her?" I asked.

His face brightened in a wistful way, as if he needed a moment to consider what it was going to feel like talking about his deceased wife. When he began to speak, his Welsh accent glittered on his sentences like something made of sugar. "I met her by the ship's ticketing office in Liverpool. I'd received a letter from my brother that day that my sponsorship was in order, and I'd come to buy my passage on the next ship that could take me. It wouldn't leave for another two weeks. Afterward I walked into a little restaurant there by the ship's offices to get a cool drink—it was a blistering-hot day—and Lily waited on me. She was so beautiful and friendly. Dark hair and violet eyes—her mother was from India, she told me. She asked what had brought me to the docks on a hot day and I told her I'd just bought my passage to America. She brought me my pint, and a sandwich, too, though I hadn't ordered one. I'd spent the last bit of cash in my pocket on the pint. I told her she'd given me someone else's sandwich by mistake. But she said she'd made no mistake. And when I whispered to her that I had no money on me to pay for it, she whispered back to me that she was celebrating my happy news of soon being on my way to America. I saw such longing in her eyes when she said it, they glimmered with it."

"Is that the day you fell in love with her?" I said it in

a lighthearted tone so he wouldn't think I had a vested interest in gauging the depth of his grief.

He didn't answer right away. "She fell in love with me that day," he finally said. "She told me so. I don't know when it was that I fell in love with her. I didn't really fall. It didn't feel like falling."

I lifted the cloth. His words interested me. Struck a chord in me. "What did it feel like?"

He closed his eyes, either in contemplation or exhaustion. "It was like . . . stepping into a room."

"Stepping into a room?"

"A new room. One I'd never been inside before. And I stepped in because I wanted to. Not because I fell. I took a job loading crates at the shipyard so that I could stay in Liverpool until my ship sailed. My mother had just died and our landlord had taken back our cottage in Cardiff. There was no reason for me to go back to Wales to count the days until I left. So I saw Lily every day after that. Two days before I was to leave she told me she wanted to come with me. As my wife. We married the day before we sailed."

The slow spin of the earth seemed to halt as Andrew spoke. I knew the feeling he was trying to describe. The way I had been drawn to Edward was not as it had been with broken-arm Otto or dashing Daniel, when I'd tumbled headlong into their charms like a schoolgirl. I had felt connected to Edward the moment I met him, as if a history had already been written about us, but the record was stowed in some heavenly place I could not visit. Eternity already knew us as a couple. We had been destined for a long, blissful earthly life together and the fire had robbed me in the cruelest of ways, taking my future happiness away when I had but tasted it.

"You felt you already knew her, didn't you? Almost as if you had met before." I felt tears brimming and I attempted to blink them away. One fell onto Andrew's chest and I rushed to blot it.

He opened his eyes slowly at my touch. I wiped the tear onto my apron, unable to pull my eyes from his. I waited for him to tell me that was just as it had been for him and Lily. But that was not what he said.

"Who did you lose in that fire, Nurse Wood?"

A thick ache rose up in my throat and I swallowed it down. I closed my eyes to shut the gates on any more tears.

"His name was Edward," I said, when I was able. "And I had known him for only two weeks." A smile tugged at the corners of my mouth. "Just as long as you knew Lily."

"You loved him?"

I nodded. "I did."

"And he loved you?"

Andrew's four-word question was the main reason I had told no one except Dolly about Edward. How could I explain that I knew Edward had loved me? We had only ever spoken to each other on the elevator. But the kinship I felt with Andrew's loss made me brave in that moment. I reasoned that he was the only person on the island—indeed, in my life—who might understand.

"He was destined to love me," I answered.

Andrew seemed to ponder this for a moment. "If he had lived . . . ?" He stopped, inviting me to finish the sentence.

"If he had lived I wouldn't be on this island. I'd be with him."

"Is he the reason you are here?"

It didn't seem fair to heap the blame for my exile

solely on Edward. "I'm the reason I'm here." I attempted a weak smile.

"You are here to forget."

The strange hope in his voice suggested he very much wanted to know that it was possible to forget what despair felt like. But I didn't want to forget anything.

I placed the cloth back in the basin. "I don't want to forget Edward. I guess I am here so that I won't."

"But then, won't you always be here?"

It had been a few weeks since I had stopped to ask myself how long I wanted to live this way, tethered to the island and unable to set my foot on the vast expanse of the rest of the world.

"I want to be able to remember and have it not hurt. I think it's possible to remember someone you loved and lost and feel blessed that you knew them, even for just a short time, without it hurting. Don't you think?"

He nodded slowly and closed his eyes.

I placed my hand on his brow, gauging his temperature, ready to have him swallow some aspirin if the cool compress had not accomplished what I had hoped. But his skin felt nearly cool against mine.

"How long do you think that will take?" His eyes stayed closed and his voice sounded as though he were slipping into slumber.

He drifted off to sleep before I could think of an answer. Indeed, as I rose from the bed I was certain there was no calendar to consult.

It would take as long as it took.

Andrew would likely survive his illness. In a couple weeks or less, he'd be well enough to leave the island. He carried his loss like I carried mine, close to his chest.

And he would carry it off this island in one way or another. I did not envy him.

I was no closer to knowing what I would do with Lily's letter. Give it to him and change his grief to a bitter wound, or burn the letter and leave him to grieve in ignorance for who knew how long?

At lunch, Dolly and I had a table to ourselves. I told her what Andrew had said about stepping into love like it was a room you wanted very much to go into. She listened to me intently and then offered again to give him the letter and be done with it. "He deserves to know," she said.

"Nobody deserves to get that kind of news, Dolly."

"I didn't say the man deserves the news; I said he deserves to know the truth."

I poked at a slice of buttered turnip and pictured Andrew reading the letter, absorbing the degrading news that he had been played a fool. I shook my head to shatter that image. "I wish I had never opened that trunk."

Dolly set her fork down hard and it clattered on the wood table. "You were meant to open that trunk, Clara! Have you thought about that? What if fate wanted you to open it because it was the only way that good man would know the truth? Nobody should have to spend the rest of his life grieving something he never had!"

At that moment a figure approached our table. I looked up to see Dr. Randall with an empty tray in his hands on his way out of the dining room. The puzzled look on his face suggested he had heard the last bit of Dolly's comment.

"Ah, good afternoon." He nodded to both of us and then turned to me. "Have you given any more thought to discussing Keats, Miss Wood?"

"Keats?" Dolly echoed, gaping at me.

"I . . . I've been busy—" But Dolly cut me off.

"Keats?" This time she said it to Dr. Randall.

He smiled congenially. "Miss Wood is a devotee of Keats. He's not my favorite poet, but that doesn't mean I won't enjoy discussing his work. Might make it more interesting, actually."

"You want to discuss Keats with Clara?" Dolly laughed lightly.

"I should like very much to discuss Keats with Miss Wood. And be allowed to address her as Clara." He smiled back.

"I don't know . . ." I mumbled.

"Why on earth would you want to talk about a dead poet after a long day at this hospital?" Dolly said. She leaned closer to the doctor but nodded to me. "Is that really the best you can do, Doc?"

Dr. Randall laughed easily. "Oh, but I happen to like poetry. Lucky for me, Miss Wood does also."

Dolly tipped her head in my direction. "Does she now? Well, that is providential."

"This place lacks something in the evenings," Dr. Randall went on.

"Indeed it does, Doctor. That is why we nurses work for the weekends. Getting on that ferry Saturday after-noon makes the long week bearable."

Dr. Randall again turned toward me, an eyebrow cocked. "Will you be on the ferry tomorrow, Miss Wood?"

"I am working this weekend," I replied before Dolly could answer for me. And it wasn't a lie. I *was* scheduled to work through the weekend.

"So am I," Dr. Randall said. "Shall we say tomorrow

night then? In the commons? I'll be waiting for you at seven o'clock."

Before I could think of an excuse for not being able to accept his invitation, he nodded to both of us and walked away.

Dolly watched him exit the room. "Nellie's right about that one. He's sweet on you, Clara."

I reached for my coffee cup. "He's bored and lonely."

She turned to face me. "What would be so terrible about that nice young doctor being sweet on you?"

"He's not sweet on—"

"And for heaven's sake, did you really tell him you were a fan of Keats? You've never said anything about that to me. I wouldn't have taken you for a—what did he call you?—a devotee of poetry." Dolly's smile broadened. She was clearly enjoying my predicament.

"It was the only name I could think of, thank you. I didn't take him for one either." I stood to gather my utensils and tray.

She stood as well. "You'd better hope there's something by Keats in the commons bookshelves that you can read tonight or you will have a very short date."

"It's not a date. And please don't tell anyone that it is." I walked away from her.

"I won't, I won't." She quickened her steps to catch up with me. "Want me to peek into the commons and look on the shelves for you?"

She apparently had not looked closely at Lily's book.

Even if I planned to meet Dr. Randall, which I had no intention of doing, I had no need to scour the shelves in the commons looking for anything by Keats.

I told her I already had a book by Keats I could read.

Fifteen

FRIDAY after supper, I wrote a letter to Henrietta, washed my hair, and polished my shoes. But the evening wore on and still I was not sleepy. After Dolly was snoring quietly across from me, I reached under my pillow for Lily's book.

I had read the minimum of literature in school, impressing no one with my insights. I was far more suited to history and science. If I had read Keats in school, I had quickly forgotten anything he had written. To drop his name to Dr. Randall had been an impulsive, reckless act.

I opened the book and withdrew the two folded pieces of paper—Lily's letter and the certificate—and set them aside.

I flipped to the first page and read what I found there.

"Ode on a Grecian Urn"
Thou still unravish'd bride of quietness

Thou foster-child of Silence and slow Time,
Sylvan historian, who canst thus express
A flowery tale more sweetly than our rhyme:
What leaf-fringed legend haunts about thy shape
Of deities or mortals, or of both,
In Tempe or the dales of Arcady?
What men or gods are these? What maidens loth?
What mad pursuit? What struggle to escape?
What pipes and timbrels? What wild ecstasy?
Heard melodies are sweet, but those unheard
Are sweeter; therefore, ye soft pipes, play on;
Not to the sensual ear, but, more endear'd,
Pipe to the spirit ditties of no tone:
Fair youth, beneath the trees, thou canst not leave
Thy song, nor ever can those trees be bare;
Bold Lover, never, never canst thou kiss,
Though winning near the goal—yet, do not grieve;
She cannot fade, though thou hast not thy bliss,
For ever wilt thou love, and she be fair!

The poem went on for three more stanzas. Line by line I read it. And then I read it again, these verses of a man describing images he sees on an urn; images of men running after women in a forest. Pipes are being played and drums being beaten. What does it matter what images a man sees painted on an urn? I didn't understand any of it, least of all the last two lines.

"Beauty is truth, truth beauty,"—that is all
Ye know on earth, and all ye need to know.

What did that even mean?
I grabbed Lily's letter and the certificate, slipped them

back inside the book, and snapped it shut. I shoved it under my pillow and turned out my light. But sleep eluded me for an hour or more as I chewed on the words in my head. What meaning had Lily found in a poem like that? Or Andrew? What had they seen that I had not? I fell asleep at last and did not dream of the fire or anything else.

IN the morning as we dressed Dolly asked me what I was going to wear that evening to discuss poetry with Dr. Randall.

"Dolly—"

"Now, don't tell me you're going to leave him waiting there for you, Clara."

"I never told him yes. He walked away before I had a chance to tell him."

She placed a hand on her ample hip. "So you're not going to show."

"Of course I'm going to show. It would be rude not to. I'm not going to stay."

"For heaven's sake, why not?"

I placed my nurse's cap on my head, tucking wisps of brown curls up underneath it. "I was wrong. I don't like poetry. And I don't like Keats. We will have nothing to talk about." I headed for the door.

She grabbed her own hat and trailed after me. "I am quite sure there are other things to talk about besides poetry."

I said nothing else as we headed down to breakfast.

Half an hour later, I arrived at the ward. Five of the men had been deemed finally free of contagion the evening before and were now preparing to be discharged. I spent the next hour helping Mrs. Meade with the final paperwork, gathering belongings, and escorting men out of the hospital and into the sunshine of a new day. I went about my business distracted by remembered snippets of Keats, and my gaze was continually pulled toward Andrew's bed. I was oddly jealous that Lily had something in common with him that I did not. His rash was now beginning its hellish transformation from scarlet to scales. In a matter of days desquamation would begin and he would need to be scrubbed repeatedly to rid his body of the remaining flakes of poison.

The last man to be discharged needed help sending a telegram to his mainland sponsors telling them that he was now free to come ashore. I offered to accompany him to the main immigration building on Ellis to find an interpreter who spoke Italian. I was able to find an available interpreter fairly quickly and the three of us continued on to the telegraph office. When asked for the address of his sponsor, the Italian man set his suitcase down, opened it, and presumably set about looking for the address. While he rifled about his belongings, I saw a flash of reddish-orange fabric and I knew at once why I hadn't seen Lily's scarf among Andrew's things since I'd rotated in to the ward.

"Wait!" I bent down and reached for the cloth that shone like flame. I pulled it out of the suitcase and turned to the Italian man, who was staring at me openmouthed.

"Where did you get this?" I said.

His eyes grew wide but he did not answer me.

I turned to the interpreter. "Ask him where he got this!"

The interpreter calmly said something in Italian. And the man said something back.

"He said it's his."

Indignation swelled within me. "I asked him where

he got it. Because I can assure you it's not his. It belongs to another patient."

The interpreter frowned and said something to which the Italian man responded angrily. He reached out to take the scarf from me. I stepped back, keeping it from his reach.

"He said it was his mother's," the interpreter said.

A tiny tendril of doubt crept up alongside my anger and I turned the scarf over in my hands, needing proof that I was correct. I ran my fingers along its hemmed edge, looking for a manufacturer's tag. I felt something hard, thin, and about the size of my little finger inside the turned-under fabric, but I quickly moved past it in search of affirmation that I had a British woman's scarf in my hands. My fingers felt raised stitches, letters of the alphabet.

Lily.

I held up the scarf and pointed to the hand-stitched name. "Still want to tell me this was your mother's scarf?"

I turned to the interpreter. "This belongs to a patient who lost his English wife to scarlet fever during their voyage. It's the only thing of hers Mr. Gwynn has left."

The interpreter shrugged. "Maybe Mr. Gwynn gave it to him."

I frowned. "Do you really think that's what he did?" Then I wheeled toward the Italian man. "Shall we go ask Mr. Gwynn if he gave you this scarf?"

The interpreter repeated my question in Italian. For a moment the man stared me down. Then he leaned over, yanked a card out of his suitcase, and slammed it shut. He stood up, faced the interpreter, and rattled off a handful of words without looking at me.

"He said he would like to send his telegram and get off this island," the interpreter said.

I took a step toward the man with the suitcase. "Shame on you!" I turned on my heel. "He's all yours," I said to the interpreter, and I left them.

The man shouted something at me and the interpreter tossed the words to my back. "He says he thought the man was dying." The red-orange tails of Lily's scarf trailed like a garland from my wrist as I continued on my way without a word.

As I marched back to island three, my anger was replaced by gratitude for having been the one to escort the Italian man to the telegraph office instead of Mrs. Meade. She wouldn't have recognized that bit of orange peeking from out of the suitcase.

I reentered the ward and made straight for Andrew's bed, Lily's scarf in my hands. He was sipping tea as I approached him and when he looked up, his eyes were immediately drawn to what I was carrying in my hand.

"How did you . . . Where did you find it?" he whispered.

"It seems that it mistakenly ended up in one of your ward mate's suitcases."

He set his cup down and slowly took the scarf. It was as if he thought it might disappear if he reached for it too fast.

"I assumed it had been taken from me to be destroyed," he murmured. "She was wearing it when she . . ." He looked up at me. "How did you know it was Lily's?"

"I . . . I remember you had it around your neck the day you arrived."

"You remembered that?"

"It's a very pretty scarf. And it's a lady's scarf and yet you were wearing it, so . . ."

"You figured it was hers."

"Yes. And then I saw her name embroidered on the edge. I knew that man had taken it from you."

Andrew's mouth crooked into a smile. "Her mother gave it to her when she was young, stitched her name inside because Lily was forgetful." He paused for a moment as he fingered the bright fabric. "She was shivering so badly from the fever. I couldn't keep her warm. Not even with this. I took it off of her before they . . . before they took her. I don't know how to thank you."

"No need. I'm just sorry it was stolen from you in the first place. I apologize for that."

"Not your fault." He folded the scarf carefully. "Is it safe for me to keep? Will it harm anyone?"

"If it is properly washed and sterilized there is no reason you cannot take it with you. Would you like me to see that it is laundered for you?"

"Yes, thank you." He handed the scarf back to me. My hands brushed his fingers as the scarf moved from his hand to mine and the sensation was remarkably tender. But Andrew seemed alarmed that our hands had touched.

He looked down at his hands. The tops were pasty and streaked.

"All those scales will come off, Mr. Gwynn. They won't be there forever."

Mrs. Meade called for me then to ready the emptied beds for new arrivals. I took the scarf to the nurses' desk and wrapped it inside a clean pillowcase and set it aside. I wouldn't take the scarf to the laundry facility, where harsh chemicals and rough hands could easily reduce the delicate fabric to tatters. I would wash it myself, carefully, and with the respect it deserved.

When Mrs. Meade and I were finished she left to

assist in the children's wards, where mumps was making the rounds. My ward was now easily managed with just an aide to assist with meals, baths, and bed changes.

An hour or so later it was time for doctors' rounds. Dr. Randall arrived, smelling of sunshine and sea breezes.

"Good morning, Nurse Wood," he said cheerfully as he donned his cloak. "I trust you have been outside this morning."

"I've been in the ward this morning."

He looked about at the remaining men who were sitting or lying in their beds, most of them out of the woods as far as the disease went and in various stages of recovery. "As soon as these gentlemen are well into desquamation, I want them outside for thirty minutes every day. In the sunshine. It's like a prison cell in here."

"Outside?"

"Let them see some sky and a bird or two. And breathe fresh air." He stepped over to the desk to check the master chart. "I see Dr. Treaver has discharged five. That's encouraging, to see the room empty out some."

"Well, yes. But the beds don't stay empty for long."

He smiled at me. "But today five are empty. Celebrate your successes, Nurse Wood."

I reached for my cart to follow him. "They are not exactly my successes, Doctor."

"Of course they are." Dr. Randall made for the back of the room to work his way forward, stopping first at Andrew's bed. "How about it, Mr. Gwynn? Would you care for an easy stroll outside on Monday? Just a few minutes of sunshine and fresh air?"

Andrew seemed surprised that Dr. Randall was asking his opinion. "Why, yes. I'd like that very much."

Dr. Randall turned to me. "See?"

"But I can't leave the others to take one man outside," I countered.

"I'll see that you get another nurse for the afternoons. Doctor's orders." He turned to Andrew again, to inspect the blistered vesicles on his chest, back, and extremities. "Let's start the scrubbing process tomorrow, Nurse Wood. Three times a day. The usual solution."

I recorded his instructions while Dr. Randall listened to Andrew's heart and lungs.

"You are making a fine recovery, Mr. Gwynn," the doctor continued. "You will be out of here by end of next week if all goes well."

With those words there was no doubt the hourglass was in play with regard to Lily's letter. As I made a mental note of the days remaining, Dr. Randall turned to me.

"So I've brushed up on my Keats and am quite ready to discuss his merits, Nurse Wood."

I snapped my head up to look at him. "Beg your pardon?"

"I said, I'm ready to discuss Keats tonight."

I could see out of the corner of my eye that Andrew's interest had been piqued. I very much didn't want Andrew to hear that I wasn't a fan of Keats after all. "I, uh, haven't had time to brush up, I'm afraid. We may not have much to talk about."

"We'll keep to one of your favorite poems of his, then. Which one?"

"I don't . . . I don't actually understand his poetry very well."

"That's why poems are best discussed. The meaning often comes across through conversation with other people. Don't you think so, Mr. Gwynn?"

Andrew nodded, but before he could say anything, Dr. Randall went on. "Which one?"

I could name only the one. "Well, I guess 'Ode on a Grecian Urn.'"

"Perfect," Dr. Randall replied. "We shall discuss 'Ode on a Grecian Urn.'"

"That's one of my favorites, too," Andrew said quietly, more to me than to Dr. Randall.

Dr. Randall moved to the next bed and cheerfully greeted the man tucked inside it.

I slipped Andrew's chart back inside its receptacle at the foot of his bed so that I could follow the doctor to the next bed.

But Andrew motioned me to come close to him. I obeyed and leaned in with a measure of nervous curiosity.

"'Ode on a Grecian Urn' is about expectation and fulfillment," he whispered.

"What . . . what does that mean?" I whispered back.

"Sometimes the expectation is better than the fulfillment."

It still made no sense to me. "How?" I whispered. "How does the poem say that?"

"'Heard melodies are sweet, but those unheard are sweeter.' Keats is saying what you can still dream about is often sweeter than the reality."

For a moment I could not move as I let these words soak into me.

I seemed riveted to the floor and Andrew's gaze.

Dr. Randall called for me and I pushed my cart away from Andrew's bed, murmuring my thanks.

Sixteen

AFTER our shift was over, and as the New York skyline across from us began to turn auburn, Dolly and I returned to our room, she to dress for her night out on the town, and I to watch her get ready. In my hands I carried the folded-over pillowcase containing Lily's scarf.

She and I and the other nurses liked to wash our own undergarments rather than send them to the laundry with our uniforms to be scrubbed and boiled by rough hands and rougher contraptions. And we used a lavender-scented antiseptic we made with carbolic and diluted with hot water to kill any contagion lingering on our clothes. It was normal to see wet things hanging in our communal bathroom after a gentle scrubbing in one of the basins. Tonight, when I returned from the commons to my empty room, I would wash Lily's scarf and allow it to dry unnoticed in my dormitory room.

While Dolly tossed her white nurse's uniform onto her bed and faced her wardrobe, I nonchalantly dropped the pillowcase in the corner on my side of the room near where my own laundry was gathered in a basket. When I turned back around, Dolly was attempting to stuff her full figure into a lime green party dress that had come in the mail that week from her sister-in-law. I reached into my own wardrobe and pulled out a navy blue skirt and plain ivory shirtwaist.

"Good Lord, no wonder Josephine sent me this thing," Dolly exclaimed. "She told me she would never fit into it again after the baby, but I bet she never fit into this thing. Help me with these hooks, Clara."

I laid the clothes on my bed and walked over to her. The bodice was already tight around Dolly's back, with a good inch of space still gaping between the hooks and eyes. "There's no way I can fasten them, Dolly. Sorry."

"Try!"

I pulled at the fabric, knowing it was futile. There was too much Dolly and not enough dress. "It's not going to work."

"Oh, bother it!" She pulled at the sleeves and shimmied her hips. After a few contortions the dress fell to the floor and Dolly stepped out of it. "You should wear it for your date tonight."

"It's not a date, and I would wear pajamas before I'd step into the commons wearing a ball gown."

Dolly bent down and picked up the dress. It made a swishy sound. "It's not exactly a ball gown. More like a . . . a party frock."

"I'm not going to a party."

"Don't tell me you're wearing that!" She waved her dress in the direction of my bed and the clothes lying on it.

I glanced at the skirt and blouse I'd chosen. "I seriously doubt Dr. Randall will be wearing anything other than street clothes. And that's what these are."

Dolly tossed the party dress onto her bed and then turned to face me in her pale pink corset. "Will you at least let me fix your hair?"

"I don't know. . . ."

She reached into her bureau drawer and pulled out a cloisonné hair comb in shades of periwinkle and cornflower blue. "I've always thought you would look good in this comb. It clashes something terrible with my red hair and green eyes and I wear it anyway. Your brown hair and blue eyes, though? Perfect. Turn around."

"You'll be late. You're not even dressed yet."

"I will not be late. And the girls won't let the ferry leave without me. Sit at the vanity and face the mirror."

I obeyed. Dolly pulled the pins from my chignon and they clinked on the vanity top as she tossed them there. My hair fell around my shoulders and then Dolly began to brush it.

"You've got the best natural curl in all of Christendom, Clara. Do you know how lucky you are?"

I closed my eyes as the bristles massaged my scalp. "It's just hair, Dolly."

"Apparently you don't."

I smiled. She continued to brush.

"Will you promise me you will try to have a good time tonight?"

"I don't think a person can *try* to have a good time," I answered. "You either have a good time when you go somewhere or you don't."

"You know what I mean. Promise me you will stay longer than ten minutes."

"I can't talk about poetry for longer than ten minutes."

"Oh, for the love of God, Clara, there are plenty of other things to talk about. Ask him where he's from. What he likes to do for enjoyment. What his favorite color is." She stopped brushing and I opened my eyes to look at her in the mirror's reflection.

She brushed one side of my hair up past my ear and slid the comb into place, leaving the other side to fall naturally past my shoulders. The effect was very pretty.

"I don't usually wear my hair down," I said.

"Well, you should. You have beautiful hair. Go put on those boring clothes."

I stood, slipped out of my nurse's uniform and into the skirt and shirtwaist. It had been so long since I had prepared for an evening out with a man, I had forgotten that getting ready for it was part of the thrill. The day of the fire, as I rode the elevator to meet Edward, I had felt a little like this. Like I had wanted to reach up to my hair and let it loose. I remember pinching my cheeks as the elevator ascended.

When I turned back toward our vanity, I was amazed at the transformation Dolly had wrangled with just a different hairstyle and a pretty accessory. Even my clothes looked better with the cloisonné comb to accent them.

"I could easily hate you," Dolly muttered. "You look like you just stepped out of the pages of *Vanity Fair*."

"I do not."

"You make even those schoolmarm clothes look nice. If I wore those I'd be mistaken for Mrs. Nesbitt."

"He will think I am trying to impress him." I touched a curly lock of my hair as it rested on my shoulder.

"He will think nothing of the sort. He invited you, remember? He's trying to impress you."

I tossed the lock behind me. "I don't want to be impressed."

"I don't believe you. You don't even believe you. Help me pick another dress."

Dolly went to her open wardrobe, slid the hangers on the rung, and pulled out a ruffled dress the color of the sky. She held the dress up to her face. "Does this make me look pale? Nellie says this dress makes me look pale."

"It doesn't make you look pale. And I know what you're doing. You're pretending not to hear what I'm saying."

She tossed the hanger onto her bed and stepped into the skirt. "I'm not pretending anything. I just don't believe you. You're in love with a dream, Clara. Sooner or later you're going to wake up from it and you'll be glad I didn't coddle you while you slept."

"Edward wasn't a dream."

"I'm not talking about Edward. I'm talking about the reason you're hiding here on this island. You're in love with what might've been. Help me with the hooks."

It took me a moment to close the distance between us so that I could grab hold of the hooks and eyes and yank them together. "What *would've* been."

"Might've." She turned to face me. "Might've. You barely knew the man."

"I knew enough! And in case you've forgotten, he died before I could know more."

"And then you came here and stopped wondering."

"What's that supposed to mean?"

Dolly stepped into a pair of dancing shoes. "I already told you. You could easily find out more about Edward if you really wanted to. But you're here where you can't."

A knock on our door silenced us. I wrenched the door open and Nellie and Ivy were standing there, both clearly having heard too much.

I'd been stupid to have this conversation when I knew Dolly was getting ready to meet the ferry to Manhattan. I should have guessed the girls would come looking for her. Stupid.

"I'll be there in a jiffy," Dolly called over her shoulder.

"Sorry you can't come with us," Ivy said to me, her voice sounding thoroughly patronizing.

"Yes, too bad," Nellie chimed in, sounding slightly less so.

I could see it in their faces. *Who is Edward?*

"Another time perhaps." I stepped aside so that they could wait for Dolly inside our room if they wished. They remained on the threshold.

"Your hair looks nice down like that," Nellie said.

"She has the hair of a goddess." Dolly doused her neck with cologne and grabbed a wrap and a plumed hat from inside her open wardrobe. She came to me and took me into her arms to hug me good night. But she also whispered in my ear, "Don't be mad at me. And be nice to the doctor."

"Don't tell them," I whispered back before she could let go of me.

She pulled away, leaving her freshly sprayed cologne on my clothes and hair. "Of course not," she said. She pressed the hat to her head and grabbed a handbag from the top of her dresser as she swished to the door.

They said good night to me, each one wearing an expression that I couldn't look away from fast enough. Dolly's was a mix of maternal care and encouragement, Nellie's a sympathetic stare, Ivy's a look of itching curiosity.

I closed the door and waited for the heat of my embarrassment to dissipate. They would pump Dolly for details on the way down to the ferry. *Who is Edward? What happened to him? How did he die?*

I didn't want Dolly to lie to them. I didn't want her to tell the truth.

I wanted her to tell them it was none of their business.

And maybe she would. But that wouldn't end their curiosity. The breach was widening in my in-between place and it seemed I was now thoroughly powerless to close it.

I sat on the edge of my bed, contemplating my options. Edward's name was no longer a secret; nor were my feelings for him. I could not keep Nellie and Ivy forever in the dark about who he was. If they came back later tonight having gotten nothing out of Dolly, they would surely press me for details. And if I didn't fill in the blanks, they would speculate, not just between each other, but probably with other nurses on the island.

There would be talk, whispers on the air—because what else was there to talk about here?—of my sad little tragedy. And once the island knew what I had brought with me, it would cease to be a place that the fire had not touched.

Maybe Dolly was partly right. Maybe I was in love with a dream as well as with the man who had spun it. But it was my dream. And on the island I could keep it spinning. It seemed the only place I could keep it.

I reached under my pillow for Lily's book and "Ode on a Grecian Urn," hungry to find those lines of poetry that spoke of the images on the urn occupying a better place than the real things they represented. I read it twice. The second time through the poem seemed on the very edge of clarity to me. It was as if I stood just outside the door of a well-lit house, but I was on the mat outside, waiting in the darkness to be let in. In that moment I longed to rush to Andrew, not Dr. Randall, to ask him about the poem. I imagined reading it aloud to Andrew and having him tell me, line by line, how the words spoke of the tension between that which changes and that which stays the same.

When it was time to go down to the commons, I couldn't decide whether I should bring Lily's book with me or leave it. I didn't want to answer any questions about where I had gotten it. Then again, I wouldn't have to.

I wasn't staying.

Seventeen

I found Dr. Randall seated in an armchair near shelves that held the staff's small lending library. He wore charcoal pants, a russet-hued vest, and a shirt the shade of butter. A newspaper was open in his hands. The seat of the matching chair next to his was covered by his suit coat.

As I neared him he looked up, smiled, and set the newspaper on the circular table in between the chairs. Then he reached for his suit coat, which he'd apparently been using to save the chair for me, though the commons was nearly empty.

"Good evening, Miss Wood! I see you've come prepared." He nodded at the slim volume I held in my hand. "I'm lucky I found Keats in an anthology in the shelves here or you would outshine me for certain."

"There would be no chance of that, I assure you." I

took the seat, but sat forward in the pose of one ready to rise momentarily and exit.

"I'm sure you are being too modest."

I shook my head. "Not at all, Doctor. I owe you an apology. I misspoke when I told you I liked Keats. I don't know why I said that."

He smiled, surely thinking I had said it to impress him.

"I was just having a bit of fun," I hastily added.

Dr. Randall's smile deepened and he tipped his head toward Lily's book. "So you don't like Keats, but you have his book?"

"It's not actually my book. It . . . it belongs to someone else."

"So you have a borrowed book of Keats and you don't like Keats?"

I mentally chewed on an answer before deciding vague honesty would actually ease me out of this doomed discussion of "Ode on a Grecian Urn." "This person happens to like Keats."

"Ah. A friend of yours?"

The book was technically Andrew's now. I considered him nearly a friend. "You could say that."

"But not a suitor." Caution laced Dr. Randall's words. I could tell he was a man of integrity, and not one to make advances on a woman who was already spoken for.

"No," I said, and he visibly relaxed.

"So what about Keats don't you like?" Dr. Randall leaned back in his chair, ready to begin an evening-long discussion.

"I don't think you will want to get too comfortable, Doctor. I've misled you. I can't even say that I don't like Keats. I have only read one poem by him."

"But you read that one and you didn't like it. That

means there is plenty to discuss. It's actually better this way. If we both liked it, what would there be to talk about? And will you please call me Ethan?"

A lengthy lock of hair fell about my face. I swept back the part that wasn't tugged into the comb. "I don't think that's a good idea. I was taught—"

"Yes, I know what they teach in nursing school. And tomorrow on the ward you can call me 'doctor' if you wish. But we are both off duty. I am just Ethan. May I call you Clara?"

I cleared away a tiny tickle in my throat. "I think you should call me Miss Wood."

He smiled. "All right, Miss Wood. Then perhaps you could call me Mr. Randall. Not 'doctor.' Agreed?"

"Perhaps."

"So tell me what you didn't like about 'Ode on a Grecian Urn.'"

I was prepared to say my piece and excuse myself. It wouldn't take but a few minutes. "It was too difficult to understand. I said as much to you in the ward today. I think if you're going to write about something, then you shouldn't be vague. Use interesting words if they delight you, but don't shroud your meaning in obscurity. I don't see the good in that."

He nodded thoughtfully. "I actually agree with you there, but I'd venture that true devotees of verse would say obscurity is part of a poem's charm."

"Which makes me, as I said, a person who knowingly deceived you. I'm not a devotee of verse. I led you to believe I was and I'm not. Forgive me." I rose from my chair to bid him good night.

"Miss Wood, you mistake me for someone who cares about all that! Please don't go. Please?" His eyes and voice implored me to retake my seat. I hesitated before slowly lowering myself back into the chair.

"I am not overly fond of poetry myself," he continued. "But when you said you liked it, I was willing to find a poem we could talk about together. The after-hours on this island are far too quiet. I don't see how you've been able to live here week after week after week. I tell you, I will be glad when my internship is up."

A queer sense of allegiance for my island stirred inside me. "I like it here."

He laughed lightly. "Truly? You don't get bored?"

"No."

"But you do look forward to weekends, when you can get away and reconnect with the real world, right? Don't you find yourself growing hungry for something bigger than this?" He motioned with his hand to include the bit of borrowed earth the hospital stood on.

I had no intention of telling him what my soul hungered for, so I simply repeated what I had already said. "I like it here."

He frowned slightly. "You're saying you *don't* look forward to the evenings you can get away?"

"We do good things here. People come to Ellis full of hope. The ones who are sent to the hospital have dreams that are twice as grand because they want so badly to get well. It's very rewarding to see them board that ferry to the mainland at last."

"Well, yes, of course. But I was not talking about them. I was talking about you. It's admirable that you are content in your post here, but I can't imagine you do not long for stimulation outside this hospital. Tell me, what do you like to do when you go ashore?"

This was a conversation I was not going to have. "If

we aren't going to discuss Keats, Doctor, perhaps I should return to my room." Again, I rose to leave.

"Then let's discuss Keats!" He had risen to his feet too. "Please?" He motioned with his hand to my chair. I sat back down and so did he.

He pursed his brows in contemplation, surely thinking that if the next thing out of his mouth wasn't a Keats question, I was going to bolt.

"Perhaps I could read the poem aloud to you? Can we start there?" he asked.

"I've read the poem half a dozen times in the last two days. I don't need to hear it again."

His face brightened at this, taking it as a compliment, I think. I'd been thinking ahead to our meeting—or so it seemed to him.

"Well, perhaps I could read it again for my own benefit." He stretched out his hand toward me. "May I?"

I stared at him. "May you what?"

He grinned. "Borrow your borrowed book."

I hesitated a moment, but then opened Lily's book to the first poem inside and handed it to him.

Ethan Randall smoothed the page and cleared his throat. He began to read and I found myself quickly immersed in a lyric fog of words that were both familiar and strange. I closed my eyes as the words fell about my ears. I was still at a loss to decipher the poem's full message, but Dr. Randall's reading voice was strong and robust and I could nearly envision the urn and its painted surface. He had been finished for a moment or two before I realized he had stopped reading. I snapped my eyes open to find him looking at me.

"Your thoughts, Miss Wood?"

"Um. What do you think it means?" I answered quickly.

"I suppose the urn is something of a storyteller. In the story there is a lovely forest, and there are maidens and men, pipers and dancers, and trees that never lose their leaves because it is always springtime on the urn. It doesn't change."

"It's an in-between place . . ." I murmured, realizing this about the urn for the first time.

"Well, I guess you could say it's in between real and imaginary. The pictures on the urn aren't real but they're not invisible either."

Whispered words echoed in my head. "Someone told me it's a poem about fulfilled expectations not being as satisfying as the dream of them," I said, more to myself than to him. "Heard melodies are not as sweet as the tunes we can imagine hearing."

Dr. Randall nodded. "Well. Yes. Yes, I could see it meaning this. Someone told you this?"

But I barely heard him ask. Andrew's words to me earlier drifted and an image of Edward standing next to me in the elevator replaced them. Edward was inviting me to come to the sewing floor a few minutes before five. Edward of my dreams, bidding me to come to a floor he should not have been on a few minutes before five. Edward, gone from me. Like an urn broken to bits on the ground after having been flung from the sky.

"Do you believe that?" I finally said. "Do you believe that an unfulfilled desire is better because it's something you can still dream about?"

"I . . . I don't know. I have never thought about it like that. When I've wanted something, I've always pursued it with the intention of acquiring it. I can't imagine being happy with just wanting it. Seems like you'd get tired of nothing ever changing."

"That is like saying change is always good. Change is neither good nor bad. Good changes are good. Bad changes are bad."

Ethan Randall smiled at me and I remembered him telling me he liked talking philosophy. "Well said, Miss Wood." He patted the newspaper that lay between us. "Speaking of change, I was reading just now about that terrible fire you survived. The criminal trial won't take place until December, but there is already change in the works for better labor laws . . ."

His voice droned on but I felt myself physically disengage from the conversation the moment he said the word "fire." The rest of what he said became like water falling out of a bucket, splashing over the sides of the widening rift in my carefully crafted island home. I had not known there was to be a criminal trial. I had avoided looking at newspapers, and my parents and sister never brought up the fire's aftermath in their letters to me, because I had asked them not to. The fire hadn't raged here and didn't live on here. But in the streets of lower Manhattan—just as I had feared—smoke was still rising. I stared down at my shoes, fully expecting to see ashes and blood all around them.

"Miss Wood?"

I heard my name as though it had been spoken from behind a brick wall.

"A trial?" I murmured, but my voice sounded far away.

"Yes. The owners are being charged with manslaughter."

I raised my hands to my ears instinctively.

"Are you all right?"

I sensed an edge of alarm in his voice.

"Clara?"

He spoke my name, but I didn't care. The room felt warm.

"Let's step outside for a moment. You've gone pale. You need air."

His arms were around me as he helped me to my feet.

"The book," I muttered.

"I have it right here. Come on. I've got you."

We stepped out into the late-August evening.

Eighteen

THE sensation of being wrapped in Ethan Randall's one-armed embrace lifted me out of the fog and by the time we were stepping outside I was fully myself again.

"I'm all right." I gently pulled away and inhaled the moist night air.

"Are you sure?"

"Yes. Yes." I turned to him, glad that the violet night was hiding my embarrassment. "I'm sorry."

"Nonsense. I'm the one who is sorry. I shouldn't have mentioned it. Please forgive me." He sought my gaze. "You're quite sure you are all right? Would you like to sit?" He led me to a wooden bench just outside the main hospital doors—a bench that family members some-times sat upon while waiting to visit a patient who likely would not survive; the dying were the only ones allowed visitors.

"I was unaware there would be a criminal trial," I said. "I was just surprised."

When he said nothing I looked up. The expression on his face was one of astonishment. "How could you not know? It's been in all the papers for weeks."

"I . . . I don't care much for the newspaper."

"But surely when you've gone ashore you must've heard about it."

I could only shake my head.

"Harris and Blanck are being tried for manslaughter, Miss Wood."

I shuddered and looked away, toward the Jersey shore and not New York. I have always hated that word, "manslaughter." Always. And sitting there, under that night sky and its ambivalent stars, I hated it as much as ever I had. "Slaughter" was a word that belonged only in stockyards. "I didn't know," I said.

"I just find that—" Dr. Randall stopped in midsentence. "Have you not been back on the mainland since?"

What did it matter now if he knew I hadn't? He would hear soon enough. Anyone who was acquainted with me on the island was aware that I hadn't.

"No."

He was quiet for a moment.

"Are you . . . Is it because of what you saw? Was it too terrible?" he finally asked.

Ethan Randall's simple question filled me with simple confidence. "It was unbelievably horrible, what I saw."

"And you really haven't set foot back on Manhattan since?"

"I haven't."

"Because back in Manhattan they are still talking about it?" he asked.

"I suppose that's part of it."

"But you could go anywhere. You could leave New York altogether. Nurses are needed in every city, Miss Wood."

"I don't want to go anywhere. I like it here."

"But you have so much to offer. You're young. Your whole life is ahead of you."

I rose. "Yes, well. Thank you very much for assisting me outside. I feel much better but I think I shall retire to my room now."

He sprang to his feet. "I've said too much. I'm sorry. You don't have to run away."

"I'm not running away. I'm going to my quarters. May I have my book, please?"

I reached for Lily's book but he did not hand it to me. "Can we not go back to the commons and continue our discussion of Keats?"

"I don't think so."

He handed it to me. "I've offended you. I'm sorry. I just don't understand."

"You haven't offended me." I took the book. I wanted to add, *And you're right. You don't understand.* "Good evening, Dr. Randall. My apologies if I have ruined your evening."

I started to walk back into the building and he fell in step beside me.

"You didn't ruin my evening." He stepped ahead to open the door for me.

"Dr. Treaver sometimes plays cards in the dining room. You might find him in there," I offered.

We stood in the main corridor, where we would part. He looked toward the direction of the staff dining room and perhaps a few games of rummy with a colleague.

"Good night, Doctor," I said.

He turned to face me. "Miss Wood, perhaps you would consider allowing me to accompany you on a trip ashore."

"That's not necessary. When I'm ready to go, I'll go."

"But perhaps if someone accompanied you, you wouldn't have to wait until you're ready."

I felt suddenly like a child in his presence.

"I'm serious," he continued when I said nothing. "It might not be as difficult to do as you think. Sometimes fear of a thing is worse than the thing itself."

I wanted nothing more than to make good my escape from him, but his words hung on the air between us. Despite his ignorance of what I longed for most, I knew that what he was saying made sense. As soon as the words left his mouth I knew the voice of reason had been whispering them to me for weeks and I'd been pretending I hadn't heard them.

He smiled. "I know I said I don't understand. But I would like to."

I just nodded. "Good night, Doctor."

I turned from him and made my way toward my dormitory. He must have been watching me walk away, for it was several seconds before I heard his footfalls on the tiles as he headed in the opposite direction toward the staff dining room.

I didn't see how I could make Ethan Randall understand what kept me planted on the island. There were times, such as at that very moment, when I barely understood myself why losing Edward had sent me here and kept me here. I had nothing of Edward's to show Dr. Randall or anyone else. I hadn't a pressed rose or a note or even the memory of a lingering kiss. I had nothing tangible or intangible to prove I had lost something precious when Edward died. All I truly possessed was guilt, because Edward had been on the ninth floor waiting for me when he should have been on the floor above, where there was a way of escape.

I possessed nothing of Edward's to prove to myself that he'd thought me worth the price he ended up paying. As these thoughts assailed me, I looked down at the book I held.

My steps stilled.

I had nothing of Edward's, and yet I had so easily kept back Lily's book from Andrew. How had I been able to think I could keep this book from him all this time?

I'd been drawn to Lily's scarf because it was all that remained of the thin slice of time Andrew and she had shared together, time that Andrew, in blissful ignorance, treasured. Except it wasn't the only tangible thing left. There was also the book. And he didn't know I had it.

I pivoted and retraced my steps back to the main corridor. There was no sign of Dr. Randall. I headed to the isolation pavilions at the far end of the island, aware of but undaunted by the fact that I had no idea what I would say to Andrew when I handed him Lily's book. He deserved as honest an answer as I could give him. I could tell him I had opened Lily's trunk by mistake, I had seen the book on top, and I'd thought he might want it when he was well. That much was true. When I had first removed the book from the trunk, that had been my motivation. And now he was on his way to being well.

But as I neared the entrance, I realized I had no good answer for why I was choosing to bring it to him now, at eight o'clock on a Saturday night, when I was off duty. Perhaps he would be so cheered at having it he would not bother to wonder why I was there after-hours, handing it to him.

The night nurse at the main nurses' station looked up when I entered the building. I told her I'd left something in the scarlet fever ward. She went back to her charting and I walked quickly past her.

The rooms were dark, as most of the patients had turned in for the night. A few lamps burned here and there. When I reached the scarlet fever ward, I saw that Andrew's bedside lamp still glowed, but he appeared to have fallen asleep reading.

For several moments I contemplated what I should do. Leave and come back with the book tomorrow? Not with everyone awake.

Leave the book on his bedside table?

But he would wonder where it had come from unless I wrote a note. I stepped over to the ward's nurses' station and withdrew a piece of paper and a fountain pen. Then I walked to Andrew's bedside, masking my footfalls as best I could. In the soft glow of his lamp, his splotchy skin appeared almost normal. An open book lay across his chest: *The Return of Sherlock Holmes.*

I waited for a moment to see whether he was merely resting, but when he didn't open his eyes, I moved the metal chair that was near the foot of his bed closer to the light. The chair squeaked a little as I lowered myself onto it.

I placed the paper on top of the book and uncapped the pen.

Dear Mr. Gwynn, I wrote. *I found this book when—* And then I stopped.

I couldn't summon the professional words to say what I had done and why. For several long seconds I just stared at the paper. And then I was acutely aware that I was being watched. I lifted my head to see Andrew looking at me.

"Nurse Wood?" he said softly, as if I were an apparition.

"I'm sorry I woke you." Heat rose to my face for the third time that evening.

"I nearly didn't recognize you. You . . . you aren't wearing your uniform."

I looked down at my clothes and then I remembered my hair was down around my shoulders and Dolly's beautiful comb was probably glinting in the lamplight. "I just . . . I just needed to bring you something."

I withdrew the book from underneath the piece of paper. The second Andrew saw it, I knew something wasn't quite right. I expected to see the same joy as when I had returned Lily's scarf to him. The look on his face was very strange, almost like dread.

"Where did you get that?" he whispered.

Accusation tinged his voice. My heart began to pound inside my chest with something like shame. I felt as if I had stolen it. "I . . . I happened across it the day you had me look for your father's pattern books. I opened your wife's trunk by accident, thinking it was yours, and when I saw this little book—"

"That's impossible."

Again the tone was unmistakably one of utter disbelief.

"I . . . I swear I meant no harm. It looked like a book your wife had loved and I thought you might like to have it with you while you recover. You are finally past the worst of it, so I thought I'd bring it down to you." I handed it to him and he slowly took it from me.

"I don't understand," he said. "I lost this the day before we set sail. You found it in Lily's luggage?"

Now it was my turn to sound dumbfounded. "*You* lost it?"

"This was my mother's." The timbre of Andrew's voice was now as tender as it was incredulous. It was plain the book was a precious keepsake he'd believed he would never see again.

For a moment I was as perplexed as Andrew was, but then the words in Lily's letter came hammering back to me.

> From the day I met you I planned to run back to the hired cab for a forgotten glove, and to find someone on the street to give you the message to look inside my trunk, where I knew you would find this book. . . .

Lily had taken the book from Andrew the day before they left England and hidden it in her own luggage with the note and certificate. She knew that when Andrew was given the message from whomever she'd hastily paid on the street to deliver it, he would open the trunk and he'd see—to his great surprise—his mother's book. He'd pull it out, this treasured book that he'd thought was gone forever. He'd open it and then he would find what Lily had left inside for him. With the beloved book planted there, he was assured of finding the letter and the certificate.

Tears had sprung into Andrew's eyes as he stared at the book. "I just don't understand. Why would she do that? She knew I was looking everywhere for it. . . ."

He did not really expect me to know the answer. But in that horrible moment I nearly told him everything. Had I not still been smarting from the sting I'd suffered earlier when Ethan Randall had unwittingly assured me that for me, the Triangle fire still burned, I might have. Just that little bit of deception on Lily's part seemed to weigh so heavily on Andrew.

And yet . . . A breach had opened in his in-between place just as it had in mine. His new bride had taken a book from him that he'd clearly valued and she'd hidden it from him in her luggage. Now a tiny fissure marred his perfect memory of her. If I gave him those terrible papers when he left Ellis, they would not have as great an impact after tonight. Because the fissure would widen in the coming days. Of course it would widen.

He inhaled heavily, like one starved for oxygen. "If you hadn't opened Lily's trunk by mistake the book would be gone now. Yes? Burned with everything else of hers?"

"Yes, I suppose it would."

"Then I am so very grateful to you. Thank you."

"It was nothing." I didn't want his gratitude. And because I knew I didn't deserve it, I blurted another confession. "I read from it. I shouldn't have. I am sorry."

He didn't seem surprised. "Had you not read 'Ode on a Grecian Urn' before?"

He'd figured it out—why Dr. Randall and I were discussing Keats.

"No," I answered. "If you hadn't told me what it meant, it would still be a mystery to me."

This didn't seem to surprise him either. "Poetry speaks slowly. My mother told me that. We are usually too much in a hurry." He sighed at this remembrance. "Hurried people miss many things. They see only what is right on top. . . ." His voice fell away.

"I should let you rest." I rose from my chair. "Good night, Mr. Gwynn."

But Andrew didn't say good night back to me. He seemed not to have heard me at all. His eyes were on his mother's book, practically entreating it to reveal how it came to be in Lily's trunk. I could not leave him without offering him some snippet of the truth I was holding just out of his reach.

"Sometimes people do things for reasons they aren't ready to explain," I said.

He turned his head in my direction, and seemed to consider what I'd said. His gaze drifted to the butterfly comb in my hair and then his eyes were tight again on mine.

"Everything is turning out so very differently than how I imagined it would," he said.

"I know." But I could say no more. My throat thickened with dread at the thought of what I would be bringing to him on the day he left. "Good night, Mr. Gwynn."

"Thank you, Nurse."

I left him and returned to my quiet room. I filled the basin in my shared bathroom with warm water, cleaning solution, and a few drops of lavender. I returned to my room for the scarf, withdrawing it from the pillowcase I'd carried it in. I took it back to the bathroom and plunged it into the soapy concoction, massaging its length to purge its threads of any remnant of Lily's terrible disease, knowing I couldn't possibly wash away everything she had done. The thought of handing over her letter made me shudder as if a winter wind had blown open the tiny window above my head. The coward in me wanted to find an easier way. . . . Perhaps I could place the letter and

certificate into the folds of the scarf when I returned it to
him on discharge day. He would take the scarf from me
and not realize there was something nestled inside. Then
when he arrived at his brother's and unpacked, Andrew
would find the letter. He would know that I'd had it, and
surely had read it, but I wouldn't have to see his face.

I'd be here on the island.

Almost a world away from him.

It was as merciful a plan as I could come up with, not
only for him but for me as well. I would wrap the scarf
in tissue, tie it closed, and hand it to him at the last moment, just before he left. He would thank me. And that
would be the last thing I would hear him say to me.

As I washed, my fingers rubbed the slender bit of
metal I'd felt the day before, when the Italian had the
scarf in his suitcase. Thinking it to be something left
mistakenly behind by the seamstress who made it, I
picked at the stitches on the turned-under edge to work
the metal fragment free. It clinked onto the porcelain
sink, and I could see that it wasn't a sewing implement.
It was a small brass key. When I picked it up, I saw that
tiny words had been hand-etched into it. I held the key
up to the light above me and squinted to make out the
words: 92 Chambers Street.

A New York City address, carved into the metal by a
slender hand.

I held the key for several seconds, unsure what to do
with it.

I set the key on the shelf above the sink while I rinsed
and squeezed out the excess water, bringing the garment
close to my nose to gauge whether there was any lingering scent of Lily's cologne. I smelled only carbolic and
lavender and soap.

Spreading a towel over the back of the tub, I laid the scarf on it flat. Then I sat on the edge of the tub beside it and worked the key back inside the hem.

The truth would wound Andrew, and he would likely hate me for inserting myself into his private affairs, but surely Dolly was right. Surely knowing the truth about Lily would be less grievous—and less prolonged—than mourning a lie.

A braver person would march right down to the ward at that very moment and hand over to Andrew what belonged to him.

But I wasn't that brave person.

Nineteen

SUNDAY morning dawned cloudy and clammy, as if it had just been let out of a simmering teakettle. I stepped outside before heading over to Ward K, as much to prepare myself for the week that lay ahead as to gauge the conditions for getting the patients outside for air, as Dr. Randall had ordered. There was no scent of rain but the air felt heavy with purpose. It seemed there would be clouds and late-summer heat but no soothing rain to calm the hours.

The men in the scarlet fever ward were awake and finishing breakfast when I arrived, including Andrew, who was sitting on the side of his bed. He looked up when I entered the room and nodded a hello. In the sallow morning light I could see three new arrivals from the previous evening's shift, whom I hadn't noticed last night when I'd brought Andrew the book.

"A late-arriving ship from yesterday," the night nurse said as she briefed me on the new additions before heading back out to the main nurses' station. I greeted the new arrivals, all of whom were being quarantined for a low-grade temperature and suspected exposure to scarlet fever. The remaining five patients, including Andrew, would need to be scrubbed today, at least once or twice, to rid their scalp and skin of the flakes of disease that still clung to them. A male attendant named Mr. Charles, an ebony-skinned, soft-spoken man whose accented English reminded me of faraway islands, arrived to help with the baths and short strolls outside. After the scrubbings, we would take the men out, one by one, for a dose of fresh air.

While the breakfast trays were being cleared away, I filled the tub in the tub room with hot, soapy water and lined my cart with scrubbing sponges and towels. While Mr. Charles helped the first patient step safely into the water, I put on gloves. Then I proceeded to scrub the man's head, back, neck, and arms. He spoke no English, so I cleansed the unreachable areas of his skin in relative silence. Mr. Charles left us to change the sheets so that the patient could return to a freshly made bed.

I'd given dozens of descaling baths during my nearly six months on the island, and had politely turned my head away as men of all ages lowered themselves into the tub. It had taken me a few weeks to get used to seeing men that way. As I had not had brothers nor been married, my exposure to the male body had been limited to photographs in the nursing textbooks, rounds at teaching hospitals, and one abscessed thigh wound the week I first arrived in New York. But on the island, where it seemed that for every sick female immigrant there were two males, I had quickly gotten used to my role as care-giver for grown men. I had stopped wondering how my touch might affect a man who had been my responsibil-ity for two weeks, separated from anyone he cared for. My goal at this stage of the disease had always been largely singular—rid the skin of the scales using as ag-gressive an approach as possible. Most welcomed the scrubbing, as the scales tended to itch, but as I rubbed Mr. Oliveri's skin and scalp I was acutely aware of how personal my ministrations were.

I'd changed the tub water four times before Mr. Charles brought Andrew Gwynn to the tub room. He seemed sur-prised to see me there and this produced an anxiety in me that I had not felt since my first week on Ellis. None of the other men that morning seemed to care that I was in the room.

"How are you feeling this morning, Mr. Gwynn?" I attempted a bright tone.

"Very well. Thank you." He was politely guarded.

"Your bathwater is ready for you." I forced a smile.

"I can take my own bath." His tone was polite but firm.

"I'm afraid I must scrub the areas you can't reach." My voice sounded meek in my ears and I cleared my throat. "But I promise to give you your privacy as you step into the tub. Mr. Charles here will help you into the water."

I turned away before Andrew could protest. I heard water sloshing as he got into the water. When I turned around, Mr. Charles moved past me to go change An-drew's sheets. Andrew was now sitting in the tub, his legs bent against his chest and his arms crossed over his knees.

"Let me know if you feel light-headed or if you need

me to stop," I said as I pulled on gloves and reached for my sponge. "I'll just be scrubbing your scalp, back, and shoulders."

"That's a grand relief," he said, and I laughed nervously.

As he held his head back, I plunged the sponge into the water and brought it up again, squeezing it over his head and neck. Then I began to scrub his scalp the way a mother might wash mud off a little boy who'd been playing in puddles. Again and again I doused his head and neck and shoulders with water and scrubbed away at the mottled skin, exposing hints of rosy pink. The more I rubbed, the more it seemed Andrew relaxed.

At least, I hoped it was a relaxed state that made him close his eyes, and not pain.

"Does that feel all right, Mr. Gwynn?" I asked. "Am I hurting you?"

The sound of my voice seemed to rouse him as if from sleep. "It's fine. I mean, you are not hurting me."

And so I kept at it. The rhythm of my hand strokes sounded like a swishing skirt on a dance floor and there was no other sound but that of water dripping off his body. As I moved my sponge across his shoulder blades, I was overcome with the intimacy of this act in a way that I never had been before. I felt a stirring inside me that I had not felt since I had met Edward on the elevator. It nearly took my breath away. I opened my mouth to explain to Andrew what I was doing, to remind myself I was only a nurse washing skin ravaged by scarlet fever.

"This is the last stage of the disease, the skin peeling. Underneath the damaged skin is a new layer. It won't be long now—" I would have prattled on, but he unhooked one of his hands from around his knees and covered mine as I washed just under his jawline.

My hand stilled under his.

"I think I can take it from here." He gently pulled the sponge out from underneath my hand.

"Of course," I managed to say as I eased away from the tub. "I'm sorry if I was rubbing too hard."

"You weren't."

"Yes, but—"

"You've been nothing but kind to me, Miss Wood."

After a moment of watching him scrub his damaged skin, I backed away, and waited at the doorway for Mr. Charles to return.

When I was free to leave the tub room, I made my way to the nurses' station to dutifully record that the morning scrubbing baths had been completed. But it was several moments before I picked up the pen to write anything down.

I had been so tuned to Andrew's loss I hadn't noticed how much I was tuned to his presence, his gentle manner, even his deep affection for his dead wife. I had let myself get too emotionally attached to a patient, something I had been warned in school not to do. And it wasn't just our common grief that drew me to him.

I had let my loss become entwined with Andrew's such that I was now having a hard time distinguishing between where mine ended and his began.

Andrew's loss, I reminded myself sharply, began with vows he had spoken to another woman the day before he sailed. Mine began with an elevator that opened its doors to hell. This attraction I felt for Andrew was simply validation that I wasn't stupid to think you could love someone you'd only just met.

That was all it was.

As soon as Andrew was clothed in clean pajamas and making his way to his bed with Mr. Charles helping him, I went back into the tub room to let the water out. I watched as the water swirled away, hurrying down the drain.

I wiped the tub clean with considerable force to reorient myself to the task at hand: following the doctor's orders so that the patient would be successfully discharged. There would be days ahead filled with scrubbing baths and taking walks outside. A week of them, no doubt. The baths and the walks were doctor's orders, nothing more. I could think of them as nothing more.

After his discharge, I would never see Andrew Gwynn again, Lord willing. Surely after he opened the scarf, he would wish never again to see me.

Over the next hour, Mr. Charles and I took turns with the men who were well enough to step outside for a breath of air. As it happened, I was not the one to assist Andrew Gwynn with his few minutes outside; Mr. Charles helped him.

When I returned to the ward with the last patient, Dr. Randall had arrived to make his rounds. All the other men were either back in their beds or sitting on the edges, waiting for their turn to be examined. Dr. Randall greeted me as the last patient and I made our way into the room. When I returned to the nurses' station, he was bent over the night nurse's notes.

"And how was the rest of your evening?" he asked.

"Fine." I didn't elaborate. "And yours? Did you find Dr. Treaver in the dining room?"

"I did. He's a better player than I. Dr. Treaver had a great evening. He won every hand."

I smiled politely and gathered what I needed for my cart for rounds. Tongue depressors, clean cloths, a cleansing basin, an otoscope.

We began to move around the room, Dr. Randall making his examinations, and I meticulously recording his findings on the patients' records.

At the end of the first rows of beds, as he washed his hands at the basin in my cart, he leaned in toward me. "Fancy a stroll outside tonight after the evening meal?"

I handed him a drying towel. "A stroll?" I said, though I had heard him perfectly.

"Yes. A stroll. A walk." He took the towel from me.

"I don't think—"

"I'm not asking to court you, Miss Wood. I just want to take a walk after dinner. Unless you'd like to come with me on the ferry tomorrow instead. It's your day off, too, isn't it? We can take a walk in Central Park." He handed the towel back to me.

I took it from him. "No."

"Just a walk in the park."

I folded the towel slowly. "No, thank you."

He moved in a bit closer. "You know, I'm only trying to help."

I could hear the genuine compassion in his voice, and the ardor all good doctors have for curing what ails someone. When I looked at his eyes, however, I couldn't tell whether the fascination I saw there was for my pathetic state or my being a woman he might actually find attractive.

"It's not right that no one has stepped in to help you with this, Miss Wood," he whispered, mindful—and I was glad of it—that some of the patients in the room understood English. "If you were my sister or friend or my beloved—"

"Let's finish the rounds, shall we?" I yanked the cart from in between us and spun it around, as much to end the conversation as to point the cart in the opposite direction.

"Think about it," Dr. Randall said as he fell in step with me and we moved across the polished floor toward Andrew Gwynn's bed.

"And how are you this morning, Mr. Gwynn?" Dr. Randall said as he reached for Andrew's record at the foot of his bed.

"Fine, Doctor. Thank you," Andrew answered.

"You're looking much better today after the scrubbing bath. Any lingering pain?"

"No, Doctor."

Dr. Randall handed me the patient record to examine Andrew's scalp and neck. But as he moved closer to the bed I saw the doctor's gaze linger on the bedside table. The poetry book lay near the base of the lamp, as if Andrew had placed it there after reading it last night.

Ethan Randall opened his mouth to say something but abruptly shut it. My breath caught in my throat. He turned to me with questioning eyes. I looked away.

"Now then, Mr. Gwynn," I heard him say. I lifted my eyes and saw that Ethan Randall was examining Andrew's skin. And Andrew seemed to know something odd had just occurred between the doctor and me. His gaze traveled to the book on his bedside table.

The awkward silence surrounding the three of us was palpable. I busied myself at my cart, as if the book hadn't caught Dr. Randall's attention. As if there were no book.

But when Dr. Randall turned from Andrew to wash his hands at my cart, his eyes sought mine. I met his gaze because I knew I must.

"Change your mind about that walk tonight?"

I couldn't read the emotion behind Dr. Randall's simple question except to know that he was at the very least concerned that I'd had in my possession last night something that belonged to a patient in my care.

What could I do but nod my head?

Twenty

THE rest of the day dragged as though it were weighted with irons.

Before he left the ward, Dr. Randall gave instructions for the second scrubbing to take place after supper, before the men retired for the night and after my shift was over. I wasn't sure of his rationale but I didn't care. It meant I wouldn't be giving Andrew Gwynn another bath that day. I didn't think I could handle another one. He was starting to remind me too much of Edward in too many ways.

In the early afternoon, two more new patients were sent to us from the main building, a lad of fourteen as slender as a birch tree, and an older man with a mustache and beard that reached to his waist. After I had both men resting comfortably in their beds, I made my own afternoon rounds: temperature taking, filling water pitchers, administering aspirin to those with fevers and chills.

When I approached Andrew's bed to fill his water pitcher, he pointed to the book beside it. "Did the doctor recognize that book? I mean, I couldn't help but notice."

Heat rose to my cheeks. "I think maybe he did."

"You had it with you last night when you met with him?"

I winced at the way those words sounded together. But I nodded my head.

"Does he think it's yours and he's wondering what I'm doing with it now?"

I grabbed his pitcher and began to pour from my larger one. "He knows it's not mine. I told him it belonged to a friend. I'm sure he's wondering what *I* was doing with it."

A drip of water fell onto my polished shoe, splattering like a raindrop on pavement.

"Are you in trouble, then?"

"I don't know. It was a stupid thing to do. It wasn't my book and I didn't even have your permission. Now Dr. Randall probably thinks . . ." But I let my voice trail away as I realized I had been thinking out loud.

"He thinks what?"

I set my own pitcher back on my cart. "Nothing." But as I exchanged Andrew's water glass for a clean one, I stole a glance at him. I could see he knew what Dr. Randall probably thought.

"You've done nothing wrong," Andrew said. "You've shown me nothing but compassion."

I nearly knocked over the glass as I backed away from both the table and the compliment. "Don't say that."

"But it's true. I shouldn't have asked you to get the pattern book. I knew it was asking too much of you. But you did it anyway. And because you did, you saved my mother's poetry book. You found Lily's scarf too, and brought it back to me. You've made sure my every need has been met here. I'll tell him myself if you want me to."

"No need, I assure you. But thank you. You should rest now."

I eased myself away from him and his gratitude, to tend to the rest of the ward's needs and to wait for the long, awkward afternoon to end.

As the day slogged on, I missed Edward more than I had in weeks. I missed where I would have been had life dealt us both a different hand. Perhaps after these last six months Edward would have asked me to marry him and I'd be choosing a dress and planning my wedding, not hiding away on this spill of earth, latched onto the grief of another.

When the day finally ended and the evening shift began, I left the ward without a backward glance. I headed to the dining room to take my meal at a corner table, where I could enjoy the solitude of not having to answer any questions about my personal choices.

The dining hall was stuffy from the day's humidity, and I hadn't much appetite. The stewed chicken was sinewy and tasteless. After eating a few bites of overcooked potato and creamed peas, I was finished. As I prepared to leave, Dr. Randall entered the dining room with Dr. Treaver and two other nurses. Dr. Randall excused himself and walked over to my table and set his tray down.

"I think we need to talk," he said, politely but assertively. He took the chair opposite mine.

"There really is nothing to talk about, Doctor. I borrowed Mr. Gwynn's book and then I gave it back. Ask him yourself."

"You said that book belonged to a friend."

"No. You asked me if it belonged to a friend and I said, 'You could say that.'"

"Is that what Mr. Gwynn is? Is he more than a patient to you?"

His words felt like a reprimand and I instinctively drew back in my chair. "You presume too much. May I remind you Mr. Gwynn just lost his wife. He is in mourning."

Ethan Randall regarded me for a moment. Then he spoke, calmly but with purpose. "I've seen the way you look at him, Nurse Wood. I've seen the way you care for him. I thought it was admirable at first. You don't treat the other patients the way you treat him. You favor him. I presume only what I see evidence of."

At first I could summon no words. Fury rose up within me and tied my tongue in a knot that loosened only as I pressed down my anger.

I leaned over the table and spoke softly so that no one else would hear and so that it would appear I was perfectly calm, which I most assuredly was not.

"I treat that man differently because he lost his bride of a week on the ship that brought him here. His bride of a week! She practically died in his arms!"

He seemed taken aback by my response, but only for a moment. "What has that got to do with you having his book?"

"I was merely borrowing it. What is the harm in that?"

"You make it a habit of borrowing things from your patients?"

"Of course not. Why are you making so much of this?"

"Because I have seen the way you are with him. And the way he is with you."

What Dr. Randall was intimating was ludicrous. "You don't know what you are talking about," I murmured as low as I could and yet with vehemence. "If you are insinuating that I am in love with Mr. Gwynn, then you are indeed greatly mistaken. And Mr. Gwynn is not in love with me. He loved his wife. And I . . . I loved someone else. It's our grief that binds us!"

Ethan Randall's earlier disapproval thinned to something more like surprise. "You loved someone else?"

I cleared my throat to sweep away the ache of having said so much in such a small number of words. "I lost someone I loved in the fire, if you must know. Someone I'd just met, but who meant a great deal to me."

"I . . . I truly am very sorry to hear that."

I knew my eyes were shimmering with emotion but I held it in check, even as Dr. Randall suddenly put it together. It all made sense to him.

"That's the real reason you haven't gone to Manhattan, isn't it?" he said. "It's not what the fire did; it's what the fire did to *you*."

I shifted in my chair at his bluntness. "I haven't gone because I've had no desire to go." I blinked back the last of the threatening tears and pointed to his tray. "Your food's getting cold."

"I am, as I said, so very sorry for your loss, but I think you haven't left here because you haven't given yourself any reason to."

"I beg your pardon?"

"You've been here nearly half a year? You haven't left the island—even once—in all that time. And you think your grief is as fresh as Mr. Gwynn's? Can't you see? It's *your* grief you are concentrating on, not his. You're keeping it alive by staying here."

It took me a moment to fully realize what he was saying. That I was in love with my grief.

That my in-between island was a place where my loss could stay evergreen and a bereaved man like Andrew Gwynn would seem like a soul mate.

I rose from my chair. "I think we are finished talking."

"And Mr. Gwynn?"

"What about him?"

"You can't be treating him differently, Nurse Wood. He's your patient. You're his nurse."

"I know exactly what I am!" I replied hotly. "And you're telling me you treat all your patients the same, even though their needs are vastly different?"

"Yes, I do," he said, as gentle as I had been angry. "Each one gets the best care I can give them, all that I can give them, regardless of what they suffer from."

I opened my mouth to protest, and shut it just as quickly. Despite Dr. Randall's flair for frankness, he was right. In my zeal to administer healing and hope to the grieving Andrew Gwynn, I had neglected to some extent every other man on the ward.

"It won't happen again. Good night, Doctor." I took a step away from the table.

He reached for my arm. "Please don't leave angry with me."

I wriggled my arm free of his grasp. "I'm not angry with you."

"I really do want to help you."

I looked past Dr. Randall's clean-shaven face, past the spectacles, to his blue eyes. "Why?"

"I like you. Is that so terrible?"

"You mean my pathetic state interests you."

He drew back a bit in his chair. "I don't mean that at

all. And I do not think you are in a pathetic state. Do you think you are?"

Truly, in that moment I didn't know what I thought. The breach now was so wide I could not feel solid ground beneath me. It was as if the island were sinking into the water and taking me with it.

I was sure of only one thing.

Everything had been under control until Andrew Gwynn had arrived. The sooner he left, the sooner I could repair what had been broken. In the morning I would request an early rotation to a different ward. It would be easy enough to ask Mrs. Crowley. Surely there was a nurse in reception who could take my place in the scarlet fever ward. When the day came for Andrew Gwynn to be discharged, I would see to it that everything I had that belonged to him was returned. Dr. Randall, who would continue to see Andrew every day, could be convinced to return the pattern book and scarf to Andrew upon his discharge. He would be only slightly aghast to learn I had kept other items that belonged to Andrew Gwynn, and if he was truly eager to help me he would do it. In the morning I would send a note to Andrew via Dr. Randall that I had been moved to another ward. I would tell him that his belongings would be safely returned to him before he left. I would wish him well, and in my heart I would pray that he would bear up under the weight of what he would soon learn. And that would be the end of it.

"Miss Wood?"

"No. I do not think that I am in a pathetic state."

"Will you let me help you then?"

"Yes."

I turned from his surprised but pleased face. And I left the dining room without telling him what I had in mind by way of help; he would find out soon enough. I hurried to my quarters to finish what I needed to do. I found a long piece of tissue paper in the trunk I kept at the foot of my bed and spread it out on my coverlet. The scarf, draped across a chair back, was dry and smelled faintly floral and yet sterile. The little key was snug under the hem. I laid the scarf out on the tissue and then reached under my pillow for the letter and the certificate. I placed them at one end of the scarf and began to fold it over, again and again, until the fabric was a tight rectangle bearing no hint of what it held inside. Then I wrapped it in the tissue and tied it closed with a bit of ribbon. It looked like a gift.

I heard voices on the other side of the door. Dolly's and others'. She was saying good night to another nurse.

I grabbed the package and tossed it under my bed.

Twenty-One

WHEN Dolly returned to our room we finally had a chance to talk alone. She wanted a full report on how my evening with Dr. Randall had gone, and I wanted to know what she had told Nellie and Ivy about what they had overheard before they boarded the ferry.

We changed into our nightgowns and sat on our beds eating caramel popcorn she had bought from a sidewalk vendor in Central Park.

Dolly said she had told Nellie and Ivy the simple truth that I had lost a good friend in the fire and it pained me to speak of him, so they were to hush up about it.

"And they were satisfied with that?" I asked.

"Who cares?" Dolly popped a golden clump into her mouth. "It isn't any of their affair. I told them they'd be unkind to bring it up. They're gossips, but they aren't cruel, Clara."

I told her everything that had transpired over the weekend, deciding to leave nothing out. I recounted fully the returned scarf, the hidden key, the poetry book, and finally Dr. Randall's bold assertion that I had overstepped my responsibilities regarding Mr. Gwynn, but that he was anxious to help me brave my first trip off the island. And all the while, Dolly said nothing, which was strange for her. She usually had a comment for everything.

Her silence unnerved me. "Why haven't you said anything?" I asked when I finished by telling her I was going to rotate early out of the scarlet fever ward.

"I hardly know what to ask," she answered. "So, are you saying you have feelings for Mr. Gwynn?"

"I said nothing of the kind!" I sputtered. "I merely said I think it would be best if I got out of that ward. Everything became far too complicated for me when Mr. Gwynn showed up."

Dolly cocked her head. "Complicated?"

"Yes, complicated. His losing his wife the way he did and then asking me to get that pattern book, and my doing it and finding that awful letter—"

"There's nothing complicated about that letter. I think you're doing the right thing by giving it to him. I've thought all along he should have it. Although I don't see any reason to put off doing it until he leaves."

"He needs to concentrate on getting well and getting off this island."

Dolly shrugged. "Well, I don't suppose it will matter much if he reads it now or next week. And you're sure Dr. Randall will return those things to Mr. Gwynn the way you want? He won't report you, will he?"

"He said he liked me. And he said he wanted to help me."

"But he was talking about helping you off this island. And other issues related to your wounded heart, I'd wager." She was thoughtful for a moment. "I'll trade wards with you. I'll take the scarlet fever ward and you can finish out my week with the tots. They're cute little things this time. No biters. And I will give Mr. Gwynn his belongings for you."

"Not until the day he leaves, right?"

Dolly clucked her tongue. "I don't think it will matter."

"It matters to me! I don't want to run into him here on the island after he's read it. He'll know I had it the whole time. And that I certainly must have read it. You have to promise."

"I think you're making more of this than what is there, love."

"I am not. That letter is going to crush him in a way Lily's dying didn't. He thinks she loved him! It's an amazing thing to believe you are loved."

Dolly looked at me, surely hearing my own longing in those words. "Indeed it is," she finally said.

"So you will wait until he's ready to leave? You promise?"

"I promise. He won't even suppose I know anything about anything. I'll hand him the pattern book and the scarf on his way out. And it will be done. Finished. All right?"

I nodded, closing my eyes.

Yes, it would be finished.

"So you'll tell him you're moving on to another ward, yes? You'll tell him you'll make sure the new nurse—that would be me—gets his belongings to him?"

"Why can't you just tell him?"

Dolly studied me. "Is that really how you want to do it?"

I shrugged and looked down at my feet. "I'm just his nurse."

"It's not a crime that you fancied him, Clara."

I snapped my head up. "I didn't. I don't."

"And I'm saying it's not a crime if you did. You can't pine after Edward forever. He wouldn't want it, you know. Have you thought about that? Would he have wanted you to be stuck on this island the way you are? I don't think he would. No, I don't."

"Stop."

"You know I'm right."

"I don't fancy Andrew Gwynn. He mourns his wife, for pity's sake."

"Then come with me and the girls next weekend. We're going to the Jersey shore this time. Come with us. It will be fun. And it won't be New York."

I didn't want to talk anymore. I didn't want to think anymore. I just wanted to crawl under my bedcovers and escape into my dreams. "I don't know, Dolly. Maybe."

"I can live with maybe." Dolly closed the bag of popcorn and tossed it onto her bedside table. "But I think you should tell Mr. Gwynn tomorrow that you're rotating to another ward. Tell him I can be trusted to get his pattern book and that scarf to him with no fuss. You say you have no feelings for him. But if you leave without saying a word, it will look as if you do."

She stood and a few stray bits of golden kernels fell to the floor. I watched as she took her toothbrush and powder and headed out of our room.

If what Dolly said was true, then I would also have to tell Dr. Randall that I was rotating to a different ward.

I rushed to follow Dolly to the bathroom. She looked up at me as she sprinkled powder on her toothbrush.

"I'd like to tell Dr. Randall that I offered to switch with you because you were needing a break from the little ones," I said.

"Dr. Randall?"

"He will also wonder why I left the ward early. He will see me on the children's ward in your place and he will make assumptions. Just like you did."

Dolly considered this request for only a second. "You can tell him that." She stuck the brush in her mouth but then pulled it out again. "And what of the doctor, Clara?"

"Pardon?"

"The doctor. Do you fancy *him* in any way?"

"No," I said quickly.

Too quickly. She shoved the brush back in her mouth, a slight grin on her face.

I went in uniform with Dolly to breakfast the following morning, though I could have slept in later, as I had the day off. But I wanted to make sure Mrs. Crowley would allow us to switch wards with just one week left on our rotation. If we were to make it, Dolly would be headed to the scarlet fever ward that morning and the floater taking my place on my day off would need to report to the children's ward.

We ate quickly and found the matron in her small office near the main reception, getting ready for the week ahead. When we asked whether we could make the switch, because Dolly needed a break from the little ones who missed their mothers, she simply nodded. What did it really matter anyway to someone who didn't know the real reason I wanted to switch? She was more interested to know why I was in uniform.

"You're off today, Miss Wood. Why are you dressed that way?"

"I thought perhaps I needed to take care of this in uniform," I said quickly.

"Well, go take that off or I am liable to put you to work." She shooed us away, obviously encumbered with more important matters.

As we emerged back into the main corridor Dolly turned to me. "I've got a few belongings in the children's ward. I'll give you a couple minutes to say what you need to say to Mr. Gwynn."

"I won't be long."

In fact, the quicker I said good-bye to him, the quicker I could regain my equilibrium, such as it was. We parted and I headed for the scarlet fever ward, earlier than I would have had I been working that day. The night nurse would still be on duty, and I would have to hope she didn't find it strange that I needed to speak to one of the patients.

As it was, she was assisting someone in the toilet, and I sped toward Andrew Gwynn's bedside to take advantage of the opportunity. He appeared to have only just awakened. He was sitting on the edge of his bed, the sheets rumpled and the comfortable look of sleep in his eyes. The skin on his neck and cheeks looked better than it had in days. His eyes widened at my approach.

"Nurse Wood?"

"Good morning, Mr. Gwynn," I said as quietly as I could without sounding like I was being secretive. "I just wanted you to know that I am rotating to a different ward today. But the nurse coming in after me is my roommate.

Her name is Dolly and she will be sure to give you the pattern book and the scarf when you leave. She won't say a word about either one until you are discharged and then she will hand them to you. All right?"

He seemed to need a second to process all that I had said. I stole a glance toward the door but no one was walking toward it.

"You're moving to a different ward?"

"Yes. We rotate wards here. I am moving to the children's ward. I just didn't want you to wonder how you were going to get your belongings. It's all been taken care of. Dolly will be discreet."

"But . . . you said nothing of this yesterday." He frowned and my heart seemed to skip a beat.

"Yes, I know. It came up rather suddenly. Dolly was needing a break from the little ones. It can be hard for them. Very hard. Most of them miss their mothers so much. It's very frightening for them."

"So I'll not see you again?"

For a second I could not answer. I had been wholly unprepared for his disappointment.

"I . . . Dolly is a fine nurse. And very friendly. You will all get on fine with her. I promise you."

He blinked, his gaze never leaving mine, and I could see he was thinking. Contemplating my words. Weighing them.

"Is this about the book? Is it about the doctor?" he finally said, not much louder than a whisper.

"No. No, not at all!" I whispered back with intensity. "We move about the wards. All the time."

But he sensed there was something I wasn't telling him. I could see it in his expression. "Is it something I've said to you? What is it? What is troubling you?"

His kindness, so like Edward's, was nearly unbearable. I could feel tears springing from the ready place they'd occupied since the fire. There is no way to hide ready tears. You can keep them from falling, but you cannot keep them from shimmering just at the rim of your lashes. They shine like silver. Especially in morning light.

The truth was, I did fancy Andrew. He was starting to fill the space Edward had left and I hadn't even realized it until that moment. And nothing good could come from that swelling attraction, not for me.

"I need to go." I reached for his hand and squeezed it. "I wish all the best for you, Mr. Gwynn. I truly do. And I . . . I hope you will remember that I said this to you."

I turned and left before he could say anything else, hurrying as I heard the pull of a nearby toilet's flush cord.

I flicked the stray tears away and made for my quarters. I pulled off my uniform as soon as I was alone in my room and tossed it onto the back of the vanity chair. I needed to get outside and drink air that didn't smell like the hospital. Grabbing a tawny brown shirtwaist from my wardrobe, I re-dressed in my own clothes and yanked my nurse's cap off my head. My hair came undone and fell about my shoulders but I didn't care. I left the room.

It was the first of September and the heat from the day before had slithered away like an unwanted guest. A teasing chill lingered and as I stepped into the sunlight, I felt my skin respond to the change in the weather. I made for the long corridor between islands two and three, passed the ferry house, and finally reached the far side of Ellis.

Once there, I watched in fascination as the New York skyline shook off its early morning cloak and embraced the sun. An ache such as I had not felt before came over me. I wanted to be back in the city, in the grip and grace of its mesmerizing hues. Back to that bit of time when it was nothing but loveliness to me. I wanted to spin the world backward, to the day Edward had invited me up to the sewing floor. I wanted to say to him, "Let's skip out early, shall we? Let's leave before the clock tells us the workday is over!" He'd smile and say, "Where will we go?" And I would say, "Anywhere, Edward. Anywhere but here."

And we'd be far away from the Asch Building when the first hungry spark grabbed hold of tinder-dry scraps.

I stood there for a long while, watching the city welcome the new day. I felt it call to me from its glistening shore. Teasing me. Taunting me. Daring me to return to the place where one doesn't know from one moment to the next what will happen, where there is no spinning backward.

I waited until that voice grew quiet and it seemed to turn its attention to more important matters.

Then I walked slowly back, lingering for a while on Ellis, watching newcomers make their way into the building, hope and desire coloring their faces.

As I passed through the ferry house I saw Dr. Randall in his blue medical corps uniform preparing to meet the next ferry. It was his day off, too. He saw me as well, and he pushed through the crowd to speak to me.

"Miss Wood! You've changed your mind?" His voice was hopeful, but also dubious. He seemed surprised by more than just my being there. My hair was down around my shoulders and I hadn't so much as a clip to keep it tamed. He looked regal and handsome in his ensign uniform, and I surely looked like a wild woman from the mountains.

"No, just out for a walk," I said, as brightly as I could.

"Are you all right?" Concern played across his face.

"Just forgot my hat. Have a nice day onshore. Good day, Doctor."

I started to move away from him, but he caught my arm gently. "I'll wait for the next one if you'd like to go fetch your hat. It's a beautiful morning in Manhattan, Miss Wood."

I looked past him for just a second to the city's beckoning, bullying towers.

"As pretty as it is here on the island," I said.

And I spun away from him.

I didn't look back. I headed toward my room, where I planned to spend the day writing letters and reading. In the main corridor I stopped to see whether the mail had been delivered and if there were any letters from my mother or sister.

The mail had indeed been delivered. And there was a letter for me, but it was from my father. I opened it as I walked back to the nurses' quarters, but stopped as I read what he had to say.

He was coming to Manhattan that week and he wanted to have lunch with me. He, my mother, and Henrietta were worried about me.

He would meet me at noon on Friday.

At the dining room at the Hotel Albert on East Tenth Street.

Twenty-Two

I sat on the edge of my bed with my father's letter in my hand, long after I had read it and read it again.

I'd assumed that my parents and sister believed me to be happily engaged in my work at Ellis's hospital, and so enamored with my post that I was fully content to spend every waking moment on the island, even on my days off.

I was nothing but cheerful in my letters to my parents. I couldn't think of one sentence I had written that betrayed my real reason for not leaving the island in nearly six months. The sad girl my parents had left in Manhattan had found renewed purpose on Ellis. But I had been a bit more forthright in what I wrote to Henrietta. As I sat there, I tried to remember what I had written to her that might have suggested that something besides dedication to the job kept me planted in one place. I hadn't mentioned Edward, but I had told her the island was filling an empty space within me, one that the fire had created. Had she surmised there was more to it? If she was concerned about me, she wouldn't hesitate to bring the matter up with our parents. But why couldn't she have asked me first whether something was bothering me? I would have assured her that I was quite content.

That was the least of my concerns, of course. I could not picture getting on a ferry on Friday to have lunch with my father. Just sitting there on my bed thinking about it made my heart race. I wasn't ready.

And I didn't have that day off.

Spinning thoughts circled in my brain as to how I could decline the invitation. I could send a telegram addressed to my father at the hotel, expressing my regrets that I had to work. He might wonder why I was not able to ask for the afternoon off when he had given me plenty of notice. I would have to say that I had tried but was unsuccessful. I would have to lie to him.

I sprang from the bed, clutching his letter. I wasn't in the habit of lying outright to my father. In fact, I never had. I had allowed him to think things that weren't true, but I had never told him I had done something that I had not done. The thought of it now was nauseating.

Perhaps I could tell Mrs. Crowley that my father had asked me to lunch but that I knew how busy the children's ward was and I could meet him another time. I could tell her this when she was busy. She would be glad not to have to think about finding a floater for me for Friday afternoon. "Fine, fine," she would say. And then I would not have to lie to anyone.

In fact, I would ask her right then. Mondays were notoriously busy and she'd remember that I'd asked a favor of her already that day, so my telling her that I wouldn't be asking for Friday off would actually sit well with her.

I stuffed the note from my father in my skirt pocket and quickly braided my hair. Then I headed down to the hospital's main reception area to find Mrs. Crowley. It was nearly lunchtime and there was only a small crowd at registration. I waited until the last patient had been properly admitted and then, as Mrs. Crowley rose and began to collect her things before heading to the staff dining room, I approached her.

"Mrs. Crowley, I've had a letter from my father asking me to lunch in Manhattan on Friday, but I will understand completely if asking for that afternoon off is too much of a complication, especially since you've already done me a favor today by allowing Dolly and me to switch rotations." I said it too fast. She blinked at me.

"What was all that?"

I repeated what I had said, overly mindful that she was now paying attention to every word. I had hoped she would be distracted with more important details and would simply nod in agreement.

"Your father, you say?"

"Um. Yes. But—"

"And when was the last time you went ashore?" She motioned for me to follow her. We began to walk.

"The last time?"

She turned to me. "Yes. I can't recall that you've left the island since I've been here. So it must have been a while."

The conversation was not going as I had hoped. "Yes," I said, but nothing else.

"So how long has it been?"

"Quite a while."

"Then you should go. No one on my staff is as dedicated as you are, Nurse Wood. But you can't let your work be your everything. Go have lunch with your father on Friday."

"But I am sure we can make it another time. I know how busy the children's ward can be."

She waved that excuse away as if it were a mayfly. "They're all busy. Just go. Be glad you've a father to have lunch with. I want you to go. You'll be no good to me if you work yourself to death, Nurse Wood."

"Oh, but I don't mind the hours I put in. I truly don't."

Mrs. Crowley frowned at me. "Yes, that's my point. You should mind. You should want a break from all this. How can you not? I want you on the eleven o'clock ferry on Friday."

She quickened her step, signaling we were through talking.

I slowed my speed to absorb what had just happened. Mrs. Crowley had practically ordered me to take the afternoon off. I could get out of it now only by feigning illness. Hard to do when all your colleagues knew when someone was faking it.

I had no appetite but I wandered into the dining room anyway, looking for Dolly and a sympathetic ear. I found her at Nellie and Ivy's table, but before I could leave unnoticed she saw me and beckoned me to join them.

"Where's your tray?" Dolly patted the chair next to her.

"I'll eat later." I sat in the chair only to allow them to go back to whatever conversation they had been engaged in before I arrived.

But Nellie and Ivy were staring at me while obviously trying not to stare at me.

Dolly sensed my unease and that something was on

my mind. "You girls wouldn't mind finishing up at another table, would you? I need to ask Clara's advice about something."

Nellie and Ivy dutifully obeyed, but with questioning looks on their faces. When they were gone, Dolly turned to me. "What is it? You look perplexed."

I pulled my father's letter out of my pocket and handed it to her. It took her only a minute to read it.

"So you are going, right?" she asked, her eyes wide.

"I don't see how I can get out of it. Mrs. Crowley is practically insisting I go." I recounted my conversation with the matron. "I think the only way I can beg off now is to pretend I'm having my monthly time."

Dolly reached out to squeeze my arm. "Don't do that, Clara. Please don't."

I stiffened a bit at her urgency. "I don't see why I have to go. Why do I have to go? It's just lunch."

"But you do know you have to go sometime. You do know that, don't you? Now is as good a time as any. Isn't it? And it's not just lunch. Not for you. And not for your father. He's worried about you. And so am I."

I extended my hand for the letter, loosening her grip on me. She handed it to me wordlessly. "I'm fine," I said.

"No, you're not. If you were, you wouldn't be looking for ways to stay here."

I slowly put the note back in my pocket as I searched for words to oppose her. But I could think of none.

"I wish I could go with you, Clara. But I don't think Mrs. Crowley would give me the afternoon off as well unless we told her everything. She might then."

I bristled. "I'm not telling her anything. It's none of her business."

"But I am concerned about you going alone, Clara, I

am. I so very much want you to go but I worry about your setting foot on the pavement without someone with you. Can't we please tell her?"

"No."

"And you are quite sure you can manage it?"

I wasn't quite sure of anything except that too many people were imposing their agendas on my life. "I guess I will find out, won't I?" The words fell hard from my lips.

For several seconds Dolly said nothing, but her gaze was on me. Her thoughts were about me.

"All right then," she said. "I will ask Mrs. Crowley if I can accompany you merely because I am your friend and I know the streets of Manhattan better than you. Perhaps she will say yes. May I do that? I can wait in a coffee shop or something while you have lunch with your father. You don't have to worry about me intruding on that conversation. All right?"

I nodded. In truth I didn't want to make the trip alone. And I wasn't completely sure I could.

We were silent for a moment as the tension between us evaporated.

"Your Mr. Gwynn is a very polite fellow," Dolly said.

"He's not my Mr. Gwynn."

"Well, he's still a very polite man. And I think he's sad that you left the ward so suddenly."

"Don't be ridiculous. He mourns his wife."

Again there was silence between us.

"I think I will get a tray after all." I rose from my chair, to prove to myself and to Dolly that I was not as fragile as everyone believed.

THE following morning as I entered the children's ward a peculiar sadness came over me. And because it did, I was as firmly resolved as ever that I had made the right choice to rotate early. There should be no sadness at ward changes. None. The wards were the same and the people in them the same. They all needed our careful attention and they all would leave the island after we made them well, if indeed we could.

The children's ward was full of little ones with mumps and a few with typhus. They were kept separate so as not to share their illnesses. Some were old enough to understand why they were being kept from their mothers, but most were scared little tykes who latched onto every adult female who offered them kindness.

I mentally prepared myself for Dr. Randall's rounds with the children, since Dolly had told me that he and Dr. Treaver were sharing that responsibility. But I was still nervous when he appeared midmorning while I was coaxing away anxious tears from a two-year-old in my lap. There were more nurses on the children's ward per patient than in the men's wards, so Dr. Randall made his rounds bed to bed with another nurse, but when he arrived to examine the little girl in my lap, who had at last quieted into slumber, he asked the nurse who'd been accompanying him to fetch him an otoscope with a smaller speculum from the main nurses' station.

When she left the room, I steeled myself for whatever he might say.

"Your roommate who took your place in the scarlet fever ward says these little ones tire her out."

I nodded. "They have a lot of energy. Even when they are sick."

He smiled. "Nice of you to switch with her."

It was obvious he didn't believe any of it.

"We are good friends. She would do the same for me."

"I'm sure she would."

I rose from my chair and placed the sleeping child on her cot so that the doctor could listen to her heart and lungs.

"I wasn't going to say anything to anyone about the book," he murmured.

"And why would you? What is there to say?"

He gently palpated the little girl's neck and stomach, and she stirred slightly.

"Look, I need to say something before Nurse Pruitt comes back," he said softly. "And I'm afraid she will soon return, so I don't have time to ease into it."

Wordless, I stared at him.

"Nurse McLeod asked Mrs. Crowley for Friday afternoon off and was denied. She can't go with you to the mainland. But I can. I've already asked for the leave, and Dr. Treaver granted it."

My mouth dropped open. No sound came out.

"I know you're probably going to be angry with her that she told me about your lunch invitation with your father. She knows it, too. But she doesn't want you to go to the mainland alone. She cares about you more than she cares about how angry you will be."

"Dolly told you?" Hot anger made the words slip out like sizzling coals.

"She doesn't want you going alone. And I don't think it's a good idea either."

"I didn't ask either one of you if you thought it was a good idea!" I raised my voice, waking the sleeping child. She began to cry and reached for me.

"Even so, I'd like to accompany you, if I may."

I pulled the now screaming child back into my arms.

"Am I some infant that must be fussed over? I can't believe you two were discussing me as though I were."

"She cares about you, Nurse Wood. And in case you've forgotten, you told her that I offered to accompany you on your first trip to the mainland. You told her that I offered to help you with this situation and you said yes."

The child's cries abated and she nuzzled her wet face into my neck.

"When I said yes, this wasn't what I meant."

"Well, it was what I meant. And I still do mean it."

"You barely know me."

"I know you're bound to this weight as much as any sick person is bound to her illness. I know that."

"And so that's why you want to help me? Because you feel sorry for me?"

"Even if that were the only reason, it would be reason enough. Yes, I feel sorry for you."

Behind me I heard the sound of footsteps. The nurse was returning with the otoscope.

The conversation came to an abrupt halt. When the nurse reached us, Dr. Randall crossed to the side of the bed where I stood with the child in my arms.

"I will hold her curls out of the way," the other nurse said, as Dr. Randall bent to look inside the little girl's ears.

"There's a good little girl," the nurse said sweetly. "The doctor won't hurt you."

The child whimpered in my arms, but the nurse's soft voice and my own gentle strokes across her back convinced her to believe it was true.

Twenty-Three

I could not stay angry with Dolly.

She was penitent to the point of annoyance the first night in our room after Dr. Randall insisted on going to Manhattan with me. And while she was sorry I was angry with her, she wasn't sorry she had told Dr. Randall about my Friday plans and the associated predicament. Not really.

"Who else could go with you, Clara?" she said. As the rest of the week unfolded, I gradually warmed to the idea of Dr. Randall accompanying me. By Thursday afternoon he and I had the plan mapped out. After morning rounds, we would both change into street clothes and then meet at the ferry house for the eleven o'clock crossing. We would land ashore in plenty of time to get to the Hotel Albert. He would take a cab with me to the hotel at noon, drop me off, and then return for me at two o'clock.

The night before the trip, Dolly helped me choose a dress and then tried out hairstyles for me to wear. I didn't care about either, but both were a welcome distraction.

As I sat at the vanity and she experimented with my hair, she told me that Andrew Gwynn would be discharged the next day.

A peculiar pain nudged me. I had learned from loving Edward that sometimes there are people you meet in life who are yours for only a moment and then they are gone. Edward had been like that, and now so would Andrew. Edward's brief time in my world had changed me forever, and I knew that after Andrew left Ellis, he might think the same thing about me, that I had changed his life, and perhaps not for the better. Still, I would play a role in the course of the rest of his life just as Edward had played a role in mine.

"Clara?"

Dolly had evidently asked me a question and I hadn't heard her.

"What?"

"I said, before you go to bed tonight, you might want to get that pattern book and the scarf out for me. I will be returning them to him tomorrow. Unless you've changed your mind and want to do it yourself."

"No. I don't. And please see to it that Mr. Gwynn isn't on the eleven o'clock ferry."

Dolly sighed and pinned a loop of my hair to my head. "He won't be. He and a couple others who were on the *Seville* are leaving first thing in the morning. He's already sent a telegram to his brother that he's being released."

"Good. I mean, it's good that he's being discharged."

"He asked about you," Dolly said after a long pause.

"In what way?"

"He asked if you were well." She pinned up another loop and then rested her hands on my shoulders.

"I trust you told him I was fine." I looked at her in the reflection of the mirror. She held my gaze for a moment.

"Of course." Dolly stepped back to admire her work. "Looks very pretty. But I think you will want to borrow Nellie's green hat. It would go so nicely with the green stripes in your shirtwaist."

I stood up from the vanity. "I don't need to borrow anyone's hat."

"Yes, you do. Don't pull the pins out of your hair yet. I am going to go ask her for it. Stay here."

Dolly pulled open the door and was gone.

I checked my best shoes for scuff marks and inspected my handbag to make sure I had money for the cab, extra hairpins, and a handkerchief.

With everything in order, I then knelt by my bed and pulled out the pattern book and the tissue-wrapped scarf. The top of the pattern book was dusty, as it hadn't been touched in three weeks. I grabbed a stocking out of my laundry basket and wiped it clean.

And then for no other reason than sentimental curiosity, I opened the book. The pages were filled with sketches of suit coats, blouses, trousers, and rows of measurements in a lovely script that made me want to reach out and touch it. Between some of the pages were folded pattern pieces, soft bits of thin muslin that smelled like leather, tobacco, and mint. I lifted out a piece and held it to my face, drinking in scents that could be described only as strong and handsome. I replaced it when

I feared I would inhale the very soul out of that treasured piece of fabric. I turned the pages, admiring the artistry that had created them, and picturing Andrew in his father's tailor shop learning the trade just as I had learned the healing arts from my father. As I turned the last page, I saw that the back inside cover of the book had been inscribed in the same flowing hand that had sketched the clothing.

My dear sons Nigel and Andrew:
I wish I'd had the pleasure of meeting your mother at an earlier age so that I would not be such an old man when God blessed me with fine sons such as you. I wish we'd had many years together and not few, and I wish the few that we had were not so crowded with my illness. Know that I am so very proud of you, in every way. I know that you will care for your mother when heaven calls me home as I am now sure it will. I have taught you everything I know to be good tailors, but I trust I have also taught you all you need to know to be good men. I spent many years alone before I met your mother, but I would change nothing if I were to live my life again. The person who completes your life is not so much the person who shares all the years of your existence, but rather the person who made your life worth living, no matter how long or short a time you were given to spend with them.

May God bless you with love such as
this—true and absolute.

> Your father,
> Alistair Henry Gwynn
> June 1902

A tear, one that I hadn't noticed, had crept to my eye-lid, slipped unchecked, and landed on the page. Startled, I pressed the edge of my sleeve against the wetness, know-ing it would surely leave a mark. I hastily closed the book and held it to my chest as I waited for my stirred emotions to settle, reminding myself that the words had not been meant for me. They did not belong to me.

I looked at the small parcel on my bed that hid Lily's letter and certificate. Doubts again assailed me. Was I doing the right thing by giving Andrew what would have been destroyed unread had I not opened the wrong trunk? Had divine circumstances, or diabolical ones, al-lowed me to intervene?

Dolly returned as I sat with the pattern book on my lap and the tissue-wrapped package next to me. In her hands was an emerald-green hat with sparkly black net-ting attached to its brim. She looked at what I held in my lap and what lay next to me.

"Give me those." She tossed the hat onto my bed and scooped up the pattern book and parcel. She laid them inside her wardrobe and shut the door on them. "Now. Let's try the hat."

I positioned myself back on the vanity stool and she placed the hat on my head, cocking it slightly and pulling the netting down to just above my brows.

"Perfect," Dolly announced. "Now you're ready."

I still said nothing as she removed the hat and began to pluck out the hairpins.

I went about the morning getting ready as one in between sleep and waking. Dolly pinned my hair up the way she had the night before and then positioned my nurse's cap carefully over the pins so as not to muss them. When we went down early to breakfast, Dolly carried the pattern book and parcel in a laundry bag, which she deposited at the nurses' station in the scarlet fever ward before any of the men had awakened. Inside the dining hall, we were the first to arrive, and it took supreme effort to eat two pieces of toast under Dolly's watchful eye. I had no appetite.

Once in the children's ward, I found myself constantly looking at the clock on the wall. First because Andrew Gwynn was leaving on the earliest ferry off the island. And I very much wanted him to have neither the time nor inclination while he waited to open the parcel that held the scarf. Throughout the early morning I told myself that of course he wouldn't open it. He knew what it was. It was Lily's scarf, washed and neatly folded and ready to be packed with the rest of his things. He wouldn't fuss with it. Unless he wanted to wear it off Ellis as he had worn it on . . .

When the doorway was darkened a few minutes before nine, I glanced up in terror, thinking it was Andrew looking for me with the open parcel in his hands, demanding to know what I had done. But it was Dr. Randall, ready to do his morning rounds before we left for the ferry house.

"You all right?" he asked.

"Fine," I answered quickly, and without conviction.

As he completed his rounds my gaze was on the clock. At ten, Dr. Randall left the ward, and half an hour later so did I. I practically jogged to the ferry house to make sure the first ferry of the day had come and gone. Relief filled me when I saw that it had long been away, but melancholy wrapped itself around me as I left to go change into my street clothes. It seemed that a chapter had ended in my life, and again, I had nothing to show for it.

I walked back to my quarters, trying very hard not to ponder that in less than an hour I would also be on a ferry bound for Manhattan. I would be stepping willingly out of my in-between place and onto the solid surface of the real world, the one where time didn't stand still.

Twenty-Four

I arrived at the ferry house in my green-striped shirt-waist and Nellie's borrowed hat with only five minutes to spare. I found Dr. Randall pacing at the gate, waiting for me.

"I was about to come to your quarters looking for you," he said, breathless.

"That would be against the rules. Mrs. Crowley wouldn't like it." I pushed past the gate to stand with him in the queue of people already boarding. The air in the ferry house was stale and warm, and I felt a trickle of sweat form at my neck.

"I'm serious. I was worried about you."

"I'm here now. Stop talking about it." I reached back to my neck and touched the beads of sweat with my glove.

"Give me your hand."

I looked up to say I didn't need him hovering over me like that. I just needed to take it one second at a time. He was making it worse. But he didn't appear to be sweating. No one else was. Without speaking, I clasped his arm. We began to move forward.

"Close your eyes if you want. I'll make sure you don't run into anything."

"I'm not going to close my eyes, for heaven's sake."

But a moment later I did. As soon as my foot touched the gangplank, I felt a heavy weight inside me surge up my throat. I clamped my other hand over my mouth and let Dr. Randall guide me.

"You're doing fine. Just fine."

"Stop talking!" I rasped between my fingers.

I leaned into him as I felt my body leave the gangplank and arrive on the ship's slightly undulating deck.

"Wait!" I whispered as the barely discernible movement under my feet set me off balance.

"I've got you. You are doing fine." He tugged me forward, and I could feel people behind me wanting to move much faster.

"I don't think I can do this," I said, more to myself than to him. My legs felt like iron and there seemed to be no oxygen on the ship at all.

"Yes, you can."

More gentle tugging. I felt as if something heavy inside me were clanging like a bell, wanting out, wanting to explode.

"We're almost there."

I peeked then and saw that Dr. Randall was propelling me toward a long row of red upholstered benches, away from the windows and the open doors. He led me to the corner of the expansive interior room and set me down, taking a seat right next to me.

"All right?" he asked.

"No. Yes. I don't know. I feel sick. I can feel my pulse in my head."

"Give me your hands." He took my hands and yanked off my gloves, so abruptly that I snapped my eyes open and pulled my hands away.

"What are you doing?"

"Give me your hands." He grabbed them back. At that moment the ship's whistle blew and I felt the ferry begin to move away from the dock. I clenched my hands into tight fists as we picked up speed and I could feel the water under us pushing us away from safety. I imagined the ferry house falling away from us, getting smaller. . . .

"Clara! Listen to me. Close your eyes and listen to me. Listen only to me."

I wanted to bolt. I wanted to jump overboard, in Nellie's beautiful hat, and swim back to my island. I could see the railing. I could see my island. I could swim that far. . . .

"Close your eyes, damn it! Listen only to me."

I swung my head around to Dr. Randall. I knew I must look like a feral child to him, or a lunatic. But he just held my hands and told me again to close my eyes. It took everything in me to do it.

"You are safe. You are safe," Dr. Randall said, and as he said this again and again, he stroked the backs of my hands with his fingers, gently and with obvious rhythm, like a metronome. And then he turned my hands over and gently pried my fingers out of the curled fists, stroking my open palms the same way he had the backs of my hands.

At some point I realized I was no longer struggling to breathe. The heavy thing inside me had stopped its lurching and now hung suspended in my chest, not altogether gone but not pressing up against my lungs either. My pulse, which had felt like a freight train only moments before, was now skipping along, far faster than it needed to, but not so fast that I felt as if I might explode.

I opened my eyes slowly. Dr. Randall's kind face was intent on mine. He appeared ready to heave his body over mine if I were to make a mad dash for the railing.

"You all right?" he asked tentatively.

"You called me Clara," I squeaked.

He smiled and I felt his body relax somewhat. "We aren't at the hospital. We're not in uniform. You're just Clara. And I'm just Ethan."

The gloves he had yanked off lay on the deck at my feet.

"May I have my gloves back?"

He let go of one of my hands as he bent down and retrieved them.

"I'm not going to jump overboard," I murmured, taking the gloves with my free hand.

"I know you're not."

"I promise."

Ethan slowly let go of my hand and I steadied myself on the bench.

"I'm really sorry about . . . about all that," I said.

"Don't be. It's nothing to be sorry about. You've just taken a huge step. You should be proud of yourself."

"I guess I did."

"No guessing. You did."

"Where did you learn the trick with the . . . the hand stroking?"

"I studied psychology before I went into general practice. I had a professor who used that technique on his patients. It's not so odd really. Gentle rhythmic stroking is how mothers calm agitated children. It's how you calmed that little girl the first day I saw you in the children's ward. You made her feel safe."

I chanced a glance out the windows across from us, wishing I didn't feel like that child and yet knowing the ordeal wasn't over. Not by any stretch. "I still have to get off this boat when we dock."

"And you will."

We were silent for a moment. "I was never like this before," I said. "Never. I could be in my dad's surgery and watch him reattach a nearly severed limb or cut dead skin away from a horrible burn and I never had to turn away. My mother and my sister? They ran gagging into the house. But not me. I was never afraid." I looked down at my bare hands in my lap. "I wasn't afraid of anything."

Ethan paused before answering. "Everybody's afraid of something, Clara. You can't be human and be afraid of nothing."

I sighed heavily. "I don't want to be afraid of this anymore."

He reached for my hand. "That's half the battle right there."

I let him hold my hand in his. And then in that tender moment, I began to tell him why I had exiled myself on the island. I thought he deserved to know. "It's my fault Edward died in that fire. He asked me to come up to the sewing room just before the workday was over. He wouldn't have been there if he hadn't. He would've been on the tenth floor, where there was a way out. I saw him jump. I saw his body hit the pavement."

For the first time since it happened I didn't feel about to burst into tears at the retelling of that horrible day. Ethan squeezed my hand.

"And I could do nothing," I continued. "I had known him for only a couple weeks. You probably think that's too short a time to fall in love with someone, but I did love him. And I think he loved me. We just . . . we just didn't have the time to tell each other. We never got the chance."

"I really am sorry, Clara. But I'm sure deep down you know it was not your fault he died. You know that, don't you?"

"But it feels like it was."

"You can't listen to that voice in your head that says it was your fault. That's not the voice of truth, Clara. And for your information, I do think two people can fall in love right away. My parents did. It happens all the time."

"Really?"

He nodded.

"That's why I felt some kind of kinship with Mr. Gwynn. He had just lost his wife and they had been married just a few days. He had known her for only two weeks before they were wed. I understood his loss and the depth of his love for her. I understood it better than anyone. I understood more than he even knew."

"I know you did. And . . . and I know about the letter you found. Dolly told me."

I gasped inwardly. Why would she do that?

"She didn't want to involve me, but she was ordered by Mrs. Nesbitt to help another patient send a telegram right at the time Mr. Gwynn was to be discharged. She needed someone to make sure he got the belongings you had kept for him in your room. She asked me to give them to him."

"Did she tell you everything?"

"Enough for me to know that you wanted to do right by Mr. Gwynn. That is admirable. But . . ."

Something in his voice spoke of disapproval. "But what? You don't agree that he should have that letter?"

"I don't think we can say which is right and which is wrong in this case. I don't see how any decision you could make would be the right one. Which I guess means neither choice is wrong. There is no happy solution to be had here."

"For the longest time I didn't want him to see it," I said. "Mr. Gwynn thought his wife loved him. I know how marvelous it is to feel that way."

Ethan looked away, almost as if I had struck a tender spot. When he turned back to me, though, his expression held no evidence that I had. "You're right. It is wonderfully marvelous. I am indeed sorry you lost someone you loved. Perhaps, if you would like, we can visit Edward's grave after lunch today. It might be very comforting to you. I lost my grandmother to influenza some years ago, and when I visit her grave, I feel less sad. I know that sounds contrary, but it's true."

"I don't know. . . ." It hadn't occurred to me find out where Edward was buried. And now, the suggestion that I might find comfort in visiting his grave was a completely foreign idea.

"We don't have to. It's just a thought."

"Well, I . . . I don't know where he is buried."

Ethan didn't seem surprised by that. And I was glad, because I didn't want to explain why.

"I'm sure the newspaper that carried his obituary

would have the cemetery listed. If you want to find out where he's been laid to rest, it won't be hard. But you don't have to."

The caution in his voice both surprised and touched me.

"Maybe," I said. "Maybe you could look up his obituary while I am with my father."

"Or we can go look it up together after your lunch. If you still want to."

"All right."

The ferry slowed and when I looked out the window I could no longer see the city skyline. It was above me. We were at the dock.

Ethan reached for my other hand and held them both tight.

"I think I might need to close my eyes again," I whispered as the boat shuddered to a stop and the weight in my chest swung heavily against my heart. I screwed my eyes shut.

"I'll get you safely off this boat," Ethan said as he pulled me gently to my feet. "Let's just let everyone else off first so you can take your time."

I felt the bustle of people around me, and I heard the sweet storm of immigrant languages as newcomers to America prepared to step onto her shores.

Someone bumped into me and I cracked an eye open. But the boat seemed to sway on its moorings when I did. I toppled a bit and Ethan closed the distance between us and wrapped an arm around my waist.

"It's okay to keep them closed," he said.

Finally, the many voices that had been all around us seemed far away and I realized everyone was off the boat except us.

"Here we go." Ethan began to walk and I leaned into

him and matched his movements. I felt the sun on my face when we stepped onto the gangplank and smelled the tang of harbor air. That odor was soon followed by the heady fragrance of the city slamming into me. I came to a halt on the gangplank.

"You're doing fine. We're almost there."

"That . . . that odor." I felt tears stinging the backs of my eyes.

"That's New York. That's all it is. The good and the bad in New York. You're doing fine."

I took another tentative step and then another, breathing in short gasps.

"Bigger breaths, Clara. Come on. Big breaths."

Ethan began to breathe deep beside me. I felt his rib cage expand next to mine and I endeavored to match it, concentrating on that. Air in, air out. Air in, air out.

And then my foot hit pavement. As solid as rock.

The place where everything had changed for me.

I paused for a moment to take it in. The sensation of solid ground beneath my feet, the odor of horses and cars and peanuts and hot coffee and dead fish; the sounds of motors and birdcalls and voices raised in absolute joy and utter annoyance; the taste of salt and steam and September morns.

And then I slowly opened my eyes to the arrogant beauty and bustle and bravado of Manhattan.

Twenty-Five

TARYN

Manhattan
September 2001

IT was the silence that most surprised me.

After the roar of the tower's fall and the first screams of terror, there was a massive hush that nearly seemed appropriate, since no words could describe those moments. There would have been cries for deliverance but our mouths and lungs were filled with a million fragments of former lives and purposes. No one could move air past their vocal cords.

Perhaps it was the absence of human voices on those crowded streets that made it seem as if the wall of destruction were without sound.

In that heavy silence where no light shone, the florist and I fumbled for survival like two children who didn't know how to swim, flailing in a rushing river.

I don't know how long or how far we staggered to break the surface; I only knew the longer we surged forward the more aware I became that my body was stinging, my hands and forehead were sticky with blood, and my throat ached for water.

I heard breaking glass as others in the same desperate plight shattered windows to get inside buildings. Several people pushed past, and as I started to pitch backward, I felt the florist grab me. More windows were being broken.

He turned us away from the stampede of people wanting shelter and water, and then I heard the sound of metal sliding on metal. I saw a shimmer of colors in this sea of nothingness and the florist pushed me toward them. I banged my knees on a shelf of some kind and started to fall. He jumped ahead of me, grabbed my torso, and pulled me toward the rainbow flecks. A metal door slammed shut against the gray wall behind us.

We were inside a van, surrounded by flowers in buckets of water.

He and I dived for the buckets, yanking out the blooms and savagely tossing them aside. I sputtered and coughed as I lapped at the water, cupping my bloodied hands to get as much as I could into my mouth and down my parched throat.

For many long minutes we just knelt at the buckets and drank. When we weren't drinking, we were spitting and coughing up a mush of pasty rubble. When I finally felt the strong return of air in my lungs, I turned to my rescuer. He was covered in ash, as white as a ghost, and was wiping his face with a roll of paper towels.

"Are you hurt?" he said.

I looked down at my hands, stinging from the water.

A narrow gash had opened on one hand and a few scrapes on the other. I didn't know how I had gotten the wounds.

"Your head's bleeding," he said. And he tore off a length of paper towel, folded it, and held it to my forehead. I reached up to hold it with the hand that hurt the least.

"Let me see your hand."

I held out my other arm and he wound two paper towels around the injury. He reached into a rubber tote behind him and grabbed a spool of florist tape, winding the Christmas-green adhesive around the makeshift bandage.

"Are you all right?" he said.

"I think so." My voice was raspy and barely recognizable as mine. I coughed.

"I don't think we can stay here."

I took in where we were huddled, two specters sitting among strewn flowers while a nightmare pulsed outside. "What?" I said, though I had heard him.

"We shouldn't stay here. It's not safe. As soon as we can see our way outside, we have to get out."

I was numb and strangely calm, as close to shock as I have ever been.

"Miss? Did you hear me? What's your name?"

But my attention was on the tossed tulips in my lap: soft, rose hued, and wet. As pretty as the woven ones on my dress, which I could no longer see.

"Miss, what's your name?" He leaned toward me and touched my arm. Gentle, but firm.

"Taryn," I whispered. My voice sounded like I'd pushed my name past gravel.

"Karen?"

I didn't correct him. I fingered a petal, so supple and beautiful.

"I'm Mick. I don't think we should stay here. We're too close. If the other tower falls . . ."

But he didn't finish. The other tower was Kent's tower.

I raised my eyes to him as the numbing of my body continued to spread warm and thick over every inch of me. "Is this real?"

"Yes." Again, the gentle tone.

"Why is this happening?"

"I don't know."

A buzz began to hum in my ears, increasing in intensity as the seconds ticked away: the sound of reality reestablishing itself. I didn't want to hear it.

"Karen, I think we need to get ready to go."

"He's dead," I blurted, the buzz in my ears hot and grating.

"I . . . I'm really sorry about that." Mick reached for my hand again, touching me just above the bandage he had made. "Very sorry."

"If it wasn't for me, he'd be alive."

Mick paused for only a moment. "I'm sure that's not true."

I shook my head and continued my confession. "I left him a message to meet me at Windows on the World at a quarter to nine. I was going to tell him we're having a baby. We've tried for so long. He wouldn't have been there if it weren't for me. He would have gotten out."

Mick grasped my hand firmly. "It's not your fault."

But I could only picture where Kent would be at that moment if I had not called him. He would have made it out of the smoking building and sped to safety like thousands of other evacuees had. "He would have gotten out."

"Look, we're going to have to go." Mick lifted the

paper towel away from my head, and then pressed it back.

But I sensed no urgency. I sensed nothing beyond the crushing weight of the choices I had made. "I should have called him the moment I knew," I mumbled. "If only I had called and told him right away. If only . . ."

Mick sat up on his knees to look out the windshield, no doubt gauging the condition and visibility of the streets we needed for our escape. He knelt back down to my level.

"I'm not going to be able to drive the van. We're going to have to get out of here on foot. Can you do that? Can you run?"

I couldn't process what he was saying. The disconnect between what had happened, which was obvious, and what was still to come in our bid for survival, which no one could predict, rendered me mute.

"Hey, you aren't to blame," he said emphatically. "You did nothing wrong. Evil people did this." His eyes turned glassy. "Terrorists killed all those people."

My eyes sought his as emotion slowly returned to me, raw and cutting. Fresh tears slid down my face. "Those people jumped." The three words tumbled out of my mouth, sharp edged.

"Yes, some jumped."

"Did it hurt?"

Mick blinked and the glassy wetness pooling in his eyes dislodged. Two tears slid down his face. "No."

I grabbed his arm. "How do you know? How do you know it didn't hurt?"

"Because it happened too fast! It was too fast. We have to go."

He tore off two long lengths of paper towels and plunged them into the buckets. After squeezing out the excess, he handed one to me.

"Cover your nose and mouth. Keep your other hand on the paper towel on your forehead."

"Are you sure it was quick?" I had to be certain that despite what I had done, Kent's death had not been agonizing.

"Yes. I'm positive."

I needed one last assurance that I deserved to live before I headed back into the thin space between death and survival, coincidence and destiny. "I was supposed to meet Kent up there. I was late."

Mick placed both hands on my shoulders, pulling my gaze to his. His hands were wet from the water in the bucket. "Then I'm sure he died glad that you'd been delayed. If I had been him, that would have been my last thought. That you were safe."

And with this new idea to give me strength, I put the covering to my mouth and Mick opened the door.

The scene outside the van was like a nuclear winter. A blizzard of yellow ash and pulverized concrete still swirled down. An acrid odor rose up from the moonscape that we set our feet on. A faint, pearly light at the edge of the stunted horizon hinted that the sun still shone somewhere beyond us. The muffled whine of dozens upon dozens of sirens and alarms struggled to be heard.

I had no idea where we were. Mick took my arm and we hurried down a street that didn't look like a street or feel like a street, but there were hulks of vehicles all around us, so it had to be. The air burned my eyes and lungs despite the wet towel I held to my face. I saw a few other shapes moving in the fog, shuffling toward the rim of pale light that seemed to hover ahead of us.

Mick stopped at what appeared to be an intersection. I could vaguely make out the street signs. We were at Maiden Lane and William Street. He turned to me and leaned in close.

"I think I should take you to the hospital so someone can look at your hand and that wound on your head."

I didn't argue. I just nodded and he took my arm again and we headed north to NYU's downtown hospital three blocks away. The closer we got to the hospital the more we could see a steady stream of refugees making their way out of the horror we had left. A thunderclap sounded behind us and instinctively we turned toward it. We could not see what had made the sound, but the boom had the same tone and timbre as when the South Tower fell: a roar, deep and guttural.

"The other tower is falling!" A man wearing a safety vest coated in white ran past us. "Keep moving!"

"Come on!" Mick yelled. He pulled me along, yanking me into a hazy half-light. We staggered toward a building that was the hospital, although I could not make out the signage. Hospital employees, some wearing street clothes, were ushering evacuees into a triage center that been set up just inside. We were given water and cool cloths to clean our faces. I was only half-aware that Mick was telling a nurse that I had a gash on my hand and a wound to my forehead. I was lowered into a chair. A woman applied antiseptic to my hand and face, and then covered the wounds with salve and gauze. As she worked, Mick knelt beside me.

"Is there someone I can call for you?" he said. "My

cell phone's not working, but there are a couple of pay phones over there. If there's someone I can call for you, I'd be happy to wait in line and do it."

I didn't answer right away and the nurse filled the silence. "No one's going to be allowed in to get her," she said, as she hurried to tape the bandage on my hand. "Only emergency vehicles can come downtown. The tunnels and bridges are closed, too. And the subways. The two of you will have to walk out of here."

"But she's . . . Can I talk to you for a minute?" Mick and the nurse stepped away from me and I noticed that the previous silence had been swallowed up by a cacophony of human sounds, all of them dreadful and wild. I covered my ears to shut them out.

Mick returned and knelt next to me. "Karen, they are going to take care of you here, okay?"

I let my hands drop to my lap.

The nurse knelt down beside me, too. "I'm going to go find a doctor. I want you to wait right here." Then she sprinted away, disappearing into a sea of hurry.

"Will you be all right?" Mick said.

"I don't want to stay here."

He covered my uninjured hand with his. "The nurse thinks you might be going into shock. You really should stay here and let them take care of you until someone can come for you."

"I don't want to stay here." I did not want sit in that crazed place where no one knew how to make sense of what had once been a beautiful morning. The only hope I had was that Kent might have left the restaurant when I was late. Maybe he decided to meet me in the lobby and ride up with me. Maybe he had been detained, just like I had. Maybe he had tried to call to tell me *he* was running late. When he got no answer on my cell phone, he would have called our landline.

I had to get home.

Mick squeezed my hand. "They will take care of you here."

It occurred to me then that I had not said Mick's name aloud. He had pulled me out of the clutch of hell and convinced me to crawl away from it. He'd made me realize that if a random phone call had made me late, the same thing could have happened to Kent.

Kent might be on his way home at that very moment just like I should be. And it was this man who had brought me out of the nightmare so that I could awaken and realize this.

I pulled my hand out from under Mick's and touched his name tag on the once-green apron that was now a sickly pale yellow. "Thank you," I said.

The weight of having taken responsibility for me was evident in his demeanor. I could see how it lifted a little when I thanked him. I think he knew I was thanking him for more than his help in leading me out of the cloud.

He clasped my hand in his for the last time, not in the grasp of runners to safety or encourager to the defeated, but in farewell. We both knew we would likely never see each other again.

"Will you be all right?" he asked. He wanted the assurance that he could leave me. I had not until that moment considered that he might be worried about someone who had been in those towers, or that he was anxious to get to a phone to assure his loved ones that he was okay.

I nodded.

Mick lingered only a second longer. He rose to his feet, squeezed my hand, and left. He turned back once and our gazes met. A bustle of people moved in between our line of vision, and when they finally parted, Mick was gone.

I didn't wait for the nurse to return.

It was easy to lose myself in the panicked crowds and be absorbed again into the mass of humanity moving toward the Brooklyn Bridge, only a few blocks away.

The lanes for cars were now a pathway for thousands of walkers fleeing downtown. Many stopped as they walked to look over their shoulders at the smoking, marred landscape of Lower Manhattan. I didn't. I looked for Kent among the walkers; that was the only reason I turned to look behind me from time to time.

On the other side of the East River, we evacuees were welcomed by a crowd of sympathizers who offered us water and hugs and rides to our homes or theirs. I accepted a lift to my apartment from a silver-haired reverend who took five of us away from the bridge in a church van.

When I got home, I couldn't get to my front door fast enough. I was already calling Kent's name as I ran down the hallway of the fifth floor, amazed that I still had my purse with me and could unlock my door.

I burst inside, but the rooms were empty. He wasn't there. I ran to the landline in our kitchen and there was my cell phone on the counter by the window. I had set it there when I had used two hands to close the stubborn thing earlier that morning. The landline blinked with eight messages and my cell phone showed I had seven missed calls and six text messages.

Three calls from Kent on my cell.

One from him on the landline.

Two text messages from him.

With shaking hands I pressed the button to hear his voice mails.

The first call was at eight forty-eight and for just a moment I thought he had called me from his office, and not the restaurant. "Taryn, there's been an explosion. Don't come up the elevator. If you're not already on your way, don't come yet. Something's happened. Call me back the minute you get this."

The second one, at eight fifty-one, swept away the infant hope I had latched onto at the hospital: "It was a plane. A plane crashed into the floors below us. There's a lot of smoke up here. God, I hope you weren't in the elevator. Please call me back. I am calling the landline just in case."

The third was at nine o'clock. "We can't . . . we can't use the stairs. I don't know why I'm calling. I'm afraid you aren't answering because . . . It's getting hard to breathe. I need to let one of the waitresses use my phone to call her family. Please let me know you are safe."

I crumpled to the floor. The text messages were sent at nine-oh-seven, nine fourteen, and nine twenty-seven.

"Did you get out? Text me!"

"Can't get to the roof. Too hot. They are breaking windows. Are you safe?"

"Only one way out now. I love you, Taryn. I'm coming."

I don't know how long I lay on the floor with my cell phone clutched in my hand. Time ceases to have substance when you are flattened by despair.

At some point the phone trilled and I managed to lift it to my ear.

My mother's relieved cries pierced the hollowness of my grief.

"And Kent is okay, too?" she asked.

"No. No, he's not."

Later I was glad that that was all I needed to say.

She didn't ask a dozen questions, thank God. Just the one. "Oh, Taryn! Are you sure?"

My parents called Kent's family, relieving me of that horrible job. And they called Celine in Paris and a few other close friends here in the States. While I was still sitting there, numb in the apartment, Celine's brother and his wife arrived to take me home with them so that I would not spend my first night without Kent alone.

It took my parents three days to get to New York from Wisconsin. Kent's parents had an easier time, arriving by train from Connecticut two days later.

But I don't remember much about those first few weeks of my new life as a widow.

I do remember telling my parents and in-laws that I was pregnant, and that when I did tell them, the heavy cloak of mourning felt lighter. At least for a little while.

And when Celine returned from Paris many days later, I remembered that I had been holding a scarf the day Kent died. A very old and beautiful scarf, which didn't belong to me, but that had saved my life nonetheless. I had no idea what had become of it.

What I remembered most acutely from those early days—and remembered still—was the burden of Kent thinking I was dead, because his calls and texts to me went unanswered.

Another unfortunate happenstance, that forgotten phone?

Or the willful hand of providence?

The magazine photograph, Kendal's questioning eyes, the impending tenth anniversary, the calls from the reporters and producers, the compassionate stares from customers and neighbors who recognized me in the photo—all of these served to remind me that I didn't know which it was.

I could have shut my mind and heart against that burning question except for Kendal, who still waited for an answer as to why I'd never told her I was across the street from the World Trade Center when the towers fell and her father was killed.

Celine had no doubt talked to Kendal, because she didn't ask me about it again. And yet this unspoken subject between my daughter and me felt dark and heavy. I knew she had questions that needed answers.

After all these years, sweet Jesus, so did I.

Three days after the photo was published, on the morning of the ninth of September, Kendal asked me whether I was going to go with her and Kent's parents to the memorial ceremony on the eleventh. It was obvious she very much wanted me to go.

I could tell her only that I was still thinking about it.

That same morning, after Kendal had gone to school and during a lull between morning and afternoon, the store's phone rang. Celine and Leslie were with customers, so I answered it.

"The Heirloom Yard. This is Taryn. How can I help you?"

"Taryn Michaels?" I didn't recognize the man's voice. Another reporter perhaps?

"Yes. Can I help you?"

The man hesitated before he spoke again. "This is Mick Demetriou."

I didn't make the connection in my head. Not at first.

"I'm sorry, who?"

"Um, from the photo in *People* this week."

For the second time that week I had to reach for a cutting table to steady myself. "The florist?"

"Yes. I'm so glad I finally found you. I have your scarf."

Twenty-Six

CLARA

Manhattan
September 1911

THE pier was a frenzy of activity, so much so that moving through the crowds, the gates, and the buildings kept me from concentrating fully on the fact that I was no longer in my in-between place, but back where life can seem like a madman's carousel. Ethan's tight arm around my waist and my hunched form earned us stares. People couldn't help but gape at me, as if I were a just-apprehended fugitive or an ill person about to vomit or a mental patient bent on chasing after everyone with an ax. And this, too, was a distraction, albeit an unkind one.

When we finally emerged onto the street in Battery Park, Ethan insisted on hailing a motorized cab. He assisted me inside and shut the door, cutting out the street noises and some of the grip of the city. I leaned back against the squeaky leather seat as the motorcar lurched forward.

Ethan took my hand again, holding it with gentle reassurance. "The Hotel Albert. And take Broadway, please," he said to the driver, and then he turned to me. "Big breaths, Clara."

"I'm fine," I whispered.

"You're pale. Big breaths."

I obeyed.

The driver turned onto Broadway and we headed north toward Greenwich Village and my father's hotel. I hadn't been to the Hotel Albert before—indeed, I hadn't been to many places in the two weeks I had lived in Manhattan—but after a few minutes of my breathing and the cabbie driving and Ethan holding my hand, the scene out my window began to look familiar.

Too familiar.

I leaned forward in my seat, my gaze intent on the world outside my window. "Where are we going?"

"It's all right, Clara. We won't be going past Washington Place. We're skirting it. If you want, just close your eyes and you can open them when we get there."

I knew where we were. We were close. Something fell outside the window and I backed away from it into Ethan's chest.

"It was just a bit of newspaper on the breeze. That's all."

But it looked like a swatch of ash and Ethan knew it. "We're three blocks away. You can't see the building from here."

I nodded, attempting to press down the heavy weight in my chest, wanting to crush it with everything I had in me. "Why does it have to be like this?" I murmured.

"It will only be so today. The next time you come, it will be easier. And the time after that, easier still."

I took him at his word and sat back against the seat, willing the panic that seemed on the edge of consuming me to dissipate. A few minutes later the cab turned left on Tenth, a street I wasn't familiar with. And then we were pulling up alongside the curb and the Hotel Albert loomed above me, twelve stories of brick and granite.

Ethan handed the driver money before I could even think of reaching into my handbag. Then he got out of the car and came around to my side, opening my door and extending his hand to me.

I stepped out slowly, breathing deeply as Ethan had instructed me, and when my feet were firmly on the pavement I gazed up at the hotel. It looked a lot like the Asch Building.

"They all look the same," I whispered.

"But they're not." Ethan closed the cab door and the car pulled away from the curb. "Would you like me to escort you inside?"

I shook my head. "I can make it." But as soon as I said it I was keenly aware of how much Ethan had done for me that morning. I knew I wouldn't be standing there had it not been for him. "I am so very grateful for your help. I don't know how to thank you."

"You just did." He smiled at me. And then he raised his hand, hesitated, raised it again, and tucked a fallen wisp of hair back under my hat.

His touch unnerved me for only a moment as I realized my cowering and clutching certainly had to have taken their toll on my appearance. "Oh, my goodness. I must look a fright!" I reached into my handbag for a mirror but could not find one.

"You look lovely."

"I've forgotten my mirror!"

"Clara, you look fine."

I pinched my cheeks and licked my lips.

Again he smiled at me. "I will come back for you at two. And I will meet you in the lobby."

"Where will you go?"

"It's Manhattan. I will find a place to haunt for two hours. Don't worry."

I was suddenly sad to think of him leaving me, but I also knew I wanted to meet my father alone.

He tipped his hat and started to walk away, but he turned back and I knew he was waiting for me to walk inside the hotel and complete my journey. I took a step toward the hotel entry. A uniformed porter opened the door for me as he greeted me warmly.

And then I was inside.

I hadn't given much thought to what I would say to my father or what he might say to me. Since I had gotten his letter on Monday I'd been intent solely on getting myself to the hotel. Now that I was making my way through the richly appointed lobby, it occurred to me that my reason for staying on the island had been dealt a blow even as I closed the distance to the dining room doors. I was off the island. I was in Manhattan. I was three blocks away from where hell had opened up right in front of me. And I was able to keep walking. An unfamiliar confidence seemed to rise up from a slumbering place inside me.

My father was seated near a window and he rose when the waiter who'd met me at the dining room entrance brought me to him. He looked just as he had six months earlier, when he and my mother had come to take me home after the fire and were unsuccessful. I wondered whether I looked the same to him.

"Clara!" He took me into his arms and kissed me on the cheek. I could smell the country air on him, and his brand of tobacco, and even a hint of my mother's cologne, from when she had hugged him good-bye.

"Hello, Father."

He stepped back from me with his hands still on my shoulders. "You came!"

"You . . . you invited me."

"But I wasn't sure you'd come. Henrietta thought you might not."

I smiled nervously. "Well, here I am. Shall we sit?"

"Of course, of course."

The waiter, who had idled by while my father greeted me, now pulled out my chair, and as I took my seat I mentally prepared myself for what else Henrietta might have said.

"So how is everyone?" I said. The waiter handed me a menu and I thanked him. "Mother doing well?"

"Everyone is fine. We're wondering how you are. We've been worried actually. I think I mentioned that in my letter."

I took a sip of water from the cut-crystal glass in front of me. A tiny spiral of lemon slice sparkled in it. "You did. But I am well, as you can see."

He folded his hands and regarded me, considering me the way I'd seen him study a confounding symptom. "You look wonderful, certainly. But . . . Henrietta mentioned you'd seemed melancholy in your letters to her. And that's why you hadn't been off the island since you arrived. Not even once."

I set the glass down carefully. "Henrietta mentioned nothing of these concerns in her letters to me."

"But you haven't been off the island until today. Isn't that right?" I could see the care in his eyes, how much it pained him to ask me this.

"I haven't. But I am here today."

"But it took effort to come, didn't it? I can see how hard it was."

One of the benefits of working closely alongside someone for so many years is that you are in tune with their unsaid thoughts and the language of their body. My father read the account of my travail to get to him like he had read the menu at his elbow.

"It was a little difficult, yes. But I managed it, Father. A friend from the hospital came with me to make sure I got here."

Again he studied my face, searching it for clues as to what I was not telling him. There had to be more; he could sense that much.

As I in turn studied him, I knew that I could probably trust him with the details of Edward's influence on my life. Having told Dolly, Ethan, and even Andrew Gwynn about losing Edward, I now realized no one had thought me silly for falling in love with a man I barely knew; nor had anyone ridiculed me for grieving his death the way I had.

But it also seemed that every time I shared Edward's story with someone, his hold on me diminished a little. And I didn't want him to disappear from me; I had so little of him to hold on to.

"I had a rough time for a while, Father. I will admit that. And the horror of the fire took . . . took a long time to ease into something I could live with. But I am not the same person I was the last time you saw me."

"So, perhaps you are thinking it is time to move on? Seek another post?"

I shifted in my chair. "I haven't been looking for another post. I like working on Ellis."

"But it seems to have kept you from moving on from the fire, Clara. At least, it looks that way to us."

"Us?"

"Your mother and I, and Henrietta. We all see it in your letters. Henrietta especially so. I agree that you are not the same girl you were when we saw you after the fire, but you're not the same girl who left home for nursing school, either. You've changed, Clara."

"Everybody changes."

He nodded. "Of course they do. But not all change is for the good."

The moment these words were out of his mouth, I heard echoes of the very same thing I had said to Ethan only a few days earlier.

"You seem sad," he went on. "And that makes us sad. I think you need to get out of New York altogether. We all do."

For a moment I could not find my voice. When I did, my words surprised me. "I am a grown woman, Father. I make my own choices about where I will live and work. Just as you made yours when you became an adult."

I had never spoken to my father like that before. It was on the tip of my tongue to quickly apologize, but he spoke before I could.

"You are absolutely right. I am not telling you what to do. I am suggesting something to you, Clara, because

I love you and I can see your life from a perspective that you cannot. You witnessed something . . . horrific. More horrific than you are telling me. I think staying in New York, staying on Ellis, is asking too much of yourself."

"But New York is where I want to be!"

"This is where you *wanted* to be. I don't think it's the same place that you'd dreamed of. Not now."

The waiter appeared then, but he saw we were engaged in a heated discussion and scurried away.

I looked directly at my father. "I am not coming back to Pennsylvania."

"I'm not suggesting you do."

A second of silence hung between us.

"You're not?"

"No. I know you love the city and I know our quiet life back home is not what you want out of life. But there are other places besides New York, Clara."

He had come to New York to propose something to me. That was clear to me now. "What are you suggesting?"

"I've a friend who's a professor at a medical school, who will be traveling to Edinburgh for a year on a research project at the university there. His wife is in fragile health and needs nursing care around the clock. He wants to hire a nurse to go with them to Scotland. You would have every other weekend off. And you'd be able to travel with them to sightsee the rest of the British Isles, as well as the Continent. I told him I would ask you about it. The post is yours if you want it."

"Edinburgh?" That one word encompassed a dozen questions. My father seemed to discern them all.

"I know you've longed to see Europe, as much as you wanted to see New York. Here is your chance. It's only for a year. When they come back to the States you can see where you want to go next. They are nice people. She is especially kind, despite her many health problems. And as sad as your mother and I would be to have you so far away, it would get you off that island."

The thought of leaving Ellis for good was both exhilarating and terrifying. I could barely speak.

"Promise me you will think about it? You don't need to decide for a week or so. They leave the first week in October."

"I promise I will think about it."

He smiled, reached across the table, and covered my hand with his. "I am so glad to hear you say that. And I'm so glad you came today. I'm sure it was harder than you've let on."

I smiled back, unwilling to confirm or deny it.

He let go and we each reached for our menus.

Twenty-Seven

MY father had an appointment with a colleague in Midtown at two o'clock, which he apologized for, but I was glad to kiss him good-bye fifteen minutes before the hour. I wanted a few minutes to myself to collect my thoughts and ponder in a snippet of solitude the proposal my father had spoken of before Ethan returned. I told my father I would send a telegram to him about the job by the middle of the month.

After he departed, I settled into the sitting area in the lobby with a view of the front doors. As I imagined myself living in Scotland for a year, traveling to the Continent, and caring for just one frail woman, a strange but welcome ache for the loss of my island fell over me: the ache of losing something that is comfortable only because it is familiar, not dear. For the first time since I'd made the island my home, I could picture myself packing my belongings and leaving.

If I was truly to let go of Edward, I needed to do so in as complete a way as I could, and yet the thought of doing this filled me with the same dread as when I had stepped off the island earlier that morning.

I was so lost in contemplating my life without the richness and sadness of Edward being in it, I was unaware that Ethan had entered the hotel and was standing before me, his hat in his hand.

"Did it not go well?" he asked kindly, when I lifted my startled gaze to his.

I stood quickly. "How long have you been standing there?"

"Not long. Did it not go well?"

"No. I mean, yes. It went well."

"That's wonderful." He cocked an eyebrow. "Is this how you normally respond to something going well?"

"I am just surprised. I thought Father was going to try to talk me into coming back home to Pennsylvania. He didn't."

Ethan took my arm and we began to walk toward the hotel doors. "Then it must have been a pleasant visit."

We stepped outside into the early-afternoon sun. "He thinks I need to leave New York."

Ethan held his hand up to signal for a cab, but he lowered it. "Because of what happened to you here."

"Yes."

"And is that what you think you need to do?"

I shook my head. "I don't know. He found a post for me with an older couple moving to Scotland for a year while the husband is occupied at the university on a research project. The wife is in fragile health and needs round-the-clock care."

"Scotland?" He sounded as if the thought of my saying yes were unthinkable.

"I've always wanted to see Europe. And I know I can't stay on the island forever. I've always known that."

"Yes, but the only thing keeping you on the island is you, Clara. You can leave it anytime you want. And you don't have to go to Scotland to get away from it."

There was truth in what he said, truth that I had long known. I was the one keeping me chained to the island. If I was going to leave it for Scotland, or anywhere else, there were a couple of things I needed to do. If I waited, I might lose my courage, especially if I went back to the island and let it lull me again into a dazed stupor. I knew that with Ethan there with me, I could manage them both.

"I'd like to drive by the Asch Building," I said.

Ethan stared at me. "I beg your pardon?"

"I would. I want to drive by it."

"You do know that just two hours ago when you thought we were driving past it, you nearly—"

"Yes, I know. But I want to try. It's different when it's something I choose. Do you see? When I thought we were driving past it and I hadn't known we would be, I felt powerless. But if I ask to be driven past it, then I am in charge."

He seemed unconvinced that I knew what I was talking about. "All right," he said slowly.

"I need to come to terms with what happened between Edward and me. I need to drive by the place where I watched him die. And I want to find the cemetery where he's buried. Just like you said we could. I want to do that."

The confidence in my voice surprised us both. "Then that's what we'll do." He tucked my arm in his and with his other hand he signaled for a passing hansom.

Once inside the carriage, Ethan told the driver to take us past the Asch Building.

The driver turned to us. "If you're looking to see what's left o' the fire, you'll not see anythin'. Been telling tourists that for a while. You can't even tell."

"Just drive past slowly, please?" Ethan said politely.

The driver shrugged and turned back around.

We set off, and in a matter of minutes Washington Square was in view, and the brick-faced tower that was the scene of my undoing. I reached instinctively for Ethan's hand.

"Have him turn down Greene Street." My voice sounded strained in my ears. Ethan repeated my instruction.

As the building began to grow in scale, such that it filled my field of vision, the heavy weight that had been pressing against my chest all day suddenly blossomed like a rose in a hothouse. I could scarcely hear Ethan's voice beside me, telling me over and over that I was safe, I was safe, I was safe.

The driver was taking it slowly, as we'd instructed him to, but out of the corner of my eye and as we turned down Greene, I saw him glance back at me.

"Stop here!" My voice came out in a rasp, like tattered metal in the wind.

"What was that?" Ethan said.

"Tell him to stop."

This time my voice carried throughout the cab and the driver pulled on the reins.

As Ethan was asking if I was sure I wanted to do this, I stepped out of the carriage in front of the green-grocer's store, at once assailed by the twin smells of earthy vegetables and remembered smoke. Ethan had jumped out, too, and I heard him tell the driver to wait for us. But I was only minimally aware of him joining me as I began to walk across the cobbled street, undaunted by the sound of a car horn and the tinkling bells of bicyclists.

My body seemed powered by some outside force as I stepped onto the sidewalk where the dead had fallen. It was bleached clean of human tragedy. All the red blooms had faded into remembrance and the handful of people who walked past did not even seem to be aware of where their feet were walking. I sank to the pavement and pressed my hand to the warm stone.

"I am sorry," I whispered. "I'm sorry."

Ethan knelt beside me just inches away, ready to catch me if I collapsed into despair, I suppose. But I did not feel despair, kneeling there on an ordinary sidewalk in the heart of Manhattan. I felt only regret that we are so fragile. Our bodies are so weak. We are capable of feeling such powerful emotion, such that if the body could match the potency of what the heart holds, I could have flown to Edward's side as he stood on the flaming window ledge, and carried him down.

Or he could have flown to me.

But the strength of what I held inside didn't match the strength outside.

"I couldn't save him," I said aloud.

After a moment or two, I felt Ethan's arms on my shoulders, lifting me up and away.

We walked silently back to the hansom. Ethan assisted me inside and closed the door. The driver's eyes were wide as he looked back at me.

When Ethan was seated next to me, he turned to me and took my hand. "Do you still want to know where he's buried?"

I nodded.

Ethan turned to the driver. "The main office of *The New York Times*, please."

The driver said nothing as he eased us away from the curb.

"Are you all right?"

It took me a moment to answer Ethan, but strangely enough, I was all right. I was still greatly saddened by what I had lost, but kneeling on that pavement where Edward had died had reminded me that he had been real. Our spark of a romance had been real. It had been sweet enough to enjoy, long enough to mourn.

"It was worth it," I finally said. "I don't wish I hadn't met him. And I am glad I can say that."

Ethan stroked the top of my hand in wordless affirmation. It should always make us happy to say that loving someone and being loved by someone is worth whatever price is paid. I felt myself relax for the first time since I had opened my father's letter. The clanging weight in my chest had diminished to a wedge of unfinished business with no dread wrapped around it. Edward had told me that his parents had lived in New York City since they'd stepped off the ferry. I could only hope that they had buried their son here so that I could at last say goodbye to him, thank him for loving me, tell him how sorry

I was that he had been on the ninth floor waiting for me when the fire broke out, and that I would never forget how he gallantly offered his hand to that young woman when the two of them were swept away to heaven.

We rode in silence, but with our hands clasped together. I was glad Ethan knew I didn't need words in those minutes as the hansom brought us farther into Midtown. We stepped out onto Broadway and Ethan took my arm as we entered the *New York Times* building. He asked the smiling woman in the reception area where I could look up the obituary of a victim of the Triangle Shirtwaist Factory fire. She led us to a viewing room where recent issues hung on poles, suspended on a wooden frame. But the issue I needed was from farther back. She returned minutes later with several issues in her arms. When she handed them to me she said there would be no charge for the issues. She must have surmised I wanted the obituary because someone I cared for had died in the fire that the city was still talking about.

I took a seat at a wooden table and laid the newspapers down. They were dated the Monday, Tuesday, and Wednesday after the fire.

"Perhaps you'd like to be alone?" Ethan asked.

"No. You can stay." I looked up at him. He seemed concerned for me. "I mean, I want you to stay."

He took the chair next to me.

I picked up the first paper, unfolded it, and immediately felt hot tears spring to my eyes as the headlines, even on the third day after the fire, shouted the continuing horror of what had happened on the Saturday afternoon before. I scanned the index quickly, looking for the page number where I could find the obituaries and get away from the front-page woes.

But Edward's obituary wasn't among the dozens listed on the several pages of obituaries, many of them short death notices of the poorer dead.

I set the first newspaper aside, reached for the second, and again averted my eyes from the headlines on page one, which were not as large on the Tuesday paper after the fire. I found the obituaries page. The moment I turned to the correct page, my breath stilled in my lungs. Edward stared back at me; his smiling portrait pulled at my eyes. He might have been waiting for me all this time to come find him.

"There he is," I whispered, though it must have been too soft for even Ethan to hear.

For a moment I sat there and looked at Edward's black-and-white face, the shape of his nose and forehead, the set of his eyes, the curls of hair peeking out from the brim of his hat. I drank him in like a desert wanderer drinks in found water. I didn't know I was crying until a tear slipped onto the paper and startled me. I flicked the tears away and suddenly there was a handkerchief in front of me. I turned to Ethan and saw that he held it out for me, a sad look on his face. I thanked him and pressed the cloth to my eyes, smelling the woodsy scent of Ethan's aftershave.

Then I began to read.

Brooklyn Native Dies in Tragic Fire

Mr. Edward Brim, only son of Mr. and Mrs. Joseph Brim of Brooklyn, died in a disastrous fire last Saturday afternoon at his place of employment in Manhattan, where he worked as a bookkeeper.

His remains were brought to his parents' home, where the funeral took place Monday. The interment was at the Green-Wood Cemetery in Brooklyn.

Edward's kind and gentle nature made him many friends, and he was a loving son and devoted brother. A large concourse of friends and relatives were in attendance to pay their last respects at his graveside service.

In addition to his parents, the deceased is survived by a sister, Miss Margaret Brim; several aunts and uncles; many cousins; and his fiancée, Miss Savina Mayfield.

The handkerchief in my hand fluttered to the floor.

Twenty-Eight

ETHAN was silent beside me.

He did not ask, "What is it?" or, "What does it say?" He said nothing at all.

This was my first clue that he had already known Edward had been engaged.

Still, I waited for Ethan to comment on my stricken state, grab the paper from me and read the shattering words aloud. When he didn't, I read the words again myself, and then the last four words, over and over.

I heard my voice whisper, "This is not possible."

How could it be? It was unthinkable that Edward would have been the way he was around me if he were pledged to another. I could not believe that he was so heartless as to make advances toward me, eye me the way he had, if he'd been engaged to be married.

Unless . . . unless in my naïveté I had mistaken his genteel manner for physical attraction.

Was that it? Had Edward merely been showing kindness to a Manhattan newcomer, engaging me in conversation to welcome me, inviting me to the sewing floor as a polite gesture only?

No.

There was no mistaking his interest in me, the desire I had seen in his eyes. No mistaking it.

A stab of pain coursed through me, growing in intensity as I fully realized the truth. Edward could not have cared for me the way I'd cared for him. How could he? He was to be married to someone else.

I'd been a fool, but not the kind that mistakes simple kindness for amorous advances.

I'd been the silly girl who believed the one she loved, loved her in return.

There were no words to describe the ache of realization. It was so fierce and demoralizing, no tears even sprang to my eyes. In mourning, tears had been a ready salve for the ache of loss, but this, *this* was not grief. It was something darker and lonelier.

Ethan shifted in his chair, reminding me he was there. I turned to him dry-eyed, but I could not look him in the face. "You knew."

"Dolly told me." His tone betrayed that he'd been a somewhat reluctant participant in my learning the truth. I didn't think he was looking at me, either. "She looked up his obituary some time ago."

"When did she tell you this?"

"Yesterday."

My mind conjured a picture of the two of them—in

the scarlet fever ward, no doubt—heads bent in conversation about poor, unsuspecting Clara, duped, deceived, and pining away after an engaged man.

"She couldn't bring herself to tell you," Ethan went on. "She kept hoping you'd finally come to the city and find out for yourself."

"Find out for myself," I numbly echoed.

"Dolly said she'd tried hinting that you should find out more about Edward Brim, but it'd been almost six months, and, well, she didn't think you ever would."

"I know how long it's been." My voice sounded strangely emotionless.

"She cares about you, Clara! She thought you deserved to know the truth. Even if it was hard to hear."

"The truth? Is that what this is?" I snapped. It did not feel like truth to me—nothing so virtuous and holy as truth. Ethan didn't answer me.

"So you must have agreed with her. That I should know this," I continued.

For a second he said nothing. I remembered then in those seconds of silence that when Ethan had suggested we find out where Edward Brim was buried, he had offered me several opportunities to leave the matter alone. Dolly had obviously had to talk him into it.

"Dolly and I were worried you might not ever leave the island if you never learned the truth," he finally said, in a voice that both touched me to my core and raised my ire like a battalion flag.

"I had no intention of staying on the island for the rest of my life! Is that really what you both thought? That I'd be an old woman there, having never left it? You really thought that?"

Ethan paused only a moment. "No."

"And yet the two of you connived to get me into this building, knowing what I would read when I arrived."

Emotion that had eluded me minutes ago sprang to life inside me. I shot up out of my chair and it made a screeching sound across the marble floor that startled us both. I grabbed my handbag and headed for the doorway, away from Ethan, and away from that open newspaper that lay between us.

I passed the woman who'd retrieved the back issues for me and caught a glance of her surprised face as I rushed past her reception desk. Behind me, Ethan called out our gratitude as he raced to keep up with me. I burst through the double-door entry into the afternoon sunshine and the ordinary pulse of the city: trolleys, horse-drawn carriages, bicycles, men in suits, men in rags, women selling flowers, women holding parasols, street vendors, and newspaper boys.

The street scene was so utterly alive and apart from me, I came to an abrupt stop and Ethan nearly crashed into me.

"Clara."

I ignored him, raised my hand to a passing hansom, which did not stop, and then to another, which did. I stepped inside without Ethan's assistance, though he offered, and he slid in next to me.

"The pier at Battery Park," I said to the driver. The hansom pulled away.

"Clara." Ethan reached for my arm, and we were too close in the carriage for me to resist him. "I'm sorry! I thought it was the right thing to do."

"In the middle of an office building in downtown Manhattan with you sitting right next to me? You thought *that* was the right thing to do?"

His raised voice suddenly matched my livid tone. "What way would have been better? Tell me! Sometimes the truth hurts, Clara. But it's still the truth."

Oh, yes, indeed, the truth hurt. I'd been a fool. Dolly knew it. Ethan knew it. And now I did. And so I said it out loud.

"You were not a fool," Ethan replied. "Loving someone is never foolish. Edward Brim was the fool. He was worse than a fool. You have done nothing to be ashamed of, Clara."

But in that very moment, at the second Ethan assured me I had done nothing I should regret, a new truth slammed into me: I had sent Andrew Gwynn off Ellis Island that very day, with the same crushing evidence of deception that Ethan had just placed before me. Andrew Gwynn was now somewhere here in Manhattan with Lily's letter in his possession, the same letter that would have been incinerated unread had I not inserted myself into his affairs. Later today or tomorrow or next week or next month, Andrew would find that letter and read it, and he would feel as I felt now, only worse. I had loved Edward but I had not been married to him. I hadn't spoken vows to him or shared my bed and my body with him or taken his name.

I had not married someone who was already married.

The bracing coolness of mourning would give way to the punishing heat of betrayal, and Andrew Gwynn would wish as I now did for the return of grief and its numbing chill.

"We don't have to go back yet," Ethan was saying.

I mumbled that yes, I did.

He sighed in near annoyance. "For God's sake, Clara. Don't disappear back on that island! He's not worth it!"

As if I were concerned only with my own tragic little life. Me and me only.

My hand flew to the side of the carriage, though we were still in motion and the harbor was nowhere in sight. I wanted out of the hansom. Out of Manhattan. Out.

"Do you hear me?" Ethan raised his voice. "He's not worth it."

I closed my eyes for a second to gather strength not to punch him. "Do not speak to me of the worth of things," I said evenly, when I was able. The words fell out of my mouth like slivers of shattered glass.

"I *will* speak to you of the worth of things," he shot back. "Somebody has to!"

My eyes sought water, harbor, ferry, distance. Island. Why weren't we at the pier yet?

"You can't run back to the island and disappear into it." Ethan's tone had wilted into something more like supreme disappointment. "You can't."

"What does it matter to you what I do?"

"Can you really not tell?"

I couldn't concentrate well enough to ponder why Ethan had any interest in me at all. I wanted nothing but the cover of silence and solitude to find a way to live with what had been done to me, and what I had done.

At last the ferry was in view.

When the hansom pulled to a stop I dashed out of it as if it were on fire.

THE ferry ride back was vastly different from the morning voyage. I wasn't clinging to Ethan with my eyes closed and my head bent to his chest. I wasn't on the edge of jumping overboard or tottering to the deck unconscious. I sat, unmoving, on the same couch where I'd sat hours before. Likewise, Ethan didn't have his hand clasped over mine and his gaze was not on me, but rather on Ellis as it grew in size at our approach.

As Manhattan fell away behind us, I became aware of an increasing sense of unfamiliarity as we neared the island, as if it had forgotten who I was, or worse, had closed its door to me the moment I'd stepped off it. A foreboding crept over me like one might feel when she has bet everything she owns and intuition is whispering to her that the odds had not been in her favor that day. I raised my head to look at the island as we neared the dock, hoping I'd merely had too hard a day and I would be welcomed again to my in-between place. But the sense that I had wronged a good man hung on me as the boat bumped along the dock and passengers stood, ready to disembark.

I did not rise to get off the ferry, which surprised Ethan. He stood next to me, waiting, obviously unsure what my hesitancy meant, since I'd dashed onto the ferry minutes earlier as if I could not wait to get back to Ellis.

"We're here," he finally said, though surely he knew I was aware the boat had stopped moving and nearly every passenger had stepped off.

He offered his arm and I took it. I stood and slowly took a step forward and then stopped.

"What is it, Clara?"

"Everything is different," I whispered, more to myself than to mystified Ethan standing at my side.

He said nothing and I was glad he didn't nudge me off the ferry as he had nudged me onto it. A moment later I summoned the courage to meet whatever reception the island was to give me. I knew even as we moved onto the gangplank that my in-between place was gone.

The gauzy veil had lifted. When my foot hit the island's welcoming shore I realized with shocking clarity that the island hadn't changed in the hours I had been away.

I had.

I kept my arm on Ethan's, and as we made our way through the busy ferry house, I sensed he didn't know what to do with me. Offer to sit with me, take me back to my room, leave me there at the ferry house?

I didn't know what to do with myself either. There seemed to be no place of sanctuary for me now.

"I don't know where to go," I said.

"Coffee?"

His one-word invitation to have a cup of coffee with me sounded polite but hesitant, almost as if he wanted to be alone, or at least away from me. I had disappointed him somehow.

I nodded and we made our way to island three.

As we stepped over the threshold of the main building, my mind recalled that it was at this very place where I had first seen Andrew Gwynn, with Lily's scarf embracing his neck. A pang of sadness shot through me. Mrs. Crowley stood at the reception desk with a ledger in her hands, talking to another nurse.

"Back so soon, then?" She arched an eyebrow in surprise as she noted that Ethan was right beside me.

I nodded.

"I gave you the rest of the day off, Nurse Wood. Did you not tell your father that?"

"He had a meeting to attend after our lunch." I continued to walk, not wishing to engage in a lengthy conversation about why I had returned early.

"Wait," Mrs. Crowley called out. "I have something for you."

I turned back to her with effort. My thoughts were far away from my duties as a nurse in her charge.

"That Mr. Gwynn in the scarlet fever ward who was discharged today? He was looking for you before he left."

My heart seemed to thud to a standstill in my chest. "He was?"

Mrs. Crowley bent forward and opened a desk drawer. "He insisted I give this to you, though I must say, Nurse Wood, I do not think a personal note from a patient is a good idea. Or gifts."

"Gifts?" I whispered.

Mrs. Crowley straightened as she pulled something from the drawer. In her hands was the tissue-wrapped package that contained Lily's scarf, the ribbon that kept its secrets still tied.

Twenty-Nine

FOR a moment I could only stare at the package in Mrs. Crowley's hands, as if I feared that if I reached out to take it from her I would awaken from a dream.

Ethan moved beside me and I heard him inhale as he, too, realized what Mrs. Crowley was holding.

"You may as well take it," Mrs. Crowley scolded. "I can't tell him you won't accept it. He's gone."

I slowly reached out my hand and Mrs. Crowley plopped the package into it, along with a folded note nestled under the ribbon.

"It's against my better judgment to have allowed him to leave it for you, Nurse Wood. He seemed very keen on expressing his gratitude to you. You don't have to keep it if it makes you uncomfortable."

I pulled the package toward my body. "Thank you, Mrs. Crowley."

I turned on my heel and sped away from her. Ethan fell in behind me.

"Clara," he called after me.

When I rounded the corner into a corridor, away from Mrs. Crowley and her scrutinizing gaze, I leaned up against the wall. Ethan followed me, concern in his eyes.

I studied the package in my trembling hands, looking for signs that it had been opened and retied. I wasn't sure. I didn't think so. I slipped the note out from under the ribbon and for a second or two I could only hold it in my hand.

"Do you want me to leave you alone?" I could tell Ethan was starting to figure out why I had reacted as I had in the cab. What he had done to me, I had nearly done to Andrew, in a far more blistering way.

But I didn't want him to leave. His nearness as a strong outsider was empowering, as it had been all day, even in the cab when I wanted to slug him.

"You don't have to go." It was not the same thing as "I want you to stay." He lingered, rather than stayed.

And then I opened the note in my hand.

Dear Nurse Wood,

Thank you for safeguarding my father's pattern book while I was ill. I worried for nothing, as my trunk was returned to me this morning with all its contents intact. Surely you knew this would be the case, yet you did as I asked, even though it was not within the scope of your responsibilities. I realize now that what I asked of you could have resulted in disciplinary action against you, for which I would have been ever remorseful. My apologies for putting you in such a place when you merely wanted to ease my grief.

I would not wish on anyone my experiences of the last two weeks, but I am grateful to have been on this island, even as sick as I was, to learn to embrace with courage what God had determined I should bear. Had I not come through Ellis a widowed sick man, I would have come through it a widowed bitter man. I believe I have you to thank for reminding me that pictures on an urn, though lovely, are not real. Life is real, in all its complexity. And though it can be painfully difficult, it can also be unspeakably wonderful. I am forever grateful you saved my mother's poetry book from the furnace that consumed my wife's trunk.

I want you to have Lily's scarf as a small token of my gratitude. You told me it caught your eye on the day we met, and that you thought it very pretty. I know you have walked a hard road, as I have. I trust the scarf will brighten your soul as it did for me, for the time that I held it.

Yours in sincere
gratitude,
Andrew Gwynn

Tears had sprung to my eyes.

From the side, I saw Ethan rifling through his pockets, most likely looking for the handkerchief he'd loaned me once already that day.

"I forgot your handkerchief at the newspaper office," I said, my voice shaky and childlike.

"Is it about that letter his wife wrote? Did he read it? Is he angry with you for having it?"

I shook my head and handed Ethan the letter. He read it quickly.

When Ethan looked up, he seemed relieved for me, but also sad—disappointed, perhaps, that Truth had been dealt a blow. Andrew Gwynn would never know the truth. And he'd left the island deceived—but full of hope.

I had pondered over many days what to do with Lily's letter, feeling spectacularly ill equipped to decide what only Solomon would have the wisdom to decree, yet deciding anyway. I'd trod uninvited, not once but twice—when I took the letter from the trunk in which it would have been burned and when I tied it up in the scarf I now held in my hands—and providence had ridden in and intervened, relieving me of any notions that I held any destiny in my hands save my own.

"I guess he wasn't meant to know," Ethan finally said.

"No. He wasn't."

"Did Dolly and I make a mistake? With you?" He sought my gaze, and I read in his eyes his ready remorse.

I had known for less than a day that I understood nothing, really, about love, only that it was the most devastating, most spectacular, most desirable force on earth. It was far too powerful a thing to leave sleeping in an in-between place. Dolly and Ethan's scheme had only precipitated the inevitable: that I would eventually leave the island hungry to love and be loved, even if it brought me to my knees again and again. I had done what I did for Andrew in the name of that same relentless love. He deserved to believe love was worth the flattening ache of grief. Love was both the softest edge and the sharpest edge of what made life real.

Ethan waited for my answer.

"I'm taking the job in Scotland." The words tumbled out as if they'd been perched on my tongue since the moment my father had mentioned the offer.

Ethan blinked in surprise. "What did you say?"

I could hardly believe I had said it myself. But I had. It was as if the voice of reason inside me had risen up and taken over. Just saying the words seemed to throw open a door that had been at my elbow all along, though closed, and I'd chosen to see it as a wall.

"I'm taking the job in Scotland. I'm leaving the island."

IT took several minutes for Ethan to convince me to please stay a moment and explain what I meant. I agreed to coffee after he persisted. We made our way down the corridor into the staff dining room, filled our cups, and took seats in a room that was empty except for a few early diners who had evening shifts coming up.

"So just like that, you're going?" he said.

"You were the one who said I needed to get off the island." I took a sip of my coffee.

"You do need to get off the island at some point. I didn't mean it had to be tomorrow."

"It's not tomorrow. It's next month."

"And I didn't mean you had to leave the country. It's like . . . it's like a different kind of escape, isn't it?"

"It's nothing like that at all." It had not occurred to me that it might appear as if I were trading one island for another. Even as I considered it, I shook my head. "I'm moving on. Like you said I should."

He frowned at me. "It's because of what Dolly and I did, isn't it? You read that letter from Andrew Gwynn and you think we made a mistake. *I* made a mistake."

I threw him a frown of my own. "It's a little late to wonder if you did the right thing. I know you and Dolly meant well, but what does it change, my knowing that Edward was engaged to be married?"

Ethan studied me for a moment. "If I hadn't taken you to the newspaper office today, would you have decided to take the job in Scotland?"

A few seconds of silence hung between us as I considered his question. I had no answer for him.

"Who of us knows what we would have done had circumstances changed and we had the chance to make different choices?" I said. "I honestly don't know, Ethan."

I pushed my coffee cup away and was about to stand when Dolly rushed into the dining room and over to our table.

"Good heavens, Clara. Mrs. Crowley said you were back already. I didn't believe her." She slid into the chair next to me. "Did everything go all right? Did you make it across? Did you see your father?"

"I saw it all, Dolly."

"Saw it all?"

"Everything. I saw it all."

Dolly looked from me to Ethan.

"I took her to the newspaper office. She saw the obituary," Ethan said.

Dolly faced me again. Her voice was firm. "You

needed to know, Clara. If you never speak to me again, I'll say it to my dying day. You needed to know."

"And so now I do." The cynical edge to my voice surprised even me.

"I have no regrets about making sure you found out for yourself what Edward Brim was up to." She whipped her head around to face Ethan Randall. "And don't you go having any regrets either, Doctor."

"I don't," Ethan said, but with only a measure of conviction.

"Good," Dolly said defiantly.

"She's taking a job in Scotland."

Dolly laughed, a short little guffaw, and she turned to Ethan. He was not laughing and of course neither was I. Dolly swung back to face me.

"What's this?"

"A friend of my father's needs a private nurse for his ailing wife while they are in Scotland for a year. I'm taking the job."

Dolly's mouth gaped open. "Truly?" she said, after a moment's pause.

"Yes."

"That's . . . that's terrific, Clara. You're really moving to Scotland?"

I sighed, as tired as I had ever been. I wanted to sleep for a week. But I answered her. "Yes."

Her wide smile comforted me, strangely. "Well, hallelujah and amen, Clara's getting off this hell of an island. Good for you. If I had champagne, I'd raise my glass. Good for you, Clara. When?"

My head was screaming for a pillow and a soft bed so that I could be alone with my thoughts. I didn't care that it was so late in the afternoon that a nap would surely make sleep that night impossible. "Next month. Look, can I tell you all about it later, Dolly? I'm . . . I'm very tired. I'm going to go lie down."

Dolly nodded. "Of course."

As I started to rise, I pulled the package and note out of my lap and into my hands.

Dolly reached out her arm to stop me. "Good heavens, is that what I think it is?"

"Yes, it is."

"But . . . but . . ." Dolly turned to Ethan. "Didn't you give it to him?"

Ethan started to speak but I cut in. "Dr. Randall did exactly what you asked him to. Andrew Gwynn left it for me at the main reception area, unopened, as a thank-you gift. He knew I liked the scarf."

"For the love of God . . . He didn't read what's inside!?"

"No."

Dolly shook her head. "I give up. I do." She pointed to what I held in my hands. "If I were you, I'd take that straight outside and throw it all into the river and good riddance. Been nothing but a damn nuisance since the day that Welshman arrived."

I turned to Ethan. In spite of everything I still felt a rush of gratitude for how he had helped me reunite with Manhattan. But I needed time to come to terms with the newest jagged edge of grief over losing Edward. Ethan's touching admiration for me was mixed up in that and I felt a desperate need to keep the two separate. "Thank you for escorting me to Manhattan today. I'm sorry you had to use one of your days off to do it."

"Clara, please—"

"It's been a very long day already and I just need some time alone."

Whatever Ethan had planned to say before I interrupted him he left unsaid. Dolly spoke instead.

"Say! Let's really celebrate, Clara! Come to the Jersey shore with me and the girls tomorrow! And we'll drink champagne and eat toffee peanuts and go dancing. Say yes, Clara. Say you'll come!"

"Fine. I'll come." I just wanted my bed.

Dolly hollered her delight and I turned from her to Ethan, who was sitting back in his chair, his eyes suggesting there was unfinished business between us.

"I meant what I said. I really am grateful for your help today," I said.

He tipped his chin toward his chest. I could feel his gaze on my back as I left the room.

Thirty

I slept until dawn the next day and did not dream.

I didn't hear Dolly come to the room after supper; nor did I hear her getting ready for bed later. I heard nothing at all after I laid myself out on my bed fully clothed, and closed my eyes.

I awoke to a rosy sunrise, feeling as if I had awakened from a spell meant to last forever. In our bathroom, I peeled my wrinkled clothes off and bathed, sitting long in the water, contemplating my future. I felt empty without Edward's sweet memory to charm me. When I dried myself off and walked back into the room, Dolly was awake.

Her eyes grew wide when I dropped the towel and took my time selecting my undergarments.

"Well, aren't you the confident girl today! Goodness,

Clara. Perhaps you'd like a horse to ride around the island on."

It took me a moment to realize my bare body was
totally out of character for me. "Oh. Sorry." I reached
for my bathrobe on the chair back behind me.

"That's more like you." Dolly stretched and slipped
out of her bed. "Don't start doing too many things you've
never done before. You're likely to get carted off to the
psych ward."

I pulled my uniform out from the wardrobe and brushed
a stray thread off the collar. Everything about the island,
including my room, the uniform, even Dolly, seemed to be
receding from me, as if I didn't belong there anymore. I
dressed and then drew out a piece of stationery from the
desk Dolly and I shared. I penned a short letter to my father,
telling him I was accepting the position with his professor
friend. And then on impulse I wrote that I would be asking
for a few days off to come home and say good-bye to Mother
and Henrietta.

I was surprised at how quickly I was able to write the
letter that seemed to chart a new life for myself. When I
was finished I read it out loud so I could hear those words
spoken, drifting on the air, words that said that I was
taking the new job, resigning my post on the island,
coming home, leaving for Scotland.

It suddenly sounded very much like I was escaping,
just as Ethan had said. "That's not what this is," I murmured to no one.

"That's not what what is?" Dolly had returned from
the toilet.

"Nothing. Hurry up. I'm hungry."

"That's because you didn't have dinner last night. I

had to check you three times last night to make sure you were still breathing. I've never seen someone who wasn't drunk sleep as hard as you did."

"I was tired."

"Obviously."

I slipped the letter into an envelope and then into my uniform pocket to mail later. When I turned to get my hat off my bureau, Dolly was staring at me.

"I'm so glad you don't hate me," she said.

"Finish! I'm hungry."

"And I'm glad you're still talking to me."

"Yes, well, I don't want to talk anymore. I want to eat. Hurry up. Get ready."

Dolly made no move to put her uniform on. "And I am very glad you are taking that job in Scotland. Really glad. Even though I will miss you. You don't need to be here."

Her kind tone was embarrassing me. "This place is good enough for you. And Nellie and Ivy. And Dr. Treaver."

"And Dr. Randall."

"Yes, and him."

"It's a great place for a job, if that's all it is to you. But it was more to you than a job. And now it's not. And I am very happy for you."

I needed her affirmation. It was at once clear to me that Dolly had been as near to me as my own sister in the months I had known her. "Are you really?"

"Yes, I am."

"Ethan—Dr. Randall says I am just looking for another island to escape to. This one's just bigger."

"Farther away, I think."

"Yes."

Dolly pulled on her uniform and began to button it.

"Ethan Randall likes you, Clara. That's why he may not want you to go. He likes you. He has from the very first day."

"I don't know why he does."

She plucked her hat off her bureau and planted it on her head. "It's because you have big breasts, of course."

"I do not have big breasts!"

Dolly smiled back at me as she slipped on her shoes. "Well, then. He must like you for you."

I didn't want to talk about Ethan Randall anymore. I didn't want to think about physical attraction, or love, or desire, or anything having to do with the opposite sex. "Are you ready? I am going to faint if I don't eat."

Dolly said nothing else and we started down to breakfast.

"I'm going to tell Mrs. Crowley this morning that I'm leaving."

"That seems wise."

"And I'm going to ask to be transferred to the inspection line at the great hall."

Dolly turned to face me as we walked. "You won't like it."

"I think it will be easier to leave if I'm not in the wards when the month is up."

She was thoughtful for a moment. "You don't have to brush him off completely just because you're spending a year in Europe. You could write letters, you know."

But I didn't want to imagine that I could possibly fall in love with Ethan Randall, or even that I might already be falling for him, when I would soon be separated from him. I still had lingering affection for the Edward I had created in my head. And Andrew Gwynn was also not far from my thoughts, much to my consternation. "I think . . . I think I need a break from all that."

"Ha!" Dolly laughed. "My girl, you need to be dead to get a break from all that. *All that* is all there is."

I didn't have time to give notice to Mrs. Crowley before my shift began on what I hoped would be my last day in the wards. I prepared myself for Ethan's arrival for rounds, but Dr. Treaver appeared in the doorway at ten thirty. I knew I would run into Ethan again in the time remaining to me. I would see him in the dining hall, in the corridors, maybe even in the ferry house if I opted for more visits ashore. But I wouldn't be Nurse Wood to him anymore, following him around with my cart and basin. I was Clara now, and he was Ethan. I was leaving. And he was staying.

I left the ward a few minutes before lunch to deliver my news to Mrs. Crowley, who was genuinely miffed to learn of my departure, but pleased I would still be around until the end of the month.

When I told her I wanted to spend my remaining time on the main island at the inspection line, she practically hugged me. No one liked that rotation. I used that joy to ask for a few days off to say good-bye to my family, and she grudgingly told me I could have the next five days off if I wanted them, but then I was to be hers until I left for good.

At lunch I broke the news to Dolly that I was going home for a few days and would have to back out on my promise to go to the Jersey shore with her and the girls. She extracted a pledge from me that I would spend my last Saturday night in New York with her and Nellie and Ivy, having fun her way.

I hurried to the telegraph office before my lunch break was over to wire my father that I was coming home, selecting the most important lines from the letter in my pocket, which now I would not send. Then I stopped by the ferry house to purchase a ticket for the first morning crossing so that I could catch an early train to Philadelphia and be home in the afternoon. I was keenly aware how amazing it felt to be buying a ticket for the ferry, knowing I probably wouldn't be tempted to jump overboard and swim in a panic back to the island the moment the boat eased away from the dock.

I regretted how I had minimized what Ethan had done for me. I'd been so intent on making him feel bad for his part in the scene at the newspaper office, I hadn't fully appreciated that he'd given me my life back. It was a new life, different from the one I had before I came to the island, and before I came to New York. But it was a life nonetheless, and I wanted to thank him for it. But I didn't know how to go about it.

When my shift was over at the end of the day, and after I'd said good-bye to the little ones in the children's ward, I met Ethan coming out of the typhus ward. He was finished for the day, too, and he would no doubt be heading to Manhattan for the evening.

We fell in step together. "Dolly tells me you're headed home to Pennsylvania for a few days."

"Yes. I leave tomorrow morning. I haven't been home in almost a year. I hadn't realized how much I had missed everyone until I bought my ferry ticket today."

He nodded. "I hope you have a wonderful time."

Impulsively, I reached for his arm, stopping him in the middle of the corridor. "I know I said things yesterday that were unkind and—"

"No, you didn't."

"Yes, I did. I'm a little mixed-up right now about . . .

about a lot of things, but I do know this: I wouldn't be able to get on that ferry tomorrow if it weren't for you. I am truly grateful for that."

I expected Ethan to politely minimize my gratitude, to tell me it was his pleasure to have assisted me, but he stared at me as if I had asked him a question he didn't know the answer to.

And so I went on.

"I wanted you to know that, because . . . because I will be rotating to the main island after I return from Pennsylvania. I will be assigned to the inspection lines. And I will be there until I leave. So I may not have another chance like this one to tell you how much I appreciate what you did for me."

For another long moment he said nothing. It both surprised me and, strangely enough, pained me. I didn't expect to have my gratitude thrown back in my face.

Then he reached for my hands, just as he had done on the ferry when I was nearly blinded with dread. "I'm so sorry for what happened at the newspaper office. And for the things I said on our way back to the ferry. I lay awake last night thinking about it."

"You did?"

"I should've realized while we were still in the carriage that you were thinking about Lily Gwynn's letter, not just that obituary. I'm sorry. And now you will be at the main island until you go. That is my fault. And I'm sorry for that, too."

When no response rose to my lips, I looked down at my hands in his and he let go.

"I just wanted you to know that," he said.

"I . . . thank you," I stammered.

A few seconds of silence hung between us. "Will you

be all right tomorrow morning?" he finally said. "Getting on the ferry, I mean?"

"I think so. Thank you."

"I am meeting my brother in Midtown tonight—"

"Oh! Of course." My cheeks flushed scarlet and I took a step back so that he could continue on his way.

"What I meant was, if I weren't meeting my brother tonight I'd ride the ferry with you tomorrow morning—just in case."

The heat on my face deepened. "I am optimistic, actually, thanks to you."

He smiled. "Just remember to breathe."

I laughed nervously. "I'll try."

We began to walk, an easy pace, unhurried.

"Promise me you will say good-bye before you leave Ellis?" he asked.

And I told him I would.

Thirty-One

A preautumn chill hugged the island like a shawl when I awoke the next morning. Outside my little window I saw only mist. I had packed the night before and was ready to go long before the ferry house would even be open. I lingered at my breakfast, imagining a dozen times getting myself onto the boat alone.

It seemed I was going back to the beginning, back to my childhood home, where everything began for me. I was comforted by this notion as I finally made my way to the ferry house a few minutes before nine. I found that I wanted more than anything to be free of the fire's last embers and the hopeless image of a treasured man falling to the unforgiving ground. And because so much of Edward was now tied to Andrew Gwynn and our twin sorrows, I was ready to be free of him, too. Before I left for Scotland I would burn Lily's letter and ask Dolly to give the scarf to one of the poorer women in the wards.

I would be finished with this. All of it.

My resolve and the persistent morning mist allowed me to step onto the ferry's gangplank with only the slightest trepidation. I couldn't see much of the New York skyline as I took a seat near a window. The city that had become something of a specter to me during the last six months was still draped in gauze, or maybe the specter was now gauze itself, weightless and thin.

When we docked at Battery Park twenty minutes later, I boarded a trolley that took me to the train station, and within the hour I was headed toward Pennsylvania.

Home.

MY time in nursing school was the only other extended period when I'd been away from my family for more than a week or two. I'd enjoyed a few visits home for holidays and term breaks. Before that, my travels had only ever taken me to New York, Boston, and, of course, Philadelphia.

My exile on Ellis had kept me away longer than at any other time in my life. The closer the train got to home, the more I realized I had missed being surrounded by people who loved me.

I wanted to complete the journey from misted island to beloved home on my own, so I'd purposely not mentioned which train I would be on. When we pulled into the station at Newton Square, I found, as I had hoped, someone I knew heading toward where I was going. My surprise arrival brought tears of joy to my mother's eyes.

That evening, Henrietta, her husband, and their little

ones gathered at my parents' house to welcome me, share a meal, reminisce about old times. The fire was never brought up, nor my long months on the island, as if everyone had been warned not to say anything about it. When I helped my mother with the dessert dishes, she at last spoke of it, in a way that surprised me.

"It was personal for you, wasn't it? The fire." She plunged a china dish into a pan of soapy water. Tendrils of fine hair framed her face when she turned to me, and I thought for the first time how much I looked like her.

"Yes."

"Sometimes I wish you had never gone to Manhattan. Most times, actually."

A response to her comment did not come quickly. I hadn't thought about it before, but in that moment I realized I did not wish I had never gone, despite everything that had happened, and was still happening.

Falling in love with Edward, watching him die, meeting Andrew Gwynn, finding the letter, reading the poem, meeting Ethan—my life seemed more fully layered because of the choices I had made, both consciously and in ignorance.

I didn't wish I'd never gone to New York, but I did wish to be free of its dark hold on me. I wanted to bury what had died within me and be done with it so that I could return someday and find only a distant memory of what had happened there.

"I'll be all right," I finally said, by way of answer.

My mother touched my face with her wet hand—a caress that felt almost like a cleansing. "I know you will be."

IN the morning, I joined my father at his practice, though he attempted briefly to talk me out of working on my first full day home. But I think he quickly understood that I was reconnecting with the part of my life that hadn't left home. When we arrived at his office, I went from room to room, inhaling the scent of newness, for a doctor's office is that way; it is new every morning. It has to be. There can be no lingering remnants of disease or decay from the day before.

The time passed quickly, sweetly. I wrote to my father's friend Professor Bartlett and his wife, Beatrice, and officially accepted the position as her private nurse. I gave them my address on Ellis and told them I was ready to set sail anytime after the end of the month.

On my last night my father asked me whether I wanted to read the news accounts of the fire. He had saved the newspapers for me, thinking that someday I would want them. My mind immediately went to the day I had read Edward's obituary, and the remembered heaviness in my chest. I declined. And he said nothing more about them. I was finished with it.

There were tears all around when my parents drove me to Philadelphia to take the train back to New York. They offered to come with me, but I could see no purpose in delaying our good-byes. As we embraced, I thanked my father for finding the job for me, and told him I was sure the months would pass quickly, as time so often does. I promised I would write as soon as we arrived in Edinburgh and had a permanent address.

I arrived back in New York late in the day, as the sun was turning the city amber and cerulean. An hour later, I stepped aboard the ferry that would take me to the island that no longer felt like mine.

THE first week back at Ellis, I felt very much like the droves of immigrants who stood day after day in the health inspection line where I now worked. They were both anxious and hopeful, just as I was. They were steps away from a new beginning, a beginning that would test their resolve, just as I was. And they had never been where they were about to go, they scarcely spoke the language of their new surroundings, and in many ways, I, too, was about to embark as a foreigner to an untried place.

I saw Ethan here and there, in the dining hall, in the corridors. But I avoided being near him, as I needed to keep a safe distance from those who were tied to the life I was leaving behind: Edward Brim, Andrew Gwynn, Ethan Randall. I could not risk the fragile hold I had on my rebirth by contemplating a future with Ethan. He seemed perplexed by my aloof behavior. Dolly thought it was plain senseless.

"He's only ever looked out for your best interests, Clara. He doesn't deserve a cold shoulder from you," she said one night in our bedroom. "You're not even giving him a chance."

"A chance at what? I'm leaving the country."

"That doesn't mean anything. You're not leaving the planet, for God's sake."

"I'm leaving this *island*."

And I went into the bathroom to end the conversation.

I was able to soothe her anger at me by joining her and Nellie and Ivy the following Saturday for an evening out in Manhattan. But even then, I was unable to give myself fully over to relaxation and frivolity. I counted the hours, silently and unbeknownst to her, until we returned. Dolly assumed I'd had a great time and I let her believe it. On Monday morning, I was ready to begin my last week at Ellis. On Saturday I would say my good-byes, including the promised farewell to Ethan Randall. I would pack my few things. I would tearfully hug Dolly, who would probably pretend she was glad to see me go so she could have the bed by the window. I would give her Lily's scarf and ask that she find an immigrant woman in the wards who needed a dash of something beautiful and give it to her. And I would take the letter and the certificate of annulment to the incinerator and throw them in myself.

Then I would be free.

I rehearsed these farewell steps in my mind often as that last week began. I tried to focus on tasks at hand but I often found my mind wandering.

Late on Tuesday, I was sent from the health inspection room to find an interpreter. I made my way into the great hall, which was busy as usual. Mrs. Meade, the nurse who had double-teamed with me in the scarlet fever ward, was also in the hall near one of the information desks. She was talking to someone, but he did not appear to be an immigrant. He carried a leather case meant to hold papers, not clothing, and his attire was that of a first-class passenger, whom we hardly ever saw at the hospital.

When she saw me, she flagged me over.

"Nurse Wood. Perhaps you can help this gentleman," she said when I closed the distance between us.

I turned to the man. He smiled politely. "Good morning. The name's Chester Hartwell."

British.

"I'm Miss Wood. How can I help you?"

"He's looking for one of the patients you cared for. Mr. Andrew Gwynn?" Mrs. Meade said.

I felt my pulse take a stutter step. Had something gone awry when Andrew was discharged? Did his brother, Nigel, not come for him?

"I'm a private investigator, Miss Wood." He reached into the breast pocket of his coat and handed me a card with a London address.

I stared at his title. My mind raced with possibilities as to why a British man in a nice suit was looking for Andrew. Nothing good came to mind.

I handed his card back to him. "I'm sorry I can't help you. Mr. Gwynn has been discharged."

"Yes, I know." The confidence in his tone revealed that Chester Hartwell already knew a great deal. "I was hoping you could tell me where he was headed after his discharge."

Despite his expensive clothes and polished shoes I did not trust this man. I sensed within my being that he was a threat to Andrew. A line of sweat opened on my brow. "I'm sorry, Mr. Hartwell, but—"

"It's very important that I find Mr. Gwynn."

"But as I have said, he's been discharged." My voice sounded weak in my ears.

Chester Hartwell cocked his head knowingly, and then nodded toward Mrs. Meade. "I understand from your colleague here that you were Mr. Gwynn's primary nurse during his stay at the hospital. Perhaps he mentioned something of his final destination after Ellis?"

"I was not his only nurse. And I'm not at liberty to discuss a patient's personal matters."

"Of course. Of course you aren't." Chester Hartwell turned to Mrs. Meade. "Thank you for your help, Nurse." His tone was politely dismissive. Mrs. Meade hesitated for a few moments before turning away from us. Chester Hartwell took my arm as though directing me to a dance floor. He stopped at a quieter spot a few yards away. I lifted my arm out of his hand.

"My employer is most anxious to find Mr. Gwynn, Miss Wood. And he's authorized me to spare no expense in locating him. It's quite important."

A second line of sweat formed beneath the first. Warning bells sounded in my head. "Your employer."

"Yes. Angus Ravenhouse."

I swallowed hard and Hartwell did not miss it. He cocked his head, filing away my unspoken response to that name.

"It's very important that I find him."

"Then you'd best be on your way so that you can continue your search. Mr. Gwynn is no longer a patient here."

He looked down at me with keen discernment, as a shrewd father might gaze upon a lying child. It was as if he could read my thoughts, could see into my mind that Andrew Gwynn had been more to me than just another patient. "You don't know what Mr. Gwynn did, do you? Or perhaps you do?"

"I must get back to my post. Good day, Mr. Hartwell," I sputtered, barely able to speak the words. I started to move away but he stretched out his arm and blocked me.

"Mr. Gwynn and Lily Ravenhouse were in a scheme together. Lily was Mr. Ravenhouse's wife. Did you know she was already married? Did you know that?"

I pushed past his arm and he grabbed my elbow.

"What they did was illegal. If you're protecting him, you're in it as much as he is, Miss Wood. And I can tell you, a man who would do what he's done is not worth going to jail for. He's not worth it."

He's not worth it.

"He probably killed Lily, you know."

He's not worth it.

The echoed words spun in my head. Nausea coupled with the sweat on my brow made the room teeter.

"I can tell you're not being truthful with me, Miss Wood. And I assure you he is not a man you can trust. He killed her, no doubt. He'll likely kill you when he's done with you."

"Let go of me." I yanked my arm free. "I have no idea what you're talking about."

The paternal demeanor fell away and was instantly replaced by razor-sharp determination. Hartwell's cold stare nearly stung. "Andrew Gwynn didn't just steal a man's wife. He stole a necklace worth fifty thousand pounds that has been in the Ravenhouse family for a century. Mr. Ravenhouse wants it back."

I didn't believe him. Not for a minute. If a necklace was missing I was certain Lily had taken it.

And if she had it with her when she crossed the Atlantic then it had been incinerated along with the rest of her things. The knowledge made me shudder. Hartwell didn't fail to see this, either.

"He didn't tell you about the necklace, did he?"

"There is no necklace." The instant I said it I wished I hadn't. It was akin to saying I knew much more than I was letting on.

Hartwell smiled—not the evil grin of a crocodile, but of a man who had played a risky hand and won it.

"Oh, but there is, Miss Wood."

"Lily Ravenhouse died of scarlet fever aboard ship, and her belongings, including whatever she brought with her from England, were incinerated upon its arrival." Again, I felt I had said too much. His smile deepened, and the paternal tone returned.

"Miss Wood, I must warn you that men like Andrew Gwynn, who carry off rich, married women within days of meeting them, have only one goal in mind. If you know where Mr. Gwynn went after he left here, you must think about the next vulnerable woman he will meet. And you must think of yourself. The more you know, the more of a liability you are to him."

My mind began to spin in a thousand directions. I needed to get away. I needed to talk to Andrew before Hartwell got to him. If Chester Hartwell had been able to discover with whom Lily Ravenhouse had traveled to America, then how long would it take him to find out Andrew Gwynn was a tailor headed for his brother's shop in Manhattan? Hartwell would confront Andrew the way he had confronted me, and Andrew would then find out in the worst possible way what Lily had done to him.

"Miss Wood, do please consider your own safety."

A new revelation suddenly slammed into me like a bullet.

Lily had never planned to see her trunk again.

She wouldn't have put a necklace worth fifty thousand pounds in a trunk that she planned to leave with Andrew when she disappeared on the pretense of retrieving a lost glove.

She wouldn't have wanted the necklace on the ship at all.

If she needed the necklace to make good her escape she would want it to be waiting for her when she got to New York. Could it be that I already knew where it was?

Could it be she had etched the address of where the necklace waited on a key and then hidden it in the hem of her favorite scarf?

I had to get back to Manhattan and see what, if anything, was at 92 Chambers Street. And I needed to find the tailor shop before Hartwell did. But I needed time, and I needed Hartwell to back off under the pretense that I was reconsidering.

"I . . . don't know how I can help you, Mr. Hartwell. But I would like to think about what you have said. Perhaps you could give your card back to me?"

He studied me for a moment before extending the card. I was certain he wasn't completely convinced that I had so quickly changed my mind.

"Sometimes I remember something a patient said long after he's said it, Mr. Hartwell," I said.

"Indeed. I am staying at the Waldorf, Miss Wood, while I make further inquiries."

"The Waldorf?"

But I knew what the Waldorf was. And where it was.

The hotel was a mere taxi ride from Greenwich Village, where I had to find a tailor shop.

"At Fifth Avenue and Thirty-third," he continued. "You can ask for me there."

"Of course." I tucked the card in my apron pocket. "I'm afraid I must get back to my duties, Mr. Hartwell."

His mouth was curved into a genial smile, but his gaze was penetrating. "Don't think on it too long, Miss Wood. I will find him. With you or without you."

I turned from him and forced myself not to run. It took everything in me not to.

As soon as I was out of the main hall I ducked into the women's restroom, and left through the back door to return to the hospital, unseen, as quickly as I could.

I had to get to Manhattan.

Thirty-Two

AS I left the main island and hurried toward the ferry house, I looked for Mr. Hartwell as surreptitiously as I could. I didn't see him following me, but I was fairly certain he would continue his search for someone on the island who was willing—for a price—to tell him what he wanted to know. I anticipated that he would use all his skills of persuasion to entice someone—a baggage boy, a clerk at the telegraph office, a hospital aid, even another immigrant—to give him a clue as to where Andrew Gwynn was headed when he left the island.

I didn't see him, so I quickened my pace, the interpreter I was supposed to find forgotten. As I made my way back to my quarters on island three, jumbled thoughts crowded my brain.

For only a moment I considered going to my room, grabbing Lily's letter, finding Chester Hartwell, and showing him that Andrew had no idea what Lily had done. But surely that wouldn't satisfy him. Angus Ravenhouse wanted his stolen necklace back. The letter in Mr. Hartwell's hands would only hasten him to find the tailor shop, where he'd plop that terrible letter down in front of Andrew and ask him where the necklace was.

The thought of Andrew reading the letter that way cut me to the core. If at last he was to read its terrible contents, I wanted to be the one to give it to him. I wanted to prepare him for Hartwell's imminent arrival.

I doubled my speed to get to my room, retrieve the wrapped package that contained the letter and scarf, grab my handbag, and board the next ferry.

IT took less than ten minutes for me to change out of my uniform into street clothes and head to the main building. I needed to tell Mrs. Crowley that an emergency had arisen and I had to leave for the rest of the day. She'd be angry, but what more could she do? I was within a week of leaving the island.

I made my way to the reception area but halted to a quick stop when I heard Mrs. Crowley speaking to someone whom I couldn't see from my angle in the corridor.

Then I heard the person introduce himself as Chester Hartwell, a private investigator on urgent business that involved a recent patient at the hospital.

I knew Mrs. Crowley would likely tell him nothing and he would soon be on his way. But I didn't want him on his way yet. I wanted him occupied with his snooping so that I could make my escape.

But how to stall him?

I turned and headed back the way I had come, looking for the first side door that led to the outside. I had gone only a few paces when the door to the doctors' lounge opened, and Ethan and another doctor stepped out.

Ethan's eyes widened as he took in what I was wearing—street clothes in the middle of a workday—and my panicked expression. "Clara. What is it? What's wrong?"

The other doctor excused himself and I waited only a few seconds before pulling Ethan close to me and telling him in rapid, incomplete sentences what had happened.

"I don't understand. What are you going to do?" he said.

"I've got to find the tailor shop before that private investigator does. I need to give Andrew the letter and the certificate. It's his only proof he didn't know Lily was already married and that whatever she did with that necklace, she acted alone."

"You don't have to do anything."

"Of course I do! This is all my fault! If I hadn't inserted myself into this—"

"Clara, if you had never found the letter it would be gone and Andrew Gwynn would be no worse off. This investigator still would have come. If he finds Andrew Gwynn, the result would've been the same. It has nothing to do with you."

But it did. It did have to do with me.

"Please just do me a favor. Go to the reception area and distract him," I pleaded. "I don't want him seeing me walking to the ferry house. Please?"

"Clara, I—"

"Please, Ethan! Don't do it for him; do it for me. Please?"

I had never said his first name out loud before. Not

in his presence or anyone else's. It surprised me how easily it fell off my lips. He seemed likewise aware that I'd said his name the same way he had already been saying mine. Effortlessly.

"I don't want you going alone."

"But I'm not afraid."

For a moment he said nothing. I could see that he was turning my request over in his mind. He wanted to please me, but he also didn't like my plan. "You don't know where to begin looking," he finally said.

"He told me his brother's shop was in Greenwich Village. How many tailor shops can there be in Greenwich Village owned by someone named Nigel Gwynn?"

A second of silence passed.

"Go back to the newspaper office," he said. "Ask the woman who helped us before to look it up for you in the business directory. If Nigel and his brother have a telephone, their shop will be in it."

I squeezed his arm in gratitude. "Thank you! I will come straight back tonight. I promise."

"Even if you can't find him today?"

I nodded.

"And try again tomorrow, I suppose."

"I have to, Ethan. It's the right thing to do. I would do the same for you if what had happened to Andrew happened to you."

The moment I said this, I knew it was completely true. I would do this for Ethan.

He nodded once and something in the way he was looking at me changed. It was as if he fully understood in that moment that I needed to do for Andrew what no one had been able to do for me: rescue something precious from the clutches of deception. I knew he would help me.

Ethan reached for me, cupped his hand under my jaw, and drew me to him. His kiss on my forehead was soft and yet urgent. "Please be careful."

"I will. I promise."

We moved soundlessly to the edge of the corridor, where we could see Mrs. Crowley and Hartwell's back as he faced the reception desk.

Hartwell apparently hadn't gotten much further with Mrs. Crowley, for now he was telling her that Andrew Gwynn had been involved in theft and the police were likely to be notified. Ethan squeezed my arm and then rounded the corner. A few seconds later I heard him ask Hartwell whether there was something he could help him with. Hartwell would have to start all over. I sped back down the corridor and out a side door. Picking up my skirts, I ran for the long connecting hall to the ferry house, drawing stares from everyone I passed. At the ticket counter I learned the next ferry wouldn't leave for another twenty minutes. I bought my ticket and moved as far forward as I could to lose myself in the growing crowd of people waiting for the next boat. I could only hope that Chester Hartwell was still in the hospital retelling his story to Ethan.

I took a seat on a bench, and then pulled the packaged scarf onto my lap, opening it and placing the letter and certificate safe in my handbag. I wound the scarf around my neck and waited, keeping my profile low. At last the passengers were told to board and again I moved as quickly as I could to secure a seat among the other travelers, glancing up tentatively to make sure I hadn't been spotted.

The ferry ride seemed to take far too long, but the only apprehension I felt was that we weren't traveling fast enough. When at last I was through the gates, I made my way to the curb and the row of hansoms waiting there.

As soon as I was seated inside one, I slipped my fingernail into the seam of the scarf, and worked free the little brass key.

The driver turned to me.

"Ninety-two Chambers Street," I said.

And we were off.

Thirty-Three

I didn't know in which part of Manhattan Chambers Street was located, and I was surprised when only a few minutes later the driver pulled up in front of a boarding-house, not unlike the one I had lived in during those two weeks when Manhattan was my home.

I also didn't know what to expect when I stepped inside, or how long I might be there, and I was reluctant to lose the hansom. I checked the contents of my hand-bag to make sure I had the money to keep the driver at the curb for me.

"Will you stay for a few minutes if I pay you?" I asked him.

"How much?" he quickly responded.

He had brought me there for fifty cents. I handed him that and an extra dollar and asked that he give me fifteen minutes. He grunted his assent.

I tightened Lily's scarf around my neck and emerged from the carriage. The building in front of me was well kept but not extravagantly so. A cat sat in the front window, which was framed by lace curtains yellow with age. The stoop was clean but cobwebs decorated a pot of thirsty geraniums. A beggar woman a few yards away nodded to me and started to approach, but when I rang the bell she slunk back to the curb.

A stout woman answered the door, wiping her hands on a dish towel.

"I've no vacancies, miss," she said, sizing me up even as I stood there. "Maybe at the end of the month I might. You're welcome to come back then."

"I'm actually not looking for a room. I'm here because, well . . ." A lie fell off my lips before I could contemplate the wisdom of uttering it. "My cousin, Lily uh," I hesitated a second before deciding to try her maiden name. "Broadman contacted you about—"

"Where the dickens is she?" the woman exclaimed, half in consternation and half in concern. "She said she'd be here nearly a month ago. Why didn't she write me? What was I supposed to think when she didn't come?"

I didn't know which question to address first. "She's so sorry about that. She's been detained."

The woman frowned, but only for a second. "Well, is she coming? Or have you come for her trunk? I've people asking about the room. It's only paid up through the end of this month, you know."

Her trunk.

"I've, um, I've actually come for her trunk. I'm so very sorry. Things haven't worked out like we thought they would."

The lies kept bubbling out of me like a frothy drink

poured too fast. My face began to grow warm. But the woman swung the door open wide and stepped back. "Well, come on in then. It's not like I was going to give the room away when she's already paid up through the month. Still. What was I supposed to do with that trunk? No forwarding address or anything. That's not usually how I operate. I don't like accepting boarders by mail and this is why. I don't care that she paid me extra."

"Yes, I'm so sorry about that," I muttered. "It couldn't be helped."

We stepped over the threshold into a narrow entryway with closed doors on either side. She opened a drawer in a narrow telephone table just inside the front door and grabbed a ring of keys. Then she proceeded to lead me to the stairs at the far end of the hallway. "Well, like I say, I don't usually rent a room to someone I've never met. I felt sorry for her when she wrote me that her parents had died. I hope whatever it was that kept you was important."

"I was . . . was ill. I should have sent a telegram. I'm . . . I'm sorry."

The woman swung around to stare at me as she put her foot on the first step. "You don't sound English."

I knew the fewer lies I told, the better I'd be able to keep up this ruse. I had no idea whether what I was doing was illegal, immoral, or plain foolish. It felt like a hearty concoction of all three. "I was born here in the States."

"I don't give money back on the month's rent. You're welcome to her room until the end of the month. If you want her room after that, I'll offer it to you first. But if you decline, you need to be gone on the last day of the month."

"I'm . . . I'm not sure what my plans are," I said, and it wasn't a lie.

The woman nodded and turned back around. "My living quarters are at the first door on the left when you come in the house. I don't like to be disturbed before seven in the morning and there's to be no coming and going after ten o'clock at night. And no men. You get breakfast with your room. I serve it at seven thirty in the dining room, first door on your right when you come in the house. There's a café across the street for your other meals. No food in the rooms. I don't want mice."

At the top of the stairs we took a right and then walked past another staircase leading up, past two closed doors and finally stopping in front of a third. The woman selected a key from her ring and opened it.

"Your key's on top of the bureau."

I wanted to thank her by name but I couldn't, and she apparently assumed I already knew it so I just said, "Thank you."

She grunted and brushed past me to head back down the stairs.

The room Lily had secured was simply furnished. A bed, a bureau, a chair, and a desk. The furnishings were clean but had clearly seen better years. On an oval rug sat a steamer trunk with a brass lock and decorated with shipping labels. Several stamped envelopes lay on top, addressed to Lily Broadman at 92 Chambers Street. The return addresses were all jewelry stores in Manhattan. I set them on the bed and then knelt in front of the trunk. The date on the shipping label was late June; Lily had sent it from London two months before meeting Andrew in Liverpool. The brass key was warm in my hand.

I thrust it into the lock and turned it, knowing it would open.

And I knew what I would find in the trunk, past the dresses, extra shoes, hair combs, and capes.

At the bottom of the trunk was a simple red velvet jewelry box. And inside, a shimmering circle of rubies and sapphires, dazzlingly bright and without a doubt costly beyond words. I had never seen anything so precious. Dozens of sun rays from the window across from me reached for the necklace like eager hands. I fingered one of the gems. It was hard and cold and unyielding.

I didn't rush down the stairs, though I'd lost track of time. I didn't know whether ten minutes had passed since I'd left the hansom or closer to half an hour. But from the window at the front door I could see the driver was still at the curb, napping. I placed my hand on the door, ready to head to the newspaper office, when my gaze fell upon the telephone table where the landlady had retrieved her ring of keys. Under the telephone was a bound book of thin pages. I reached for the phone base and moved it to read the lettering. The book was a Manhattan business directory.

I grabbed the directory and fluttered through its pages to the Ts. With my finger I traced the names of the tailor shops. It took only seconds to find it, which was both exhilarating and disconcerting. Greenwich City Tailor Shop, Nigel Gwynn, proprietor, Seventh Avenue and Morton, New York, NY. I slapped the directory back to its place under the telephone and opened the front door.

I hurried to the carriage and climbed back in. The driver swung his head around. "Where to now, love?"

"Seventh and Morton."

As we drove it occurred to me that Lily might have taken only what Angus had taken from her. She had written in the letter that Angus Ravenhouse had ruined her father financially. Not only that, but Ravenhouse had made off with Lily's inheritance when she was forced to marry him. It seemed a shame that Angus Ravenhouse would get the necklace back and never be held accountable for how his actions had led Lily to make such disastrous choices.

I nearly felt Ethan beside me, telling me I couldn't single-handedly right all the world's wrongs. I had tried to do right by Andrew Gwynn; indeed, I had given love every opportunity to stay golden in his eyes, as I wished it had stayed golden in mine.

I prayed silently as we neared Seventh Avenue that Andrew would not despise me for my blatant and uncalled-for dabbling in his private affairs.

At least he would find out the truth from someone who cared enough about him and the virtue of love to have wanted to protect them both.

When the hansom pulled to a stop, I paid the driver and stepped out, trying to gather strength from the beat of the city as it pulsed around me. The Greenwich City Tailor Shop was one of several small businesses arranged like children's building blocks in a long row. The paint on the shop's window frames and door was cracked and peeling, but the panes of glass were freshly scrubbed. On the other side of the window I could see two wooden tailor forms, one with a completed suit coat hanging on it, and the other bare. There was a long wooden counter and behind that, the back of a man's head—surely Andrew's—as he bent over a sewing machine. I could smell the wool and gabardine and linen even before I opened the door, steeled myself, and went inside.

The tinkling of the bell on the door startled me and I wanted to hush it so that I could stand there for a moment before launching into my confession. But the bell had alerted him and he turned to me. The courage I had summoned as I had opened the door now seemed to evaporate with the dissipating trills of the bell. As Andrew's face filled the doorway, I reached into my pocketbook to touch the letter, to remind myself again why I was there.

And then he spoke to me. "May I help you?"

For a shimmering second I could almost believe it had all been a dream, that it was March again, I had only just arrived in Manhattan, and nothing bad had happened to any of us. Andrew didn't know me and I didn't know him. That was why he didn't recognize me. It had all been a dream.

But then I realized as I opened my mouth to speak that the man in front of me wasn't Andrew. It was a man who looked very much like him.

His brother.

"May I help you, miss?" he said again.

"Nigel." The name came from remembered conversations while Andrew had lain riddled with fever and loss, and I had cooled his brow.

"Yes. Do I know you?"

"I'm . . . I am a nurse at Ellis Island. I have some news for your brother, Andrew. I was his nurse when he was a patient at the hospital there."

"Oh. He's not here at the moment, I'm afraid."

I was about to ask him how long Andrew might be gone when the door behind me opened and the tinkling bell announced someone else was stepping into the store.

I turned to see whether perhaps it was Andrew, but that was not who it was.

"Good afternoon, Miss Wood." Chester Hartwell tipped his hat and smiled at me, as polite and genteel as a table host.

I should have guessed Chester Hartwell had planned to
follow me from the moment he met me in the great hall.
Chester Hartwell... Miss Wooley... her
... thanked

Thirty-Four

I should have guessed Chester Hartwell had planned to
follow me from the moment he met me in the great hall.
He had come to the hospital not to ask questions of Mrs.
Crowley, but because he had trailed me there. And he
had waited in the hospital reception area as long as it
might take an ordinary woman like me to change out of
a uniform into street clothes and get to the ferry house.
He had concluded his hopeful questioning at the hospital, thanked Mrs. Crowley and Ethan no doubt, and
then made his way to the ferry house to see whether I
was among those waiting for the next boat.

Of course he had seen me without my seeing him.

He saw me get into the hansom and so he got in
one. He followed me to Chambers Street and saw that
I'd paid my driver to wait for me. So he waited. And
when I came out alone some fifteen minutes later and got

back in the carriage, he instructed his driver to again follow me.

Right to the tailor shop.

He had watched from the street as I went in. Seen through the window that I was talking to a man who surely met the description of Andrew Gwynn he'd been given.

And then he had come in, ready to pounce.

A great sense of defeat fell over me, thick and cold.

"I'm afraid I'm a little lost here," Nigel said.

"Allow me to explain, Mr. Gwynn. You are Mr. Gwynn, aren't you?"

"Yes, but who are you?"

My voice seemed to have been encased in stone and I couldn't summon the energy to smash the granite.

"I'm Chester Hartwell. I'm a private detective." He produced a business card and handed it to Nigel.

And I could say nothing.

"Is there something I can do for you, Mr. Hartwell?" Nigel said politely. His accent was just like Andrew's. Soft and melodic. My own voice seemed light-years away from me.

"There is, indeed. You see, I'm under the employ of Angus Ravenhouse. I'm sure you've heard of him." Nigel's blank stare made Hartwell laugh. "Let's not play games, Mr. Gwynn. It's far too late for games."

"I'm afraid I've no idea what you're talking about." Nigel's polite tone was so much like Andrew's. It gave me the strength to throw myself into the conversation. I knew that once I did, I would change its course.

"You're talking to the wrong man!" I exclaimed. "This is Nigel Gwynn, not Andrew."

Mr. Hartwell needed only a moment to process this

information. "Then I shall wait to speak with the right man."

"What is going on?" Nigel said, his courteous tone giving way to concern. "I'd like to know. Especially if it involves my brother."

"Yes, Miss Wood. We'd all like to know. I'm sure the authorities might like to know, too." Hartwell smiled effortlessly, as if threats of calling in the cops were something he said as easily as his own name.

A tremor of fear started to blossom inside me, growing in intensity as seconds ticked by. Truth is truth, Ethan had said, but sometimes the truth was ugly. Truth itself was not beautiful or hideous. It was like change, neither good nor bad. And there was nothing I could do to make beautiful what Lily had done to Andrew, what Angus done to Lily, what the fire had done to me.

I looked down at Lily's scarf around my neck and I saw the tattered threads where I had removed the key. And I thought of the letter she had written that I held in my handbag. A letter that spoke of what she had done but also what she had suffered.

And I realized that while I couldn't beautify what was ugly, I could hide the hideous under the cover of mercy.

What is mercy for if not to cloak ugliness?

I had the power to do it.

Everything that had happened until then had led up to that moment. I turned to Nigel. "When is Andrew expected to return?"

"Soon. What is all this about?"

"Will you lock up the shop for a few minutes? Please? This is important."

Out of the corner of my eye I saw Mr. Hartwell raise an eyebrow. He wasn't expecting me to take charge. I was surprising him. And he didn't like it.

"I'd say it's more than just important—" he began, but I cut him off. I would cede no more power to him.

"You will be silent, Mr. Hartwell." I turned back to Nigel. "Will you please close the shop for just a little while, Mr. Gwynn?"

Nigel Gwynn walked over to the store's entrance, locked it, and pulled down the shade. When he came back to us, he motioned to chairs that someone might sit in while waiting to be fitted for a suit. We sat.

"What is all this about?" he asked.

I drew in my breath. Where to begin?

"It's about your brother marrying someone who was already married and stealing a necklace," Hartwell said confidently.

The words sounded so ridiculous that I marveled that they had struck fear in me only a short time earlier. "You are incredibly misinformed, Mr. Hartwell. And may I remind you that I have the information you seek. I know everything you want to know, so I suggest you be quiet."

"Miss Wood, please, what is all this?" Nigel entreated me.

I pointed to Hartwell. "This man will tell you that only days before he sailed, your brother falsely married a woman who was already married, that the two of them conspired to steal a necklace belonging to this woman's husband, and that Andrew somehow had something to do with her death on the ship that brought them here. None of it is true. And I have the proof."

Hartwell was absolutely silent next to me.

I pulled out the letter and certificate from my handbag. I opened the certificate and showed it to them both.

"Andrew had no idea Lily was already married. She didn't tell him. But she was planning to tell him by letter the day they arrived at your tailor shop. That's why she had this. But she never made it to America. She contracted scarlet fever on the ship and died before reaching New York.

"When your brother was admitted to the hospital he was numb with grief over losing his wife. I had recently lost someone, too, so I was especially aware of how difficult that day was for him. When I asked whether there was anything I could do for him, he asked me to retrieve your father's pattern book from his trunk in the baggage room. I would've told him that wasn't possible but I felt such sympathy for him, I told him I would try. When I found his and Lily's luggage in the baggage room, I thought the smaller of the two was his. It wasn't. The smaller one was hers; I knew that as soon as I opened it. I would've just closed the lid but I saw she had a book of Keats's poetry in her trunk. And it looked like a well-loved volume, so whether I should have or shouldn't have, I decided I would take the little poetry book to Andrew. I thought it might comfort him to have something of hers. I didn't know that the book had been your mother's. Nor that Lily had taken it from Andrew's trunk and put it in hers so that when he opened the trunk in New York after she disappeared, he would find it. And he'd see what was inside."

I unfolded the letter. "I didn't mean to read it. It fell out of the poetry book along with the certificate. When I saw what was written on the certificate, I confess I could not help but read it."

I cleared my throat and began to read the letter slowly, line by line. When I was finished neither man said a word.

"Andrew still doesn't know about this letter, Mr. Gwynn," I continued. "I hadn't the heart to tell him. There were times when I wanted to. Times when I thought I should. And the day he left, I thought I had." I touched the scarf around my neck. "This scarf was Lily's. I'd offered to wash it for him so that it would be free of disease when he left. On the day he was to be discharged I put the letter and the certificate inside the scarf and wrapped it in tissue so that he would find them later. But he left the scarf, wrapped, as a thank-you gift to me when I was away from the ward. And the note he included led me to believe he truly was better off not knowing. He still believes in the sacred beauty of love, Mr. Gwynn. Of all the things I have trifled with, I very much do not want to trifle with that."

"And the necklace?" Hartwell asked.

"I know where Lily put the necklace, and since that is all you care about, I will see that you leave with it, provided Mr. Gwynn here doesn't think we should do otherwise."

Nigel shook his head. "I hardly know what to make of any of this. If what you're saying is true—"

"It's all true," I assured him.

"Then this necklace is not mine or my brother's to lay claim to."

"But I am telling you this, Mr. Hartwell." I went on. "You will leave New York, and you and your employer will not trouble the Gwynn family again. You will say nothing to Andrew Gwynn about this—not now and not ever—and if you or Mr. Ravenhouse does, I will let the British police have this letter. They might find of interest

Lily's accusation that her father was defrauded by Mr. Ravenhouse. Do we have an understanding?"

Chester Hartwell nodded once. "Where is it?"

I unwound Lily's scarf. The necklace circled my neck, its gems warm on my skin.

BEFORE he allowed Hartwell to leave, Nigel insisted that he sign a statement that he'd received the necklace in question. It took a moment for Hartwell to agree, but in the end he did as Nigel asked. I signed it as witness and so did Nigel. Nigel then folded that piece of paper and tucked it into his pants pocket.

Hartwell tipped his hat and turned from us. He left the shop without a word.

Nigel and I watched him board a trolley and take off down Seventh Avenue.

When he was gone, I turned to Nigel and offered him the letter and the certificate. "I don't know what to do with these. I keep thinking I do. I don't."

He stared at them for a moment. "Why didn't you put them back in her trunk after you found them?"

"I tried to. When I went back to the baggage room Lily's trunk had been taken to the incinerator. The luggage of all those who had succumbed to the fever on that ship was confiscated and burned."

"You could have given them to Andrew."

"Could I? Could you? Could you have looked at your grieving brother, sick and separated from everything that mattered to him, and given him *that* letter?"

He did not answer me, and we were quiet for a moment.

"What made you do all this?" he finally said.

I knew the answer. It came quickly to my lips.

"I did it for love."

Nigel's eyes widened. "You're in love . . . with my brother?"

For a moment I wanted to believe there was a way that I might love Andrew Gwynn purely and without pretense, and that he could love me, but how could that be? I could never share with him the terrible thing I knew, nor my own part in shielding him from it. How could I love a man completely to whom I could not bare my soul? My hand went instinctively to my neck, where the scarf rested against my skin now that the necklace was gone. Peeling myself away from the fire, from Edward, from the island included this: releasing Andrew Gwynn from that part of my being that wanted to rescue him and keep him close.

"I did it for love's sake," I finally said. "Someday you might think Andrew will need to see that letter. But I pray that day never comes. I truly do. Mercy would keep him from ever learning what he cannot change and what would change nothing. I saw hope in your brother's eyes when he left the island, Mr. Gwynn. He still believes in love. Even though it cost him."

Nigel Gwynn stared at the papers in my hand. "They'd be ash now if Andrew hadn't asked for the pattern book, yes?"

"Yes."

Again he stared at the papers, willing them, it seemed, to speak of what should be done with them. "I see hope in his eyes too," he finally said. "Every day a little more."

Nigel Gwynn took the papers from me. Then he reached behind the counter and drew out a pair of shears.

I left the tailor shop a few minutes later. Nigel asked whether I would like to leave my address with him should

Andrew wish to contact me or in case Chester Hartwell showed up again. But I shook my head. Chester Hartwell would not be returning.

"Are you sure?" Nigel pressed. He knew I had bound myself to his brother and was now choosing to loosen the strings.

"I am."

Nigel kindly offered to hail a carriage for me, but I declined and stepped onto the busy street alone.

For a moment I stood there watching life zoom and saunter past me, in all its severity and magnificence. I was shedding my skin, becoming raw and new. Everything that had kept me bound to the island was sloughing away with each brave step I was taking.

As I stood there, familiarizing myself with my renaissance, I knew there was one thing left I needed to do. Wanted to do.

I boarded the next trolley headed in the direction of Chambers Street.

We had gone no farther than two blocks when I saw Andrew Gwynn walking down Seventh Avenue with a bolt of cloth on his shoulder. The trolley was slowing in traffic and for a moment our eyes met. Instinctively I raised my hand to the window glass that separated us. At first his stare was that of a stranger. It took him a second to embrace the notion that in that moment, his two worlds had collided—the sad life he knew on Ellis with me and the hopeful one he was building here with his brother. Then his eyes burned with recognition. The trolley began to accelerate and he seemed to vacillate between running after me and continuing on his way back to the shop. I kept my hand to the glass, and smiled at him, feeling tears sliding down my cheeks unchecked and landing on Lily's scarf. And then he raised his hand to me, waved once, and lowered it slowly. He did not run after me. I turned to face the back window as we passed so that I could continue to watch him. He stood facing the trolley with his hands on the bolt of cloth until I could no longer see him in the distance.

Thirty-Five

TARYN

Manhattan
September 2011

I had always assumed I had lost Mrs. Stauer's scarf in the maelstrom of my escape on September eleventh. The most I had ever hoped for was that I might find its closest match. It hadn't occurred to me that the florist might have had it all this time. I hadn't thought to try to contact him; nor could I have done so. Until the photograph had turned up I hadn't even known Mick's last name; nor could I remember which florist employed him.

As I stood with the phone to my ear, the words "I have your scarf" echoed in my head. I couldn't believe that the scarf was no longer lost to me. In all the years I had spent looking for its match, I had never fully considered how I might feel when I found it. Here now was not just its match, but the scarf itself, safe in the hands of the very person who had used it to pull me back from the rim of hell.

I hurried to the back room and shut the door so that I could talk to Mick alone. Even before the photo, Celine knew that a florist had helped me escape the tower's fall, but she didn't know everything that Mick Demetriou had done for me in the single hour that had defined our relationship. No one knew.

"What did you say?" I asked, when I was safely behind the closed door.

"I said I have your scarf."

Mick's voice sounded different than it had on the day I'd met him. Deeper. Softer. I would not have recognized it.

"I found it in my delivery van," Mick continued, when I said nothing. "I went back for my vehicle after the roads opened again. Your scarf was on the floor by the buckets where we . . . where we waited. I almost didn't recognize it, it was so covered in dust."

"Oh." I willed away the mental images of those remembered moments. The buckets. The water. The flowers. The searing pain in my chest. The ghostly figure next to me guzzling water like an exile in the desert.

"I have tried for years to find you. I thought you said your name was Karen. I couldn't find you on any list of surviving family members. I kept looking for someone named Karen."

"Oh. Right. Sorry about that," I mumbled, remembering clearly the moment he had asked for my name.

"No, it's my fault," he said. "I didn't hear you right."

"There was a lot going on."

He paused. "Yes. Yes, there was."

Another moment of silence stretched between us.

"The reporter told me you'd been identified. I'd like very much to give you your scarf back," he said.

"I should probably tell you it's not even mine," I confessed.

"Pardon me?"

"I was supposed to match it for one of my customers. I had just picked it up that morning. That's why I was late."

A third stretch of silence followed before he said, "But you want it back, don't you?"

His tone was distinctly hopeful, as if he needed me to want the scarf. After all these years trying to find me, it was important to him that I have it. As I contemplated his question I could sense that the scarf was near him. Perhaps he was holding it in his hand as he talked to me.

Mick's question hung between us, unanswered.

It was the wrong question. What I wanted didn't matter. It never had. None of this was ever about what I wanted.

"Are you still there?" Mick asked.

"I'm here."

"Don't you want it?" Sadness coated his voice as he repeated his question a third time.

His tone hinted to me that he had ascertained the weight of what he was asking. To an outsider it would seem such a simple inquiry: Did I want a lost scarf returned to me or not? But Mick was no outsider. I answered him with the one question that had obsessed me for a decade.

"Do you think everything happens for a reason?"

"Do I what?"

A door inside me seemed to fling itself open and the ponderings of more than three thousand days flew out. "Do you believe it was just a fluke the photographer found that memory card, and that there was a photo of you and me on it? And here you've kept the scarf safe all these years while you looked for me. Do you think that was a coincidence?"

"Well, I . . . No, I guess I don't."

His quick confidence in providence awed me. "You think the photographer was meant to find our photo?" I insisted. "That it was meant to be published? You were meant to see it? You were meant to keep the scarf all these years so that you could get it back to me?"

A second or two passed before he answered.

"All I can say is I've looked for you for a decade. At every 9/11 event, inside every subway station, in the face of every woman on the sidewalk who reminded me of you. And yes, I've asked God to help me find you."

"To give me back that scarf."

"Well, yes. But it's not just about the scarf."

He was right. It wasn't just about the scarf. It was about what I was willing to live with. If fate had twice orchestrated the whereabouts of an insignificant piece of neckwear, surely fate didn't stop there. It was far better for me to believe that chance alone impacted my choices.

I didn't want to play destiny's game anymore.

I didn't want the scarf back.

"I told you it's not mine," I said. "It was never mine."

"Yes, but—"

"I will see if I can locate the woman it belongs to. I am not altogether sure she is still living but I will find out."

"But—"

"Look, I can't play the game anymore."

"Game? What game?"

It was time to end the conversation. "I will always be grateful for what you did for me. Really. I have to go.

Someone will be in touch with you if we can find the owner of the scarf."

"Wait. There's something else—"

"No. There's nothing else. I can't do this anymore."

"Taryn, please don't hang up!"

"Good-bye, Mick. Thank you again. For everything. But please don't call me back."

I pressed the button to end the call and pulled the phone to my chest, which was heaving now with anger, sorrow, and trepidation.

Surely I had made the right choice.

The reasonable choice.

I stayed in the back room until I had thoroughly tamped down the tide of doubt that had swelled inside me.

KENT'S parents arrived the next day, Saturday, to attend the anniversary services on Sunday. As a treat for Kendal, I let her stay with them at the Marriott downtown, just a short walk from the newly opened memorial grounds. I decided at the last minute to attend with them but I arrived just as the service began and left before it was finished. I stayed long enough to achieve a measure of peace. Kendal and I found Kent's name on the North Tower's shining, watery monument, and we ran our fingers over the letters etched in granite. We stood for a moment under the shade of the lone surviving pear tree and marveled that it had been loved back to health and replanted there. The grounds were hallowed to me, but also private. I knew it was selfish of me, but I didn't love the idea that Kent shared a final resting place with so many, because that meant I had to share it, too.

Yet I knew this day was important to Kendal and I wanted to have the memory of the event to share with her, even if its very public nature was still too much for me. I didn't want to be recognized as the woman in the photo, and I didn't want to run into Mick, though the crowds were in the thousands, and it was easy to stay in the shadows.

It was a moving ceremony, even from an emotional distance, and I was glad I went, though I didn't know whether I would ever be able to commemorate that day without wishing I could just fall asleep before midnight every September tenth and wake up on the twelfth. When Kendal and I returned to the apartment later that day I was exhausted.

Kent's parents stayed through Tuesday, a welcome distraction for me. By the time they left, the city had returned to its normal day-to-day hum.

I tried to return to mine.

I found I could not.

Restless and moody, I was unable to concentrate on anything. Mick's phone call kept replaying itself in my mind. The hope in his voice when he said he wanted to return the scarf and the disappointment when I said I didn't want it haunted me. It was as if he, too, was struggling to comprehend what to make of our intersected lives, and he had hoped I would be the key to his making peace with similar thoughts.

The worst part was, I still owed Kendal the truth. She deserved to know why I was on the street on 9/11 instead of at the Heirloom Yard, where she and nearly everyone else thought I had been.

I lay awake every night on the edge of sleep, wanting the ease of thinking that everything that had happened on the day Kent died was mere coincidence.

But I woke every morning hungry for more than a random life for me and for my daughter.

As the month bent toward the beginning of autumn and the first leaves began to blush with a tinge of color, I knew that I had been kidding myself. The steady cadence of the seasons was proof enough that I still believed there was divine order in my world. And yet I continued to let the days go by, one by one, without sitting down with Kendal and without making inquiries about Rosalynn Stauer.

I thought about telling Kendal the truth.

I thought about trying to find Mrs. Stauer.

I thought about the scarf.

I even dreamed about the scarf.

But day after day went by and I chose to do nothing.

I was helping a customer choose fabric for a quilt on the last day of summer when the most remarkable thing happened. The woman had in her hand the quilt pattern for a Tangled Irish Chain, one of my favorites, and she was struggling to choose between a blue or green color palette. There were hues of both colors that she loved and hues of both that she hated, and the pattern, which was the same for everyone who bought it, did not dictate which color she must have.

As the woman stood there contemplating her options with the pattern in her hand, clarity suddenly fell upon me. The answer I was looking for had been right in front of me the whole time. I had the power of choice, just like the woman who was now faced with choosing which fabric to buy. I could believe that a photographer had been destined to come upon a lost memory card, or that Mick Demetriou was destined to find me after a decade, or that I was destined to be a phone call away from being reunited with the scarf and yet chose to do nothing.

That was the beauty and terror of choice.

I chose to love Kent. It had been my greatest joy, choosing to love him. I hadn't understood the beauty of this freedom to love until I began to understand, at that very moment, that it was countered by the freedom to hate.

This was what Mick had meant when he told me, as we sputtered and coughed in his delivery van, that it wasn't my fault that Kent was at the top of the North Tower when the first plane hit. My choices that terrible morning had been prompted by love. What others had chosen had been prompted by hate. The effects of our choices had spilled onto each other. They always did.

Which must be why, in the midst of all this freedom to choose, a scarf had been sent my way. So that Kendal could be born and so that I could continue to hope love would triumph.

THE next day, the first of autumn, I told Celine that the man in the photo had Rosalynn Stauer's scarf and that I needed her help in finding her. A decade ago, Mrs. Stauer had been quick to forgive me for losing her scarf, considering the circumstances, but we had not seen her in the store for a long time. Celine, initially surprised that I had said nothing of Mick's phone call until then, thought she could find Mrs. Stauer, if she was still living. Celine seemed to understand rather quickly that I'd needed time to process the scarf's sudden reappearance in my life— and Mick's, too, perhaps. I was still in the midst of that process when I told her. If I was meant to have the scarf returned to me, then I needed to find out why. Perhaps the reason was bigger than me, just as it had been the first time. Perhaps it wasn't about me at all, but about Mrs. Stauer. The scarf had been precious to her. Maybe the scarf was reappearing now for her sake, not mine.

I wanted to share the scarf with Kendal before I handed it over to Mrs. Stauer. Kendal's life had been spared because of it. The scarf was a key part of the story I owed her, the only beautiful part. If she could see the scarf and touch it, perhaps it would soften what I had to tell her about the rest of that day.

Mick would surely bring the scarf to me if I asked him, but I wanted to go to it, just like I had done the first morning I saw it.

A few minutes after ten, I tapped his phone number into my cell.

A male voice answered. "Athena Florist."

"Mick?"

"Speaking."

"It's Taryn."

I made arrangements for Celine to pick Kendal up from school.

Before I left for the subway station and Greenwich Village, I went upstairs to the apartment. I had a sudden and surprising urge to feel pretty. I changed into a honey-hued blouse, linen capris, and coffee-brown pumps. I pulled my hair out of its ponytail and clipped a gold barrette into it.

It was a Friday afternoon and the sidewalks were already teeming with people heading out early for the weekend. It still felt like summer. I boarded the number one train to the Village and twenty minutes later emerged onto the sidewalk at Christopher Street, just a block away from where I needed to be.

I walked slowly, preparing my heart and head to see the scarf again.

To see Mick again.

I saw the blue awning first and then the stylish sidewalk arrangement of flowering plants in pots.

His shop was small like mine, but bursting with color that no other store on the block could match. The tinkling of a little wind chime tied to the door handle announced my arrival. I breathed in the scents of a dozen different kinds of blooms.

Mick was at the register just a few feet from the welcome mat, ringing up a purchase. The last time I had seen him he was covered in ash. But the first time, he had looked very nearly like he did now. Even his apron looked the same. A slight sprinkle of gray that had not been there before touched the black hair at his temples. He raised his head when I stepped in and a smile broke across his face.

A dark-haired woman who looked a lot like Mick, but much older, started to come toward me.

Mick finished with his customer and stepped out from behind the register. "I got this, Mom," he said to the woman. "Do you want to take the register for me?"

She smiled at me and took Mick's place. I had not moved from my spot just inside the door. Mick came to me with one arm outstretched, his hand open. I moved toward him and tentatively placed my hand in his. He pulled me gently toward him and kissed my cheek.

"So good to finally see you again," he said.

I nodded dumbly, my eyes filling with tears for no reason that I could think of.

"Here, let's go to the back." Mick led me past wrought-iron displays of African violets, potted bamboo, and cyclamen, past shining glass doors where flowers of every color stayed cool and fresh. We entered the workspace used for creating the arrangements. A young woman who looked college-age was working on a centerpiece, but she excused herself and left. He thanked her. Mick had obviously told her beforehand he'd be needing the room and that privacy would be appreciated. He indicated a corner where shelves held vases and ceramic pots, spools of ribbon and netting, and boxes of florist's wire and tape that loomed over a little table.

He pulled out a chair for me.

"Thank you," I said.

Mick took the chair opposite mine. "You are well?" he asked.

"Yes."

"You . . . you look great."

"Um. So do you."

"I'm so glad you called me back."

"I am, too. Look, I'm sorry I was so harsh when you first called me. I . . . I needed to sort some things out."

"You don't owe me an explanation."

I leaned forward in my chair. "No, I do. I didn't realize that I wasn't in a good place mentally until that photo was published. I . . . I was in a weird, in-between place where I didn't know what I believed and I didn't even know I was stuck there. And then you called me out of the blue and said you had the scarf."

I stopped to gather strength, and Mick reached across the table to squeeze my hand.

"I know exactly what you mean," he said. "I wasn't the same after that day either. And my losses weren't nearly as huge as yours. I was in a weird place for a long time, too."

For a moment we just sat there, looking at each other and remembering what had bound us together then and kept us bound now. Then he released my hand and stood. He walked over to a desk in a far corner of the workroom, opened a drawer, and drew out fabric as brilliant as sunlight.

The scarf.

He walked back and I could not keep my face from erupting into a smile. He handed the scarf to me and it was as if he were handing me a bouquet. The marigolds were practically shouting a greeting to me. The scarf was just as beautiful as I remembered it.

"You can't even tell what happened," I said, fingering the bright threads.

Mick retook his seat and laughed. "It took several washings to get all the dust and debris out. My wife— ex-wife, I should say—said I'd never get it clean. But I was determined to have my way. The marigolds insisted I not give up. They are very resilient flowers, you know."

I laughed lightly, too. It felt good. "Are they?"

"Oh, yes. They aren't fragrant like roses and sweet peas, but they can stand against odds that the more fragile flowers cannot."

"Really?"

He nodded. "They can bloom in the fall, even after a frost. Even after other flowers have given up."

"No wonder I couldn't stop thinking about them then," I said, attempting to sound nonchalant, but my words must have hit Mick in a deep place.

For a moment he said nothing.

"I tried to find you. God, I tried." Mick's voice was noticeably apologetic. He sounded as if he wanted my forgiveness. "My . . . my ex-wife said I should get rid of it, be done with it. She said it was stupid to hang onto it when it was obvious I would never find you."

"Ex-wife?"

Mick sighed. "We were already having some issues

and I . . . I had a hard time after that day. A cousin who was a firefighter, and whom I was very close to, died in the North Tower—"

"I'm so sorry," I interjected.

"On top of that, I couldn't find you. And I couldn't stop thinking that I should've stayed with you at the hospital. I shouldn't have left you there."

He was sounding more and more remorseful. I had no idea why.

"You had already saved my life, Mick. I'm sure I would have died on that street were it not for you. There was no reason you should have stayed with me."

He shook his head. "But you're wrong. I should have. I almost did. I should have followed my instincts. If I had stayed, I would've figured out your name isn't Karen. I probably would've learned what your last name was. I would have been able to find you later when it really mattered."

I didn't understand the depth of his regret. And I was intuitively sensing that his unsuccessful quest to find me might have been the last straw in a marriage that was already crumbling. It was my turn to lean across the table and squeeze his hand. "There was nothing else you could've done for me."

"But there *was*, Taryn. The scarf wasn't the only reason I couldn't stop looking for you."

"What do you mean?"

Mick looked down at my hand on his. "A text message that was sent to me that morning was delayed because of the overload. I didn't get it until later that day."

I still didn't have a clue what he was getting at. "And?"

He raised his head to look at me and meet me eye-to-eye. "It was a reply to a message I had sent earlier. To your husband."

The air in the little room seemed to become a solid thing. I felt the weight of it. "What?"

"He got the text message I sent for you. He replied at nine twenty-eight."

"Oh, God almighty," I whispered, and it was as much a prayer as any other I have ever uttered. Tears of relief and shock filled my eyes. I could barely remember what I had told Mick to text to Kent a decade earlier.

I had to think for a moment.

Tell him I'm safe.

Tell him I love him.

Tell him he's going to be a father.

Kent's last text message to my forgotten cell phone had been sent at nine twenty-seven, when he assumed I was already dead and his own death was only moments away. He had received my message from Mick's phone a minute later. What I had wanted Kent to know, with all my heart, he had known.

I had an answer for the question Kendal had been asking since she was four years old.

Does he know I'm here?

"What did the message say?" I whispered.

"'Tell her, "Be happy."'"

I pulled the scarf to my face and let my tears fall into its threads for the second time in my life. The scarf had found its way back not for Mrs. Stauer. Or even for Mick.

It was for me.

Thirty-Six

CLARA

Manhattan
September 1911

ONLY a few hours of daylight remained when I arrived exhausted back at Lily's rented room. Not enough time to complete my last task before leaving for Scotland.

And as I stretched out on Lily's bed to rest, I knew what I would do.

I did not need to rush back to Ellis on the next ferry. I had a room to sleep in, even clothes to wear if something happened to the dress I had on. But I knew people would worry about me if I didn't show up at dinner on Ellis.

Ethan would worry.

Ethan.

For as much as I was sloughing off, I was keenly aware that everything about Ethan was hanging on. Part of me found that thrilling, but a bigger part shrank back in hesitation. My heart was nearly free from the crucible that had tested it and it would soon be mine again—as bare and vulnerable as a newborn—to give away. I could not picture myself handing my heart over again so soon.

Especially not until I had taken care of one last detail.

I drifted into sleep and awoke to the sound of a fire engine's clanging bell as evening shadows were creeping into the room. I rose from the bed, disoriented and ferociously hungry and thirsty. It had been nearly twelve hours since I had eaten or had a drink.

I checked my reflection in the mirror above the bureau, pinching my cheeks to restore color to my face. I smoothed back the stray wisps of hair that had sprung free of my chignon while I slept. Lily's scarf was still wound around my neck. I unfurled it and lay it on the bed.

The first order of business before finding a place to eat was using a telephone. I had to call the island and let Mrs. Crowley know where I was so that she in turn could tell Dolly and Ethan.

I checked my handbag to see how much cash I had left. I needed to save enough for transportation in the morning and my ferry back to Ellis. And I needed to eat. I had less than five dollars. Not enough to inspire confidence. I was fairly certain the landlady didn't let her boarders use her telephone without paying her something.

Kneeling at Lily's trunk, I rifled through the contents, looking for something of value to trade with the woman for the use of the phone.

I came across a small wooden box no bigger than a pound of butter. Inside were several folded British banknotes, a string of pearls, a silver ring with a single ruby, and several lovely bracelets, none of which looked inordinately dear, but neither were they cheap. I chose one, closed the lid, and rose to my feet.

Minutes later I was knocking on the woman's door. She answered with what I was beginning to believe was her customary frown.

"Sorry to trouble you, but I would like to use the telephone if I may."

Her frown deepened. "It's an extra dollar a month for use of the phone."

I held out the bracelet to her. "I'm a little low on cash, and the call I need to make is very important. May I trade you this bracelet to make the call? Please?"

She hesitated and then reached for the trinket and curled my fingers around it. "Don't be giving away things that are special to you. Keep it short." The woman disappeared back behind her door.

I lifted the phone off the table, put the handset to my ear, and raised the base to my mouth. When the operator came on the line I asked for the switchboard at Ellis Island and gave her the exchange.

Seconds later I spoke my message slowly to the operator on Ellis so that she could write it down and give it to Mrs. Crowley when she found her.

"From Clara Wood: I am staying overnight in Manhattan. It couldn't be helped. My apologies. Please relay to Nurse McLeod and Dr. Randall that all is well and I shall return tomorrow."

I had hoped a different woman might be working in the reception area when I returned to the newspaper office the following morning. But the woman was the same one who had assisted me when Ethan brought me there. And she remembered me. Concern for me was etched across her face when she recognized who I was.

I decided honesty would be in my favor with this woman. She would respond to grief with compassion.

So I told her I had survived the Triangle Shirtwaist fire but had lost a good friend to it, and I apologized for having dashed away the last time I was there.

"Not to worry. It's quite all right."

And then I told her I wanted to read all the news stories that had followed in the days after the fire.

She nodded, knowing without my saying it that I was performing something of a ritual cleansing, long overdue.

She took me to the reading room where I had been before and set me down. She left and returned a few minutes later with a stack of back issues. The woman squeezed my shoulder when she left and shut the door, giving me privacy that I didn't know I would treasure until she was gone and I was alone.

I unfolded the papers, which she had given me in chronological order, and prepared to look down at the ghastly headline for the March 26 issue, the final death toll not even complete:

141 Men and Girls Die in Shirtwaist Factory Fire; Trapped High up in Washington Place Building; Street Strewn with Bodies; Piles of Dead Inside

A sound escaped my throat, not so much a whimper as a single note, like a tiny scrap of a hymn. I lifted my eyes from the words, waited for strength to return to me, and then I continued to read the account of the day that had forever changed me.

Three stories of a ten-floor building at the corner of Greene Street and Washington Place were burned yesterday, and while the fire was going on 141 young men and women—at least 125 of them mere girls— were burned to death or killed by jumping to the pavement below.

The building was fireproof. It shows now hardly any signs of the disaster that overtook it. The walls are as good as ever and so are the floors; nothing is the worse for the fire except the furniture and 141 of the 600 men and girls who were employed in its upper three stories.

Most of the victims were suffocated or burned to death within the building, but some who fought their way to the windows and leaped met death as surely, but perhaps more quickly, on the pavement below. . . .

One by one, I opened and read the newspapers from the last week in March, pausing often to blink back cleansing tears that I should have shed long ago. Each new headline felt at first like a blow to the chest, and then a remembrance for the dead, and then a stone to be cast across the wide sea of my memory.

When I was finished, and the papers refolded to hide again their terrible news, I rose from the table and opened the door.

The woman who had helped me watched me emerge with a kind and knowing smile on her face.

"Thank you so much for letting me read the papers,"

I said, but I was thanking her for more than that and we both knew it.

"Is there anything else I can do for you?" she asked.

There was.

"The friend of mine who died was named Edward Brim. He was one of those who fell. And I . . . I was there to see him step out of the window."

"Good gracious," the woman whispered, a sheen of wetness glossing her eyes.

"He . . . took the hand of a young seamstress who was too afraid to go alone." My voice was breaking as I spoke. "He took her hand. He helped her down. He helped her down."

I could not continue. The woman was now openly crying.

"I am so sorry for your loss," she said when she was able.

"I would very much like to tell his parents—and his fiancée—that he died a hero," I said.

"Oh. Of course."

"But I only know that his parents live in Brooklyn. I was hoping you could look up the address for me. And I don't know where his fiancée lives at all."

"Oh."

A strange look passed over her face and I wondered whether she thought I was asking too much of her.

"Well," she continued, "I can give you the Brims' address, but the woman he had been engaged to, I do believe she has married and now lives in Chicago. Or maybe Minneapolis. I would have to check. The announcement was printed last month."

"What was that?" I could not wrap my thoughts around the words "she has married."

"Yes, I am pretty sure that was the name I saw in the announcements last month. Savina Mayfield?"

I could only nod my head.

"It was an unusual name. I remembered it from Mr. Brim's obituary. And so it caught my eye when I saw it last month in the wedding announcements."

"She married someone else?"

The woman shrugged. "It happens that way sometimes."

Words failed me. I had only just now been able to release Edward, and in the same time Savina Mayfield had already married someone else?

As I stood there, incredulous, the woman told me to wait for a moment and she would return with Mr. and Mrs. Brim's address. A moment later she came back and handed me a slip of paper.

MY mind was a tumble of thoughts as I sat on a train bound for Brooklyn. Reason bade me to concentrate on what I knew, not on what I didn't. Savina Mayfield's reasons for marrying so soon after Edward's death were her own. She owed me no explanation, and since I surely wouldn't get one from her, I focused on preparing to introduce myself to Edward's parents and share with them what their son had done with his last seconds on earth.

I exited the train seven blocks from where the Brims lived off Fulton Street. A ticket taker at the train station was kind enough to tell me in which direction I would find their house. I decided to walk to clear my head and also save my money. I still needed to get back to Battery Park and on the ferry.

My feet were sore when I arrived at the brownstone row house, one of twenty just like it on the Brims' street, but the ache was a welcome distraction. I wanted to know what had happened with Savina. I truly did. And within me, I felt I had the right to know. Surely the Brims knew. How would I get it out of them politely? I knocked on the door the moment I arrived on their stoop so that I wouldn't suddenly change my mind and leave.

But no one answered my knock.

I kept at it long past the moment when I knew no one was home. I wanted an answer. I needed one.

A fresh wave of mental exhaustion was falling over me as I kept up with my pounding. At first I didn't hear the voice behind me. When I did, I realized the woman who had spoken to me had asked me the same question twice.

"Can I help you, miss?"

I pivoted in embarrassment to face her. She was standing on the stoop next to me with a tiny dog in her arms that now barked a warning to me.

"I . . . I was just . . . I wanted to speak to the Brims."

"Oh. They're out of town for a few days. Were they expecting you, hon?"

"No. No, they weren't."

"You can come back on Monday. They'll be home then."

I shook my head. It seemed heavy on my shoulders. "I'll be gone."

The woman cocked her head. "You want to leave a message with me? I'm watching their place while they're away. This is their dog."

It would have been easy to tell her no, there was no message, and leave. But I did want the Brims to know what Edward had done for that young, frightened girl who had shared the fiery ledge with him. Perhaps they had questions like I did. Perhaps they wondered, maybe wondered every night, why he was on the ninth floor instead of the tenth, where his office was.

"May I borrow a piece of writing paper?" I asked.

"Come on over."

The woman introduced herself as a longtime neighbor and friend of the Brims, while the dog steadily announced he was not pleased I was there. She sat me down at her own little writing desk and handed me a pen and a sheet of lavender paper.

I smoothed the paper and wrote the words that I would remember Edward by:

> My name is Clara Wood. I was a nurse in one of the offices at the Asch Building and I was there the day of the fire. I met Edward in the elevator two weeks earlier. He was very kind to me, as I was a newcomer to Manhattan. He had invited me to see the sewing floor the day of the fire. That is why he was on the ninth floor. I was safely on the street when those trapped in the burning building began to fall from the windows. I saw Edward on the ledge. A young girl was next to him and the fire was all around them and she was afraid to step off. He took her hand and they left the ledge together. I wanted you to know that. His last act was one of kindness. I am so very sorry for your loss.
>
> Clara Wood

I blew the ink dry. The woman handed me an envelope. I tucked the note inside but I did not seal it shut. I didn't care whether the woman read it and I figured she would when I left.

"So you knew Edward, then?" I asked, as I addressed the note to Mr. and Mrs. Brim.

"Oh, yes. Poor fellow. You heard what happened?"

"Indeed. I did."

"Such a tragedy. Such a needless tragedy."

I nodded. "And him engaged to be married."

The woman snorted. "Yes, well. It wouldn't have been much of a marriage to that one. None of us liked her. I think toward the end there, Edward was starting to see what we all saw. She was nothing but trouble wrapped in a pretty face and sweet talk. I wouldn't have been surprised at all if Edward had called the wedding off. We were all hoping he would. He told his mother he had met someone and was having second thoughts. And then . . . that terrible fire."

I let her words wash over me, words that held within them a sticky balm that soothed even as it raked across the remnants of the wound.

"He didn't love Miss Mayfield?" I asked.

The woman seemed to think this an odd question. "Well, I don't know. Maybe in the beginning he did; Lord knows why. But I don't think he did toward the end. And she certainly didn't waste any time finding someone to take Edward's place. You know she got married already, right? I feel sorry for that man; I do."

For a moment I sat there in the neighbor's chair, inhaling the sweetness of the air around me.

The grieving heart could still believe in love.

And so could I.

"Can you tell me where Green-Wood Cemetery is?" I asked.

HALF an hour later, after splurging on a taxi for the three-mile jaunt and walking the length of several rows of headstones, I found Edward's place of rest.

The grass was lush and thick on the spot where he had been buried. Flowers that had been fresh a few days ago lay across the rounded top of his headstone.

I bent down to trace the curves of the letters in his name.

Edward Allen Brim.

He had been twenty-four.

Only two words came in a whisper off my lips as I knelt there. A passerby would have stared at me, aghast, for they are not words heard often in a cemetery. But I was alone and this seemed the only thing I wanted to say, needed to say, to Edward.

"Thank you."

I stayed a moment longer, blew the stone a kiss, and then turned back to the waiting cab.

Thirty-Seven

I returned to Lily's room with one purpose: to erase from the world the last remnants of her deception.

I tugged her trunk down the boardinghouse stairs and pushed it out onto the street. The beggar woman from the day before was now a block away, but easily visible from where I stood. Today, a raggedy little child was with her. I waited perhaps five minutes to hail a passing hansom. With the driver's help we loaded the trunk into his vehicle.

"I want you to take the trunk to that lady over there," I said to him, pointing toward the woman.

"What lady?"

"That one." And again I pointed to the woman who stood next to a light pole, her arm stretched out and a tin cup for coins in her hand. The child held on to her skirt.

The driver shrugged but said nothing.

A minute later we were at the curb. We pulled the trunk out and I set it down in front of the woman. I opened the trunk, lifted out the jewelry box, and handed it to her. The little girl at her skirt backed away from me, smiling but clearly shy.

"Can you take the trunk, too? There are some clothes that might fit you. Do you have anyone to help you get it home?"

Her smile, slow in coming, was wide and missing several teeth. "Yes, miss. I can take this trunk! I can take it."

I smiled back at her. I pulled Lily's scarf out of the trunk and was about to drape it across the little girl's shoulders, but it seemed too heavy to lay across such an innocent child. And I was still drawn to it, as much as I had been the first day I saw it around Andrew's neck. I wasn't ready to part with it. I coiled it about my own neck.

"Thank you, miss! Thank you, miss!" the woman said, her eyes now shimmering with gratitude.

I got back in the cab and shut the door.

I had taken the ferry to Ellis only four times. The first time, when the fire sent me there broken and battered. The second, after having just learned Edward had been engaged. The third, when I went home to say goodbye to my family and bury forever what had happened to me. And now this time, when what I thought I'd needed to bury was instead returned to me.

As the ferry neared the island, I felt I'd been gone for far longer than a day. I was aware of a weightlessness, as if Lily's letter and certificate had been made of iron, and now that they were gone, I was returning to the island lighter. My eyes misted at the indescribable relief that was swelling inside me the closer we got to shore. It had been a long time since happy tears had slid down my cheeks.

Minutes later, as the ferry docked and the gangplank was lowered, I hurried to queue up with the other passengers waiting to disembark. I wanted to tell the island all that had happened, to tell Dolly. To tell Ethan.

It was late in the afternoon and the ferry house was crowded with immigrants waiting to get onto the ferry that I had just gotten off of. A flurry of languages floated on the air above me as I eased my way past the entry gates and beyond the throngs of people waiting to board.

"Clara!"

I heard my name above the din. I turned my head this way and that, searching for the source.

"Clara! Here!"

And then I saw Ethan, moving toward me.

I rushed to him, surprising myself with the urgency I felt. I had so much to tell him.

When he reached me, he pulled me to his chest as though I had been lost for weeks. "Are you all right? What happened?"

"I'm fine! I'm all right."

He pulled back from me to study my face. "Why did you stay? Did you find him?"

"Yes! I found him."

People were brushing past us as we stared at each other. Me with a hundred things to tell him, and him surely with a hundred questions. Then a look of profound loss swept across his face and all the questions in his eyes seemed to disappear. I realized why.

Ethan thought I had not only found Andrew Gwynn, but that I had stayed with him. Spent the night with him.

The anguish I now read in Ethan's eyes I knew intimately. I had felt the same grief when I thought Edward was in love with another woman. It was the same anguish

I had fought to spare Andrew from. Ethan wore the look of a lover terribly wronged, suffering a trespass of the ugliest kind against the most beautiful of virtues.

He could feel this way only if one thing were true. And I was sure now that it was.

Ethan was in love with me.

As I had been in love with Edward.

As Andrew had been in love with Lily.

And that love had blossomed in the span of three weeks.

In my heart I knew I did not yet love Ethan the way he loved me. But I felt the sure stirring of possibility and desirability. If I stayed, I would surely fall for him. The mere thought of that surrender made me shiver. I needed time to regain the strength I would need to withstand the cost of loving someone. I felt fragile inside, as if the pieces of my shattered life had been put back together but the glue had not dried.

I remembered what Andrew had said when he explained what the Keats poem meant, that what you can still dream about is often sweeter than the reality.

I wanted to dream about loving again before I embraced the reality of it, in all its wonder and risk.

I raised my hand to his face and rested it on his cheek, the most comforting gesture I could think of.

He leaned into it, hurt still shining in his eyes.

"I am not in love with Andrew Gwynn," I said. "I didn't stay with him last night. I didn't even talk to him."

His eyes widened in surprise, mixed with equal parts hope and hesitation.

"And I *was* in love with Edward. But I know he's gone."

Ethan covered my hand on his face with his. "What does this mean, Clara? For me? For us?"

"It means I do want to love again, Ethan. Someday."

For a moment neither one of us said anything.

"Don't go to Scotland," he finally said. A glassy tear shone at the corner of his eye.

"It's the one choice I can trust right now, Ethan."

He gently pulled my hand to his lips and kissed it. "You can trust me."

He bent his head toward mine and he kissed me, soft and long, right there in the ferry house with a hundred languages falling around us like rain.

Like stars.

The world seemed to tilt and I broke away before I plummeted into that kiss. I could not go to that uncertain place where Ethan had already gone. After what I had been through, I needed something far steadier than love. Our eyes met.

"Right now I need you to trust *me*," I whispered. "Please, Ethan. I need time for my heart to be still. It just needs to be still right now." If he truly loved me, surely he would grant me that.

He studied my face. "All right," he finally said. "You will write?"

"I promise." I slipped my other arm through his. "Now walk with me? I want to tell you what happened with the letter and the necklace and Mr. Hartwell. It's an amazing story."

We made our way out of the ferry house. A teasing autumn breeze followed us, lifting the marigolds from around my neck as if it might scatter them heavenward. I reached up with my free hand to press them gently back down over my heart.

Thirty-Eight

TARYN

Manhattan
September 2011

HAD I not received the text from Kendal asking me whether she could sleep over at a friend's house, I might have declined Mick's invitation to dinner, but with Kendal taken care of, I had no reason not to go. I was surprised by how glad I was to say yes.

I felt an unexpected kinship with Mick, a bond I had not sensed with anyone since Kent was alive. The trauma of what Mick and I had survived together explained the connection in part, but there was more to it than the hour we'd shared on the worst day of my life. For the last ten years Mick and I had both been on a search. When our two quests collided, we were there to share the moment with each other.

We walked to a Latin fusion bistro near his store and

sat at a sidewalk table while we ate and talked. I was right about the aftermath of the disaster undermining Mick's already fragile marriage. His ex-wife, Denise, hadn't had the motivation to understand why Mick was obsessed with finding me. She didn't want to understand that his spirit had been crushed, just like mine had been, even if what crushed him had been different from what flattened me. Denise ended up looking for intimacy in the arms of another man and, two years later, she divorced Mick.

He stayed with the family floral business, taking over its management several years ago, after his father had a debilitating stroke. All that time he continued to look for me, even when it seemed I had never existed.

I showed him pictures of Kendal and the Heirloom Yard that I had on my phone. I told him how wonderful it was to be her mother, and how much I enjoyed my job, and my little niche on the Upper West Side. I told him how surprised and shocked I was when the photo of us had appeared. I also told him what I had finally discovered the day before while helping a customer choose between green and blue fabric—that I had been living an in-between existence that had kept me cushioned from the hard and beautiful aspects of a full life. I hadn't realized it until the photo had shown up. And then the scarf.

"What will you do now?" Mick asked, as we lingered over coffee and flan.

"Do you mean with the scarf?"

"I mean with everything."

In his eyes I could see what he was asking. Now that he and I had reconnected, was there room in my newly begun life for his friendship?

"Well, I'm going to try my best to find Rosalynn Stauer. It is her scarf, after all. And then I need to tell

Kendal why I was on the street that day. I don't know if she'll ask me what would have happened to Kent if I hadn't left the message. But I think she might. That's why I've never told her."

Mick reached for his coffee cup. "But you know what the answer is, right?" He took a sip.

I half smiled. "I know what my heart says would have happened if I hadn't left that message."

Mick set his coffee cup down and reached across the table for my hand. "The heart always wants to believe the best. About everything. I wouldn't change that for the world. But the heart doesn't run the show."

I blinked back ready tears. "I know it doesn't."

He squeezed my hand. "Only God knows what would have happened if you hadn't left that message, Taryn. That's the answer you give your daughter. Because it's the truth."

I smiled at him, afraid to trust my voice. I knew he was right.

"I am so glad I can tell her Kent knew about her before he died," I finally said. "It will make the hard part easier for her to hear, I think. I can't even tell you how glad I am that you found me."

"That makes two of us," Mick said. We both laughed.

"What would you have done if I hadn't called you back? I mean, I know I told you not to call me again. But would you have let me believe, for the rest of my life, that Kent had died not knowing I was pregnant?"

Smiling, Mick reached into his shirt pocket and drew out a letter-size envelope and placed it on the table between us. The envelope was addressed to me.

"I was going to give you until the first of October and then I was going to send this to you, with the scarf."

I picked up the envelope. "Do you mind?"

"Not at all."

I opened the flap and drew out a single sheet of cream-colored stationery stamped in green with the Athena logo.

> Dear Ms. Michaels:
>
> Please forgive me if I am making a mistake by writing to you and returning the scarf. For a decade I have looked for you to tell you that your husband replied to the text message I sent on your behalf. I didn't receive it until many hours after I left you at the hospital, even though he sent it at 9:28 a.m.
>
> The message he wrote was, "Tell her, 'Be happy.'"
>
> I hope you have been.
>
> Or I hope now you will be.
>
> Your friend,
> Mick Demetriou

WE ordered second cappuccinos, talked for another hour, and made plans to see each other in the coming week. Then Mick walked me to the subway, and kissed my cheek before I went down the stairs.

I was glad to return to an empty apartment so that I could be alone with my thoughts, and the scarf.

Celine called me a little after nine to ask me about my meeting with Mick and to tell me she had found Rosalynn Stauer, widowed now and living in New Jersey with her son and his wife.

"You told her about the scarf?" I asked.

"Was that okay? The son wasn't going to tell me where she was until I told him why I was asking about her. Sorry if I spoiled a surprise you were planning."

"It's okay," I said. "Does she want me to mail it to her?" I was hoping Celine would say yes. If I waited until next week, Kendal and I could have a few days with it.

"She didn't say, Taryn. She just said she will be in touch. She still makes trips into Manhattan, apparently. Maybe she's not in a rush."

Celine had sensed my reluctance to part with it so soon.

"All right," I said.

"So, you had a good visit with Mick Demetriou?"

"Yeah, I did."

For the next twenty minutes I told Celine all the reasons I had had a good visit. After we hung up, I got ready for bed and my phone vibrated.

The text message was from Mick.

"I had a really good time tonight. Sleep well."

I draped the scarf across my bedside table so that the marigolds by night-light were the last thing I saw before closing my eyes.

I woke late the next morning and hurried through breakfast to get downstairs before we opened. Autumn Saturdays were always busy, since the promise of winter motivated our clientele to shop for the frigid days to come. Our first hour of business flew by. I had only a moment to text Kendal and ask her when I needed to come get her. She texted back that they were going out for an early brunch and Melissa's parents would bring her home before noon.

A few minutes after eleven, while I was finishing up

an order at the cutting table, a familiar voice at the front of the store made my heart sink.

Rosalynn Stauer had just walked into the Heirloom Yard and was now happily greeting Celine.

The timing couldn't have been worse. Kendal wasn't even home yet. I had so very much wanted her to see the scarf before Mrs. Stauer reclaimed it. I doubted she would let me keep it another few days, since she'd already gone to the trouble of coming to Manhattan, though of course I would ask her.

As she made her way to me, I heard Mrs. Stauer tell Celine that she missed seeing us, but she couldn't sew anymore because her arthritis was so bad. If not for her recognizable voice, I wouldn't have known her. Mrs. Stauer had aged considerably. Her hair was now left to its natural silver, and a jewel-topped cane suggested she was perhaps a bit unsteady on her feet.

And she was widowed. I knew firsthand how the death of your husband could steal years from you.

When she arrived at my table, Mrs. Stauer leaned forward to wrap me in a one-armed hug. The cane clattered against my knee. Celine flashed a sympathetic grin and left us to wait on other customers.

"Dear Taryn! So the scarf is found at last!"

"Yes," I said. "Finally."

She broke away. "I never expected to see it again."

"I'm sorry it took so long."

"Not to worry. It wasn't your fault."

"Would you like to come to the back room?" I asked. "Your scarf is there, quite safe this time."

Mrs. Stauer's smile widened. "I would like that very much."

I ushered her into the back and asked whether she

wanted to sit down for a moment, hoping she would say yes. I would need to explain why I wanted to keep the scarf for a little while, and she would probably need to be seated.

"Oh, thank you so much, dear." She eased herself down on one of the chairs and leaned her cane against the wall behind her. "I can still get around pretty good. Not so great going up and down these days. Makes traveling by train harder because of all those stairs, you know. But I still like to come to Macy's. I can take a cab from Penn Station to just about anywhere. My daughter-in-law or son comes with me sometimes, because they worry about me. But I didn't want them coming today."

I listened with half interest as I retrieved the scarf from my desk. I caught the faintest fragrance of floral notes as I brought it to her.

"Oh, my goodness. Would you look at that!" She beamed and held out her hands.

I gave her the scarf and sat down in the chair on the other side of the little table.

"It looks the same as the day I last saw it. How remarkable!" she exclaimed.

"The person who found it worked hard to get all the dust and ash out of it. He took good care of it."

Mrs. Stauer unfolded the entire length and then ran her fingers over the embroidered letters that spelled the name Lily.

"Oh, Lily," Mrs. Stauer murmured. She brought the scarf to her nose and inhaled. "Smells like roses. Isn't that funny! The marigolds smell like roses!"

"Yes. Um, Mrs. Stauer, I wonder if you could possibly consider allowing me to hold on to the scarf for just a little while longer," I said, my heart pounding in my chest. "I really wanted to show it to my daughter before I gave it back to you. I know this is going to sound crazy, but that scarf saved her life. Only . . . she doesn't know the story and I . . . I wanted her to see it when I tell her."

Mrs. Stauer looked at me, wordless, her smiling eyes visible just above the scarf that she still held to the bottom half of her face.

"I should have told her a long time ago what happened that day, but I didn't have the courage," I continued. "I don't know if you saw the photo in *People* magazine a few weeks ago, but—"

"Oh, yes." Mrs. Stauer pulled the scarf away from her face, but she was still smiling. "I saw it."

Heat rose to my cheeks. "I am so sorry about that. I had looked in my purse for a tissue. And there wasn't one. The scarf was the only thing I had. I'm afraid that's why I lost it. It wasn't inside my purse when the first tower . . . when I had to run."

Mrs. Stauer set the scarf down on the table and tapped it with a finger. "This scarf made you late, didn't it? That's what you told me that morning. You were supposed to meet someone, but because you came to see me, you were late."

"Yes. My husband."

"And that's why it saved your daughter's life. You were pregnant?"

I could only nod as my eyes brimmed with all-too-familiar tears. I fingered them away.

"Your first?"

"Our only."

Mrs Stauer hesitated a moment before continuing. "I think I know a little bit about what you've been through, Taryn. I didn't know how much you could miss a person until my Roger died. You'd think I would be glad that we had such a long, happy life together. But I miss him all the more because we did."

More tears sprang to my eyes.

Mrs. Stauer reached into her jacket pocket and handed me a tissue. "I didn't come today to take the scarf home with me."

I paused in the middle of dabbing my eyes, sure I hadn't heard her correctly. "What was that?"

"I just wanted to see it. But I'm not taking it. I want you to have it."

I could only stare at her.

"I've only my son and his wife for family," she went on. "This scarf would mean nothing to them. But I know what it means to you. Please take it."

"Oh, Mrs. Stauer . . ."

"It would make me very happy if you kept it."

I laughed to dispel the tears. "It would make me very happy to have it."

She beamed at me. "It's all settled then!" She pushed the scarf toward me.

I pulled it from the table and held it to my chest. "Thank you."

"Now then," she said, obviously pleased with the situation and ready to be on her way. "Would you be so kind as to hail a taxi for an old woman?"

"Of course."

I walked Mrs. Stauer to the front of the store, the scarf draped over my forearm.

"May Kendal and I come visit you sometime?" I asked.

"That would be lovely, dear. Just lovely. You call me anytime."

I reached for one of my business cards in my apron pocket and handed her one. "If there's ever anything at all I can do for you, you call me. That number is my cell."

She thanked me and I opened the door for her. As she slipped the card into her purse, she stopped.

"Oh! I almost forgot." Mrs. Stauer withdrew a plastic sandwich bag from her purse. Inside I could see a yellowed envelope, discolored by the passing of time. She opened the bag and handed the letter to me.

"What's this?" I took the envelope from her as we stepped outside. On its face, one word was written in beautiful script. *Eleanor.*

"My cousin Corrine—the one who wanted a copy of the scarf?—she died last year and I was sent some of her things, including a jewelry box that had been our aunt Eleanor's. That letter was in it."

"Oh?"

"It was written to my aunt before she left Scotland by the woman who owned the scarf before her. I thought you'd like to have it."

My skin tingled with instant curiosity. "Oh, my goodness. And you're sure you want me to have it?"

"Oh, yes. Very sure. I think whoever has the scarf should have that letter. Go ahead. Read it. My aunt was a housemaid—you need to know that before you read it."

I turned the envelope over and opened its ancient flap. Several sheets of writing paper were tucked inside, crisp with age. I opened them carefully.

November 16,
1911

Dearest Eleanor,

I shall miss saying good-bye to you, as
my train leaves for Liverpool early in the
morning and you are not expected back
until nightfall. It has been my pleasure
getting to work alongside you these last
six weeks.

I have tendered my resignation and am
going back home to America. It had been
my intention to stay for the entire year,
but my heart is not here, as I am sure you
must have guessed; it is back home with
someone who loves me and whom I know
now I love in return. Dr. Bartlett has been
most kind to allow me to go. He can find
another nurse, he told me, but I cannot
find another heart. He understands, bless
him, because he so dearly loves Mrs. Bartlett.

My dear Eleanor, I leave you knowing
you are in a place of great distress. You
loved Wesley with all your heart, and now
he loves someone else. Perhaps you are
thinking, as I once did, that love is too
precarious to want to lavish it again on
another. I want you to know that love is
not a person. It is not of this earth at all.
It wasn't until now that I realized I had
mistakenly come to believe that love came
from a place inside me and therefore I had

to protect that place. It comes from heaven, Eleanor. It is given to us not to hold on to or hide from, but to give away.

I want you to have the scarf that you found with this letter to remind you of this. The scarf came to me twice, in the most amazing of ways. I was meant to have it, just as I believe that you are meant to have it now.

This scarf was given first to a woman named Lily by a mother who loved her. Life sent Lily to the valley of decision, just as it sends all of us there from time to time. She made difficult choices based on despair. If I have learned anything this past year, it is that despair is love's fiercest enemy.

Do not choose to abandon love because you are afraid that it will crush you. Love is the only true constant in a fragile world.

Don't despair. Be happy. Choose hope.

Yours, Clara

For several seconds I could only stare at a letter that seemed to have been written to me, and not to a Scottish maid a century before.

"I can see why my aunt kept that letter, can't you?" Mrs. Stauer squeezed my forearm.

I nodded. "Yes, I can."

"She did love again, by the way. She and my uncle Steven were married fifty-nine years."

I smiled and slipped the ancient pages back inside the envelope. "I'm really glad to hear that. Thank you for this."

I hailed a cab and helped her into it.

Mrs. Stauer patted the purse on her lap. "That's a lovely saying you have on your business card, Taryn. I'd forgotten that was your store's motto. 'Everything beautiful has a story it wants to tell.' It's very lovely."

I smiled. "I think so, too."

"You will give your daughter a hug from me, won't you?" she asked.

"Of course," I said, and bent to kiss her cheek before closing the cab door.

I watched the taxi until it disappeared into the steady stream of Saturday traffic. Moments later, a red MINI Cooper sidled up to the row of parked cars ahead of me and Kendal stepped out. I heard her thank Melissa's mother and then she closed the car door. I waved from where I stood and the MINI Cooper beeped a response.

Kendal walked toward me, hiking her backpack onto her shoulder.

"Hi," I said. "Have a good time?"

"Yes, but Melissa's brother : . . Hey! Is that the scarf you had in the photo?" Kendal pointed to the marigolds cascading over my arm. And I knew the scarf would pass from me to my daughter that very day. I didn't need it any longer. I had made my peace with destiny. Kendal, on the other hand, was just beginning to understand that the freedom to love and be loved, though it shook you to your core, made life exquisite.

"Yes, it is," I said.

"But . . . where was it all this time?"

I slid my other arm around her and pulled her close. "Now, that is a long story, and I'd like to tell it to you."

ODE ON A GRECIAN URN
John Keats

Thou still unravish'd bride of quietness,
Thou foster-child of Silence and slow Time,
Sylvan historian, who canst thus express
A flowery tale more sweetly than our rhyme:
What leaf-fringed legend haunts about thy shape
Of deities or mortals, or of both,
In Tempe or the dales of Arcady?
What men or gods are these? What maidens loth?
What mad pursuit? What struggle to escape?
What pipes and timbrels? What wild ecstasy?
Heard melodies are sweet, but those unheard
Are sweeter; therefore, ye soft pipes, play on;
Not to the sensual ear, but, more endear'd,
Pipe to the spirit ditties of no tone:
Fair youth, beneath the trees, thou canst not leave
Thy song, nor ever can those trees be bare;
Bold Lover, never, never canst thou kiss,
Though winning near the goal—yet, do not grieve;
She cannot fade, though thou hast not thy bliss,
For ever wilt thou love, and she be fair!
Ah, happy, happy boughs! that cannot shed
Your leaves, nor ever bid the Spring adieu;

And, happy melodist, unwearied,
For ever piping songs for ever new;
More happy love! more happy, happy love!
For ever warm and still to be enjoy'd,
For ever panting, and for ever young;
All breathing human passion far above,
That leaves a heart high-sorrowful and cloy'd,
A burning forehead, and a parching tongue.
Who are these coming to the sacrifice?
To what green altar, O mysterious priest,
Lead'st thou that heifer lowing at the skies,
And all her silken flanks with garlands drest?
What little town by river or sea-shore,
Or mountain-built with peaceful citadel,
Is emptied of its folk, this pious morn?
And, little town, thy streets for evermore
Will silent be; and not a soul, to tell
Why thou art desolate, can e'er return.
O Attic shape! fair attitude! with brede
Of marble men and maidens overwrought,
With forest branches and the trodden weed;
Thou, silent form! dost tease us out of thought
As doth eternity: Cold Pastoral!
When old age shall this generation waste,
Thou shalt remain, in midst of other woe
Than ours, a friend to man, to whom thou say'st,
"Beauty is truth, truth beauty,—that is all
Ye know on earth, and all ye need to know."

AUTHOR'S NOTE

I strive to be as accurate as possible when I create an imagined story in a historic place and to carefully choose when to use literary license to bend fact. I have in these pages proposed how one nurse might have experienced Ellis Island Hospital in the second half of 1911. While physicians in 1911 would have been Marine Hospital Service Commissioned Corps officers, nurses would not. Between the years 1930 and 1944 the Commissioned Corps was expanded to include dentists, nurses, and other health care specialists, as well as physicians.

The eight so-called measles wards on island three were in fact buildings where immigrants with any number of diseases were cared for, including those with scarlet fever. I chose to place Andrew Gwynn at Ward K, one of the isolation wards at the farthest end of the island, because I wanted him to be at the island's edge and secluded. This location suited the story.

Any deviations from actual history were made for sake of story, or imperfect conjecture on my part.

I am donating a portion of the royalties from the sale of *A Fall of Marigolds* to the Save Ellis Island foundation for the much-needed restoration of the hospital buildings on islands two and three. You can learn more about this important project at http://saveellisisland.org. I encourage you to join me in supporting this timely effort.

—Susan Meissner

ACKNOWLEDGMENTS

I am enormously grateful to . . .

Everyone at NAL and Penguin, especially my insightful editor, Ellen Edwards, for knowing exactly what I needed to do to take this story where I wanted it to go.

Chip MacGregor, for tenacious encouragement from the very moment I mentioned I had an idea for a novel set on Ellis Island, and for countless words of affirmation in the years you have been my agent and friend.

Gifted and generous Ellis Island Hospital experts: Janis Calella, president of Save Ellis Island, Inc.; eloquent Lorie Conway, author and producer of the documentary *Forgotten Ellis Island*; historian, librarian, and author Barry Moreno of the National Park Service; and historian Rear Admiral Arthur J. Lawrence, assistant surgeon general, USPHS (ret.). For your kind and thorough responses to my many inquiries, I am profoundly thankful.

I am also grateful for the tremendous research done by National Park Service historian Harlan D. Unrau.

Early readers Judy Horning, Debbie Ness, Barbara Anderson, and especially K. C. Wilt for much-appreciated feedback.

Dear friends and virtual watercooler coworkers Mary DeMuth, Tosca Lee, Ariel Lawhon, Marybeth Whalen, Jenny B. Jones, Nicole Baart, and Jennifer Lyn King, for being sounding boards, a cheering section, and a support group all in one. And Davis Bunn, for sharing with me your memories of being in Lower Manhattan on 9/11.

Siri Mitchell for translating the French phrases; quilting maven and lifelong friend Kathy Sanders for inspiring me to imagine the Heirloom Yard; and Nicole Shepard for showing me the beauty and bravado of Manhattan.

The survivors of 9/11 who bravely shared their stories, their wounds, their hopes. I am awed by your resilience.

My parents, Bill and Judy Horning; my husband, Bob; and our adult children, Stephanie, Josh, Justin, and Eric, for believing in me.

God, for bestowing on all of us the freedom to love and be loved.

Photo by Amber Dawn

A native of San Diego, **Susan Meissner** is a former managing editor of a weekly newspaper and an award-winning columnist. She has published fourteen novels with Harvest House and WaterBook, a division of Random House. She lives in San Diego with her husband and has four grown children.

CONNECT ONLINE
www.susanmeissner.com
facebook.com/susan.meissner
twitter.com/susanmeissner

A FALL
of
MARIGOLDS

SUSAN MEISSNER

A CONVERSATION WITH SUSAN MEISSNER

Q. What inspired you to write A Fall of Marigolds?

A. A couple years ago I viewed Lorie Conway's compelling documentary film *Forgotten Ellis Island*, about the history and former glory of the now crumbling Ellis Island Hospital. I was transfixed by the haunting images, because unlike the immigration station on the main part of Ellis Island, the hospital buildings have yet to be restored. I knew there had to be thousands of stories pressed into those empty halls and forsaken rooms, and I wanted to imagine what one of them might have been. I considered writing a story about an immigrant woman who, arriving ill to America, is sent to Ellis's hospital and is suddenly stuck in between the life she left and the life that awaits her. But as I toyed with ideas, I began to see that my main character was instead a nurse, stationed at the hospital by choice. She is desperate for a place to hover, where time can stand still. I pictured her as having survived something terrible and needing the odd space between what was and what will be, to come to grips with what had happened to her. Ellis Island Hospital was the perfect place for her, because it was a place where people waited for their situation to change. When I decided this nurse would be a survivor of the 1911 Triangle Shirtwaist fire, I knew the contemporary story that would frame the historical one would involve a survivor from 9/11.

Q. *Although this is your first novel with New American Library, you've written many other novels. How does* A Fall of Marigolds *compare to them?*

A. In my last five books, I've dovetailed a contemporary story around a historical subplot or vice versa. I like mulling over how the past informs the present. History shows us what we value, what we fear, what we are willing to fight for, and what we don't want to live without. When two separate and perhaps even unrelated story lines revolve around the same theme, we can see that there are aspects about us that don't change, even though the years change. I also like to incorporate into my novels a physical element of some kind that appears in both time periods: a tangible tie that loops the two stories together. In *The Shape of Mercy*, I used a diary. In *Lady in Waiting* it was a ring. In *A Sound Among the Trees* it was a house. And in *A Fall of Marigolds* the item that links both stories is the scarf.

Q. *I was particularly fascinated by the ethical dilemma that lies at the heart of Clara Wood's story. I so rarely see such situations explored in fiction. What inspired you to include it, and have you explored similar situations in your previous fiction?*

A. The best novels I've read have made me ponder what I would do if I were that character on that quest with those kinds of odds against me. The more difficult the choices a character must make, the more emotionally invested I become as a reader. Ethical dilemmas suggest the most challenging choices, because someone must decide what is right and wrong, and then they must live with the consequences. That kind of scenario nearly always creates tension, and tension creates interest. I admit it's my goal to craft stories that are memorable, that are hard to put down, that keep you up at night, that make you want to talk with your book club friends, and that resonate with you long after you've moved on to another book. I want people to like my books not only because they were entertained, but also because they discovered things about themselves that they didn't already know.

Q. What do you hope that readers will take away from reading A Fall of Marigolds?

A. I really do believe that the capacity to love is what gives meaning to our lives, even though we are never more vulnerable than when we let down our guard and trust our hearts to others. The world isn't perfect; nor are other people. It's quite possible that loving flawed people in an equally flawed world is going to subject you to the worst kind of heartache. But I like to think that the heart is capable of surviving the costs of loving because it was meant to. The heart is made of muscle; we are meant to exercise it. This is what Taryn and Clara come to realize. It seems to me the best kind of takeaway I could hope for.

Q. *Can you tell us a bit about how you first became a writer? Are there people or other writers who have particularly inspired and encouraged you?*

A. I usually answer this question with: It wasn't so much that I became a writer as that I realized I already was one. According to my mother, I was composing poems aloud when I was four, before I knew how to scribble all the letters of the alphabet. I've always been driven to process what I see happening around me by writing about it. I am grateful to two teachers for seeing that I was wired this way, even before I knew it myself: my second-grade teacher, Virginia Work, who gave me a little red journal to write my stories in—it was years before I realized this was something she did for me only, not for everybody in the classroom; and my ninth-grade English teacher, Frank Barone, who told me with complete confidence that I would be published someday. I can't adequately express how much that early affirmation means to me, even all these many decades later. I salute all teachers who make the effort to water and tend the seedling talents of their young students. I don't know that I would have had the confidence to attempt writing my first novel without that early encouragement.

Q. *Would you share something about your writing process? How do you tackle such a daunting project as writing a novel?*

A. I need to see that pivotal, climactic scene in my head before I can start on page one. I have many writing friends who write by the seat of their pants, and who can confidently start a novel without knowing how the story will end, or how they will get there. I must be able to visualize how the story will progress—from the scene in the beginning when the story quest becomes evident, to the middle scenes that ratchet up the tension, to the dark moment when all seems lost, to the final summit when the quest is at its zenith. I need to know why my character wants what she wants and why that matters to anyone reading her story. All that is to say that I create an outline before I start. I don't always know what every big transitional moment will be when I'm first starting to write the outline, but I do know where those key moments need to fall. When I am outlining my plot, scene by scene, I may just write, "Something big happens here," at a point of major escalation, just so I will be anticipating it as I write. I call this outlining by the seat of my pants.

Q. *What do you most enjoy about being a writer? What do you find most onerous?*

A. I heartily enjoy the creative process of imagining something out of nothing, even though that is also the very thing that makes writing fiction so hard. I started writing professionally as a reporter for a small-town newspaper and eventually became an editor, so I had ten years of nonfiction writing experience before I tried my hand at my first novel. A blank page with no parameters was what scared me most—and still does. Back in my newspaper days, when I wrote a feature story about an avid butterfly collector or a Bataan Death March survivor or a female hog farmer, I didn't have to do anything special to make those people seem real to my readers. But with novels, I am creating—out of thin air—characters who have no biography unless I imagine one for them. If I can't make those characters seem real to you, you won't care about them, and if you don't care about them, you'll put the book down. It's a delicious challenge that sometimes gives me heartburn.

Q. *Do you belong to a book club?*

A. For the last five years I have been in a book club with the most amazingly astute and insightful women. We have a long list of across-the-board favorite books, including *The Thirteenth Tale* by Diane Setterfield, *Snow Flower and the Secret Fan* by Lisa See, *The Help* by Kathryn Stockett, *Molokai* by Alan Brennert, *The Language of Flowers* by Vanessa Diffenbaugh, and *People of the Book* by Geraldine Brooks. We usually pair our monthly meeting with a lunch menu to match the book. As I am writing this, the last novel we read was *The Age of Miracles* by Karen Thompson Walker, and we had at lunch, among other dishes, End of the World Chocolate Cake—which was, of course, to die for.

Q. What's next for you? Do you have any long-term goals as a writer?

A. I am in the middle of researching the London Blitz and pulling on different story threads. As a mother, my heart has always felt a tug when I consider how hard it must have been for parents to put their children on trains and send them out of the city before the bombing began. I can't help but think that for every child and every mother, there was a story to tell. The Londoners who lived through the Blitz were ordinary people—merchants, teachers, chefs, writers—but they found themselves on the strangest of battlefields, armed with nothing but blackout curtains. They were people just like you and me. I am plotting a story in which a London mother sends her daughters to the countryside, but something happens, and the two sisters become separated. Seventy years later, an American college student studying abroad interviews the older sister, who up to that point has never told anyone what happened the day her younger sister disappeared, the same day the Luftwaffe began to bomb London.

My long-term goal is to write something worthy of being remembered, something that breaks new ground or rises above mere entertainment. I can't imagine ever retiring from writing. Perhaps I will have to slow down a little, but I see myself in my twilight years tapping out stories from a sunny corner in a pleasantly appointed assisted-living facility, which I hope very much has a view of the ocean.

QUESTIONS FOR
DISCUSSION

Spoiler alert: The questions that follow tell more about happens in the book than you might want to know until you read it.

1. What did you most enjoy about *A Fall of Marigolds*? What do you think you'll remember about it six months from now?

2. Discuss the ways in which the contemporary and historical sections of the novel relate to each other. What story elements do they share? How do they echo and amplify each other? Did you enjoy going back and forth between the two narratives, or did you much prefer one over the other?

3. When Clara Wood finds Lily's letter to Andrew and the certificate of annulment, she faces an ethical dilemma—should she tell Andrew the truth about the woman he loved and break his heart, or leave him in ignorance?

What would be the most ethical choice? What would you have done?

4. Have you ever gone to, or wanted to go to, an "in-between place"? Would you share that experience?

5. Despite the little interaction they had, Clara is convinced that Edward would have become her lover and eventually her husband. Have you ever experienced a similar certainty about someone after just meeting them?

6. Ten years after her husband's death, Taryn seems to be living a full life, but once her photo is published, she begins to realize that she has also been in an "in-between place." How has she been held back? How are her circumstances similar to and different from Clara's?

7. Discuss the role of the marigold scarf in the story. Trace its path from Lily to Taryn. How does the scarf enrich the experience of the characters? Would you react to the scarf in the same way that the characters do?

8. Andrew plays a key role in Clara's life. Is it okay with you that she doesn't end up in a romantic relationship with him? Does Ethan seem a better or worse choice to you? The book ends with Taryn and Mick heading toward a romantic relationship. Do you find that believable and satisfying?

9. Taryn and Clara each experience a horrific tragic event in which someone they love dies. Have you ever been

personally touched by tragedy? Would you be willing to share how your experience compares to what Taryn and Clara go through?

10. Do you believe in destiny? That God has a purpose for each of our lives? Discuss how these ideas play out in *A Fall of Marigolds*.

RECOMMENDED RESOURCES

Forgotten Ellis Island: The Extraordinary Story of America's Immigrant Hospital, a book and film by Lorie Conway, Smithsonian, 2007. http://forgottenellisisland.com.

The Illustrated Encyclopedia of Ellis Island by Barry Moreno, foreword by Lee A. Iacocca, Fall River Press, 2010.

Cultural Landscape Report for Ellis Island: Site History, Existing Conditions and Analysis, by J. Tracy Stakely, National Park Service, Olmstead Center for Landscape Preservation, 2003. (Available online at: http://www.nps.gov/history/history/online_books/elis/clr.pdf)